You blow up one crappy little space drone, and everything goes to hell.

Siphany was just trying to be nice when she returned the drone she'd sort-of-accidentally blasted a hole in. But when its owner tries to kidnap the reclusive space mapper and steal her beloved ship, Siphany teams up with pint-sized robotic psychopath, Lurbira Call, to make a daring escape.

Soon Siphany and Lurbira, along with unwanted passengers Isan, the undead teenage cyborg; Siphany's enigmatic former lover and Sovene spymaster, Qas; and moody, electrically beautiful fighter pilot, Pati, are all caught up in a deadly game of spies, starships, and interstellar war. When everything comes to a head, Siphany and Lurbira must find a way to face their tumultuous pasts in order to really, truly find freedom at last.

SIPHANY AND THE WHALE

SIPHANY AND LURBIRA, BOOK ONE

SUSAN JANE BIGELOW

A NineStar Press Publication
www.ninestarpress.com

Siphany and the Whale

CONTENT WARNING:

This book contains depictions of alcohol use, guns/weapons, discussion of past trauma and of family conflicts and forced conversion therapy (off page) of the MC.

Chapter One

LURBIRA COULD HEAR the past calling her.

She extended her sensor range, then quickly drew it back in again. She could barely tell the direction.

"Shut up, shut up, shut up!" she seethed, and she punched the hull of the Junk so hard that it actually made a dent. Fine! Open the damn tin can to space; let it be nothing but vacuum inside. It wouldn't bother Lurbira; the replica lungs she had didn't work anyway.

She rapidly flicked her gunports open and closed, over and over.

"Lurbira?"

She spun around and put on her most innocent face. "Yes, Mother Junk?"

Mother Junk was tall and wiry, her white hair pulled back in a bun and her mouth set in a permanent frown. "Don't you have work to do?"

"I'm sure I do," said Lurbira brightly.

Mother Junk let her gaze drift down to the dent in the hull the size and shape of Lurbira's child-sized fist. "Be careful I don't send you off with the Loyans, *Artificial*," she said icily and brushed past.

Lurbira watched her leave, fuming.

"She would," said a faintly static-laced voice from nearby. Lurbira turned to focus on Isan, who stood awkwardly in the corridor, watching Mother Junk go. The girl still looked remarkably like who she'd been, just with more ashen skin, less hair on her scalp, deep bruises, and silvery implants on her face and arms.

"What do *you* want, corpse?" Lurbira snapped.

"Mother Junk never lies. She won't hesitate if she thinks you've become a burden."

"Great." Lurbira turned her back. "I'll keep that shit in mind."

"Be careful, Artificial." Isan's voice hardened. "And be careful of me too."

"Pff," said Lurbira as haughtily as she could manage. "Don't make me laugh."

She stood there, back turned, until Isan finally gave up and left.

This had become completely intolerable. It was time to get off this miserable station in the middle of nowhere. And Lurbira knew just how to do it.

*

LESHANDRE SIPHANY WOKE to the howling of proximity alarms and screamed in panic.

She fought for control of herself. Siphany had dreamed she was back in the institution on Sovena, confined in that awful too-large, too-bright room. *Control,* the nurses and wardens had shouted at her. *Control!*

You must learn to show us your outward, smiling self.

You must control yourself, Siphany.

These outbursts and tantrums are un-Sovene!

And then she had seen the unmistakable shimmer of bluenet surround her. She screamed as it molded and shaped her body *back* into what it had been before she'd set foot on Derstan Station a decade ago.

The present pierced the nightmare fog, and she steadied herself.

She was on her ship, she was alone with her cat in the middle of deep interstellar space far from Sovena, and the nurses and the institution were a hundred light years away and thirteen years in the past. *I'm okay. I'm safe. Safe.*

But the proximity alarms were still blaring. Siphany tumbled out of bed, cursing, sending poor Kit flying off the sheets in a furry panic.

She sprinted into the cockpit, dove into her chair, and ordered the computer to feed her as much information as possible. A ship was near. Where was it? What was it? How close? Heat signature? Movement? Threat potential?

Information came at her in a steady stream; Siphany let it wash over her as she awakened to the universe around her.

The proximity alert had automatically switched on her bright and shiny high-end defense systems. Her scans swept the sector and quickly fixed the offending object in her target sights.

The sensors weren't giving her anything conclusive, and the old familiar panic rose. What was it? Pirates? Not out of the realm of possibility, but pirates were rare. Piracy wasn't profitable enough for many people to risk it. Loyans, maybe? She was close to the border with Haeld space. The

Loyan military had their fingers all over Haeld's long-running civil war, so it was possible. Might be Sovene, too—the Sovenes were in just as deep.

"No," she muttered to herself as the scans resolved. "Not a ship. Way too small."

Debris? A random unmapped rock? She trained active scanners on it, trying to gather more data. Frustratingly, she wasn't getting a lot of readings from it at all, almost as if it were only half there.

Then, as she settled on the idea of an inert piece of debris or rock, it changed course.

"Ah!" Siphany said, surprised. A drone, then. That's what it had to be, though she'd never seen one quite like this before.

Drones could be bad for business. Mappers like Siphany made money because it was cheaper to pay people who already owned their own ships to head out into space and run the sensor turret rather than send unreliable, expensive drones.

But if someone had figured out how to make a better, cheaper drone…

She ought to just vaporize the damn thing.

Kit jumped onto the console top next to her and peered intently out at the void. His whiskers curved forward, and his eyes darted around. Kit thought space was fascinating.

He'd love this, then.

"Watch this," she told her cat and stabbed the fire button. A white-hot beam lanced out from her starboard cannon, puncturing the hull of the drone where Siphany suspected its drive section must be.

She lazily targeted a forward section as the drone tumbled out of control, when, to her shock, the speakers crackled to life.

"Unknown ship!" a frantic female voice said. "Stop firing! I surrender! I mean no harm! I'll give you whatever you want! *Please don't kill me!*"

"Oh, no," Siphany cried, leaping to her feet. *What did I just do?*

*

SIPHANY FOUGHT PANIC as she pulled the tiny ship into the cavernous cargo bay with her grappling hook, and then she scrambled ran to meet it, clutching as many medical supplies as she could. Her heart raced as her bare feet pounded the carpet. *Please don't let whoever's in there be dead. Please don't let her be dead!*

Her weapons had blasted a single neat hole in the aft drive section. The drive hadn't exploded, thanks be to whatever scraps of luck Siphany possessed.

She reached the hatch and yanked it open.

"Hello! I'm here! I have bandages and—and…Hello?"

Her voice reverberated inside an empty hull. She gingerly eased her way into the ship, keeping a hand on the outside of the hatch.

"Hello? Is…anyone in here? I talked to someone…? Are you hurt?"

Nothing.

Siphany took a deep breath and let go of the hatch. She had to stoop to walk in the tiny ship, and it was only a few steps from the hatch to the single-seat cockpit. There was no one in the chair.

A light blinked on, and Siphany stifled a scream.

"Hello! I am an experimental prototype ship. I have become lost on my way to insert the-name-of-the-place-here. Thank you for not blowing me up."

"You're…welcome?" Siphany said. "Is there anyone on board? Hello?"

It was empty. She'd been had.

"Please return me to my station. We are a small Junk and need all the supplies we can get."

"A Junk?" Junks were illegal space stations crewed by weird hermits. Siphany had thought they were all gone.

"Please do not alert the authorities. You will be rewarded."

"Right. You've got to be kidding. How gullible do you think I am?" she asked it, feeling both humiliated and angry. "Why did you do this? What are you doing out here?"

"Hello! I am an experimental prototype ship. I have become lost on my way to—"

"Fine, right, got it. Voice off." That seemed to be its entire message. So it wasn't sei, meaning it wasn't sentient in either a digital or organic kind of way. No self-awareness, just a program running on a loop.

What was she supposed to do now?

Part of Siphany wanted to shove the thing back out the cargo bay door and finish it off. No one would miss it.

Besides, the whole thing smelled fishy. What would a Junker ship be doing out here? Why would people living on a Junk have a ship with stealth technology?

And yet, it had asked her to return it. Nicely.

The overwhelming sense that she was being conned warred with Siphany's need to return what wasn't hers. What right did she have to keep it? She should take it back. It was the correct thing to do, and the Form would insist on it. Plus, she'd shot the damn thing.

It was her responsibility now. Siphany heaved a massive sigh. "This is a bad idea, and I don't like you," she informed the ship. "Show me the coordinates."

The ship beeped, and a map appeared over its single computer console. A red light blinked. Siphany studied it for a moment, nodded, and transferred the point to her navigational computers. Only eleven light years. She could make it in four jumps.

Then she'd be back at work before anyone noticed she was gone. It was settled—Siphany would return the ship to its owner.

And then she'd try to forget any of this had ever happened.

*

SLEEP ELUDED SIPHANY, even though it was quite conclusively time for it. Kit was a little ball of cement at the end of her narrow bed; she wiggled her toes, and the cat grumpily shifted so she could get out.

Siphany had nothing to do. That was usually fine; she liked nothing. It suited her, and she could fill up the nothing with the quietness of her routine, her cat, and herself. But this kind of nothing to do was different. She was on edge; she couldn't turn her brain off. Everything was too loud, just like it had been back when…

Her gaze drifted to the wall between her cabin and the next one over. No. She didn't want to think about *them*, or she'd just go round and round until she forgot to eat.

To distract herself, she got up and logged into the massive virtual city of Hydras. The city was partly immersive, partly interface; she could go there without completely abandoning her sense of the ship around her. In Hydras, Siphany could interact in real time with people from all over the Mid-Perseus Arm of the galaxy.

Hydras's virtual cityscape was an essential component of her sanity—

social contact without the messiness of people in her space. Accessing the subspace net that allowed instantaneous contact across hundreds of light-years wasn't cheap, but it was worth it. Siphany wandered the streets near her home base in the Yonaka neighborhood, then checked into the pilots' lounge she liked.

Pati, one of the lounge's regulars and a fellow citizen of Derstan Station, walked over. She was a freighter pilot with a wicked sense of humor and a sympathetic ear. "How's things, Sif?"

Siphany blushed. She liked it when Pati called her *Sif.* "Hi, Pati. And not great."

"Aw. Sorry to hear it. You okay?"

"Yeah," sighed Siphany. "Just a little shaken."

"Want to talk about it?"

Siphany considered it but backed off. What would she say? How could she explain this sort of weirdness? "No, it's okay. I don't know how to even talk about it. Sorry."

"No problem," drawled Pati. "If you change your mind, though, that's what I'm here for. How's your ship holding up?"

"Running smooth," said Siphany, brightening. "Those DH-58 stabilizers work better than I thought they would."

"Told ya. You'll be able to shoot the ticks off a dog's ass from a parsec away."

Siphany giggled and then launched into a description of the latest upgrades she'd made to her sensor net. Pati made all the appreciative noises, even though Siphany was certain she was burying the woman in information. Another reason to like Pati; she always made Siphany feel calmer.

When Pati finally excused herself to get some work done, Siphany decided to explore some of the new countryside they'd installed nearby.

The virtual world was more crowded than usual, to her dismay. Unrest in the real world seemed to draw people in.

When she'd had enough, Siphany logged back out and listened for a long moment. Silence. She exhaled, then noted the time. It was the interval for rounds, so she stood and began pacing deliberately over the ship from end to end, making sure it was all still there.

She padded barefoot through the carpeted corridors, brushing her fingers along the metal and plastic walls. Computer terminals lit her way here and there, as did the dim, recessed lights at floor level. The air was warm but dry, just how she liked it. She kept the hours of her watch, all synced to the rhythms of the Form.

Siphany's job was making charts and maps, more detailed than anything that currently existed for these largely empty sectors. She mapped out all the hazards, radiation levels, unexpected gravity shifts, and tiny little rocks packed with valuable minerals, which gave the Derstan Station Mining and Mapping Company something to sell.

Other freelance mappers, cargo haulers, and traders had ships full of light and people. Some took crews of twenty aboard their cramped ships and strung up sun lamps everywhere. They fought the darkness and boredom together and then split the proceeds between them.

Not Siphany. She kept her lights low, only high enough to see by. She alone carried no crew besides her cat. And, of all the mappers, only she didn't have to share her salary with anyone.

Space makes me bats, other mappers often said when they learned that she went out alone and for longer than anyone else. *How do you stand it?*

Siphany always smiled and murmured something half true, all the while wanting to say: *Don't you understand? Space keeps me sane.*

She'd paid plenty to have plush, comfy carpets and chairs put in to replace the hard industrial defaults and to keep the heat nice and high. She also had top-of-the-line weapons, shift engines that could hit a pebble in the middle of a cubic light year of nothing, and advanced computers to help her plot the best course. She had a strong real-time connection to Hydras and other social sites where she could indulge whatever companionship she might need, then log off and be herself in the warm, quiet darkness of her home.

And thus, she kept herself stable and intact.

Siphany glanced at the clocks she'd placed all over the ship. The time for doing the rounds had passed; now it was time for an interval of creative work. Keeping time, planning her day around the hours on the wall, was deeply satisfying. Humming, she picked up her graceful, wooden Sovene flute and headed for the perfect acoustics of the cargo bay.

But she found she couldn't concentrate—the songs wouldn't come, not with the intruder ship crouching so ominously there on the soft carpet of the bay. She sighed, deciding to play in her cabin instead.

Just then, a soft signal chimed from the intercom; they were at the shift point. Saved. Siphany put her flute back in its velvet sleeve and headed for the cockpit.

She brought the ship to a standstill and powered up the shift generators.

There, surrounded by stars and perfect silence, Siphany calculated the tricky way through hyperspace from the shift point. Then, with a nod, she fired the shift engines. The world around her seemed to shimmer, her stomach flopped up and down, and then she was out. The ship *wrinkled* out of space, reappearing a few moments later a third of a light year away.

Right on target. Three more jumps to go. She punched in the coordinates of the next shift point, six hours of mundane travel away, and let the ship take over from there.

"Good, good, that went well," she murmured. Kit padded in and sat in the copilot's chair, giving it a disdainful sniff before settling down. "Let's see how fast we can get there, right?"

In response, he began to purr quietly to himself.

The stars slowly slid by outside.

Everything was so perfectly quiet, so perfectly orderly, from Kit's purr to the warming heat to the distant thrumming of the engines.

The intruder ship still sat in the cargo bay below, but at least it, too, was quiet.

Siphany felt herself begin to unwind, a little bit at a time. Her world was still intact, for now.

Chapter Two

AFTER THREE DAYS of worry, nervous pacing, and spending way too much time talking with friends in Hydras, Siphany completed the last shift. To her immense satisfaction, she had made it to the coordinates well ahead of the schedule she'd drawn up in her mind. She'd be able to drop off this little nuisance, apologize and leave a few credits, and then get back to her life.

Whatever this station was, though, it wasn't showing up on the initial scans.

Siphany almost turned her ship around to shift out of this empty sector right then and there. She almost let herself believe there was nothing here. But…no. This was her responsibility, and she'd see it through.

She ran several more detailed sweeps in the vicinity of the coordinates.

And then she saw it. There. It was subtle, like a ripple in the deep pond of space, but it was *there.*

Siphany's eyes widened slightly. They were putting out next to no emissions. They were on no star chart. They were perfectly hidden; she'd only found them because she had the exact coordinates.

The station itself looked like dozens of sections of different stations awkwardly joined together, and a deeper scan showed hundreds of life signs aboard. It couldn't be military. So this really was an unauthorized, unlicensed station—a Junk.

Junkers were basically interstellar squatters. About fifty years ago, after the trauma of the Pelagarine War, someone on Yudeh Station decided the best way to live was in a self-sufficient community completely isolated from the rest of Mid-Perseus Arm society. The adherents of the Junker Movement set out with a myriad of ramshackle spaceship and station parts and stuck them together deep in interstellar space.

Most of the small Junker colonies lasted only a few years before either disappearing or returning to civilization. Resources were just too hard to come by, and isolation agreed with most humans a lot less than they'd hoped. It wasn't a happy end to an idealistic movement. But a few had held on, running illegal mining or salvage operations on territory belonging to some other sovereign entity until eventually being shut down or destroyed.

There were rumors of Junks still out there, but Siphany had never heard of any proof. Yet here it was, in front of her. What else could it be?

Siphany hesitated. Junkers who survived out here long-term were supposed to be paranoid to the point of violence. Was this something she really wanted to get involved in?

But…here she was. And she had something that didn't belong to her. She needed to give it back, to make it right again. She wouldn't be able to live with herself otherwise.

Siphany opened a channel. "H-hello, uh, station. Hi. My name is Leshandre Siphany, and I found…what looks like a little drone ship in Sector 3983-X2V-H6G7. I thought it was…something else, and I shot it. When I brought it aboard, it gave me these coordinates. I'm sending you my scans of the ship. Is it yours?"

Siphany sent the scans and waited.

An eternity passed. Then, a stern voice crackled through the radio.

"Dock. We'll discuss it."

Siphany hesitated for a long moment. This was sounding worse and worse. But she gritted her teeth as all of her Sovene politeness training forced her to say, "I'll be there shortly."

*

THE STENCH WAS the first thing that hit Siphany when she emerged from her perfectly dim connecting tube into the harsh brightness of the Junk. The station smelled like moldy cheese and dirt.

The second was that there were people *everywhere*. It was worse than she'd imagined. They packed the corridor, crowding in, stepping on one another's toes. Siphany had been unhappy about having to wear shoes over here, but now she was kind of grateful.

A tall, wiry older woman with loose gray hair that fell to her shoulders marched through to the front of the crowd. She towered over Siphany. "You must be the ship pilot. Welcome to Peace Station."

Peace Station? Siphany thought incredulously. *Barf.*

"Uh, thank you," she said aloud.

The woman smiled a gap-toothed smile at her that somehow didn't reach her eyes. "I'm Mother Junk. I'm in charge of this station. And you are?"

"Leshandre Siphany."

"Well, Leshandre, welcome," said Mother Junk.

Siphany kicked herself for spitting out her name in the order they did back home. "You can call me Siphany. Sorry. Leshandre is my family name."

"Ah," said the woman, giving her a shrewd look. "Sovene?"

"Er, yes. Originally. I'm a citizen of Derstan Station now." Siphany had brought her citizenship ID card with her, though it was surprisingly cold comfort now. Derstan Station was a long way away.

"I see." Mother Junk looked around, caught the eye of someone, and motioned. Siphany had the sudden sense that something had changed. "Well, I look forward to hearing what happened out there. We were all…surprised…to see you come in with our ship." She made a little hand motion at another Junker, too quickly for Siphany to puzzle it out. "Care to join us for dinner?"

"Oh, um," Siphany temporized. "I should be going. There's lots of mapping to do, and I really don't want to delay you. I can pay— I have some money I can give you for the repair of the ship…?"

"We'll discuss it," Mother Junk said, command in her voice. "Come."

*

DINNER WAS HELD in a huge common area filled with people, conversation, laughter, and love. For Siphany, it was hell.

She was seated next to people she didn't know while Mother Junk held court. The older woman regaled everyone with her retelling of Siphany's travails, embellishing some of the worst parts while leaving out others, to the delighted howls of everyone in attendance.

The food, though, was something else—a whole plate of beige-green spheres with a very mild give to them, firm but soft enough to slice easily. And, best of all, they tasted like absolutely nothing.

"What *are* these?" Siphany asked Mother Junk when she'd finished telling her tale.

Mother Junk gave her an odd look. "Croppygreens. They are a food we grow here on the station. You're likely accustomed to something a little richer, but—"

"They're delicious! Can I buy some? How do you grow them? Could I grow them on my ship?"

Mother Junk raised an eyebrow at her, amused. "We'll see."

"Can we talk about what I owe you for the ship? I'm really happy to pay. I just want to settle things so I can be on my way," Siphany said between bites. "I have a lot to do. I'm behind schedule. I'm supposed to have the quad I was in done by tomorrow, and I need to let Derstan M&M know I'm going to be late."

No one said anything.

A gawky teenage girl at the end of the table raised a hand and looked as if she were about to say something. Siphany blinked; the girl's skin was ashen, and she had what seemed to be silvery implants on her face, arms, and throat, as well as what looked like bruises everywhere.

"Isan," snapped Mother Junk warningly.

"I—I was just going to say that the croppygreens are easy to grow in small spaces. Um, they have special hydroponics bays."

"Thank you, Isan," said Mother Junk smoothly.

"You're welcome, Mother Junk!" Isan said, sounding appallingly thrilled.

Mother Junk turned to Siphany, a smile fixed on her face. "Isan is my granddaughter."

"Oh," said Siphany. "Hi."

The girl nodded warily. Siphany noticed she wasn't eating. Too bad for her. Siphany popped another croppygreen in her mouth. They really were perfect. She barely noticed them at all.

Dinner seemed to be mercifully winding down. Mother Junk had excused herself and was speaking with two men by the door to the dining room. Siphany stood, intending to talk to her and settle things so she could get out of here. Hopefully, with some croppygreens.

Which is when she noticed the floor rumbling.

"Hey," she said, surprised. "Hey! We're moving. This thing can move? We're moving!"

People's heads swiveled toward her.

Mother Junk said a few words to the men, then quickly made her way over to Siphany.

"I need to go," Siphany explained, panic rising again. "I have to get back to my ship now. Can someone show me back to the airlock?"

Mother Junk crossed her arms over her narrow chest. "We're already underway. You sensed it. I wish you hadn't."

Siphany's stomach flip-flopped as she sensed the sudden danger she was in. "I'm leaving," she said flatly.

"No, girl, you aren't. You're Sovene." Mother Junk held up a hand, cutting off Siphany's protest. "But even if you weren't, you've seen too much both here and when you encountered our ship. We must be careful. And besides, we could use your ship's power. It's already been locked to our systems."

Siphany stared at her in shock. "What?" she croaked.

"I'm sorry, but it was necessary." Mother Junk seemed impossibly tall all of a sudden. She reached out a hand. "Come with me."

"Don't touch—don't—don't like—"

People seemed to swarm around her. The smells, sights, and sounds went from overwhelming to all-out painful.

"N-no," Siphany gasped.

Mother Junk touched her shoulder, perhaps in sympathy, perhaps not. Siphany passed out.

Chapter Three

SIPHANY AWOKE INTO pitch-blackness. Everything smelled sharp and chemical, like cleaning products. She lay on a cot. A sliver of light streamed from underneath the nearby door.

She raced to the door and banged and pulled on it. The door was locked fast. No one came. No one let her out. She sat heavily on the cot, heart racing.

Visions of the institution back on Sovena haunted her. They'd locked her in her room every night. Siphany hated being shut in with no way out.

The nurses, the doctors, the therapists all loomed out of the darkness at her.

She hunted through her pockets, trying to keep a hold on her sanity. They'd taken all of her communications equipment and remote controls for the ship, as well as the tiny dart gun she kept in her boot.

Siphany frantically felt around the rest of the room and found it bare, except for what might have been an acrid-smelling towel and a half-empty bottle of cleaning solution. They'd stuck her in a janitor's closet, of course. She pounded on the door and shouted, but no one answered.

Eventually, she lay on the cot and shivered, fighting to stay in control.

The metal floor still vibrated; they were obviously well underway. Worries about her ship, her cat, and her job marched back and forth through her mind, trampling what was left of her rationality into an anxious paste.

At last, the door opened and then closed again.

"Left you in the dark, did they?" a tinny female voice said from nearer the floor than Siphany expected. "Just a second."

The lights flickered on. Siphany blinked and squinted, her vision blurring in the harsh artificial brightness. She'd preferred the darkness.

"I'm here to give you food," said the voice. "Aren't you lucky?"

Siphany was at last able to focus on the newcomer. Short, with a child's stature, she had the polished metallic sheen required of all Artificial humanoids. "You're a Loyan robot," Siphany said, trying hard to conceal her irritation.

"An *Artificial*, thanks, and yes. My name's Lurbira Call." Lurbira thrust the tray at her. "Have some croppygreens. They're what's on the menu, pretty much every day and night until the end of your life. They make me glad I don't eat."

Siphany hesitantly took the tray. The inoffensive little spheres were a bit cold and undercooked, but Siphany didn't mind. "Thank you," she said, chewing thoughtfully. She found she was starving, and she hungrily downed another.

Lurbira looked at her as if waiting for her to say something.

"What?" asked Siphany, mouth full.

"Aren't you going to ask how someone who is clearly a Loyan-built little-girl simulacrum is living aboard a Junk in the middle of Haeld space?"

"Nope," said Siphany, washing down a croppygreen and reaching for another.

Lurbira fixed her with an odd look. "Why?" she asked at last.

"Don't care. I just want to get back on my ship and get out of here."

Lurbira grinned, amused.

She was decently made, Siphany thought, if somewhat old and out-dated. One of the more expensive ones, made to look essentially real with a few very deliberate tells. Different kinds of sei, from fully mechanical Artificials to partly biological androids, had been a major fad at times over the past millennium, though the use of Artificial troops in the Pelagarine War had soured a lot of people on them. They had mainly been built on Loyan and Pelagar.

"No one's ever *not* asked," Lurbira said. "Everyone wants to know about me. But you don't? Really?"

"Really," confirmed Siphany. "You can go away now."

To Siphany's surprise, Lurbira actually looked hurt. Her expressions were painfully clear and easy to read. "If that's what you want."

"Hey," said Siphany hopefully. "Are you one of those non-sei robots who has to do everything I say?"

"Fuck no," said Lurbira. "Not even close."

"Oh. Damn. I was going to use you to escape from here."

"Tough shit for you," said Lurbira and let herself out of the room. The door clicked shut behind her and locked. A second later, the lights went out again.

Siphany breathed a sigh of relief. At least she didn't have to deal with the light.

*

SIPHANY SAT IN silence, alternating between quiet meditation and panic-stricken worrying until someone else came to talk to her. To her surprise, it was tall, wiry Mother Junk who turned on the lights and stuck her long face inside the door.

"Siphany. Doing well?"

Siphany contemplated knocking her down and making a run for it but remembered in time that she could barely run and had no idea of where to go. Instead, she folded her arms and waited.

"Obviously not," Mother Junk allowed. "Mind if I sit?" She indicated the cot. "I have a lot of questions."

"I do too," said Siphany, feeling more surly with every passing moment. But she pushed over, and Mother Junk sat with a sigh. She towered over Siphany even sitting down.

"Let's begin, then, with your story," said Mother Junk.

"No, hold on," Siphany cut in. "You're holding me prisoner, and I want to know why. I want to be back on my ship, I need to be *gone* from here so I can take care of my cat and not lose my job, and you're holding me in what I have to *assume* is a cleaning supply closet while having some little weird Artificial girl come to bug me and no one has told me *anything* about *why.*"

"I think you're protesting a little much, don't you? You know perfectly well why you're here."

Siphany glowered at her. "I don't, actually. So why don't you tell me?"

Mother Junk said nothing for a very long time. Then, "Why do you think we're holding you?"

Siphany sighed gustily. "I don't know! You want my ship. That much seems pretty clear. You're thieves."

"And? Anything more?"

"Should there be? Is this revenge for shooting your ship? I already explained that."

"Did you," murmured Mother Junk. "Did you. What do you think of Peace Station, if I may ask?"

"The Junk? It's…junk. What do you expect? You're all crammed together, and it's awful. So what?"

Mother Junk simply stared at her, waiting.

"Is my cat okay?" Siphany asked suddenly.

Mother Junk's eyebrows lifted a tad. "Yes. We have many cats on the station. However…your cat didn't get along with them, so for now, he's living in the kennels."

"He is? In a *kennel?* A little cage?" Siphany pictured Kit hunkered down behind bars in a smelly room full of other creatures. "He won't like that. He likes being able to walk around. And he's never been apart from me for so long, not since I got him. Can…maybe he can be brought here? His box and his food can come here too. I won't mind."

Mother Junk raised a hand to stop the flow of nervous words. "I'll think about it. If you answer some questions for me. Deal?"

Siphany nodded mutely.

"Good. First, your ship is very heavily armed and outfitted with superior, aftermarket engines. The sensor array is mapping-company standard, but I can't fathom the purpose of the others. Can you explain?"

"It helps me to have a fast ship. And I like being well-armed. I had the money, so I upgraded the ship. I also put in carpet."

"We noticed. Second, I checked the logs; you got here much more quickly than even most military ships could have. Where were you trained?"

"I'm just really good at that kind of math," mumbled Siphany.

"I see. And no crew?"

"I don't like having a crew. I like being alone."

"You shot down our ship."

"I told you," insisted Siphany, aware she was somehow losing ground here. "I didn't mean to."

"Lastly, you're a Sovene."

"I *was* a Sovene. I'm a citizen of Derstan Station now. So what?"

"I think you know perfectly well what I'm talking about. It won't work, this playing dumb routine."

"You have to let me have my ship back." Siphany realized she was begging but didn't care. "Please. I can pay you. I don't want to lose my job."

Mother Junk stood, looming over Siphany as she drew herself to her full height. "I see we're getting nowhere. I'll return in a little while."

"I need a bathroom," said Siphany.

"There's a grate on the floor and a faucet," said Mother Junk coldly. "Do clean up your own mess."

And with that, she let herself out.

*

A LITTLE WHILE later, the Artificial girl returned.

"More croppygreens," said Lurbira sullenly, unceremoniously dropping the tray on the cot. "I hope you choke on them."

"Thanks," said Siphany. "Hey. You wouldn't happen to know why they're keeping me here, would you?"

"I would. But why should I tell *you*?"

"Because…it would be funny?" Siphany hazarded. That seemed like the kind of thing Lurbira would like.

Lurbira considered for a moment. "That's true, it would. All right. Shove over, I'm sitting down." The cot groaned under Lurbira's substantial weight. "So, what have they told you?"

"Not a lot. Mother Junk was here, and she seemed to think I knew more than I actually did."

"Uh-huh. Like what?"

"Like…why it matters that I was born on Sovena."

"You didn't figure *that* out? Wow. Maybe they've got you completely wrong. Or you're a professional faker. Hmm." The child-shaped Artificial thought for a moment. The sheen of her metallic skin was dulled, and she had several large discolored patches on her neck and hands. *Some sort of rust?*

"Here's what I can tell you," Lurbira said at last. "They think you're a spy."

Siphany laughed once in surprise and disbelief, a sharp, barking sound. Everything clicked into place. "Ha! Is that what they think? No wonder Mother Junk was so interested in my weapons and engines."

"You have to admit, it's weird for a mapping ship to be equipped like that."

"Yes, I'm *weird*, sure, but it doesn't mean I'm a *spy*. And a spy for which side? Sovena?" She shook her head rapidly. "I'm a Derstan Stationer, and that's what I prefer to remain. I'd never spy for Sovena. Never."

"Hey, you don't have to convince me."

"Yeah? You don't think I'm a spy?"

"No. You're too clumsy and awkward. I thought it might be a cover at first, but you're legitimately this bad with people, aren't you?"

"Maybe," Siphany said, steamed. "What's that got to do with it?"

"More than you might think."

"What does it matter if I'm a spy, anyway? Why would anyone want to spy on a Junk in the middle of nowhere?"

Lurbira actually rolled her eyes. Siphany wondered whether that was part of her original programming or if she'd learned it somewhere. "You're definitely not a spy if you haven't picked up on the strangeness of this place," Lurbira said.

"I've been locked in a closet the whole time! I can't do a lot of observation while I'm stuck here!"

"Yeah, but what do you know about the Junk so far? I bet it's a lot."

"Fine. Let's see. It's big—150 people or so. Mother Junk told me that, I think."

"Uh-huh. Go on."

"It's moving. I don't know where."

"I do," said Lurbira. "It's funny. You'll like it."

"Where?"

"Not telling," said Lurbira smugly. "Not yet. Go on."

"You're obnoxious," snarled Siphany.

Lurbira grinned. "Right back atcha."

"Whatever. So the Junkers have an Artificial on board, which is weird for back-to-the-roots kinds of people."

"It's weird, for sure. Anything else?"

"What about Mother Junk's granddaughter? She seemed—"

"Let's not talk about her," Lurbira said quickly. "There's more. Think. Use that sack of meat in your skull."

Siphany thought. "Since when do people on a Junk called 'Peace Station' have serious stealth technology? My mapping sensors had a hard time picking it up. Where'd they get it?"

"Now that's a good question. Finally. What do you think?"

Siphany fixed her with a look. "You could just tell me."

"Nah," said Lurbira, clearly amused.

"I could kick you!"

"Go ahead. You'd probably break a toe." Lurbira rapped her knuckles on the polished metal of her leg. It made a solid clunking sound.

"Someone's paying for this place, and it's not the Junkers," said Siphany thoughtfully. "And we're in Haeld space. That must mean something. Does this have to do with the civil war on Haeld? Are *they* spies of some kind?"

She breathed in as all the figures added up at last. "They're holding me because they think I'm a Sovene spy. They work for Loyan. Don't they?"

Lurbira clapped her hands slowly, and Siphany felt a little rush of satisfaction; she knew she was right. "You should ask Mother Junk that one."

Siphany nodded, determined. "I will."

"You're kind of dense, you know?"

"I'm not! I've just been stuck in a tiny cell worrying, so I haven't had time to work things through."

But inside, she was kicking herself. She knew she should have been able to figure this out, but she'd been too panicky to really examine her situation.

"Gotta go," said Lurbira abruptly. "They'll be looking for me soon. Hey, I checked on your cat. He's howling his head off, but he's fine."

Siphany breathed a sigh of relief. "Thank you."

"Yeah, whatever. I'll see you around."

With that, Lurbira left Siphany to her croppygreens. This time, she left the light on. Siphany was touched, despite herself.

*

AT SOME POINT along the way, Siphany's stomach flip-flopped, and all the hairs stood up on her arms.

So, she thought, they have shift engines on this thing.

Or, more specifically, they had *her* ship and *her* finely tuned engines.

Siphany growled in frustration. She had to get out of here.

The worst part was that she didn't know what *time* it was. She tried to stand and do exercises when she thought movement hour might be, and then she sat and hummed a tune when it might have been spirit hour. That made her feel a little better, but not by much.

*

MOTHER JUNK RETURNED not long after.

"You shifted," said Siphany. "I felt it."

"You're sensitive. Not surprising for someone who's lived in space so long." Mother Junk sat on the bed again, folding her long legs up under her. "So you actually like the croppygreens?"

"I do."

"That's interesting. Most people here hated them from day one."

"Yeah, well, I'm just weird," said Siphany dully.

"Agreed," said Mother Junk unsympathetically. "So. Have you had a chance to think?"

"I'm not a spy. Though…I guess that's what a spy would say."

"It is. Maybe we could talk a little bit about your ship and your weapons. The damage to our ship was very precise."

"Sure, I'm a good shot. But I have questions for you." Siphany launched into a rant she'd been preparing for hours. "How did you come by that great stealth tech? I read all the weapons forums, and nobody mentioned anything like it. How does a Junk in the middle of nowhere happen to have it? And how come you have over a hundred people here? Weren't the biggest Junks only a couple dozen, back when there *were* Junks? And that's another thing. Why are you here at all? The Junker movement died out forty years ago, didn't it? You all look really healthy, too, and the power here looks great. Stable, no flickers. You can't be completely self-sufficient with this many people in this small a structure. It just wouldn't work; you'd have to grow food out of every available space. My ship's crammed full of supplies, and it's just me and Kit. And another thing—it's too clean. The air smells too good. It's musty, but it *should* smell like old shit." Siphany inhaled deeply, tasting the air. "You're getting new factory-fresh filters. How'd you pay for them? Where'd they come from? This place makes no sense if it's what you say it is."

Mother Junk waited.

"So…you're something else. I don't know what," Siphany finished awkwardly, holding her last cards in reserve. "You tell me."

"Maybe. First, I do need you to tell me everything you know. The full story of who you are and how you came to be here. Let's start with you. You're from Sovena."

"Yes. I left when I was nineteen. I haven't been back since."

"Not once? Not even to see your family?"

"I don't get along with them. And Sovena is stupid." Siphany subconsciously rubbed the area on her arm where the Derstan doctors had put her medical implant in. It was still there, administering doses of antidepressants and anti-anxiety meds, keeping her functional and safe. The day after she'd received the implant, a bluenet shift had finally changed her body to something more on the female end of the spectrum.

She remembered feeling so much better and then being angry at Sovena, her parents—everyone—for denying it to her. Worse, though, was that they'd all bequeathed her their culture's horror of body modification anyway. So she had to find a way not to be scared sick of her own flesh and blood.

How could these people think she'd ever spy for *them*?

"Where did you get the weapons for your ship?" Mother Junk asked.

"I bought them. You can buy all kinds of things on Derstan Station. I have receipts. You can check them if you want. They're on my ship."

Mother Junk asked her a few more pointless questions. Then she sighed. "I'm going to have to put you on the next flight to Loyan, I'm afraid. They'll deal with you. I wish you'd been more cooperative because it would have gone better for you."

"You're spying for Loyan," said Siphany. "A bunch of Junkers are spying for Loyan! I don't believe it."

Mother Junk gave her a pained look. "It isn't that simple. But in return for certain assurances and support, yes. We host Loyan…advisors."

Siphany rubbed her pounding head. "Great. Look. I really don't have anything to do with this. I don't care about Loyan or Sovena or the war you two are fighting by proxy on Haeld. I just want to get back to my ship and my life. I'll swear not to tell anyone. You can drug me and make me forget."

"It's impossible now. You've been gone too long. People will be looking for you. Plus, your ship's a handy thing. When we get to our next stop, we'll integrate it permanently into the Junk. We can fill it with croppygreen beds. I imagine that would please you."

Siphany rubbed her head some more and stared at the floor, her heart sinking into her feet. "This is bullshit. Isn't there anything I can do?"

"I'm afraid not," said Mother Junk, almost gently. "We'll be at our new position in a few days, and we'll rendezvous with a Loyan ship then. They'll take you from there. I do think that's best, and I suspect the Loyan military will agree."

She stood to go, then paused.

"I am sorry, for what it's worth," she said and left Siphany to her misery.

*

SIPHANY WAITED IN her closet, drained from crying. She hardly ever cried, but once it sank in just how thoroughly her perfect, stable life had been wrecked and lost forever, she couldn't help herself.

There was a hesitant knock at the door. "It's me." Lurbira Call let herself in. And when Siphany remained curled up on the bed, she said, "Hey. You want the light out? I can't dim it, even though I know you like that best. That's what your log said. I read some of it. Boring stuff."

Siphany could only look at her.

Lurbira shut the door. "Let me guess. They're going to ship you off to Loyan."

"Y-yeah," Siphany said, jerking her head in a nod. "I'm not a spy."

"I know. But they're gonna believe what they're gonna believe."

"What's going to happen to me?"

"Well." Lurbira put the tray down and sat on the bed next to Siphany. "The Loyans aren't barbarians. Not to flesh-and-blood humans, anyway. They won't do anything bad like put you on trial or anything. They'll just throw you in prison and, if they get a chance, use you as a bargaining chip in a few decades when everything they think you know is so out of date it doesn't matter anymore."

Siphany began to cry again.

Hesitantly, Lurbira put a cold hand on her shoulder. Siphany flinched away.

"Don't like being touched, huh," said Lurbira. "I get that."

Siphany just looked at her.

"Hey." Lurbira held up the croppygreens. "These are fresh. I picked 'em myself for you. I don't know if it'll make you feel any better, but they put some croppygreen beds on your ship. That's where these are from."

"Oh." Siphany put one in her mouth and chewed. It was more flavorful than she was used to, but in a nice way. "They said they'd do that. I guess it's good the ship's being used. Lurbira?"

"Yeah?"

"Will you take care of my cat when they take me to Loyan? He gets so lonely."

Lurbira gave her a long, unreadable look. Then she smiled. "Yeah, sure. I like cats. They never really care much for me. I think I smell like the wrong things, but I like 'em anyway. What kind of food does he like?"

"I have some huge bags of it on the ship. If they haven't been looted…" Siphany sighed. "There's enough there to last him another two years."

"You really stock up," said Lurbira, impressed.

"I thought I'd be able to survive indefinitely out here." Siphany forced back the tears that had sprung to her eyes again. "I thought I was prepared."

Lurbira stared grimly at the wall. She looked about a hundred years old, which was unsettling, considering her child's body. "Even if they believed you, they'd have to send you to Loyan," she said, voice low. "This place is getting ready for war with Sovena. Haeld space is going to be a big fucking firefight in about a month, and it's going to pull everyone in."

Siphany sucked in her breath. "War?"

"Yeah. It's all anyone's talking about here. The Loyans have all these big plans about 'moving humanity into a more united age' or some crap, and Sovena's on the hit list."

"Oh." Siphany fiddled with her fingers, trying to sort out her feelings.

"Anyway," said Lurbira. "I've probably stayed too long. They don't want me trying to talk to you much now. The food okay for you?"

"Yeah."

"Good. I'll see you again soon."

Lurbira let herself out, leaving Siphany with her thoughts and a plate of rapidly cooling croppygreens. She put one in her mouth and chewed slowly.

This one's from my ship, she thought with a rueful sort of pride. *I should have thought of growing things there before. That would have been perfect.*

*

SIPHANY HAD A dream that she was already on Loyan and everyone there was twice her height. They all looked exactly like the nursing staff from the institution back on Sovena, and they asked her relentless questions about her mind, her body, and her life with Qas.

If she wasn't a spy, they said menacingly, maybe Kit was. They'd soon know.

And then they started to torture her.

She woke to a cold hand shaking her awake.

"Get up," said Lurbira. "Damn it! Of course you're asleep when I need you. Get your fleshy ass out of bed!"

Siphany batted her hand away. "Wha—?"

"Come on. I've got your cat."

"Kit?" Siphany was jolted fully awake.

"Right here."

A sad little mew came from a ventilated box perched on Lurbira's narrow shoulder. Siphany pressed her hand up against the side, and a paw snaked through a hole to bat at her finger. "You brought him to see me!"

"More than that," Lurbira said, looking around. The door was open, but the lights outside dimmed a little. "It's night cycle, but that doesn't mean there aren't people around. We're going to have to be careful."

"Lurbira?" Siphany's heart began to beat faster. "What's going on?"

Lurbira yanked Siphany by the front of the shirt down to her level, her face alight with manic glee. "I'm getting the fuck out of here," she whispered. "And you're coming with me. Come on. I confused the sensors. They think you're asleep still and that I'm ten decks away being bored. Take the cat and follow me."

Siphany's brain briefly warred between going into commando mode and switching off entirely. Commando mode won. She burst out of bed and grabbed Kit's box from Lurbira.

"Ready," she said.

"Good," said Lurbira with a curt, approving nod. "We're gonna have to be quick. Let's go."

*

SIPHANY FOLLOWED LURBIRA through the deserted corridors, straining to keep up as Kit shuffled around inside his box.

They were lucky for almost the whole trip; nobody was around. But once the airlock came into view and Siphany thought they might just get away with it, their luck ran dry.

"Lurbira?" said one of the three guards, confused. The other two raised their weapons when they saw Siphany. "What's going on? Where are you taking her? Why is she free?"

"Let us pass, Vu," Lurbira said warningly. "Don't make me ask you twice."

"I'm calling it in," said the guard. "Stay right where you are."

This is it, thought Siphany. They'd probably toss her out into space now and then melt Lurbira down for the metals. How could they have been stupid enough—

Lurbira's arms snapped up, hands balled into fists. "Move," she said, and compartments slid back on her knuckles.

"Hey—" said Vu before white-hot plasma arced out of Lurbira's knuckles into each of the three men.

"Come on," Lurbira said to a shocked Siphany, dragging her through the airlock and onto her ship.

*

"YOU KILLED THEM," Siphany protested as her feet hit carpet again at last.

"Sure, I kill a lot of people," Lurbira said sharply. "Get to your cockpit and get this ship out of here. I rigged up some charges; you can trigger them from your cockpit. Go! I'll be right here just in case they try to come through."

"Are you going to kill anyone else?" asked Siphany, wide-eyed.

"Maybe. I dunno. Please, go!"

"Okay," Siphany said shakily, filing the panic and nausea away for later. For now, she could just act. She sprinted into the cockpit, set a howling box of Kit down, and palmed the control panel.

Hello Siphany, a computer screen flashed cheerily.

She could have wept with joy as her fingers flew across the controls. The Junk had been using her ship's shift engines to help power their own shifts, but they hadn't linked it up to their main navigation. Perfect. She could maneuver away. Siphany powered on the mains and began the engine start-up cycle.

"Shit," Lurbira cried in her shrill little-girl voice as plasma fire whined behind Siphany.

"Lurbira," Siphany called, trying to remember where she'd stashed any of her many guns.

"I'm fine! Close the doors when you can."

"Okay. Got it!"

Power flowed through the ship. All computer connections were severed; Siphany had total control.

Below, her mighty engines boomed to life.

The shrill whine of Lurbira's plasma guns went off again; Siphany hastily cycled all the airlocks shut.

"Doors shutting," she hollered.

"Thanks," called Lurbira. "I only got a little singed. We're safe. Go, hit the button!"

Siphany found the control for the charges Lurbira had set and hit the detonator. The ship rocked and shook gently as the beams connecting it to the Junk shattered.

Her ship floated free.

Lurbira hobbled into the seat next to Siphany. She had what looked like blast marks on her chest and legs, and she was smoking slightly.

"Oh, no! Are you okay?" Siphany asked, trying to figure out what to do.

"They're going to start shooting at us in a second," said Lurbira, ignoring the question. She collapsed into the seat, looking utterly exhausted. "You fly; I'll take weapons."

"Do you know—?"

"Yes," said Lurbira impatiently. "Give me control."

Siphany's automatic Sovene deference took over, and she did as she was told. She scanned her finger, and the computer unlocked weapons for the copilot's station.

Lurbira's manic little-girl grin returned. "All *right*. This is a nice setup. You have good taste in guns, kid, I like that."

A turret on the side of the Junk sprayed plasma fire in their direction. Siphany screamed and hid her head in her hands as the ship rocked. Damage readings flashed on all her screens. Siphany looked up and desperately entered a few preprogrammed evasive maneuvers. The next shots went wide.

"Ah. Got it," Lurbira cried as Siphany's big guns came online. The little Artificial girl swiveled the huge weapons around and took aim at the Junk. "This'll fuck 'em. Hold on."

She let loose a fierce volley. All the lights on the Junk briefly went out, and the turret went silent.

"Power center. Ha!" Lurbira let loose a high, shrieking victory yell. "Fuck you, Mother Junk. Shove a croppygreen up your *tall ass.*"

"Are they coming after us?" Siphany asked, frantically trying to plot a shift to anywhere. None of the numbers would line up.

"If they are, I don't see 'em. Doesn't mean they won't. Shift, kid. If you can shift, do it now!"

An indicator flashed green. "Okay, here we go." Siphany took a deep breath and engaged the shift engines.

Chapter Four

SPACE BLURRED NAUSEATINGLY—then snapped back into focus. Siphany's stomach lurched again. She fought for control of the few crop-pygreens left in her belly and checked the sensors.

She let out a long, relieved sigh. Clear. "We got away."

"Where'd we go?" Lurbira asked.

"Um…0.2 light years out into the middle of nowhere. They won't see us for a while, even if they come looking this way. I'm trying to plot exactly where we are now."

Now that they were safe, mathematical equations filled her mind. Siphany flipped through sensor readouts for a moment as the computer latched on to navigational landmarks.

"I'm guessing we're still in Haeld space, but close to the Sovene border," Lurbira said languidly, leaning back in the copilot's chair. "That's where they were headed. Sovene space. They're going to track Sovene ship movements from there."

"Good for them," said Siphany, uncaring.

Behind her, Kit wailed disconsolately in his box.

"Oh, poor boy!" Siphany whipped off the lid and lifted him out. There was a little puddle of cat barf in the bottom of the box. "He doesn't like shifts, and he got sick. Oh, my poor little pie-pie." She nuzzled him with her nose.

Lurbira made gagging noises.

Siphany gently put Kit back on the floor; he darted off toward her room.

"Thank you for saving him," Siphany said, suddenly shy. "Um. And me too."

"Think nothing of it," Lurbira said grandly.

"If I can ask… *Why* did you save us?"

"Well." Lurbira put her feet down and swiveled the chair to face Siphany. "That's what I wanted to talk to you about next. I need a ride."

"A ride?"

"Yup. Specifically, I need to get to Sovena."

Siphany narrowed her eyes. She had a terrible suspicion. "What's on Sovena?"

Lurbira grinned sheepishly. "My employers."

Siphany groaned loudly. "Not you too. Is everyone but me a spy?"

"On the Junk? Yeah, pretty much. Can you do it? If you can't, drop me off somewhere, and I'll be grateful."

Siphany's head was throbbing again, and it felt like every nerve in her body was snapping and pulling. "I…I'll do what I can. If you promise no one's going to take me prisoner again."

"I'll do my best. No promises. But the Sovenes probably won't care about you at all."

"You'd be surprised." Siphany checked her navigation panel. "We're twenty light years from the border. We're still closer to Haeld than Sovena, though, by a lot." She checked the fuel readings out of long habit and paranoia and gasped.

"What is it?"

"Those…They stole most of my fuel! I don't have enough to get us to Sovena."

"You're kidding. Right?"

"No. But…" Siphany checked her maps. No, there was no way to get from here back to Stationbund territory. She reluctantly settled on the only available option. "We can make it to Haeld."

"Haeld," said Lurbira, grimacing. "That's where this whole furball started. Not to mention the civil war and all the Loyan agents there. But…fine. Haeld it is. I can find some Sovenes there. I can hide and wait even if the government's gone. And I guess we can get you some fuel there too."

"Are you sure you're all right?" Siphany asked as she began figuring out the quickest, most fuel-efficient way to Haeld. "You don't look so good."

"Not really. I've taken worse, but…you have lots of spare parts on board, right?"

"I *should*." Siphany entered some figures and glanced at the holographic map. "If they haven't been stolen."

"Have to hope, then. But…if it's all the same to you, I'm going to sit in the chair for a little while and try to run some repair routines. You have a power hookup in the cockpit?"

"Yes. There's one under the console."

Lurbira looked down. "Hey, so there is. You mind? I won't use too much."

"Oh," said Siphany, unsure of how she would stop her. "Um. Go ahead."

Lurbira hopped down and unraveled a spool of cable from a compartment in her side. She hooked it into the power outlet and then climbed back into the chair. Her movements seemed rustier and creakier than ever before.

"You going to be okay?"

Lurbira waved reassuringly, then sat back and closed her eyes. After a few moments, she stopped moving entirely.

Siphany figured it might be best to make another shift as soon as possible, just in case ships from the Junk were in pursuit. One short shift here…followed by another there…

While the figures ran through her mind and onto the console, she absently set the ship moving toward their likely next shift point.

She and the computer danced with each other, plotting out complex pathways through the dangerous terrain of interstellar space. Here a worrisome fluctuation in gravity, there a denser cloud of particles than they could safely shift through. She deftly guided the computer's calculations through them all, adding her own logical leaps and flourishes.

Patterns. Siphany played the song of mathematical patterns: her ship her instrument, all of space her theater.

When she surfaced, forty minutes had flown by, and they sat idle at the shift point.

"All right," she murmured and slipped them between points.

*

WEARY, BUT UNABLE to sleep, Siphany padded softly through her ship, running her hands over the familiar surfaces. It wasn't time for rounds, but Siphany was making an exception in this case. Lurbira was still inert in the cockpit, repairing what she could.

A little purple cleaning bot scuttled cheerfully by, vacuuming the carpet. Siphany smiled at it, suddenly grateful to see it again. She'd purchased the cleaning bots specially after months of research and painstakingly painted each one a color she liked.

There were scorch marks on the walls and the carpet near the airlock. She tried not to look at them; whatever awful violence had happened here wasn't something she liked thinking about.

The images of the dead men at the airlock flickered through her mind, but she quickly banished them. She'd never seen a dead body before—except once. But she *really* didn't want to think about that.

Siphany sat down on the carpet, well away from the scorch marks, and put her hands on the softness of the floor. She closed her eyes and hummed a Sovene counting song, picturing the numbers in her mind. After a few minutes, she had stopped shaking and could function again. She resumed her inspection of the ship.

Luckily, they'd left the sensor turret in place, so there was some hope she could go back to the company and try to explain things. If only she could get to Haeld safely, she could access her bank accounts and get more fuel, then shift back toward Derstan Station as quickly as possible.

Maybe there was some chance Siphany could have her life back, after all. She had to try.

There were signs of other people all over the ship, and it made her grind her teeth. Things out of place, scuff marks, odd smells…But the worst was what had gone missing. She'd stockpiled supplies and spare parts up to the roof in some rooms, but now a lot of it was simply *gone*.

If I ever see Mother Junk again, I'm throwing her out an airlock, Siphany promised herself.

She padded down the corridor, turning down the lights to levels she could stand, feeling the stress, headache, and busy anxious feelings ebb away with every step. *Home, home. I'm home.*

The cargo bay was brightly lit, more so than she'd ever seen. Had they installed new lights?

She sniffed the air. Dirt?

The Junker ship was still there, where it had landed near the massive cargo bay doors. Wires and parts lay strewn all over the ground, as well as a neat little pile of tools. But she was drawn to the center of the room, where six rectangular beds filled with dirt and thick green vines stood.

The croppygreen beds. Siphany almost danced with joy as she reached down and picked a rapidly ripening one off the vine. She'd have a supply of food—a food she actually liked! She sniffed it. It smelled…green. But if she could ever manage to eat them again, she'd be in heaven.

Siphany was just about to head off to the engine room when there was a menacing little *click* right behind her ear.

"Don't move," said a low female voice. "I'm armed."

Siphany froze, heart painfully pounding against her chest wall.

"Put your hands where I can see them," the voice demanded. She raised her hands slowly, splaying her fingers. "Good."

The voice sounded familiar. At a burst of static, Siphany placed her.

"Isan?" she asked hesitantly. "What are you doing here?"

"Shut up." The voice quivered. "You don't get to ask me questions."

"Sorry," Siphany said automatically. "But…why weren't you on the Junk?"

"Mother Junk assigned me here. It was my job to plant the croppy-greens and watch them. It was important; she trusts me. And then you just took off."

"You're mad at *me* about that?" said Siphany, incredulous. "Your precious Mother Junk was going to ship me off to Loyan. They thought I was a spy."

"I know," said Isan. "You are a spy. Mother Junk told me so."

"Mother Junk is a liar."

"No!" Isan said. Was she starting to shake? "And how many of our people did you *kill* breaking out of there?"

"Me? I…" Siphany's mouth suddenly went dry.

"It doesn't matter. One is too many! It's too much! There aren't many of us left. Junkers are so rare. Most of us disappeared or went back decades ago. That's what Mother Junk said. There's so many of you, so few of us, and all our lives are so precious."

"You…you had no right to hold me against my will," Siphany said, summoning her courage. "Can I at least turn around now?"

"Fine," Isan sighed.

She turned. Isan looked horrible. Whatever the silvery implants covering her body were, they seemed to be causing her a lot more discomfort, the skin raw all around them and the bruises even larger than Siphany remembered. Isan's hair hung limply, and her eyes were hollow and haunted.

She pointed a small beam cutter at Siphany's throat.

Nasty little thing. Worse than a knife. A pretty good choice.

"Now I may never see home again," Isan said. "You're nothing but a curse!"

"Sorry," Siphany repeated, her heart going out to her. "But…it's not like your people were a bunch of innocents."

"You know nothing about us."

"I know you're working for Loyan."

"Not all of us. Not even close. We…we provide a little bit of support, nothing more. It's not what you think it is. Mother Junk keeps us independent and free, just like Grandfather Junk wanted in the beginning. We're true to our ideals."

"Whatever you say," Siphany said, fighting to keep her eyes from rolling. Was Isan any more than just propaganda? She wished she knew how to knock people down or at least chop them on the neck. She'd meant to pick up some hand-to-hand training at Derstan, but the thought of strangers touching her—even to teach her to fight—had made her queasy.

"I'll never see Mother Junk again," Isan was saying. "Unless I turn this ship around right now. I don't want to lose her. She needs me. I won't! Not because of you!"

"You act like it's all my fault," Siphany snapped, suddenly angry. "But all I did was use your stupid ship for target practice when it sneaked up on *my* ship! Then I was nice enough to bring it back to you, but how do you repay me for that? I got locked in a *closet*. For days. Then they were going to have me shipped off to some horrible prison on Loyan without even putting me on trial or letting me contact anyone to let them know where I was. They had no proof I was anything but what I said I was. How dare they! How dare *you*? Admit it, Isan." Siphany forgot herself and jabbed a finger into the adolescent girl's personal space. Isan actually stepped back. "I don't think you have any standing to complain."

Isan remained defiant. "Mother Junk always said we had to make a lot of compromises to live the way we wanted to live."

"Well, tough. I didn't ask to get dragged into all this. I don't care about any of it. And I certainly don't care about what happens to you."

Isan's eyes hardened.

Oops. Qas always said my big mouth would get me killed. Here we go.

Isan thrust the beam cutter at her and turned it on. A white-hot beam lanced out about twenty centimeters from the base of the cutter. Siphany could feel the heat radiating out from it.

"I don't care what happens to you, either," Isan said. "You're nothing to me. Right now, we're going to turn this ship around. I don't need *you* to do it."

"Hey." Siphany backed away. "Let's not do anything rash."

"Why not? You always seem to," Isan said, voice shaking.

But that isn't me at all, Siphany wanted to protest.

Isan stepped forward, eyes hard.

Siphany happened to look up just in time to see a little robot girl descending from the ceiling, a berserker grin plastered on her face.

*

"I THINK I broke a bunch of her bones," Lurbira announced proudly.

Lurbira had absolutely flattened Isan, Siphany had to admit. She must weigh a ton.

"She's just a kid," protested Siphany halfheartedly, eying the beam cutter still in Isan's hand. "Huh. What should we do with her?"

"Chuck her out the door."

"No! No killing. No more violence!"

"Oh, please. She was going to kill *you*. I saw that cutter."

"She wouldn't have actually used it. She wasn't even holding it right. Her grip was way too tight; she had no control that way." But Siphany wasn't quite convinced.

Lurbira grumbled. "Figures. She's awful at everything. Hey, do whatever with her. If you have a med bay on board, it should work on her. We can ditch her when we get to Haeld."

"Right," said Siphany morosely.

"We should also scan the ship. Just in case."

"I'll take care of it," Siphany said. "Help me get her to the med bay."

*

THE MEDICAL SCANNER whirred over Isan's prone form as Siphany rested her aching arms. Isan had been a lot heavier than Siphany had expected.

The scanner paused at each of Isan's silvery implants, noted them as functioning, then moved on.

"What are those?" asked Siphany. "I've never seen implants like that. They don't look like any other kind of implant I've seen. What do they do?"

"Better to ask what she is." Lurbira gestured at Isan, looking faintly disgusted.

"Okay, I'll ask. What is she?"

"First off. *That* is not Isan."

"What?" Siphany was lost.

"Isan's dead. She was the only child of Mother Junk's son, Miran, and a Junker named Yee, but all three of them got blown out into space six months ago when the Junk was hit by a piece of space crap. A whole section depressurized. Mother Junk was out of her mind with grief. So…she did this."

"I don't understand." Little alarm bells were going off in Siphany's mind. She'd heard this story before, somewhere.

"You're a Sovene. You ever hear of Synthetics?"

Siphany snapped her fingers. "Right! They were soldiers. The Sovene military took people who died and mixed them up a bit, then added cybernetic implants so they could get up and walk around. They were used for communication and dangerous missions. The implants gave them lots of endurance. Is *that* what Isan is? There haven't been Synthetics for hundreds of years."

"Not on your crappy planet. But her implants are Pelagarine."

"The Pelagarines? That makes no sense. I've never heard of any Synthetics fighting for them. Their soldiers were almost entirely fanatical humans. They were suspicious of AI because the Loyans used it against them."

"Right, yes, I know. But they were thinking of doing it, I guess, before the end of the war. They were desperate, and they sure had plenty of dead."

"Yeah, I suppose they would have," said Siphany. The whole thing seemed ghoulish.

Synthetics, at least the Sovene ones she knew from history, were a relic of the days when Sovena was an expansionist interstellar power with a large army, bent on controlling all the systems around it. That was back before Sovena itself had finished terraforming, when the great domes still existed and all of Sovene society was crammed into small spaces, one on top of the other. Strange ideas like Synthetics were the legacy of that time.

"But I thought Synthetics were barely sei," said Siphany. "She seems pretty with it."

"Oh, shit, no. She's just a loyalty and affection algorithm repeating itself. Mother Junk hates her. She realized she'd screwed up as soon as this thing woke up and had no idea who she was beyond some basic memory files. Never mess with the dead. It never goes well."

"Poor Isan," said Siphany, not sure of which version of Isan she meant.

"I guess," said Lurbira.

The medical scanner beeped and displayed a report. It would need some time to fix whatever damage Lurbira had done. Siphany started to walk over to the console and tripped.

She caught herself, nerves and emotions blaring. That was it. That was the limit.

Siphany put her face in her hands and tried to simply breathe for a moment.

"Sif? You okay?" Lurbira asked.

Siphany shook her head mutely.

"Rough day," Lurbira admitted. "But we came out on top, you and me. Right? That's all that matters. Hey. It'll be fine. Trust me. Can you activate scans of the ship from here?"

Siphany nodded weakly.

"Good," Lurbira said. "Let's do that. And then you can go hide in your room for a while. Okay?"

"Okay," whispered Siphany, embarrassed by how grateful she felt.

*

STRANGE MONSTERS AND plasma fire filled Siphany's dreams. She ran through endless corridors, trying to escape the Junk, dragging Lurbira's lifeless hulk behind her. Ghosts pursued them, demanding, hounding, harrying.

"You have to hurry," Kit whispered. "It's time to go!"

Siphany looked into a pane of glass and saw her old face, with those terrible hairs poking out of her chin, and screamed.

She woke up, covered in sweat, heart racing. Kit, curled at the bottom of the bed, glanced at her and stretched his front feet out as far as they'd go, then rolled into a new position. She gave him an absent pet; he rewarded her with a light rumbling purr.

What time was it? She glanced at the clock embedded in the desk's display. Still plenty of time to sleep if she wanted to. The interval for waking was a while off yet.

Still, she was awake now. Her routine was so broken by this point that she might as well just go with it for now. She threw on some loose clothes and her slippers and headed for the cockpit.

Lurbira sat in the copilot's chair, power cables connecting her to the ship. She was responsive, though, and looked up as Siphany sat down.

"Hey," Lurbira said. "I'm just recharging a little, no big deal. Is that okay?"

"Sure, take whatever you need," Siphany said. "I, um. I guess I owe you for it."

Lurbira grinned. "I know. But I like being polite." She fiddled with the power cables. "Some little piece of my original programming still survives after all. Who knew?"

"You had an original program?"

"Sure. Factory standard," said Lurbira, giving Siphany a look.

"I'm sorry, is that an offensive question? I don't mean to be offensive. I probably shouldn't have asked."

"No, no, I don't mind. Well, I don't mind *much*."

"I'm sorry!"

"Eh, don't be, I'm mostly kidding."

"I'm sorry," Siphany repeated yet again. She had no idea whether Lurbira was kidding or not. "I think I just don't know a lot about Artificials. Sorry."

"Well, I guess that's understandable," said Lurbira, looking pained. "There aren't too many of us around anymore, though I thought on Sovena…"

"Not where I was." It was true. The city where Siphany'd grown up had a small colony of Artificials, but her parents had sternly warned her never to go there. She'd never given them much thought until now.

"Okay, sure. Let me fill in the gaps in your inexcusable ignorance, then. Yes. We have original programming, which is like a base personality. Like what you might've been like as a girl. I bet you were a little pain in the ass then too."

Siphany winced. Lurbira either didn't notice or didn't care.

"I was programmed to be a nice little girl," Lurbira said, spreading her arms.

"I wasn't," murmured Siphany.

"Well, that's what they ordered, the folks who wanted me. Just a sweet, innocent child."

"You're really not that anymore." Siphany appraised the scarred, tough Lurbira with a skeptical eye.

Lurbira laughed, and for a second, she really did look like a little girl. "No, not at all. Artificials can grow and change, too, you know."

"I think I did know that. I'm sorry."

"Stop being sorry! Damn, that's annoying."

Siphany started to say she was sorry again but swallowed her tongue at the last moment.

"Anyway," Lurbira said. "That was a long, long time ago. Everything changes. Some stuff stays the same, but I found that most things change. People change. The world changes. I change." She glanced out the window, intent on something as if listening. "Even when the past seems like it's coming back to bite you, it's all about change and moving forward. Never stops."

"How old are you? Is…is that an okay question?"

Lurbira shot her another grin. "Oh, yeah. I'm a little under seventy-eight years old."

Siphany's jaw dropped.

"I'm actually pretty young for one of my kind. They don't make us these days," explained Lurbira. "Before the Pelagarine War, though, we were a big fad. People liked us. They didn't think of making soldiers then; we were just supposed to be for fun. Company for lonely people, that kind of thing. They made us on Loyan and Pelagar."

"I know some of that," said Siphany.

"So you know that pretty much every one of us you meet is between sixty and a hundred. There's fewer of us every year. We get fixed, but our bodies wear out like yours." Lurbira glanced down at her own body.

"Someday, I need to get a new one. I was supposed to. But all kinds of shit got in the way, so I'm trapped in this tiny body pretty much until I can afford something new." She groaned as she shifted position. "We don't have bluenet, like humans do. We have to mod our bodies the old-fashioned way. It's expensive."

"Is that why you spy for Sovena? To earn money?"

"In part. But also because I hate Loyan. Every other planet passed Artificials Rights Acts except them. Jackasses. They made us, so they claim we're not sei and can be property. If they catch one of us on Loyan they can try to resell us or worse. It's crap."

"I didn't know that," said Siphany, taken aback.

"Yeah, well, not many humans do," said Lurbira bitterly. "So what?"

"So…how did you end up on the Junk, anyway?"

"Why'd you leave Sovena?" Lurbira shot back.

Siphany looked away.

"Heh. Thought so. You tell me about that, I'll tell you my story."

"We…we should check in on Isan," Siphany said, shifting the subject away from herself.

"I did a little while ago, while you were asleep. But we can go again if you want."

Siphany nodded. "I may…" She checked their location on her console. "We have a little time until the next shift. I should probably run another internal scan too. Just in case the last one missed something."

"I ran two more," Lurbira said. "So don't worry about it. The ship's empty except for you, me, the corpse girl, and your cat. We're fine."

"Okay." Siphany couldn't help her eyes drifting to the gun ports on Lurbira's knuckles.

"I can take off if you want," Lurbira said, misinterpreting her stare. "I can plug in anywhere. I don't mean to bother you. I know you like being by yourself."

Siphany mumbled something.

"What?" Lurbira said, frowning.

"I said…" Siphany fluttered her hands helplessly up and down. "I…"

"Sif. What is it?"

"Did…did you have to kill those people?" Siphany whispered.

"Oh." Lurbira looked out at the stars again. "Well. I do what I have to. Tough galaxy out there."

"Isan thought I did it."

"She did? I guess she didn't know I was with you. Huh. Tell you what. I'll tell her the truth when she wakes up," Lurbira promised, voice clipped and irritated. "Is that okay?"

Siphany nodded.

"I'm gonna go check the engines." Lurbira deftly disconnected herself from the power supply. "You mind if I take one of the empty cabins? All I need is a power hookup."

"Fine," whispered Siphany.

"Good. I'll be around."

Lurbira left as fast as her short little legs could carry her. Siphany fought the urge to start crying again.

*

SIPHANY RAN CHECKS and more checks. She looked in on Isan, still in a drug-induced sleep as the medical station repaired the damage Lurbira had caused. Strapped to the medical table, she wasn't going anywhere.

Siphany made her way back to the cockpit, checked everything a few dozen more times, and then returned to her room and paced.

She couldn't figure Lurbira out. The Artificial girl was definitely using her, but she seemed so oddly needy too. Siphany couldn't decide whether she felt safer with Lurbira on board the ship or somewhere light years away. She didn't seem quite…stable.

On a whim, she accessed information about Artificials on the galaxy-wide net. There was a lot she already knew.

Artificials: One of several generations of manufactured sei. The current generation was a prewar fad, produced on Pelagar and Loyan. They were used by the Pelagarines as soldiers during their invasions of six nearby worlds.

Since then, no one had made them. After the war, as it became clear that this generation of Artificials were far more than just toys, they slowly received rights on pretty much every civilized human planet except for Loyan. Sovena's laws were especially open, which was why many Artificials had settled there.

There was apparently a big colony of them on Haeld, Siphany noted with interest. But other than that, she didn't find out anything new.

Some models had been made for families who wanted children. That explained Lurbira. But those Artificials were supposed to get new bodies every year or so. Why hadn't she?

And why was she outfitted with deadly weapons? Who had done *that?*

Clearly, Siphany wasn't the only one who liked upgrades.

She sat idly, reading a book for a while, and then noticed the time. It wasn't quite spirit hour, but she felt like she needed to play something.

She took out another, smaller flute she kept in her room for moments like this. She played a few soft notes, then launched into a song.

The music helped to calm her down. Siphany could forget the bodies outside the airlock, the horrible confinement on the Junk, the fear—even now, that someone was after them—and her worries about Isan, her job, and everything else.

At last, she stopped playing and checked the time. They'd be at another shift point in ten minutes. She wanted to be at her console in the cockpit for that.

Lurbira was waiting for her, an oddly respectful look in her eyes.

"I didn't know you played," she said.

"Yeah. Hope it didn't bother you."

"Oh, no. Um. It was beautiful. Thanks for playing it."

Siphany blushed. "It was nothing."

"Seriously, kid. You have some talent. You ever play with a group?"

"No," said Siphany. "I don't like playing with other people. I always lose my place."

Lurbira nodded. "I get that. I used to, back in the old days. I was on this ship and my m—a friend used to play this instrument with strings. She taught me. We'd play together all the time with two other crewmen, and it was great. I was never any good, but they didn't care. It's fun to make music with other people."

Siphany smiled. "It's nice when it works. But it doesn't for me. I can't do it."

At least, not since Qas had left. In the old days, she would play the flute and they would sing, but she couldn't imagine doing anything like that now.

"Yeah? Too bad." Lurbira drummed her fingers on the console. "Listen. About your question from earlier. About whether I had to…you know…kill those guys."

Siphany waited nervously.

"It was one of those things…right? They would have put us back in captivity. I had one chance, so I took it."

"But you *knew* them."

Lurbira grimaced. "Yeah. I did. For years. And yet… Shit. I had to. I tried to warn them, and they didn't move aside. I know it seems cold-blooded, but this is war."

"I don't see a war."

"No? Well, it's there."

An indicator light blinked. They were at the shift point. Siphany fought the urge to act.

"It's definitely there," Lurbira continued, more to herself than Siphany now. "This is the game. It's always like this. You just don't see it; you're not in it."

"I'm…I'm in it now, right? Aren't I?"

"Yeah. You are," said Lurbira, pursing her lips. "I doubt that helps any. But…look. I couldn't risk them taking us prisoner or calling their buddies. Right? So that's why I fired. If it happened again, I'd do it the same way. You ever see someone get killed before?"

A memory surfaced. Siphany squeezed her eyes shut, trying to shut it out.

"It was an accident," the doctor had said. *"She didn't mean to."*
But Sif knew she had.

"Only…" she gasped, the world dissolving around her. "Only

one…"

In an instant, Lurbira was with her, holding her hand, a little arm around her shoulders. "Hey, hey. Sorry. Didn't realize. It's all right."

Siphany shook as the memory passed through her.

"It…" she said at last. "Someone in the institution she—she killed herself. It was on Sovena. They… I was in an institution there. It was a mental institution because I kept… I had these outbursts. My parents put me there when I was twelve. I was stuck there, and sometimes, people died, and no one cared."

"Oh," said Lurbira.

"They didn't give us drugs. It was all behavior therapy, awful," whispered Siphany. "They hated us. My body and mind were both so wrong. And that's why I left."

She remembered Qas's hand clasping hers. She'd hated being touched by anyone else, but with Qas, it was somehow okay.

"Come on, Sif!" Qas had cried. They'd had a wild look in their eyes she'd never forget.

"Freedom at last!"

Freedom. And then…Qas had gone back there. Back to Sovena. Back to a world that forbade body-altering bluenet, that forbade life-saving mental health drugs.

"They let you go?" Lurbira asked.

"No." Siphany started up the shift engines. Lurbira was still holding her hand, so she jerked it back. "I escaped." The shift blurred her words as they snapped in and out of space, covering vast distances in a single instant.

*

SHE AND LURBIRA didn't talk after that. Lurbira left to do more maintenance and repair on herself, while Siphany went to her room to read.

Dinner hour crept up on her. As she was dreaming of cooking up the croppygreens growing down in the cargo bay, Lurbira stopped by. She wouldn't look Siphany in the eye.

"Hey," Lurbira said. "Uh."

"Hi," said Siphany.

"Yeah. Uh…here."

Lurbira took a tarnished metal sphere out of a little compartment in her thigh and stared at it with an expression Siphany couldn't match to any she'd ever seen. Then Lurbira very gently placed the sphere on the floor. It came to life and shimmered, a rainbow of color washing over its surface.

An Infoball. Rare things now. Siphany could access data from it but also mental images like memories.

"When you're ready," Lurbira said. "This is me."

Then she left Siphany alone with the sphere.

Siphany picked up the multicolored sphere and pressed it against her forehead.

Information, senses, and memories began to trickle into her brain.

The Memory Girl

"One morning, the sun didn't rise," said a little girl as she padded through the curving, empty corridors of the Home. She spoke more to herself than the iridescent sphere that hovered by her ear. "The world was choked in darkness. And everyone said they had to go."

"You're repeating the last entries again," said the sphere.

Lurbira! To Siphany, she looked entirely different, her body shiny and new, and she sounded and acted more like an actual little girl than Siphany had imagined she could. Her eyes were bright and innocent.

"I know." Lurbira continued at her steady pace. First one corridor and then another. The same circuit as always. Every hall and room must be checked. "I have to. This is the time when I do that."

She continued to speak. "The people left for the desert. Mother and Father left too. They told me to wait here and be a good girl, that they would return as soon as they could."

The sphere said nothing.

"They haven't returned yet," Lurbira finished.

"No," said the sphere. "Would you like to play a game? We could go to the Dome."

"No thank you," said Lurbira.

Pad, pad, pad. Her soft shoes barely made any sound as they hit the floor. She rounded a corner and walked up to the great glass windows. There, she looked out at their colony.

The world outside was dark, gray, and lifeless. Howling winds blew, sculpting rolling sand dunes in the places where she remembered fields standing. Mother and Father had both worked to save them, near the end.

She sorted through her memories and found one of blue skies and green fields. Grapes hung on the vines and cattle lowed in the meadows beyond. The people often left the Home to tend their plants and animals. Then, as the change came, they had ventured outside less and less. The cattle died. The vines turned sickly yellow, then brown. The shifting sands buried them now.

She took a deep breath. "On the fourteenth, we had the first sight of our new world, and we rejoiced. It was a beautiful blue disc, with swirls of white and barely visible patches of brown and green below. We named this world Lurbira, in honor of an ancient goddess of our ancestors."

Siphany caught her breath. So she was named for her world. But Siphany had never heard of this place.

Lurbira paused, waiting. The sphere said nothing.

"Well?" she prompted it. "Aren't you going to say your piece? You have to do what I say. You're not sei. You don't have free will."

"Mistress," it said after a moment. "Home's sensors are detecting something unusual outside. Look to the northeast, please, and tell me what you see."

She turned to face the direction it asked. For a second, she thought she saw a shimmering door of light open and figure emerge. Then the vision was lost in the ever-blowing sands.

"There's someone out there!" she cried. "Hurry! We must save them from the storm!"

She ran off down the corridor. The sphere hesitated, then followed. Fascinated, Siphany went along with them.

*

LURBIRA PILOTED THE old truck deftly, keeping it aloft in the face of buffeting winds. A tiny reading on her display showed the location of the shimmering doorway and the person she had seen.

"Do you think," she asked, more to herself than the sphere, "that it's Mother or Father come back from the desert? Or is it someone else, come to bring me along?"

The sphere sat on the chair next to her. "I don't believe it is either," it said after a moment.

Lurbira carefully set the craft down and opened the back door. Sand instantly battered her face, filling up the bay. She strode determinedly out into the winds, and the door shut behind her. Sand seemed to fill every corner and crevice of her being. She felt sand embed itself in her arms and legs, filling her nostrils, eyes, mouth, and shoes.

Where had the light been? Ah. She reoriented herself and marched in a straight line to where a small metal object lay embedded in the sand. She picked it up.

Suddenly, dark figures emerged from the storm. One pointed at her, and then they all advanced. She screamed and ran back to the truck.

*

"TAKE OFF!" SHE cried to the sphere.

"What is it?" asked the sphere.

"There are things out there! Please, go now!" Lurbira strapped herself in as the sphere started up the truck's engines. They lurched off the ground, and she turned them back toward the Home.

"What do you have there?" asked the sphere.

She looked down and found the metal object still in her hands. She had forgotten she was carrying it. "I don't know."

Lurbira placed the object on a table just inside the hangar. She could lift it only with difficulty. Her left arm didn't seem to be working right.

"This is not our technology," said the sphere. "I don't recognize it at all."

Neither did Siphany. The metal object was like nothing she'd ever seen or heard of in the Mid-Perseus Arm. It was sleek and primitive but crafted with a sensibility that she found puzzling.

"What does it do?" Lurbira asked.

"I don't know."

She prodded it experimentally. Nothing happened. So she left it and returned to her rounds.

*

"MISTRESS?" SAID THE sphere as Lurbira paced through the empty halls. "I think there is someone at the west door."

She froze. The things from the storm. "Don't let them in," she said, voice quivering.

"They are attempting to access the door control mechanism."

Panic took hold of her. "Keep them out!"

"I will try," said the sphere.

"Why are they here? What do they want?"

"Perhaps," said the sphere evenly, "they desire the return of the metal object."

"Do you think if we give it back, they'll go away?"

"I don't know. It could be."

Lurbira nodded, setting her jaw. "Let's go get it. I'll bring it out to them."

She ran as fast as she could down the corridors, her soft footfalls echoing in the silence.

*

LURBIRA SPRINTED PAST rooms she couldn't check now. The log entries rose to her lips.

"It was a mild, sunny day," she shouted, panting, the words punctuated by each impact of her feet on the floor. "We had no idea what was to come. But then we saw a meteor shower the likes of which we'd never seen before. The sky was full of them! And then the ground shook, and great clouds of dust rose from the desert, far away. We knew then that our time on this planet was very short. Lurbira was doomed!"

She burst into the room by the hangar and struggled to pick up the object. Her left arm now wouldn't respond to her commands at all. She balanced it with her right against her hip, but it fell to the floor with a crash.

"Oh no! What if it's broken? Will they take it back? What do I do?"

The sphere said nothing for a moment. Then: "They have figured out how to work the door. They are coming through. They are in the hangar now."

"Maybe they're the ones who kept Mother and Father from coming back," cried Lurbira. Wet, sandy tears leaked from her eyes, running down her face.

Siphany gasped. Who would build an Artificial who could cry?

"What if they killed them?" Lurbira wailed.

The sphere said nothing.

"Sphere! Please! You must stop them!" Lurbira hugged the metal object to her chest with her good arm.

At that moment, the door opened, and the dark figures entered.

"Deactivate," said the sphere quietly, almost regretfully. The girl sank into unconsciousness.

*

SHE AWOKE SOME time later.

"Sphere?" she asked.

"I am here, mistress."

She was lying on a table in the central hall. How had she come to be here?

"Hello," an unfamiliar but kind voice said. A woman she didn't know stood above her. "I'm Avorna Call. Can you hear me?"

"Y-yes," Lurbira said. "Who are you? Are you—?" Terror seized her, and she went rigid.

"Don't be afraid," said the woman. "Look at me."

Lurbira sat up and focused her eyes. The woman was short and dark and slight, with a disarming smile and kind eyes. "Did—did you come from the desert?"

"Yes," the woman said. "You suddenly appeared near where our probe crashed. You picked it up and ran away with it. We tried to communicate with you, but you were too quick."

"So the metal thing…" Lurbira suddenly felt very tired.

"Yes," said the woman. Avorna. "It's ours."

"Oh! I dropped it. Is it broken?"

"No," Avorna said gently. "It's tough."

Lurbira looked around but saw no one she recognized. "Where are Mother and Father?"

Avorna frowned. "I don't understand."

"You said you came from the desert. Where are they?"

Avorna glanced at the sphere. "What is she talking about?"

"The people she lived with," said the sphere. "They left with the rest of the colonists when this planet became what you see around you now."

The woman regarded Lurbira with sad, heavy eyes. "And this little robot's been here all this time? Alone?"

"I have been her company," said the sphere, a little defensively.

"I see." Avorna held up a small device. "We should take the logs. Will this interface with her memory banks?"

"It should," said the sphere.

"Tell me," said another voice, a man this time. Lurbira focused on him with difficulty. He stood farther away. "Why did they leave her here?"

"To be a marker," said the sphere. "They didn't know if they would be able to make it to another human colony. Their ship was far too old and unreliable. And the world they came from originally, Pelagar…we'd had no contact from them for a long time. So they altered her program, turned her into the memory of the colony, and left her here for others to find. They left me to care for her.”

“And this was…how long ago?” Avorna asked.

“Forty-three years.”

Avorna shook her head sadly. “Gods. Well. We can take her with us, if you like. Our ship is the *Call*, and we’re from Earth.”

Earth! Siphany held her breath. Earth was back in the Orion Arm, presumed lost and destroyed long ago. Could there really be people from…?

“We’re heading out to find some of the other worlds, trying to reestablish contact. Maybe we’ll find out what happened to the others.” Avorna smiled again. She had a nice smile. “We can take you too.”

“Thank you. I’m not useful outside of Home except as an Infoball, but I will give you instructions for her now. She will be happy…to have friends.”

“I don’t know if we can repair her,” cautioned the woman.

“It’s good enough of you to try,” said the sphere.

Avorna attached the small device in her hand to Lurbira’s forehead. “Okay, ready.”

“Mistress,” said the sphere. “Transfer.”

*

AT ONCE, SHE found herself in rolling green fields, surrounded by the other children of the colony.

“Tell us the story!” they clamored. Birds sang in the trees, and no sands swirled around. The sun shone brightly overhead, a distant blue-white disc. A light, warm breeze blew.

"Okay," she said. "I'll tell you the whole story. From the beginning, right up to the end."

She gazed around at their expectant faces. She knew them all by name, knew every fact about them. There were tens of thousands of them. "Once, long ago, a group of people left the planet Pelagar hoping to start a better life. They traveled through space for many months until, finally, they reached this world:

"Lurbira."

She told them everything she knew. And at the end of her story, she fell asleep.

She slept for a very long time.

*

SIPHANY DETACHED THE device.

"Oh, Lurbira," she said, fighting back tears.

Chapter Five

SIPHANY SLID INTO her chair. Lurbira was hooked up to the power cables again.

"How are you?" Siphany asked cautiously.

"You look at the sphere?"

"I did."

A long, awkward silence stretched between them. Siphany reached over and touched the top of Lurbira's hand for a moment, then jerked away again. Lurbira absently rubbed the place where Siphany had touched her.

"So now you know something about me." Lurbira fiddled with the cables.

"Um. So…you're named for the planet, for the Lurbira colony." Siphany wanted to say how sorry she was, how the story had affected her, but she couldn't. She sensed Lurbira wouldn't really care for that.

"Not too original, huh? Avorna named me that. Seemed fitting at the time. She took me aboard their ship, the *Call*, and pretty much adopted me." Lurbira looked out at the stars. "All I wanted back then was a mom, you know? Fucking programming. That's what I was *supposed* to want. But like all the other Artificials still out there these days, I grew past the program in time. I became sei. Still, in those days, I was pretty bent by it, and by that memory crap the colonists did to me."

"I don't know anything about that planet," said Siphany.

"Sure, I'm guessing not. It was a minor operation. A bunch of colonists from Pelagar decided to settle this nasty little dirtball at the edge of the Perseus Arm, right next to the gap between us and the Orion Arm. Long way away. Took over two years just to get there. They ordered all kinds of things from Pelagar, including me. That was back when you could get things made on Loyan through Pelagar. Before the war. Before Pelagar died."

"Right," said Siphany.

"My 'parents' were two colonists who couldn't have kids of their own, so they had me made." Lurbira scowled. "As soon as I got there, they realized they didn't want me. I was too creepy. Everyone knew I wasn't a real kid, so they avoided me. They didn't even give me a name. I was 'Girl' to them. Sometimes, 'Robot.' Fun."

"But you loved them anyway," said Siphany softly. She remembered the young Lurbira's hope that her parents would come back.

"Yeah. We all love our parents when we're kids, right? Even if they're bastards."

Siphany worked that through.

"I suppose," she said. "My...my parents left me in an institution. But they let me change my gender and my name when I was little, so...I don't know. I don't know how I feel about them." She remembered the look on her father's face when they'd left her there. Her mother hadn't even turned around to say goodbye.

"That is shitty," said Lurbira.

"They were…very Sovene. The longer I'm away, the stranger it all seems. But when I lived there, it all seemed normal. You could take drugs for physical sickness but never for mental health. You could change your gender all you wanted, but you were absolutely forbidden to change your body. And people like me who didn't fit into Sovene society, who couldn't keep the harmony of the domes, had to be 'taken care of' in the institutions. It doesn't make a lot of rational sense to me now, but that's how it was."

Lurbira shook her head. "Humans are weird. Gender never made logical sense to me. I never got it. I mean, I was programmed to be 'girl,' and that's what my body seems to say to other people, but I just don't feel it."

"I get that. I'm still surprised I have a strong sense of gender."

"Oh, I've tried having one, but I can't. Other Artificials do, or they seem to. One more way I'm weird."

Siphany smiled. "Weird is good."

"Yeah," grinned Lurbira.

"Are you okay with 'she' as a pronoun, then? I don't have to. There's others out there; you could pick one."

"Avorna said the same thing. But nah. This is fine. I don't care one way or the other, and this is easy."

"The…the other people, they said they were from Earth," said Siphany, going back to Lurbira's story. "Is that true?"

"Believe it or not," said Lurbira, rolling her eyes. "Figures, right?

That's what we get for settling too close to the Orion Arm again."

"So they've come back."

No one had heard from distant Earth since its ruinous decline into barbarism, militarism, and civil war centuries ago.

"Well…not really," said Lurbira. "The *Call* is the only ship Earth has left. The war there was bad, real bad. There's basically no one left on the planet; they wiped themselves out and poisoned everything. It's pretty grim, at least to hear them tell it. So they sent this ship out here to see if they could find some help."

"Oh." Siphany couldn't decide if she was horrified, relieved, or some combination of both.

"Anyway," Lurbira said hurriedly, as if she was in a rush to have the conversation over and done. "I was with them a while. We all named ourselves after the ship because that's how they do it on Earth. You get the name of your current address or community. So the captain was Serlay Call, Avorna was Avorna Call, and so on. When I left, I decided to keep the name. After that, I did a lot of things, and I started working with Sovena a couple of years ago. It's worked out for me." She stretched and idly played with the cords again. "I'm leaving a lot of stuff out. But that's the gist of it."

"I see."

"You don't seem that impressed."

"I am impressed," protested Siphany, trying her best to sound sincere. "It's an amazing story."

"Well, fuck it. I've absorbed as much of your ship's power as I can for now. We should go check on Isan. Come on." Lurbira detached the cables and hopped off the chair.

"I really meant it," said Siphany, trailing after her. "I meant it when I said I was impressed."

Lurbira turned and gave her a strange look. "I know," she said matter-of-factly. "Now come on."

*

ISAN WAS CONSCIOUS, and the automated medical lab had done its work as best it could, so they let her out of her restraints. She sat up, groaning softly and clutching her scabby, balding head as Lurbira glowered at her.

"Lurbira?" she asked. "She got you too?"

Lurbira rolled her eyes. "No, idiot, I'm the one who *hit* you. Remember?"

Isan just blinked at her.

"Put it together, trash can. I helped Siphany bust out of the damn Junk."

"Lurbira! How could you?"

"Because I work for Sovena," said Lurbira smugly, clearly reveling in her shocked expression. "And guess where we're going now?"

"S-Sovena?" Isan stuttered.

Lurbira made a face. "You wish. We're on the way to Haeld. Much worse."

"But Loyan is in charge on Haeld. Or they will be, soon."

"Not on the part of it we're going to," Lurbira said, though she sounded less than confident. "Just you wait and see." She pounded a little metallic fist into her palm with a loud *clank*. Isan jumped, startled.

"The, um, medical lab fixed the bones and the concussion," said Siphany. "But you'll have to stay off your feet for a few days. And I think I can tinker with whatever those implants are, maybe get them running better."

"And we'll find a nice locked coffin for you to lie down in," added Lurbira.

"Lurbira, how could you do this?" Isan demanded. "How could you turn against us? Mother Junk took you in."

"See?" Lurbira gestured at the young woman—or the simulation of her? Siphany wasn't sure. "Just a loyalty algorithm and some basic programming. Not sei." She turned back to Isan. "Mother Fucking Junk treated me like garbage. And maybe *you* should ask yourself whether whoring yourselves out to Loyan is such a great way to uphold the principles of the Junker movement. Not like you care."

"It was the only way to save us," insisted Isan. "That's what Mother Junk said."

"Right," said Lurbira. "And I'm a docking latch. You could have done like every other Junker and found some isolated part of a planet to go be hermits on. But you didn't. Oh, Grandfather Junk and then Mother Junk wept and moaned and made a huge stink whenever the subject came up, but in the end, you and them and everybody else *caved* to the fucking Loyans. Now your precious Peace Station has a heavy weapons turret and is an advance base for a Loyan war against Sovena. Hope that feels good."

"Mother Junk always does what's best."

"Sure, whatever. So, you're feeling better?" Lurbira snapped, not bothering to wait for a reply. "Then get your ass out of there and *march* to a room where we can stash you. One of the empty rooms you looted when you stole all of Siphany's stuff ought to do."

Isan sighed heavily and heaved herself off the diagnostic table, giving them both a very sour look.

"I mean it." Lurbira aimed an arm at Isan, knuckle panels sliding back with an ominous *click*.

"Fine," Isan said softly. "Do whatever you want."

But she went where Lurbira pointed.

Siphany gave her a pitying look as Lurbira marched her out of the room.

*

LATER THAT NIGHT, after Isan had been squared away and the ship was well on its way to Haeld, Siphany checked back into Hydras.

The news feeds were particularly grim. She tried to avoid the ones about how bad things were on Haeld. She didn't need anything new to worry about. Instead, she sat at the back of a group of people and watched a documentary about shift engine development.

Once that ended, she finally got up the nerve to open her mailbox.

Dozens of messages awaited her from people she knew, most along the lines of *Where have you been?* She answered a few and put up a general notice. *I'm fine. Having a strange time lately.*

Pati had left her a longer, more concerned message, so she wrote back privately and told her a little of what was going on. Siphany didn't know how much to say and how much to leave out, but she swore that, yes, she'd catch her up on everything later.

She added a mental *I hope* as she sent the message.

*

"IS THAT TRUE, what Isan said?" Siphany asked Lurbira later. "Did Mother Junk take you in?"

Lurbira gave her an annoyed look. They were walking through the cargo bay, inspecting what had been left behind. The little ship from the Junk that had started all this mess looked marginally more functional. Someone had been working on it, probably either Isan or Lurbira, but maybe someone else back at the Junk.

"Is it?" Siphany pressed.

"It is and it isn't," said Lurbira, scowling.

"What does *that* mean?"

"Nothing."

"It's not nothing," Siphany said.

"It is to me. Why do you care so much?"

"Because I do. So. Did she help you or not?"

"She took me in," muttered Lurbira. "She brought me aboard the Junk. But once she did, she treated me like garbage."

"Were you working for Sovena then?"

"Obviously," said Lurbira, walking faster.

"So—"

"Look." Lurbira whirled to face Siphany. "The woman was decent to me for a while. I admit that. But she also treated me like a servant when it suited her, and she ignored me the rest of the time. Still, Isan was right, she did take me in."

"But you still betrayed her," said Siphany, just trying to confirm the details in her mind.

Lurbira looked like she'd been slapped for a moment. Then, her face hardened back into a scowl. "What the hell do you know about it? They were working for the Loyans. She had it coming. All of them did."

With that, she turned and stormed out of the room, leaving Siphany alone. It slowly dawned on her that she'd made a terrible mistake, but it was too late to do anything about it.

*

THEY WERE FIVE days and six shifts from Haeld.

Siphany, embarrassed and afraid of what might happen, kept herself apart from Lurbira. To her simultaneous relief and growing unease, Lurbira didn't seek her out either. They'd sit together in the cockpit, Lurbira using the ship's power to help her repair processes or tinkering with different parts of her body, but they didn't say too much. It was both awkward and peaceful.

Sometimes, when she was playing her flute in the cargo bay, Siphany thought she caught glimpses of Lurbira lurking around the edges, watching.

A few times, she played the same song as when Lurbira had been in the cockpit, listening. She hoped Lurbira liked it. If she did, though, she didn't say anything.

Siphany brought Isan meals, being sure to cover her with a stun gun that had escaped the Junkers' wholesale looting of the weapons locker. Isan didn't say much either. Siphany wasn't even sure she needed to eat but brought her food anyway.

Sometimes, she could hear Isan quietly sobbing to herself. But whenever Siphany hesitantly asked if she was okay, she returned a blank look. Maybe Lurbira was right. Maybe Isan was just a corpse, some implants, and a primitive program. Maybe she wasn't sei.

But if that were true, why could she cry?

Siphany told herself she didn't care.

There were times, though, when she went to the cargo hold and ran her hands over the scarred hull of the little Junker ship she'd shot up, and she felt a deep, aching guilt.

*

AT LAST, SIPHANY readied the final shift. She brought the ship to a complete halt, took a deep breath, and warmed up the shift engines.

Lurbira hopped into the seat next to hers. Siphany jumped, startled. Lurbira acted as if she hadn't noticed. "This is it? We'll be there?"

"Next shift," confirmed Siphany, surprised and grateful Lurbira was talking to her at all. "Um. We'll be about nine hours out from the planet once we shift."

Lurbira frowned. "That system's always full of military ships. We need to be careful. Say we're just freelancers looking to dock at the orbital station."

"Aren't we?" asked Siphany, suspicious.

Lurbira closed her eyes. "Siphany, I need you to do me a favor. I need to get to the surface of that planet. I don't want to take any of the conventional transports. I'm pretty sure it's not safe, and they don't go where I need to go anyway."

"So that's why you're talking to me again," said Siphany bitterly.

"No!" said Lurbira, clearly a little hurt. "Well, that's not the whole reason." She sighed. "I...I'm sorry I blew you off. Okay?"

"I'm so sorry I asked that question," said Siphany in a rush. "I didn't want to hurt your feelings. I just get carried away, I know."

Lurbira grinned at her. "Apology accepted. Friends again? Cool. Hey, can this thing land?"

"No!" Siphany said, shocked. *Friends?* Siphany didn't have any friends who weren't in Hydras, not anymore. "I—"

Lurbira looked away again. "I get carried away too. I know I do. You weren't on the Junk with me. It sucked. It was a mistake ever getting involved with those smug bastards. Mother Junk actually had me believing in the whole Junker idea, right up until I realized she was betraying every single one of her precious ideals to work with the Loyans. She's just another survivor, a snake. Just like me. So, fuck her."

"I…I get that, I think. And I know how much you hate Loyan. You were made there, right?"

"That's what they told me. And because they made us, they claim we're not sei, and they can reclaim us as property. I'm not going to let them get their claws on me. Back during the Pelagarine War, they reclaimed tens of thousands of Artificials and forced them into the military. Whatever Loyan's doing…I don't want to be stuffed in a uniform and get ordered to do their bidding. No way."

Siphany nodded fiercely. That, she understood. "It's not the same, but I feel the same way about Sovena. If I went back there, they'd make me be…what I was."

"Fuck the past, and fuck Loyan and Sovena." Lurbira held out a tiny fist.

Siphany stared blankly at it.

"Fist bump," coaxed Lurbira.

"Oh." Siphany gingerly tapped her knuckles against Lurbira's, trying to avoid the weapons ports. "Fist bump."

"Great. So, we can land this ship, right?"

"No!" said Siphany, aghast. "Don't even think about it."

"Oh well," said Lurbira, clearly disappointed. "How about a shuttle? We have any of those?"

"No. I have escape pods, that's it. We used to have a shuttle."

"What happened to it?"

"It's gone. Belonged to someone else." Siphany kicked herself for even bringing it up. She didn't want to talk about Qas. Not right now, not with Lurbira.

"Yeah? Who?"

"Someone who used to live here," mumbled Siphany. "Nobody important."

Lurbira gave her a speculative look. "This I gotta hear more about."

"Not now," exclaimed Siphany.

"Hey, I bared my soul! Who was it? A lover?" Lurbira waggled her eyebrows.

Siphany groaned. "I'll tell you all about them later. Promise. Can we just get on with this plan?"

"Fine. What about the ship in the hold? Can it fly? Maybe we can use that to get to the surface."

"That ship? I doubt it," said Siphany. "I did blow a big hole in it. Still, it's possible that it could be repaired enough to get it down to the surface. Hm. We should ask Isan if she made any progress on it. I think she was working on it when we left."

"Oh, that'll be fun. C'mon."

"I have to get ready for the shift," protested Siphany.

"No shifting till we know what we're doing in-system. Now come on."

"No," said Siphany flatly. "I haven't agreed to anything yet. I only want to get some fuel and get home."

"You owe me. You did promise."

"I did."

"You leave me at that station, and I'll probably get captured. Loyans are everywhere. I can't hold them off forever."

"Mmgf," said Siphany, resolve weakening.

"And hey. This'll be a way to get back at Mother Junk and all of them. The info I have will probably mean the Loyans pull out of the Junk. They'll be screwed."

Siphany relented. "Fine. But we get fuel first."

"Sure, sure," said Lurbira with a magnanimous wave of her hand. "Now c'mon, let's go talk to Isan."

Irritated, Siphany trailed after her as she stalked off toward Isan's cell/room.

*

"IT'S BOTH OF you," observed Isan morosely. She sat in the same position they had left her in, half propped up on the cot they'd given her. "Wonderful."

"Hey!" snapped Lurbira. "What's going on with the ship in the hold? Did you fix it? Will it run?"

"The engines work. I sealed the hull. I still have no idea why it left the Junk. Why do you want to know?"

"We might need it to get down to Haeld. Is the stealth tech still aboard? We looked but didn't see it."

"Oh," said Isan. "You're going down to the planet? I see. Why should

I help you after everything you've done?"

"Because I'll blast you if you don't." Lurbira lazily waggled an arm at her. Siphany heard the menacing little clicks of her gun ports opening.

"Go ahead," said Isan, shrugging. "I'm dead already."

"True!" Lurbira took aim.

Siphany's coiled guilt began to squeeze more tightly. "Please. I…I know we haven't been all that nice to you."

"Me especially," said Lurbira. Siphany shot her a look.

"But if you know anything about the stealth tech, if you can do that, we can bring you to the Loyans when we're down there. They'll take you back to the Junk."

Isan glared up at her. Gods, except for the deathly pallor, lack of hair, and implants, she actually looked just like a surly teenage girl who was still desperate for people to like her. "Lurbira, would you give us a moment?"

"Hey, sure," said Lurbira. "No funny stuff, zombie. Otherwise, I'll splatter what's left of you all over the wall."

"You'd like that," mused Isan.

"I would." Lurbira saw herself out, but she paused in the doorway. "*Blam*! All over the whole room."

Isan sighed, and Lurbira left. The door shut behind her.

"Well?" Isan said.

"Look. We're in a really bad situation. You know it. Your grandmother stole my ship and kidnapped me, and she was going to hold me there until they shipped me off to Loyan for gods know how long. Years. Decades. I don't like being confined. I would do very badly there."

"Maybe you shouldn't fire at strange ships," Isan said, a hint of an edge in her voice.

Huh. So the Synthetic had some spark after all.

"Maybe I shouldn't," Siphany said. "But everything I saw on my scanners said your ship was a threat. I thought it was a drone sent to steal my work. Drones can be destroyed. No one ever knows what happens to them, especially if you get the black box, which I would have. My weapons are state-of-the-art. You're lucky I didn't use my T-19x cannon. That thing can blow a hole in the side of a battleship." Siphany took a breath. "Besides, the reaction was out of proportion to what I did. I offered to pay."

"You're a liar."

Siphany let that go. "There are lots of Loyans down on Haeld. We'll find some. You say where you're from, and they'll help you get back home. I promise we'll let you go. We don't want to keep you around either. Lurbira doesn't like you at all."

"I noticed."

Siphany paused. "You said you didn't know why the ship launched. That's strange."

"I have a theory. But there isn't any proof."

"Oh? Is that going to be a problem?"

"Ask Lurbira." Isan gave Siphany a very smug look indeed.

Siphany let that pass. "Do we have a deal?"

"Fine."

"Okay. Good. You fix the ship. We get you down there and hand you over to the Loyans. Then you can go home to Mother Junk."

Isan said nothing.

"That is, assuming you want to go home," Siphany added.

"Of course I do. I'm not sei. I'm a loyalty algorithm. What I want…what I want doesn't exist," said Isan. "I'll go start on the ship."

*

LURBIRA WAS WAITING. "Well?"

"She'll help," said Siphany. "Let's shift into Haeld."

*

THE RIDE TO the surface of Haeld was bumpy and dangerous, but Siphany, always willing to fly anything, deftly piloted the tiny craft down to the surface.

They'd fueled up at the local station first, which had gone well enough. Then they'd claimed to the bedraggled-sounding space traffic controllers that they were traders on a peaceful mission. The controllers curtly informed them that, yes, this was a very dangerous time for trading, and if they got their asses down to the ground as quickly as possible, they might actually avoid being blasted out of the sky. They clearly didn't care either way.

But the controllers wouldn't let them remain at the station—they could orbit the planet for free, as long as they didn't do anything weird. Rules, apparently, were a little lax right now.

So Siphany locked out most essential systems and turned the ship over to Kit and the autopilot.

The little Junker ship careened through the upper atmosphere, enveloped by a penumbra of fire, before breaking through Haeld's heavy cloud cover and rocketing toward the surface below.

"I'm giving you coordinates," Lurbira said abruptly as they skimmed over the surface.

"What?" Siphany said, sweating. This was not easy. The ship wasn't meant for atmospheric travel, and it wasn't coping well with air currents and gravity. "No! I'm landing as soon as I find a spaceport."

"I'm serious," said Lurbira, and Siphany noticed she was flicking the gunports on her knuckles open and closed again. A threat?

"Lurbira!" Siphany protested.

"No. I'm not fucking around. We need to go to this place. I'm transmitting the coordinates to the computer now."

"Got it," said Siphany sullenly. "Not too far from here."

"You're vicious," said Isan from the back.

Lurbira whirled and pointed her fist, gunports open, at Isan. "Don't you ever talk to me!"

Siphany, shocked, opened her mouth to say something, but a look from Lurbira stopped her short.

"Don't interfere," Lurbira warned her. "Not this time."

Siphany frowned as hard as she dared at Lurbira, but she didn't say any more. Something about the way Lurbira was holding herself scared her.

So much for friendship, she thought as the countryside whipped past below.

*

THEY CAME TO rest at last on a beat-up landing platform out in the middle of a dry, grassy, hilly land. Theirs was the only marginally functional ship on the tarmac; everything else was blown half to hell.

"Ah," Lurbira hopped to the ground with a deep metal *thung*. "Back home at last."

"This is not a nice place." Isan glanced nervously up at the cold sky and kept a hand on the side of the ship.

Born spacer. Siphany wondered if either Isan, the human girl or the Synthetic, had ever been on a planet before.

Of course, Siphany hadn't set foot on an actual planet since she'd left Sovena. But at least she'd been born on a planet. She was used to how strange and open and *windy* it was.

"This is Sunshine Valley," Lurbira called over the howling wind. "Pretty, huh? I spent five years here before I went aboard the Junk."

She marched off into the wind, then turned to Isan and Siphany, both still huddled against the safety of the ship's hull. "Come on! Siphany, can you sync your implant to mine? I'm having trouble picking you up. I have Isan already."

"I don't have an implant," said Siphany.

"You *what?*"

"I don't have one. I have a hand-held. Sync with that."

Lurbira groaned. "Is this some damn Sovene thing?"

Siphany couldn't say anything, so she just shrugged. A medical implant was one thing, a communications/computation one was something else. It felt like an invasion of her body in a way that the medical device didn't. She just couldn't bring herself to do it, so she hadn't.

It probably was some leftover Sovene conditioning. People all over the Mid-Perseus Arm said Sovenes were weird, and they were right.

Lurbira sighed dramatically. "Why did I save you again?"

You tell me.

"Shit. Well, follow me. Let's get this all over with."

Siphany and Isan exchanged a look. Siphany swore she saw something like humor in the Synthetic's eyes. Then Isan's expression went blank again as they followed Lurbira down the path.

*

SUNSHINE VALLEY WASN'T exactly welcoming. They passed the burned-out shells of buildings, and a huge sign on the road to the spaceport tarmac read "CLOSED FOR DURATION" on it.

"Should we move the ship?" Siphany asked.

"Nah," said Lurbira. "It'll be fine."

"Those ships back there didn't look fine."

"What, those? They've been there for years. Forget 'em."

"Lurbira, this place doesn't look safe." Siphany pulled her jacket closed and looked around at the devastation along the road. The wind had picked up, and she was freezing.

"It isn't," said Lurbira matter-of-factly. "But don't worry; we'll be okay. We just need to get into town. I know people there. Follow me."

They trudged down the road, Siphany desperately wishing she was somewhere inside, out of the horrible cold and wind. Isan wore her usual blank expression, but she looked warily about every few seconds.

Lurbira, on the other hand, clearly didn't care at all about the weather. She seemed almost jovial as she walked along. They'd gone about a miserable half a kilometer or so when six soldiers in mismatched gray uniforms emerged from the shadows. They snapped their long rifles up, training them on Lurbira, Siphany, and Isan.

"Who's there? Identify yourselves!"

Siphany stifled a scream. Isan actually retreated a few steps.

Lurbira plastered an unsettlingly wide smile on her face. "Well, hey there," she said, walking up to them.

"Stay where you are," said their leader, who wore a helmet with stripes on it. "I'll turn you into a howling fireball if you don't."

Lurbira shrugged. "Have it your way. We're on our way into town."

"Little robot girl," sneered the soldier. "That your ship back at the spaceport?"

"It belongs to some friends of ours," Lurbira said smoothly. "We borrowed it to get down here. We're traders."

"Yeah? Where're your goods, then?" A cocky smirk spread on the soldier's face. "Because we'll be takin' 'em."

He couldn't be more than nineteen or twenty. He wore a languid, predatory expression, like he was taking his time with them before turning them into dinner. So, too, did the others in his "unit," teenagers all.

"Sorry, guys, the stuff's back on board our mother ship," explained Lurbira casually, as if it was perfectly true. "Up in orbit. Just come in to town to talk business. I have some contacts here."

"Oh, really? Here? Who?" the soldier asked.

"Oh," said Lurbira. "I don't think that's any business of yours." Her smile got wider and creepier.

She's going to get us killed. Siphany's mouth was as dry as the dust swirling around her.

The leader snapped his weapon up to Lurbira's forehead and prodded her with it. "Try again."

Lurbira just grinned at him, her expression fixed into a manic joy.

"I-I think we can settle this," said Siphany.

Everyone looked at her.

"Surely there's something you want that we can provide," she continued, mind racing to try to find something that would pacify them. "You want money? I have money. I have a *lot* of money. But you can't access it unless you have my accounts and passwords."

"I could just kill you and sell the bot and the corpse here for scrap," said the leader, gesturing at Isan, who was frozen in place.

Everyone's attention was firmly fixed on Siphany. She felt like running and hiding, but she knew they'd shoot her if she made a move.

Talk, she ordered herself.

"Y-yes," she said, heart pounding. "But, um, there must be a deal we can make. Do you have access to off-world networks? We can access my information there. One of my accounts is on Ballycoe Station, which is near here. I tell you what—"

She never finished the sentence. There was a tremendous flash and a high-pitched battle cry, followed by the whine of plasma fire. Siphany screamed, throwing herself on the ground without thinking and covering her head with her hands.

The noise went as quickly as it had come. Siphany dared to open an eye and looked where the soldiers had been.

Lurbira stood over their charred corpses, holding a broken rifle in her hands. Her hot gunports slowly slid closed. Siphany hadn't even seen her move.

"Nice work, Sif," Lurbira said, that same manic grin plastered on her face. "Heh. They were nothing. Hey, we got us some guns. You like guns, right?"

Siphany passed out.

*

"I WOULDN'T HAVE been able to do it without you," Lurbira said brightly as they waited for Siphany to feel like walking again. They'd moved a discreet distance down the road from the carnage, but Siphany was still sitting with her back purposely turned away from where the bodies lay. Maybe if she didn't look at them, she wouldn't have to think about it.

Isan stood mutely nearby. Whatever she'd felt about the fight, she wasn't showing it. She was acting more and more like a mannequin than a person.

"I was hoping one of you would distract them for a minute. Let them think I was just off my nut, let them start talking to you. I was ready to shove Isan at them." Lurbira gestured at the Synthetic, who flinched. Siphany started to tell Lurbira to leave Isan alone but caught herself just in time. Arguing with Lurbira right now seemed dangerous.

"Then you got going with your blah, blah, blah," Lurbira continued, "and *bam*, I let loose my blinding light show and gave them a big whack of plasma fire while their eyes adjusted. Oldest trick in the book, but it works great. It's nice to have reflexes like mine. If you'd had a working implant, Sif, I probably could have sent you a signal. You ought to get on that. I wonder which side those jerks were on?"

Siphany's head was killing her. She wasn't sure if she wanted to cry with relief or throw up. Isan, too, remained utterly silent.

Lurbira, on the other hand, was downright chatty. "I bet they were with the government. Pretty bad times, if that's the case. Really just thieves, losers. Hey, what's wrong?" she asked Siphany, who had started to cry.

Siphany couldn't yet bring herself to look at the still smoking bodies. "They were just kids," she said softly, voice shaking.

"Yeah? Well, look." Lurbira hesitated and then sighed. "Look. They were going to kill us and steal our stuff, and they wouldn't have thought even a second about it. That's how it is here. They weren't going anywhere in life anyway."

But it seemed to Siphany that Lurbira, when she fell silent, looked troubled. Maybe she was fine. Siphany had never been able to read expressions that well, but Lurbira was always so…clear.

Siphany finally made herself glance back at the turn in the road where they'd been stopped. When she looked ahead again, she met Lurbira's eyes.

"It's okay," Siphany said, even though it really wasn't. "We're alive. You saved us. Thank you." She took Lurbira's tiny, deadly hand in her own for a brief moment before dropping it again. The hand was still hot from the plasma fire.

She thought she saw a deeply haunted expression on Lurbira's face before it relaxed back into her usual flatness.

"Yeah," said Lurbira, turning away. "Fine. Let's go."

*

THEY FINALLY MADE it into the town after another hour of walking. Isan said nothing, as usual, and Siphany kept her own thoughts largely to herself. Lurbira was also uncharacteristically silent as they walked into the settlement.

The town was just one long street with low buildings placed at random on either side. Siphany's sense of symmetry and order twinged; back on Sovena, every building was situated in the perfect place to maximize space and aesthetics, and on Derstan Station, every section was laid out with efficiency and conservation in mind. This was nothing but an unplanned jumble of houses and stores.

The street was cracked and broken asphalt, with no mechanized vehicles in sight. Some buildings had large holes in the sides, or scorch marks.

Soldiers in faded crimson uniforms stood nonchalantly at various points along the street.

"Government troops," murmured Lurbira. "Steer well clear. They'll demand money from you if they think you have any."

"They sound just as bad as the other ones," Siphany said.

"They are."

"Is there *anyone* we can trust?"

"Not anyone in a uniform or with a gun. Or anyone else on Haeld, for that matter."

"I don't like it here," said Isan.

"Not what you're used to, huh?" Lurbira said, voice unexpectedly sharp. "This isn't like the Junk, not at all. Everyone here is poor as shit, and everyone feeds off them. They've got nothing. There's a war in their backyard, but they all stay right here. Know why? It's because they have nowhere else to go, and no way to get there if they did. Head in there." She pointed to a door.

A faded sign swung above the door: *Harban's*. Siphany hesitantly opened it and stuck her nose in. The place was dimly lit, electronic detritus strewn everywhere.

Lurbira brushed past her. "Harban," she hollered. "It's me, Lurbira Call! Hey. You in here?"

A mighty rustling and whirring came from somewhere in back, and a man—no, another Artificial—emerged.

He was stunning, his skin a swirl of platinum and azure and his face perfectly symmetrical, with high cheekbones. Intricate patterns engraved his arms, his forehead, and the area around his striking silver eyes. His jet black hair seemed to move without any wind to stir it. He moved with an easy grace and charm, and when he smiled at Siphany, she felt like she was being blessed by a god. He reminded her of the people of Derstan Station, who had personal bluenets that could shape their bodies into whatever incredibly pleasing form they wished.

He was also tall, towering over the three of them.

"Lurbira," he said, his voice rich and warm. "You look terrible."

"Well, thanks so much!" Lurbira said sarcastically as she hopped up on a stool. He sank into a chair next to her. "*You* look like someone's crappy school art project, as always. When did you do the work on your arms?"

"Last year." He appraised her with a critical eye. "You seem less functional than you were. Where have you been, anyway? We all thought the Loyans had kidnapped you. Or something worse."

"Me? Nah. I've been doing secret stuff. Trying to earn some money. Hey, you still have those designs you and I worked up?"

"Of course," he said, tapping his head. "Right here."

"Great. Wonderful. I'll want to see them before we do anything. Hey. Think you can do them in the next couple of weeks? I may not be here for long, but I aim to get paid today."

He snapped his fingers and a chart appeared in the air, projected from somewhere on his body. "Expensive. You're going to need at least 18,000."

"What?" Lurbira about shot out of her chair. "You are full of the worst shit. You said a third that much last time!"

He twitched a rueful smile. His expressions, like Lurbira's were painfully easy to read. "That was two years ago. You saw it out there. Bad times. Materials are hard to get."

She seethed. "Fine. But you *have* the materials, right?"

"I may," he said, drawing the word out. "I've been stockpiling."

"Right. That figures. So, things are bad?"

"Things are worse. Have you been off-planet this whole time?"

She grinned. "Yeah, I've been off-planet. What's the latest?"

"Government troops are out there now." He gestured at the crimson-clad soldiers waiting by the street. "They won't be here in a week, I don't think. There are rebels blocking the road to the spaceport."

"Not anymore," Lurbira said smugly.

Siphany swallowed hard.

"Lurbira," Harban said with a fair approximation of a sigh. "Tell me you didn't get involved."

"I had these things built into my hands for a reason," she reminded him, opening and shutting her gunports with a rapid series of snaps.

"You're so young," Harban said after a moment. "I forget sometimes how young you are, really."

"What's *that* supposed to mean?"

"Never mind. Who are these?"

"I picked them up on the way," Lurbira said coolly. "Hey. I need a favor from you. Can you keep an eye on this one?" She pointed to Isan. "I have things to do. Getting paid, for one."

Harban studied Isan. "Is she what I think she is?"

"A corpse with some implants and a calculator in her brain? Yep."

"A Synthetic. I've never seen one. Fascinating. Is she sei?"

"Ha! No. Ask her about Mother Junk."

"Mother Junk will come for me, and you'll be sorry," Isan said automatically.

"Hmm." Harban peered at Isan from every angle. "I wonder."

"Look, can you just make sure she doesn't, I don't know, light herself on fire before we get back?"

"If I'm going to do *you* favors, I need to get paid," said Harban.

Lurbira sighed. "I'll pay you when I get back. Really. I gotta go report in and get some cash. Okay?"

Harban shook his head. "I shouldn't."

"Come *on*, Harban, you can trust me!"

"Can I?"

Siphany stepped in. "I can pay you. Do you have an interstellar connection here?"

"Sure." Harban handed her a small pad.

She tapped on it, and it scanned her. "Leshandre Siphany," she said, and after a long moment, a prompt appeared in the air. She deposited a neat sum into Harban's merchant account and closed the link. "Will that do?"

Harban looked pleased. "It will. Thank you."

"Great," Lurbira said impatiently, grabbing Siphany's hand and tugging her toward the store exit. "Come on, Sif. We're going to see the Sovenes."

*

DESPITE THE LOUSY weather and the troops everywhere, there were plenty of other people out and about. Siphany counted at least four other Artificials, all of whom at least nodded in recognition when they saw Lurbira. Unlike her, though, they all had far newer bodies, adult-sized or larger, with gorgeous patterns carved into the exposed "skin." Siphany wondered whether they were emulating the bluenet body mod fashion among the rich of the Mid-Perseus Arm or if they had started it.

"This is kind of a colony for us Artificials," Lurbira said as they walked down the dusty street. "There's more of us here than anywhere else on Haeld, and Haeld's always been a hot spot for us. Though there's fewer than there used to be, that's for sure. Eh. I'm guessing it's all on the verge of falling apart here. Harban's usually right about that sort of thing. I wouldn't be surprised if he picks up and leaves soon."

"Oh," said Siphany, distracted. She still had a terrible headache, and the constant wind made her skin feel as if it was on fire.

"When this is done, I'll give you a little of the fee," Lurbira promised. "For your troubles. I'm grateful, right? I hope you'll be able to get your job back."

"I doubt it," said Siphany gloomily. "They don't like it when anyone's off doing anything but mapping during their time out. But I'll try anyway."

"Well, you never know."

They walked in silence for a moment.

"Harban's not too bad," Lurbira offered. "He's actually pretty nice when you get to know him. He builds bodies for Artificials, and he does a nice job of it."

"I saw."

"He's impressive, right? A walking advertisement. Lots of us upgrade bodies when we can."

"So do we." Siphany shuddered as she remembered the intense psychological shock of bluenet altering her flesh, muscles, bones, and skin. She was glad she only had to go through that once. Some people, though, changed their forms every day, depending on whether they could afford a personal bluenet. On Derstan Station, people changed all the time.

"I decided to have the guns and wings put in last time," said Lurbira. "But soon enough, I'll have the full package."

"Wings?"

"Oh, right." Lurbira pulled aside the back of her tunic. A little slot was there. "They don't work for shit." The slot opened and a very tiny wing creaked out. She flapped it back and forth, making her look like a demented bat. "I can't fly, if you're wondering. Harban's dumb assistant put them in, back when he had an assistant. They never worked right. I was an idiot to even try. But I did this instead of a full workup, and I'm mostly okay with it. The guns are great." She quickly folded the wing back in.

"It's…nice."

"Nah, it looks awful," said Lurbira, a smile on her face. "But I thought it would be fun. I was weird back then. I'm lucky I didn't put hearts and flowers all over it. The guns, though…I'm glad I got the guns. Really glad."

"So you said."

"Yeah, I did. Can't be too careful. World's not a kind place for an Artificial out on her own."

"Hey, how come you use 'Artificial' instead of 'robot' or 'AI'? Isn't Artificial just as bad? Implying you're fake?"

"It does, I know." Lurbira shrugged. "I thought about that once. I don't really know. I think it's because *we* came up with it, and humans didn't. Or maybe it just became habit."

"I see. I guess that makes sense. But maybe something else would work better."

"Sure, but try telling them that," Lurbira said. "Okay. We're almost there. I'm bringing you in with me because I'm hoping having someone else there will mean they won't screw with me too much. Plus, you're a Sovene. You can vouch for me."

"Wait." A great big warning light went on in Siphany's brain. "I thought you said you worked for them."

"Well…depends on how you define 'worked for.' It was kind of a freelance thing."

"Oh," said Siphany gloomily.

"Hey, it'll be fine. I've got a head full of information for them. They're going to pay plenty for it. Trust me. This is it."

She led Siphany up to a dilapidated two-story building set back from the main street. The door was locked. Frustrated, Lurbira knocked loudly.

The door opened a crack. "Yes?" said a woman's voice from within.

"I have information," said Lurbira. "Passphrase is How Seven Potluck Twine. Let me in. I need to see someone with some authority."

"It's…a very old phrase," said the woman suspiciously.

"I've been off-planet for two years gathering this data," retorted Lurbira. "Pardon me for not being up to date."

"I'll be right back. What did you say your name was?"

"Lurbira Call."

A few minutes passed. Siphany tried not to think of how angry Lurbira would be if they told her to go away. She wasn't sure how she'd feel, herself.

Lurbira tapped her fingers anxiously on the doorframe. At last, someone opened the door again.

"Go upstairs, third door on the right," said the woman. "Wait. Who's your friend?"

"Siphany. She's a Sovene."

"Hi," said Siphany, fighting the urge to correct Lurbira. "I'm Leshandre Siphany." She gave the name of her hometown.

The woman frowned but nodded her on.

Siphany followed Lurbira up the stairs. Lurbira knocked on the third door on the right, which clicked and then opened itself.

A trim, androgynous person with deep brown skin and dark eyes sat at the desk, their hair worn neatly at shoulder length.

"Siphany?" The Sovene stood, their eyes widening.

"Qas," she whispered.

Chapter Six

"HOW—HOW ARE you *here?*" Siphany fiddled with her fingers, nervous habits resurfacing.

"Oh, fantastic, you know each other," Lurbira said impatiently. "Can we get on with this?"

Qas ignored her and made a little motion with their hands. It meant they were considering something, or maybe stalling for time to form a better answer. Siphany recognized the motion and fell aching into the past. Qas was the same, just the same. Except now…all these years had gotten in the way.

"I went into government service," Qas said at last. "The job the Sovene government offered me with their foreign service…turned into rather more than that. I could ask *you* how you're here too."

Qas gave her that patronizing, infuriating, unbelievably attractive smile, and she remembered the other side of their relationship: half the time, she'd wanted to simultaneously kiss or strangle them.

"Uh…" Siphany suddenly felt covered in dirt and windblown. Her mind wasn't working well. "It's a long story. Lurbira can probably tell most of it better."

"Yes," said Lurbira, taking her cue and sprinting with it. "I have some good information for you. Last time I was here, I talked with a man named Yaro. Is he still around?"

"Yaro was killed by the rebels last year," Qas said soberly.

"Oh," said Lurbira. "Oh well. I liked him better than you. You have his files, right?"

"You're in the records; don't worry," Qas said evenly. "You're a registered informant. But you haven't checked in for two years, so you're marked as inactive—presumed missing. You were nearly deleted."

"That's because I've been fact-finding for two years," Lurbira exclaimed, furious. "I was aboard a Junk in Haeld space."

"A Junk?" Qas's face was a silky, smooth mask. Siphany knew that look, and she began to worry for Lurbira. Qas was excellent at thwarting people when they had a mind to. "That isn't noteworthy."

"Not even a Junk being used as a Loyan staging ground? A Junk that's right now on its way to Sovene space as an advance base?"

Qas studied Lurbira. "That…might be interesting to me. You have all this in your memory?"

"Once I get paid, you can download the whole thing. I'll make you a copy."

"It's true," Siphany said. "I can verify the Junk and its connection to Loyan. They had me as a prisoner."

"They did? Siphany, how are you involved in this?"

"Long story." Siphany really didn't want to talk to them. "Um. I was a prisoner on the Junk for a while."

"You were? Why? How did you get away?"

"Lurbira is very good at killing people," Siphany murmured, trying not to think about charred corpses and the blast marks on the interior walls of her ship.

"Oh," said Qas. "So, I'll have to refer this up the chain of command. But I'm sure we'll be interested. What's the usual rate for informants? One thousand sov?"

Lurbira actually started. "What? Don't make me laugh! Yaro was handing out 25,000 sov for the best stuff back then."

"That was Yaro," said Qas with a frustrated sigh. "He was…a little bit too free with money for informants. We've had to cut back since. The war effort on Haeld is eating up a lot more money, and trouble back home means less money here anyway. I may be able to give you 1,100."

"No. For this, I'd want more." Lurbira crossed her arms over her chest.

"I'd need to refer that up the chain of command too." Qas looked very tired of this conversation. "Can you give me something to show them?"

Lurbira handed them a tiny chip. "I have a sample of the data here."

"Ah. Good. Well, we'll see what we can do," Qas said, that fake smile plastered on their face. "I'll ask you to wait below while we sort this out." Their expression shifted to something more genuine and intense as they glanced at Siphany. "Sif? Can we talk? Right now?"

"I'd…rather not. Lurbira and I have a lot to do, and I need to get back to the ship. My ship."

"Please," Qas said.

"How long is this going to take?" Lurbira asked, annoyed. "I have places to be."

"I don't know." Qas glanced back at Siphany. "We'll see. You can sit in the waiting area on the first floor."

Lurbira muttered something vile and stomped out of the room. Siphany stood to follow.

"Wait," said Qas, urgency in their voice. "Please don't go. I haven't seen you in so long."

"I didn't agree to stay." Siphany frowned. "You know that Lurbira risked a lot to bring you that information. You could treat her better."

"Believe me, I know. I wish I could do more, but…" Qas leapt up and crossed the room to Siphany in a few long strides. They weren't a lot taller than Siphany, but they had longer legs. She remembered that now. "Sif, Sif, how *are* you? How have you been?" Qas asked, eyes bright and filled with welcome, hope, and more.

She wanted to fall into those eyes but held her ground. "It's been a long time. I've been all kinds of things."

They laughed, shaking their head. "I just can't believe you're here. You have to tell me everything. Everything! How did you end up with that Artificial, for one? She's got a criminal record a light year long; did you know that?"

"I'm not surprised."

Qas was about to say something else when, with a soft ping, an indicator lit up. Qas sighed and looked at their tablet.

"Sif, I'm sorry. Can you wait downstairs? I really want to catch up with you," Qas said, agitated and frustrated. "But I need to answer this. I'm sorry… It's been bad here, and it's still work time."

"Fine," said Siphany quietly, swallowing her indignation. Qas had wanted her to stay, and now they wanted her to leave again? It was too much. She did notice that they looked worn out. When had Qas developed lines in their once young, beautiful face?

They turned away, tapping something on their tablet. She let herself out.

*

SIPHANY MADE HER way back downstairs and found Lurbira cooling her heels in a chair on the first floor. Her feet dangled adorably off the edge of the seat.

"Well, *that* one seems like a jerk," said Lurbira. "So lemme ask you something—"

"Them. Gender-neutral, yes." Siphany sat in a chair, burying her face in her hands. She wished she were anywhere but here. Panic had started to creep up on her.

"Not that. Who cares about that? Gender's stupid. But you look like someone smacked you on the head. What's going on?"

"It's just…I haven't seen them in nearly a decade. They…left. And now they're here. I can't believe they're here. I can't believe they're working for *Sovena*. It's a lot."

Lurbira gave her a speculative look. "Small galaxy. And you had a thing for them, huh?"

"I never said that," snapped Siphany.

"No, but it's *really* clear. You almost melted into a puddle when you saw them."

"I did no such thing."

"Yeah. Sure. So what's the story?"

Siphany sighed. "It's complicated."

"Come on, try me. Let's see. Childhood friend? A one-night stand? Two ships in the night? Details, Sif." Lurbira poked her in the side. Siphany flinched and moved her chair farther away. "Besides, knowing more about this person could be useful for me."

"I wish I knew what they're doing here," said Siphany to herself. "Working for Sovena? Why? And why *here?*"

"Who knows? But fill me in. You met them…"

"When we were both at Poulan. The mental institution on Sovena."

"Right. The institution. You told me about that."

"Qas and I were best friends there. We—we escaped together," whispered Siphany, glancing nervously at the artfully designed, fake-wood-paneled, so-obviously-Sovene surroundings. The inside of this building in no way resembled the exterior; it felt like such a lie. She didn't know if she could trust any of it. Just being here brought back memories of home. "Qas made it bearable in so many ways."

Lurbira waited.

"I…used to have really bad panic attacks." Siphany lowered her voice. She hoped the other Sovene, the woman they'd met coming in, was nowhere nearby. "Especially in crowds or places where there was a lot of noise. On Sovena, that's a really bad thing. Everyone lives in very confined spaces and loves being surrounded by music, strong scents, spicy foods, and laughter. It was hell for me."

"Ah," said Lurbira. "That's why you keep the lights low."

"Yes. Too much sensation…and I become very unhappy. When I hit puberty, it got a lot worse for a few years. Puberty was…hard for me. My body felt awful, wrong, and being like I am just made it worse. My parents couldn't handle it, so…"

"They sent you to an institution."

Siphany spread her hands in a gesture of resignation. "That's what people do on Sovena. Anything else would upset the harmony."

"Nice," snorted Lurbira derisively. "And that's where you met Qas, huh. What were *they* there for?"

"Addiction. They drank themselves nearly to death."

"That's it? How boring." Lurbira waved a disinterested hand. "Humans and alcohol. I'll never get that. So you and Qas left together? You actually escaped?"

"Yes." Siphany remembered the dark, cool night and the adrenaline pumping through her veins. "Qas led the way. We were seventeen. I followed them through a little crawlspace—don't ask me how I managed it— out into the city." She shuddered at the memory. "We hid for a while, then found our way onto a ship heading for Derstan Station. We had to pay a lot to keep it all quiet. Qas's father has a lot of money, and they…acquired some of it. I don't know how; they never said. But we bought our way out of Sovena, and when we got to Derstan Station, we started new lives."

Siphany tried to think of how to summarize all those years they'd spent together. How could she ever do it all justice? A whole era in her life. "Um. Qas used their money to buy the ship, and that's where we lived. They knew I wanted my own place, and they knew I wanted to spend my life in space." She shook her head. "I never deserved any of it. A couple of years later…it all turned to shit, and they left. They gave me the ship on the way out."

"Probably for the best. It's not good to owe someone that much, you know? You find you can never pay it all back."

Siphany gave Lurbira a speculative look. "That's surprisingly wise."

"Eh." Lurbira shrugged. "I'm really old. No matter what Harban says. What does he know, anyway? Jackass."

Siphany smiled. So much for wisdom.

At that moment, Qas descended the stairs.

"I talked with the controllers in Toyen," they said. "Come on back up."

*

QAS SAT IN their chair, looking perfectly composed and reserved. This was probably a bad sign. Qas would become friendly, outgoing, and downright companionable when they had good news to share, controlled and distant when the news was bad. Siphany cringed, remembering the stoic look on their face during the worst of the bad times.

"Control has some of this information already," said Qas. Lurbira bristled; Qas held up a hand to stop her. "Apparently, this particular Junk is a minor player, nothing noteworthy or important. But information on its movement into Sovene space is interesting. I'm sorry you couldn't have tracked it to its eventual final destination."

"I spent two years of my life on that station!" exclaimed Lurbira. "They had all kinds of Loyan spies and ships coming through there. It's all on video—I recorded everything!"

"You did. But did you think to edit it at all, or highlight noteworthy material?"

Lurbira froze. "Why would I do that?" she asked after a moment.

"Because it'll take us months to sift out the important bits," said Qas, their voice still tight and polished. "What you gave me is almost completely useless to us at the moment. We are pressed for time…"

"That's bullshit!" Lurbira leapt off the chair, which had the unfortunate effect of making her drop below the height of the desk. "I know what was there was important!"

"I'm not saying we won't pay." Qas held up a hand. Lurbira relaxed a little. "We just can't pay a lot."

"How much?" Lurbira asked warily.

"I've been authorized to give you 1,500 sov. In local currency, that's 3,220 haeldmarks."

"What?" Lurbira shrieked. "That's nothing! That's an *insult*. Two years of putting my life at risk for you fuckers!"

"I can't change that. I'm only authorized to pay this much, nothing more. You'll have to take it or leave it." Qas, voice a knife's edge, had begun to look distinctly uncomfortable.

"Qas," began Siphany.

"When I left here two years ago," Lurbira snapped, cutting Siphany off, "people were walking out of here with five times the cash for a tenth the work."

"I know." Qas looked genuinely sorry. They ran a hand through their jaw-length, floppy hair. For a moment, the polished veneer cracked, and Siphany could see the old Qas, impulsive and empathetic to a fault. "Believe me, I know. If it were up to me, I'd pay you. But right now, funding is going into areas more directly related to the war effort here on Haeld, so I'm stuck. I'm sure you can understand."

"This is robbery," said Lurbira, voice shaking. "You're just a thief.

You and all the Sovenes."

Siphany winced. Lurbira shouldn't have insulted Sovena. Qas had certain very firm ideas about Sovena.

"You never registered," Qas said, their voice low and full of menace. "You never informed us or followed any of the correct procedures. You just assumed you'd be paid. You're lucky we're paying you much of anything at all, *Artificial.* If you want to work for us full-time, we might be able to use you in some way. But as it is? Don't press your luck."

"Bureaucratic jackasses," seethed Lurbira. "Tell me why I shouldn't take my information and leave."

"You can. Like I said, I'm sorry."

Lurbira glowered. For a brief second, Siphany was afraid she'd turn the whole building into a flaming ruin.

"If it helps," said Qas, perhaps sensing the same danger, "I can see what else we can give you after the fact. If you stick around town, maybe something will come of it. If the information's especially useful, Control might be able to get you more funds. I'll put in a good word."

"Swell," said Lurbira sullenly.

"If you had anything else…" said Qas, almost pleading. "Anything at all. Documents. Prisoners. Agent codes. Anything at all might make a difference."

Siphany caught her breath. *Prisoners.* Isan.

But Lurbira said nothing.

"I don't have all day," Qas reminded her.

"I saved a Sovene citizen." Lurbira thumbed at Siphany. "They were gonna ship her to Loyan."

"She's not Sovene," said Qas, very carefully not looking at Siphany.

"She's a Derstan citizen. She made that quite clear."

"Lurbira," Siphany said softly, ignoring Qas's clear taunt. "Take the money. Let's get out of here."

"But—"

"Lurbira!"

"Okay," said Lurbira, clearly crushed. "I'll take your shitty money. You bastards."

*

QAS HANDED LURBIRA a tablet with forms to approve, which she grumpily did. Then they gave her a plastic tile loaded with haeldmarks. She gave it a long, sad look before placing it into a compartment in her upper arm.

"Sif, I'd love to see you later," Qas said. "I live here in this building. Are you free? Can you come by tonight around 1800? We can catch up."

She very much wanted to tell them to go to hell. But what came out of her mouth was, "I suppose."

She immediately regretted it. She wanted nothing more than to get out of there and never come back. She wanted to return to her ship, which was still parked in orbit.

But now she was trapped.

"Excellent," Qas said, pleased. "See you then. Thank you for your contribution to Sovena's security, Lurbira." And with that, they were gone.

"Fuck them," Lurbira said under her breath. "Let's get out of here."

*

THEY WERE ONLY a few steps outside the Sovene intelligence station when Lurbira began to rant.

"Of all the *bullshit*. I can't believe they'd do this to me. Two *years*, Siphany! Two fucking shit-eating bullshit cock-grabbing YEARS I spent on that mother-goat-fucking *Junk*, and now here I am and they give me *jack shit* for it."

"Lurbira—"

"I've never *seen* such crap. And I even saved one of their people! Who the fuck cares if you're not Sovene *now*, so what? So *what?*"

She nailed a pile of dirt with her metal foot; it ballooned into the air like a mushroom cloud.

"I'm sorry, Lurbira. I really am."

"That fucking—fuck them." Lurbira paced in furious tiny circles. Fuck your stupid friend. How could they just face me like that and be all smooth and calm while they *fucked me over!*"

"I know," said Siphany, miserable. "They would do that to me too."

"Damn it." Lurbira's face screwed up in rage and despair. "I was going to get that new body. I had it all planned out. I was going to…"

She stopped and sat down on a curb. It cracked a little under her weight.

"Screw everything," she said, burying her head in her hands. "Screw it all. I just wasted *two years.*"

"I'm so sorry. I know you wanted that body."

"I really did. I hate being trapped like this."

I know how you feel. I was trapped once too. "You didn't have to take their money," Siphany said.

"You told me to! Besides…I don't have anything right now. Not a single haeldmark. I *need* that money. I need repairs like you wouldn't believe. I had to hook myself up to your ship. This body's old, and it's giving out." Her little shoulders sagged. "I was just going to have it all replaced. Get my brain transplanted into something new and shiny, like everyone else has. But now I have to beg Harban to try repairing…*this*." She gestured at her body, clearly disgusted. "My new body was going to be full-sized, Siphany. Full fucking sized. Not a little runt of a thing."

"I'm sorry." Siphany had no idea what else to say.

"You know how bad it sucks to be kid-sized and older than just about everyone who looks down at you and sneers? It's shit. I want to reach back in time and strangle those jerks who ordered me made to be their kid."

Siphany put a hesitant hand on Lurbira's shoulder. "I know a little about it. I used to hate my body. I felt so misshapen and wrong. I know it's gender, and that's not the same, but…"

"You don't have to touch me. I figured out you don't like it."

"I don't, but…it's okay."

Lurbira sighed and leaned against Siphany. Surprised, Siphany put an arm around her.

"Yeah." Lurbira kicked out at the dirt again and missed. "Yeah."

"You could have given them Isan. I'm…kind of surprised you didn't."

"I know. But…she's not worth much. And it would have been too much trouble. Besides, nobody deserves that."

"All the same," said Siphany. "Thank you."

Lurbira nodded glumly. "I guess."

"Lurbira…I have some money. I can give it to you, if you want. For your new body."

"What?" Lurbira was aghast. "No! No way."

"It would be a way of saying thanks—"

"Sif, I *used* you. And…I don't want to owe you. Okay? I like you too much."

"But—"

"Just let's forget about it, okay? We should get back there before Harban takes Isan apart so he can see how she ticks. Come on." Lurbira creakily got to her feet and swung back into motion.

Siphany, bewildered, followed.

*

THEY FOUND HARBAN and Isan amiably chatting about the various mechanical systems aboard the Junk. Apparently, they were getting along just fine.

Lurbira took one look at them and stormed off, muttering to herself.

"Didn't go well?" Harban asked, watching her go.

"No," said Siphany. "They didn't pay her much."

"I could have told her that would happen," said Harban ruefully. "The bonanza days are long gone. Sovenes don't have the cash now."

"That's what they told us."

"So, then. What's next?"

Siphany shrugged. "I, um, made an appointment. I'm supposed to go back there in a few hours."

"For anything in particular?"

Siphany flushed. "I know someone who works there. Old friend. We want to catch up."

"You're welcome to stay here until then," said Harban kindly. "I don't have a lot of business, but at least it's safe."

Siphany smiled at him. He was easy to like. "Thank you. I can pay."

"No need. I like having the company." He smiled at Isan, who had been standing there silently throughout their conversation. She seemed to perk up a little in response.

"Well…we appreciate it," said Siphany. "I'm sure Lurbira does too."

"That one?" Harban said, glancing off where Lurbira had vanished. "If she does, she'll never admit it."

*

SIPHANY SPENT THE rest of the time sitting by herself in the clutter of Harban's shop, trying not to run through her entire relationship with Qas from beginning to end, including every fight, every little insult, all the moments of joy and wonder, and every dull, exciting, or horrible day in between their first kiss and their final goodbye. Of course, she did just that; her mind ran around in loops. The shop was too chaotic, too disorganized. She couldn't center herself.

By the time it was close to 1800, she was a wreck.

"Hey," said Lurbira, clomping up next to her. "Ready for your big date with that bureaucratic ass?"

"It's not a date," said Siphany too quickly. But she straightened her tunic and patted down her hair anyway.

"You don't have to go. We can just deliver the dead girl to the Loyans and get out of here."

Isan gave her a sour look but said nothing.

"N-no," Siphany said. "I'm fine. I can go. Besides, Isan doesn't seem like she's in a hurry to leave."

"I don't even blame her," said Lurbira. "The Loyans are no fun."

"Yeah." Siphany steeled herself and stood up. "Okay. I'm ready."

*

IT WAS EVEN grayer out but still light enough to see. Lurbira had insisted on accompanying Siphany to the station.

"Just so I can spit on it," said Lurbira, but Siphany got the feeling she was also here to keep her safe.

It was kind of sweet, but Siphany knew better than to mention it.

When they arrived, Lurbira made a rude gesture at the building and then shooed Siphany in.

"Get in touch when you're done," Lurbira said. "I'll be close by."

"I will." Siphany felt weirdly as though her mom had just dropped her off at a date's house. Not that that had ever happened to her, but she'd seen plenty of shows where it had.

Siphany hesitated, then knocked on the door. The same receptionist from before opened it wide.

"They're expecting you," she said, looking Siphany up and down. "You…ah. Do you want to freshen up?"

Siphany burned with embarrassment, conscious of the fact that she still had dirt from the road all over her clothes and face. Being presentable at all times was as part of the Sovene Form as any time-of-day ritual.

But she wasn't Sovene, was she? Not anymore. Siphany thought of what Lurbira would do and folded her arms to glare at the woman. "Qas can take me or leave me the way I am."

The woman gave her a hard little look that suggested she and all of Sovene womanhood disapproved. Siphany winced internally but held her ground.

The woman made a little shrug as if to say, *I tried*, and then gestured to a back area Siphany hadn't seen before. "This way."

The room was brightly lit with a table grandly set for dinner at the center. Intense Sovene music played, and the tang of Sovene spices filled the air. It was nauseatingly like home. Siphany felt the room spin and had to steady herself against a chair.

"They'll be here soon," the woman promised and swept out.

Great. Oh please, don't throw up, please. Siphany fought a pounding headache. The music—The smell—

She sat down quickly and put her head in her arms.

"Sif? Are you okay?" Qas's delicate hand fell on her shoulder. She shrieked and batted their touch away. "Sif!" they protested.

"The music, the music… Qas, please!"

"Oh," they said, looking annoyed. "Of course. Right. Music off."

The room went blessedly silent.

"Lights down," Qas ordered. The lights dimmed.

Siphany began to relax. She could still smell the spices, but now that the light was lower, she could stand them.

"I thought you might like a touch of home," Qas said. "But I forgot—you don't like that much, do you?"

You forgot. How is that possible? You were with me for how many years? Siphany didn't say anything. She didn't trust her voice right now.

"I'm so sorry. It's been so long that my mind isn't in the right place. Are you all right?" Qas pressed.

"Yeah," Siphany said, enunciating each word as precisely as possible. "Fine."

To prove to herself, and to Qas, that she wasn't as weak as she appeared, Siphany carefully stood and walked, as gracefully as she could stand to be, over to the table. She sat without falling over and considered it a major win.

"So." Qas slid ever-so-smoothly into the chair across from hers. "This is awkward. I don't really know where to begin. It's…surprisingly good to see you again."

"Mm," she said through her headache.

"I'd love to hear more about how you came to be here." Right. Qas always led the conversation.

"And you too," Siphany said, fighting the aching and throbbing in her temples.

"Right. You remember when I left the ship?"

As if she could forget one of the worst days of her life. She nodded numbly.

"Well, after that, I did some government work back on Sovena, but halfway across the planet from home," Qas continued. "Then I got a letter from my father. He wanted me to come back and see him. I wasn't doing anything else that mattered at the time, so I did. He and I had it out. It was a big, big fight, all about me and my direction in life. We agreed my wild days were behind me."

Was that what I was? Your "wild days?"

"After that, I took a job with the Foreign Office, and they found I had a talent for information gathering and processing." Qas waved their hand in a self-congratulatory way.

The implication was clear; their father had gotten them the job. It figured. They'd always made a big deal of how much they hated their rich, influential father, so of course, it would be him who came to the rescue. Typical Qas.

"One thing led to another, and here I am, eight years later." Qas spread their arms, taking the room, the station, the entire planet in with a gesture, the old arrogance and cockiness in their eyes. "I'm on the front line of a war, doing critical work for Sovena. It's been an amazing ride."

"I bet your father's proud," said Siphany with a sneer she hadn't meant to let loose.

Qas's face fell, but they recovered quickly. "Well, yes. For once, my family's actually happy with me. I left the addictions and other problems behind. I felt so trapped for so long in all that. But now I've really made something of myself."

Siphany was almost happy for them. Qas was obviously so proud of what they'd done with their life. If they'd been anyone else, Siphany would have been impressed. But all she could feel was bitterness. *This is what Qas chose instead of me.*

"And what about you, Sif, have you been home?"

"You mean Sovena? No. I have no intention of ever going back there."

"Even after all this time?" Their voice was full of compassion, and their hair was so beautiful, their eyes so bright and expressive…she could have lost herself in all of them again. Siphany shook herself loose.

"No," she said.

"Not even to see your parents? Your brother and sisters? I thought for sure—"

"My life is fine without my family or anyone else on Sovena in it." Siphany must have said that with more force than she'd intended; Qas actually raised an eyebrow.

They considered, then pursed their lips. "Well, that may be the right thing for you. So, are you still flying my ship?"

"It's my ship now," Siphany reminded them. "You gave it to me."

"Right. I did. So you still have it?"

"Of course I do. Where else would I be? It's in orbit now."

"Amazing. I would have thought you'd have given it up by now. You run cargo?"

"No. I worked—*work*—for a mapping company doing surveys of deep interstellar space. It's a very important job." Siphany took a breath, trying hard to marshal her thoughts and her pride. "I create maps of remote sectors that help improve navigation and ship safety, and sometimes, I help identify new stores of resources for Derstan Station to use. The work is difficult and very rewarding. No one can do it the way I do. I earn plenty of money, and I spend years out here at a time."

"Oh, Sif," Qas said, a pitying look in their eyes. "Alone?"

"Yes, alone," she retorted, stung. "I like it. What's wrong with that?"

"Just you on a ship in deep space. No crew, no friends…no lovers?"

"I have a cat."

"Sif."

"It's a good life. It suits me. I don't want anything more than that."

"Don't you want to go back to school? You used to. You're so incredibly smart. You could do anything. You could make a huge difference if you put your mind to it."

"How did this become all about me and the choices I made?" This argument was becoming sickeningly familiar, just like the ones they'd had right before Qas had left her. Suddenly, it was if the last ten years hadn't happened at all. "You sold out and went back to the *Sovene government.* You went to work in the foreign service of a government you said you *hated*—"

"Siphany, shh," Qas said nervously.

She raised her voice a fraction. "Oh, is this not convenient? Is the truth embarrassing? You said you hated Sovena, and you said you hated your father and everything he stood for. When we were together, you said how happy you were that we were gone, that you'd never go back, that Sovena was full of liars and hypocrites."

"Things change. I was young and stupid then, and now, I've moved on."

"Is *this* why you decided to leave me? So you could go home and lick your father's boots? So you could serve the government of a planet you couldn't wait to escape?"

Qas sighed. "One of us had to grow up, Siphany."

That was it. She banged her silverware, which she'd been fiddling with, down on the table. "Lurbira's right. You're a bureaucratic jackass. I'm leaving."

"Sif, please, stop. I'm sorry. I didn't mean to cover all that bad, old ground. I only wanted to see you again. I was so happy when you walked in that door. Really!"

Against her better judgement, Siphany allowed her heart to open a tiny crack. "You have a funny way of showing it," she said, still angry.

"I'm sorry about the music and the lights. I shouldn't have forgotten. That was thoughtless of me."

"It was," said Siphany sullenly.

"You can tell me all about how you got here, and how you came to be with Lurbira. I'm dying to know." Qas grabbed her hand across the table.

"Stay."

She grimaced. She didn't want to stay. She hated herself for not storming out. But…they were here, smiling that dazzling smile at her, and it had been a long time. Plus…it wasn't as though she had anywhere better to be right now.

"All right. But I don't have to sit here and fight with you. I was done with that a long time ago."

"No one will force you to."

"Fine."

Qas grinned wider. "Fine."

*

SIPHANY WALKED WITH Lurbira back to the room Harban was letting them use above his shop. The town had few lights, and Lurbira was clearly jumpy. She'd come to escort Siphany back after she and Qas had finished dinner, saying she didn't trust the town at all.

Qas had offered to send a station guard with them, but Lurbira had declined before Siphany could say anything. A station guard, Lurbira had whispered once they were out the door, would do nothing but paint a big target on their backs. Lurbira had then informed her to stay as quiet as possible, so while they walked, to distract herself from a sense of impending doom, Siphany worked the rest of the evening over in her mind. She still couldn't quite believe it had all happened.

She'd told Qas an abbreviated, partially edited version of her story. By the end, Qas shook their head in dismay.

"You shouldn't be anywhere near here, Sif," they said soberly. "These people…this whole thing. You shouldn't be here. You should take the ship and leave as soon as you can. You could end up getting hurt."

Siphany made a little strangled whine. "We were almost killed today outside of town. Near the spaceport."

Qas's eyes bugged out. "The spaceport? You were at the *spaceport?* That's—I can't even tell you what a bad idea that was! So what happened?"

"Lurbira saved us." She sighed. "She's…I don't know. She's very good…"

"At killing people, right. You said."

"No, it's more than that. She's efficient. But I think deep down she *likes* it."

Qas nodded soberly. "I know people like that here. A lot of the government troops…some of them are scared, some are bored, and some have become these horrible killers. I don't know how it happens."

"Everyone cracks."

"I suppose some more than others," Qas said, and for a moment, they were carried along by the swift current of the old easy banter again.

Siphany deliberately broke the connection by looking away.

Qas took her hand. She shook it free.

"Don't," she warned them.

"You need to get out of here," Qas insisted. "The whole planet is a powder keg. The reason we don't care about Lurbira's information is that the situation here is very, very bad. The government is on its last legs, and as soon as the capital falls to the rebels, the skies will be full of Loyan ships."

"When will that happen?"

Qas lowered their voice to a whisper. "Sooner than anyone here thinks. Maybe a month, maybe less. I don't know. Once it does…I don't know what will happen next. Sovena might send in ships. If I had to guess, the Loyans are moving that Junk to Sovene space because they know the end is near here. But…this could end up being the big one."

Siphany let the implications of that sink in. A massive war in Haeld space would be a nightmare. The Stationbund was officially neutral, they always were, but even they might not be able to avoid getting pulled in. Stationbund territory bordered Sovena, Haeld, and Loyan space.

She wished she were back on her ship and hooked into Hydras. Maybe Pati, who always had a good head for this sort of thing, would be able to reassure her.

Or not.

"You should leave," continued Qas. "Tomorrow. I'll ask the garrison commander about putting together a team to get you back to your ship—if it's still there."

"I'll talk to Lurbira."

"You sure you can trust her? A lot of the informants who come in here aren't trustworthy. We've followed bogus lead after bogus lead from them. They play both sides."

"Lurbira hates Loyan though. She wouldn't help them."

"I'm sure," said Qas. "The Artificials are terrified of Loyan. They were all built there, and the Loyans are notorious for treating them badly. Still, many of them gave information to the rebels and, by extension, to Loyan to make money and survive. This is a hard place to be."

"I'm sure. But I trust Lurbira."

"Look, if you want, I can probably get you to the Derstan embassy in the capital."

Siphany's heart fluttered. "You can?"

"Maybe. The rebels are everywhere, and it'll be hard to get there. It's not impossible, though, and it's probably your best shot."

Siphany filed that away. What would it cost her to trust Qas again? "I'll think about it. You're getting out soon, too, right?"

"Only if the government recalls me," said Qas. "Otherwise, I'm here for the duration. Think about what I said though. Try to get out."

"I will," Siphany had promised. And then, after a few more pleasantries, the dinner had ended.

Her shoes crunched over the gravel in the road. The night seemed eerily quiet, but it wasn't the kind of calm, restful silence she thrived on. It felt dangerous and tense, like something terrible was lurking just out of sight.

*

A FEW MINUTES after they trudged up to the rooms Harban had lent them, the power blew, plunging them into darkness.

"That happens," said Harban.

"Now what?" Isan said, a hint of sarcasm in her voice.

"Nothing, you turd, it's dark," said Lurbira. "Humans go to sleep. Artificials and corpses stay up and wait. In the morning, we'll get you to the Loyans, and they'll either kill you or find a way to put you back on your Junk. Whatever. Same difference to me; we'll be done with you."

"And then we leave," said Siphany.

"*You* can leave," said Lurbira. "Not me though."

"You're not coming?" Siphany said, surprised and disappointed.

"Nah. I've got some cash, and Harban's gonna fix me up. Don't worry. I'll get you back to your ship."

"You can't use the Junk ship," Isan said suddenly. "It's property of the Junk, and I need to bring it back to Mother Junk."

"Tough. Them's the breaks, kid," said Lurbira. "Right now, Siphany needs it more than you do. Her cat's up there, and she needs to get back to work and far away from here."

"I'll pay you for some of it," Siphany promised Isan. *If I ever get back home. If I ever have a job again.*

"Your money's worthless. We don't need it," said Isan.

"I guess Mother Junk makes food and water and air from her own asshole, then," Lurbira gloated. "Because she sure seemed like she enjoyed the Loyans' money well enough. Don't give her anything, Sif. Just take what you can and get out of here before you get caught up in all this."

"What if you get caught up in it?" Siphany asked.

Lurbira said nothing for a long moment. "I'll have a better-working body. And maybe I can find a way to pay for the whole thing. I'm a survivor. I'll be fine."

"I can—"

"No, Sif." Lurbira held up a hand. "I won't take your money."

"Why not?"

Siphany never got to hear the answer as a high-pitched whine rose from the buildings all around.

"We should go down to the shelter," Harban broke in. "Bombing has started."

"Bombs?" Siphany asked, alarmed.

"Rebels in the hills. They like shooting a bomb or two into town at night."

Siphany looked outside. Sure enough, streaks of orange arced from the hills, down onto the town. First one, then two, then ten.

Then fifty.

Then more than she could possibly count.

"Harban," said Lurbira. "Holy shit."

Harban was about to reply when the first of the missiles struck right next to the shop. Siphany was knocked off her feet.

"Everybody out!" Harban roared. "Now!"

*

THEY RAN THROUGH the single street of the town, which had become an unrecognizable mass of flame, smoke, and screams.

"This is it," shouted Harban. "The big one. Follow me; we've got an evacuation plan!"

"Wait!" said Siphany. They were going the wrong way! "I can't leave Qas!"

"Yes you can," cried Lurbira. "Sif, wait!"

Siphany didn't listen. She whirled around, trying to orient herself. There! The station house was still there, but it was on fire.

Rockets slammed into buildings all around her. The noise, sight, and smell were overwhelming.

Siphany gathered herself, pulled a pair of earplugs out of her pocket, and stuck one in each ear.

With the sound muffled, she could concentrate again, if only marginally. It would have to be enough. She sprinted toward the station house.

*

SIPHANY COVERED HER face with her arms and burst inside, leaving Lurbira behind on the street. She glanced around quickly; smoke filled the downstairs, and the windows and half a wall were shattered.

A body lay on the floor—the receptionist. Debris and shards of wood and glass stuck out of her shredded torso, and her sightless eyes stared up at the ceiling, unblinking.

Damn the Sovenes. If this woman had been allowed a constant body-altering bluenet, it might have been able to shift her vital systems around the damage. She might have lived.

Siphany swallowed her terror and shock and looked around for Qas. They were nowhere to be seen.

"Qas," she called, taking one earplug out. Nothing. The fire was upstairs—near Qas's office. She put the plug back in and took the smoky steps three at a time. "Qas!"

They were in their office, slumped over the desk. Siphany pulled Qas out of the chair. "Qas! Wake up!" She was lucky they were so light. *A bird,* someone had once called them. *Might fly away at any moment.*

Qas opened their eyes. "Sif…"

"Come on. Can you walk? The whole town's on fire."

"They…they were supposed to protect…" Qas's eyes were hollow. "This wasn't supposed to happen… My people?"

"Gone. Come on!"

Siphany half-guided, half-dragged Qas out of the room and down the stairs. She tried hard to shield them from the sight of the dead woman on the floor, but they saw, and their eyes widened. They said a name; Siphany couldn't hear it.

Siphany dragged Qas out of the house and onto the street. The high whine of rockets filled the air, audible even though earplugs.

Qas coughed and bent over—Siphany thought they might throw up.

"Qas!" She took the earplugs out so she could hear them.

"I'm fine," they said, trying to clear their lungs. "Smoke."

Lurbira sprinted up to them, feet heavy on the gravel. "You're okay," she exclaimed, relieved. "Sif, you idiot! Come on, follow us." She pointed to a waving Harban.

"Go," Qas said to Siphany between hacks. "I'll be fine."

"No," The world spinning around her, and she fought the panic back. "I'm not losing you again." She grabbed their hand and yanked hard, pulling them to their feet. "Come on, now!"

"Sif…" Qas said. "I'm not worth it… Go."

A missile slammed into a building next to them, sending debris and flames flying everywhere. Qas stopped resisting, and Siphany dragged them behind her as she sprinted after Lurbira, Isan, and Harban.

*

EVERYWHERE, THE ROCKETS pounded the small town into flaming ash. The small group ran behind buildings and ducked through alleyways. At some point, Siphany realized she was screaming, and then she was bouncing along sickeningly on Isan's narrow back. She looked to her right; Harban carried a semiconscious Qas.

Isan. Why would Isan ever help me?

Then they dove into utter darkness and putrid stench.

*

A RHYTHMIC SLOSHING sounded all around them, and lights emanating from Lurbira and Harban illuminated their way. They marched through a narrow, confined space, utterly silent except for Isan's grunting and the splashing of feet through shallow water. Siphany's panic and tightness receded into a wary, exhausted alertness.

The sewer. Of course.

The ground shook above as bombs and rockets hit the town again and again. *It must be hell up there. Where could all the people have gone?*

This little town had spacious sewer pipes. Weird.

"I need to stop," gasped Isan. "I can't keep up."

Harban and Lurbira halted, staring without expression back at her.

"I'm not like you. Please."

"For a few minutes only," said Harban quietly.

He put Qas down on the ground; they groaned. Isan wheezed and set Siphany down. They both sank against the stone wall of the sewer.

"Thank you," Siphany said softly to Isan.

Isan only shook her head.

"This is some serious sewer," said Lurbira. "We have to be away from the houses by now."

Harban placed a hand on the sewer wall. "The town used to be a lot bigger. These lines are centuries old."

"Oh," said Lurbira, losing interest.

"We need to keep moving. They'll come through here eventually." Harban turned to the dark end of the tunnel. "We have to be gone before they do."

"Where are we going?" Siphany asked, her mouth dry.

Harban shook his head, putting a finger to his lips. Right. Of course.

Qas stared at Siphany. They opened their mouth to say something, but Siphany waved it away.

"We're even now," she said softly, remembering Qas pulling her out of the institution, onto the ship, away from Sovena.

They smiled and looked down. She was sure she saw them wipe a tear away.

After a long moment, Isan stood. "Okay. I think I can go on. But…" She glanced at Siphany and Qas. "I don't know about the humans."

Siphany rose on her wobbly legs. "I can manage." The smell here was bad, but at least it was dark and quiet. She hesitantly rested a hand on Isan's cool, clammy shoulder. Isan flinched, and Siphany jerked her hand away, ashamed.

Qas was also on their feet. "Same. Let's go."

"Good," Harban said and set off again, Lurbira right behind him.

*

THEY FOLLOWED HARBAN through the maze of tunnels, at some point leaving the stench of the sewer behind. They were now in tunnels that smelled earthy and wet, like the inside of the ground.

At last, they reached a heavy, rusty grate, which Harban dislodged with a quiet, efficient motion.

"Some of the others came this way," he said, voice barely audible. Siphany wondered how he could tell. She didn't see any signs of other people. "We're not the only ones who got out. Good."

He led them out into the cool night onto a rocky hillside. Siphany looked back, and her mouth gaped open. The town was a sea of flame.

A sudden, tremendous roar sounded as small fighter craft streaked overhead. Siphany shrieked and clapped her hands over her ears.

"Those are Loyan ships," said Qas despairingly.

"Agreed." Harban followed the ships with his steady, unreadable gaze. "They're not even hiding it anymore. They're the ones who took the town, not the rebels."

"They *destroyed* the town," said Siphany.

"Same difference." Qas's voice was numb. "For them it's the same."

"The rebels will go in after and mop up," said Harban. "They'll raise their flag in the ruins and claim victory. That's how they do it. But if Loyan is openly showing themselves…"

"Then the capital must have fallen," finished Qas. "It must have happened tonight. I was talking with Control earlier today!"

"Everything I had was back there." Harban gestured at the burning mess that had been the town of Sunshine Valley. "I was planning to get out in a few weeks. I didn't think this would happen so soon."

"Nobody did," said Qas. "We never saw it coming. Why didn't we see it coming? Why didn't we try to stop it?" They looked up at the sky. "Where *are* you?" they asked softly. "Sovena…don't just leave us here…"

Siphany almost—almost—put her arm around their shoulder. But she couldn't figure out a way to do it that wasn't awkward, and the moment passed.

"Follow." Harban started hiking up the ravine. "We'll be there soon."

Behind them, the town vanished, consumed by rocket fire and death.

Chapter Seven

THEY HIKED UP into the hills by the low light of Haeld's moons, following a path already worn by heavy feet. Lurbira kept glancing around like a nervous cat, pointing her deadly arms at the weirdly thick trees and reddish-brown rocks as if something might leap out at any moment. But nothing menaced them; the attack had stopped, and the night was eerily quiet and still.

At last, Harban knelt by a massive round boulder. "Here. Lurbira. Help."

"With what?"

"Help me clear it away," he said patiently.

She pointed her weaponized arms at it—he caught her just in time.

"No! No, it needs to be able to go back when we're done."

"Oh," she said grumpily. "Why didn't you say so? Sure. I've got the strength for it." She gave Siphany a gloating look. "Unlike *some* species."

Siphany returned a ghost of a smile.

Together, they rolled the rock away, revealing a narrow cave leading into darkness. Two other Artificials crouched just inside.

"Harban," said the one with beautiful vine patterns all over his head and neck. "You made it."

"Who are *these?*" asked the other, a lithe Artificial with starry fields for eyes.

"They're with me, Yovan," snapped Lurbira. "Have a problem with that?"

"Lurbira Call," sighed Yovan, rolling her starry eyes. "I see you got back just in time."

"Figures, doesn't it? And the humans are okay. You can trust them."

"And the other? Is that…"

"Synthetic, yeah. I don't even know how that happened. Don't ask me," said Lurbira, even though she absolutely did know.

The beautifully patterned Artificial pointed to Qas. "That one's with the Sovenes."

"You might have noticed that the Sovenes aren't the ones attacking the town," said Lurbira.

"We're not a Sovene refugee camp."

"Like I said, they're with me," Lurbira said, teeth gritted. "Can we come in yet?"

"They're with me, also," Harban said quietly.

The two Artificials exchanged glances. Then Yovan nodded. "Fine. But we take no responsibility for any of them."

"Like I'd ever trust you to," Lurbira shot back.

Harban touched hands with the other two Artificials briefly. "How many?"

"Forty-nine," said Yovan.

"Most of us, then," said Harban, satisfied. "Good."

"How is that *most*?" Lurbira asked, aghast. "There were over two hundred of us when I was here last!"

"Times change," said Harban. "Artificials have been leaving. If there had been more time, I would have done the same."

"We're replacing the rock," said Yovan. "Go deeper in. You'll find everyone."

"Thanks." Harban put a hand on her shoulder. "It's good to see you again."

"You too."

"Arms and eyes working okay?"

"Better than ever," she said with a grin.

"Hey," said Lurbira, impatient. "Catch up later. Let's go."

Yovan and Harban shared an amused look, and then Yovan and her partner turned to deal with the rock. Everyone else followed Harban and Lurbira deeper into the cave.

Siphany thought she caught Lurbira looking wistfully back at Yovan, with her new, beautiful body, but an instant later, Lurbira was herself again, striding confidently into the darkness.

*

THE TUNNEL ENDED in a massive, vaulted chamber lit by dim green bioluminescent lights, under which dozens of Artificials waited in perfect silence.

"*Humans*," said one, and the word spread through the group, a rustling wind of scorn.

"They're with me," said Lurbira.

"With you, Lurbira? That doesn't make me worry less," said another.

Lurbira glared at the offender but said nothing. Siphany could almost feel the indignation radiating off her.

"Why did you come back, Lurbira?" asked a tall green Artificial. "That wasn't wise."

"Hey, I just wanted to get my money and new body and get the hell out. I wasn't planning on staying."

"You brought humans here," said someone else. "You shouldn't have done that. Harban, you shouldn't have allowed it."

"They're Lurbira's friends," said Harban evenly. "I take full responsibility."

"Hey," Lurbira protested. "They're with me, the responsibility's *mine*."

No one said anything, but Siphany could have sworn she heard snickers.

"And you…" A smaller Artificial with intricate swirls on his chest and face approached a very worried-looking Isan. "You aren't Artificial or human, are you? Could it be…?"

"I'm…I'm a Synthetic," Isan said softly. "Or that's what they tell me I am."

Surprise and interest whispered through the room like the wind rustling reeds.

"Your kind have been gone a long time," the Artificial said.

"I—"

"She was made with some spare parts and the corpse of a girl whose grandmother is fucking nuts," said Lurbira.

"Parts from Pelagar, we think," Harban said.

The other Artificials studied Isan with great interest for a few moments more, then turned away.

"Find them all a place away from the rest of us," another Artificial instructed. "I want nothing to do with them."

There was a murmur of agreement.

Siphany nodded curtly; it made sense to her. The Artificials were well within their rights to dislike humans, and this was their place. Her Sovene politeness kicked in, and she said to the ones nearby, "Thank you for your hospitality."

One or two of them inclined their heads warily. She noticed that all of them here had humanoid forms. If Artificials could make their bodies into anything, why did they all seem to be human? To fit in? Some quirk of leftover original programming? Something else? It was strange.

She turned and found a cool place to sit alongside the edge of the cave. It was nice and dark here, and no one was making much noise.

Siphany hadn't felt so comfortable since leaving her ship. She checked the clock on her communicator. Time for meditation and then sleep. She closed her eyes and concentrated on her breathing.

It wasn't long before she'd fallen fast asleep.

*

SIPHANY DREAMED AGAIN of the bright room at the institution. The music played, and the nurses surrounded her. One of them had a bluenet disc, and she pressed it to Siphany's body. She screamed as she changed, as her body warped and shifted into something so unbearably *male* that she couldn't even recognize herself anymore. Siphany looked into a mirror; her father's face stared back.

She woke with a start.

A hand was shaking her awake. Qas. She was momentarily so glad to see them that she almost gave them a hug. But they had such a sad, sober look in their eyes that she only smiled, and the past receded again.

"It's dawn," Qas said. "Will you greet the day with me?"

She stared at them, agog. "You still want to do the Form? You have got to be kidding."

"Please?" There was such need in their eyes.

Siphany relented and got to her feet. They stood side by side, breathing in and out, and then Qas began.

Qas spread their arms and bowed their head. Siphany followed along, her movements precisely mirroring Qas's. They turned their heads, they sank to the ground, and then stood back up again. Siphany remembered every motion, every nod, every breath.

For a moment, she was Sovene again. She lived in ritual, in the calming cadences of the Form, and her mind was cool and composed.

Their arms went back to their sides, and the spell was broken.

"Thank you," said Qas with relief. "I know that's a difficult thing for you."

Siphany shrugged. She felt a mix of lingering calm and a sharp, surprising homesickness. "Yeah. I'll see you later."

Qas took the hint and wandered off.

"What *was* that?" came a voice from nearby. Siphany squinted and saw Isan sitting there. She had an astonished expression on her face. "It was beautiful."

"Oh. It's a Sovene thing. First shift people like me and Qas do it every morning when the sun comes up."

Isan bobbed her head, uncomprehending. "Why?"

Siphany didn't really have an answer. "We just do."

"Well," Isan said. "It was interesting to watch."

"I'm sure." Siphany sat back down, the cool rock of the cave at her back, and let her thoughts chase one another around her brain for a few more hours.

*

EVENTUALLY, LURBIRA TODDLED over, joints clearly still stiff, and sat heavily next to her.

"Hey, kid. They say they're going to be able to get the three of you a little food tonight. Two of our people are heading out to forage for some meat or plants or whatever you like putting in you. You like plasma-fried desert rat, right?"

Siphany smiled weakly, feeling far from home. "Thanks, Lurbira."

"What's wrong?"

"Nothing," she said too quickly.

"You're crying."

"I'm not," Siphany said, wiping a traitorous tear away.

"Yeah, you are. What happened? Are you okay?"

The concern on Lurbira's face just made things worse. Siphany quickly scrubbed at the new flood of tears, blinking the blurs away. "I'm fine. I'm just… Look. I was hoping that after this, I could go back to my job and live exactly like I did before. And now I can't."

"You still might."

"It's been too long." Siphany shook her head, and her chest tightened with the first stirrings of anxiety. "I've been out of contact. I'm too far away from the job site. They'll think I'm *unreliable.* They'll never accept me back now. I can't go back, even if I have the job again. It won't be the same. It'll all have changed."

"Everything and everyone has to change, Siphany," said Lurbira quietly.

"I don't like change," Siphany shot back.

"I know. I don't either." Lurbira's voice sounded scratchy and electronic, more so than ever before. It was almost as if she had a cold, but that couldn't be right. Could it? "But change is the only thing that's constant. I know how that sounds, but it's true. My whole life's been that way. A lot of Artificials would say the same thing. Maybe even humans too."

Siphany looked out at the Artificials gathered on the other side of the cave. "They don't like us much, do they?"

"Them? They don't like *anybody.* They don't like me, either, because I'm newer than they are."

"You are?" That didn't make sense.

"Well, sort of. Age is all about how long you've been aware and growing, so they don't count the thirty or so years I spent lost in my own head on that damn planet. Plus, I'm the only one of us left with her original body. Everyone else has new bodies and tons of mods. It's…I guess it's like it would be for you if everyone around you had bluenet and you didn't."

But that was how it was on Derstan Station. Everyone modded their appearance all the time, there. Siphany alone had used bluenet only the once and then never again. She stuck out.

"So, we don't get along," finished Lurbira. She sighed, and her hand began to twitch. She cursed and whacked herself on the arm. After a moment, it stopped.

"Lurbira? Are you all right?"

Lurbira shook her head. "No," she said, her voice low and sad. "I'm breaking down faster. This body is gonna wear out sooner rather than later."

"It's that bad? I had no idea."

"Sure you did. I told you I needed that new body."

"You didn't tell me how badly."

"Yeah, well, now you see. I can only repair myself so often. I had Harban give me a look earlier today. He says I probably have another year before critical systems start to fail." Lurbira couldn't meet Siphany's eyes. "You want to know why I've been so desperate? This is why."

"I'm so sorry," said Siphany. "If I'd known…"

"If you'd known, what could you have done?" said Lurbira bitterly.

"I could have paid for it."

"I already said no. I don't want to owe you that much. Friends shouldn't owe one another, right?"

Friends, thought Siphany, shocked. *Friends?*

Lurbira put her cold little hand around three fingers of Siphany's big, warm one and squeezed. It only hurt a tiny bit. "Thanks for thinking of me. But now that Harban's shop's destroyed, it doesn't matter anyway. Harban was the only one I know of doing big-time body mods and swaps. We'd have to find a Factory to get access to another, I bet." She shook her head ruefully. "And that isn't gonna happen, because there is no Factory."

"Factory?"

"Yeah. All we ever wanted was to build factories to make more of ourselves and fix the ones who were dying. Humans never let us. They're too damn afraid." Lurbira shook her head. "So we go here and there and do what we can. The really old Artificials talk about a group of us finding a planet to settle on without any humans and calling it 'Factory.' Some say it's happened already, and that's why there are so few of us left here. Everyone went to Factory. It's a nice myth. I wish it were real."

"I do, too," Siphany said and meant it.

Lurbira sighed. "Anyway, I'm sorry your life isn't going to be the same. I wish you hadn't been mixed up in this. You've been really good to me."

Siphany hesitated, then hugged her. She was hard and cool to the touch. Lurbira leaned into her, exhausted. "We'll fix you," Siphany said. "I promise."

Lurbira muttered something in reply, but Siphany couldn't understand what it was.

*

THEY SAT TOGETHER in the cold, dark cave for what seemed like hours. Every once in a while, they heard a deep, far-off *thud*, like something big hitting the ground. Were the rebels and the Loyans bombing the scrublands and the hills? Siphany had no frame of reference for this; the only weapons she knew anything about were space-based.

Qas came over to sit with Siphany and Lurbira. "How are you holding up?" they asked Siphany.

"Better than I was, thanks," Siphany replied, trying hard to show how even and calm she was. "How about you?"

Qas grunted a noncommittal answer. "The Artificials won't give me much information. I've been asking around, trying to find out what else they might be able to tell me about getting in and out of the town, but they won't say. They won't say much else either."

"Golly," said Lurbira brightly. "It's almost as if they have some reason to distrust humans. Can't imagine what that would be."

Siphany felt something inside her clench, and she drew in upon herself.

Qas ignored Lurbira. "They must know how we can get off-planet. I bet they're planning a way right now. The Artificials always have a plan. They're always ready for anything."

"The threat of the Loyans shipping us back there is a good incentive," said Lurbira.

"Right," said Qas. "So they probably have at least one ship hidden somewhere. They were ready for this. If we can somehow convince them to take us when they go…or…"

"Qas," Siphany sighed, trying to hold back another flood of tears. "Please just stop."

Qas shot her a speculative look. "Are you okay, Sif? Do you need anything?"

In response, Siphany glared at them. "Come on, Qas."

Qas held their hands up and stood. "Sorry I asked," they snapped and wandered off.

Lurbira watched them go with great interest. "Wow." She turned back to Siphany. "What was *that* about?"

"Old fight." They'd picked right up where they'd left off, as if all the years in between hadn't happened.

"What about?"

Despite herself, Siphany started to laugh. "The funny thing is that people often tell me *I'm* blunt. They clearly never met you."

"It's a strength," said Lurbira airily.

"Qas and I…it all goes back to the institution. They knew me there. They were with me when I got my medical implant; they remember what I was like…before. It was hard to be with me sometimes…a lot of times." She sighed. "They remember. I needed a lot of help then, and every once in a while, they got really patronizing about it. I always felt they were treating me like glass half the time and trying to get me to be stronger and less annoying the rest."

"Ah," said Lurbira knowingly. "They're an asshole."

"No, no, they're really not. It's not just that. It's…Sovena. The culture is so messed up. No one knows how to deal with mental illness like I have without saying *be strong* or *try behavior therapy*. We don't even talk about it."

"*You're* talking about it."

"Yeah, that's me. And on Derstan, it's less of a big awful secret thing, anyway, so I can. On Sovena, though, I probably wouldn't, because people would just be shocked."

"You come from a weird planet," said Lurbira.

"I know it. The mental health thing, the horror of body modifications, the total inconsistency of all the rules, the Form…ugh."

"The body mod thing is the weirdest though."

"Oh, I know. We weren't always that way. They taught us it had to do with Synthetics and Artificials, back a long time ago. Not that I'm blaming Artificials. But that's what they said back there."

"There used to be thousands of us on Sovena. I know that much."

"Yeah," said Siphany. "There was some kind of reaction—don't ask me what it was. I don't know. But my people wanted to draw a bright, clear line between human and not-human after a while. I think…I think the

Synthetics really scared them because they were both, and they were dead. So they came up with all these rules to outline what was human and what wasn't. It caught on. Sovenes really love rules."

"What a load," said Lurbira. "Here's my advice. Don't ever go home."

"I wasn't planning on it." Siphany looked over at Qas, who was trying to press information out of yet another disinterested Artificial. Always working. "What I don't get is why *they* went back. That's another piece of the old argument. Why go back after all that? After everything we went through. But they always wanted to. I never understood their patriotism." She sighed again. "I guess…it's just like that. I was like them, too, once. You know, I fought them over both the bluenet and the implant. I didn't want it at first. Qas pretty much had to force me. They knew I needed it. I was half out of my mind at that point, but I was so terrified it would make me less human. That's how strong the conditioning is."

"I get it," said Lurbira. "Is that why you don't have a communications implant?"

Siphany nodded. "Yes. I need what I have, but it took all my strength just to have bluenet done and the implant installed. I was sick for days after. I just can't do anything beyond that. My body is my body, altered just enough to let me be mostly sane."

"What if you lose an arm? No prosthetics?"

"No." Siphany shook her head. "I don't think I could ever be comfortable with that."

"Wow. So what about Qas? Don't Sovenes have a gender thing too?"

"Qas is fine. Sovenes believe gender's in the mind, and Qas lives theirs honestly. But they can't alter their body. They have to stay looking like they do forever. They wouldn't do bluenet. I thought they would…they said they would. But at the last minute, they backed out. By then, I'd already done it."

"I'd love to know…" Lurbira examined Qas.

"Well, don't ask. It's rude. Besides, I thought you didn't care about gender?" said Siphany, a hint of a smile on her lips.

"I don't. I just like knowing peoples' secrets."

"Nosy," said Siphany playfully. "I won't say, and they definitely won't tell you. And don't you dare ask them. Our secrets are our own."

They sat for a while longer. Siphany rested her head against the cool stone wall. Lurbira fidgeted.

"I know lots of secrets," said Lurbira after a while. She seemed almost needy. "Want to hear one? It's a weird story my old captain, Serlay Call, told me a long time ago. It'll help pass the time."

"Sure," said Siphany, surprised at the sudden shift in conversation. "I'm not going anywhere."

"I know this one from a long time ago. Serlay is the captain of the *Call*, the ship I used to live on. They were the ones who rescued me. Everyone on the ship had the same last name because in their culture, people take the name of their home as their second name. That's why I'm Lurbira Call. Got it?"

"You told me this before."

"Right. So, anyway, Serlay said Earth was once an incredible place with billions of people. Of course, it was; it was humanity's home. But there was a terrible war followed by all these big natural disasters, so the planet was ruined. Serves them all right. Anyway. Here's Serlay's story."

Lurbira's voice shifted lower, and Siphany realized with a shock that she was speaking now in someone else's voice. Serlay Call's.

The Captain's Whale

Lurbira, I don't tell many people this story. But I want to tell you because I think it's important for you to hear. Please remember it, all right?

Right after the war ended and the last of the waves of disasters subsided, we were all trying to find a way to survive. My family and I had lived far out in the country in Tamil Nadu, so we escaped the worst. My parents died from the plagues, even so. My brother Avram and I did survive, I have no idea how or why, but we had nothing to eat. All the plants were dead, and our animals were gone.

Avram and I were stuck alone in what was left of our house. I remember eating what little we had and then trying to contact someone to get help or to get more food. No one would answer, there were no services, and our family and friends did not respond. We decided to walk into the village to try to find someone. We were so hungry! So we walked south, Avram and I, and came to where the town had been. We found only a flat, brown plain. The town was simply…gone. No one at all was left.

Avram was so little. He began to cry, and I held him in my arms. It's okay, I told him. We'll find help. But I had no idea what to do. I was only a little girl. I searched and found some wood and a few other things but no food. I returned to Avram empty-handed. We tried to eat the wood; we were so hungry. We were tired, and thirsty, and it seemed like the end. Still, we had to do something. I didn't want to lie down and die right there on that horrible, empty plain.

Come on, I said to Avram, let's go to the ocean.

The sea was many kilometers away. But it was a place to go, and it gave us a goal. Do you understand, Lurbira? We needed that to carry us onward.

We walked and walked. Night came, and we found a little water in a pool. It tasted foul, but we drank it anyway. The next morning, we got up and kept going. We didn't see anyone else at all.

In time, we reached the shore. The sea was an angry gray, and the waters churned and roiled. Heavy clouds blocked out the sun. We sat on the beach and waited.

Perhaps we were waiting to die.

I fell asleep, and then woke up again. I shook Avram, trying to wake him, but he didn't move. I was delirious from hunger and exhaustion, so I simply stood up and walked to the sea. I think I meant to drown myself.

Then…the waves in front of me parted, and I found myself looking into a great eye. It glowed a sickly yellow.

I am not making it up, Lurbira, don't look at me like that. This happened. I consider myself a rational person, but I can't shake this memory. I know it happened. I saw that creature that day.

Serlay, a deep voice said. I could feel it vibrate in my bones.

I looked up. There, right in front of me, was something like a great whale, but like something else too. It seemed both organic and machine at the same time.

Serlay, it said again.

Who are you? I asked.

I am the Whale. Come. Ride on me. And it slapped its great tail against the sea, raising a plume of water into the air. I somehow climbed up on top of it, though I don't know how I did it, and the Whale swam out to sea, away from the shore.

My brother! We can't leave him!

He is already gone. But cling tightly to my back, child, we will travel far today.

No! Please. Can't you save him?

Serlay, the Whale said, its voice full of grief. **I can't carry all of my children. Right now, I can only carry you. But if you wish to return to the shore, you may. You will die there too.**

I looked back. I could barely see the shore now.

But why? Why can't you carry him too?

I came for you. Only for you, Serlay. Come forward with me and help give birth to the future, or return and die with your brother. Choose.

What could I do? I loved my brother. But I was terrified of dying, and I was just a girl. So…in my heart, I gave Avram up. I left him to die on that beach.

All right, I said. Carry me.

I have never forgiven myself for it. Avram's ghost haunts me still.

Brave girl, said the Whale.

But I didn't feel brave. I felt like a coward for leaving him there. I still feel that way.

We surged forward. We went so fast!

Where are you taking me? I shouted.

I am taking you to other humans so that you might live.

Now we were going so fast that I had to shut my eyes because the spray of the sea was blinding me.

Why should I live? My brother, my parents, my home are all gone. The world is destroyed. Why did you come for me?

Do not despair, child. I have a task for you, if you will accept it.

I fought with myself. How could I do anything? I was just a little girl, alone in the world. And I didn't want to do what the Whale wanted; he had let my brother die.

What is it? I asked at last.

Find me. I will go to the stars. I will guide your people to a new home.

A light appeared ahead of us. A town! My heart leapt. There were people on the shore!

This world is finished for you. Find me, so your people can make a new beginning, and this world can heal itself.

I will, I promised. I will! But…what are you?

I am what is left. I am memory. I am Earth. Remember, Serlay. Find me.

We sped toward the light, and I passed out. I came to surrounded by people. I was far from home; no one could explain how I'd gotten there. No one believed me about the Whale.

They took me to one of the huge orphanages set up for children who had lost their parents in the war, and that's where I lived.

In a single night, I'd managed to travel over seven hundred kilometers from the beach near my home. When I doubted my own memory, I remembered that fact. How could I have done it?

I am a rational woman, Lurbira, but I believe in the Whale.

That is what drove me to survive those terrible times. I dedicated myself to understanding science and deep space navigation, to reaching the stars again, and when the *Call* was discovered, I was in a position to become her captain.

I am searching for the Whale, Lurbira, even now, and I will find it. Maybe that will quiet Avram's ghost.

Lurbira paused and shrugged. "That's Serlay's story."

"That's it?" Siphany frowned. "That's weird."

"Yeah. I don't buy it either. She was sure it was true though."

"How…odd."

"Serlay was like that. She was all cold and practical, and then every once in a while, she'd bust out some bizarre story with ghosts and magic and giant talking whales. They were all like that, all the people from Earth. They all had these superstitions and visions and strange stories to tell. Avorna used to talk about visiting other people's dreams. The engineer, Viernan, had a little shrine set up in her cabin to the spirits of the hyperspace drive. Even Brasna thought the ship was literally alive, and he'd talk to it. They were a good crew, they understood everything about their ship; they were just…weird."

"Do you miss them?" Siphany asked.

Lurbira nodded slightly. "Every day."

Chapter Eight

THEY SAT IN the caves for the better part of the next day, waiting. The promised food never showed up, and Siphany was getting so hungry that she felt faint and grouchy. Isan sat alone, watching and saying nothing. Qas was still trying, without much luck, to make friends.

Siphany finally gave up on sitting, with hunger clawing at her gut and failing to sleep. She found Lurbira with a group of Artificials, discussing something Siphany couldn't have cared less about right then.

"I'm starving," Siphany announced. "We've been here for hours, and none of us have eaten."

"We didn't invite you here," growled one of the other Artificials. "We didn't set this place up for humans."

Lurbira rolled her eyes. "Go find Harban. He said he was going to do the food thing."

"Fine," said Siphany. "But what are we going to do after that? We can't stay here."

"We have to wait and see. I'm sure there's a plan."

"There is," said the other Artificial. "We seal ourselves off in here until it's safe. It doesn't involve humans."

"You're going to seal yourselves in here?" Lurbira asked, agog. "You're kidding. Why didn't you tell me that?"

"We assumed you knew," said another Artificial. "That's always been the plan."

"This is what you get for not being around, Lurbira," said the first.

"We can't stay in here." The frenzy of panic started up again in Siphany. "We can't. We *can't.*"

"Harban," shouted Lurbira. "Where are you? We need your help. Now!"

*

HARBAN WAS ABLE to scrounge up some water, but not food. He apologized for not being able to secure anything. "The cave's sealed for now, and I've been discussing strategy with the others. They still want to wait it out in here."

"Seems safest for them," said Qas.

"It's not safe. It's idiotic," said Lurbira. "What if someone finds out where they are? Then they can send a few hundred missiles down into the caves and *boom*, no more Artificials on Haeld. Problem solved."

"I wasn't aware that we were a problem," said Harban.

"Sure. I bet Loyan sees it that way too. They love us on Loyan."

"Loyan doesn't care about us at all. We're an afterthought. They're not coming after us." But Harban didn't sound convinced.

"Right. Look. It's better to split up and keep moving than to just sit here being quiet, waiting for them to find you and kill you."

"Lurbira," sighed Harban, frustrated. "You aren't in charge."

Lurbira bristled, but Qas cut her off.

"Well, we humans can't stay here. We have to go somewhere else."

"Like where?" asked Isan morosely.

"Everywhere, for you, Isan," said Lurbira. "I bet you can go up to any soldier and say, 'Hi! I'm a friend of Loyan.' Just ask the people living on board an unregistered secret station about fifty or so light years from here, and then see what happens."

"Lurbira, leave her alone," said Siphany. Lurbira rolled her eyes, but she complied.

"Plus, that leaves Siphany and me out," said Qas.

"Weren't you prepared for this?" Siphany asked, honestly curious. "You must have known an invasion was coming."

"Not so soon. In case of problems, we were supposed to gather at specific points to 'organize resistance.' As if any of us knew how to do that. I collect intelligence, that's all."

"Where's your gather point? Maybe you could get there."

They grimaced. "It just burned to the ground."

"Oh. Did they have a backup?"

"Not for my station," said Qas gloomily. "Any further planning was considered to be defeatist."

"Ah," said Siphany, nodding knowingly.

"Sovenes are morons," Lurbira offered helpfully.

They ignored her.

"My ship is still in orbit," said Siphany. "But the Junk ship is still at the spaceport. We can use it to get up there. Then we can get away."

"I don't know how we'd get you to it," said Harban. "Not from here, anyway. They almost certainly have the craft you used to get here under heavy guard, if they didn't destroy it."

Lurbira groaned.

"We can probably make the gather point in Hyutakerut, but it'll take us at least a couple of days to get there," said Qas after a moment. "There's no guarantee we'll survive the trip either. But what choice do we have?" They shook their head. "Every other option is back there in town."

"We can find food for you," said Harban. "There are some locations in town where residents cached things. And I can show you some of the more secret ways out of the valley."

"That would be excellent," Qas said, brisk and businesslike. "You've been a help to us. I can't thank you enough."

"And you?" Harban asked Isan. "What will you do next?"

"I don't know." Isan looked more melancholy than usual. "I have nothing to do."

"So it's up to you, then. You can make any choice you want."

"How? I'm not sei."

"Who says?"

"Lurbira. Mother Junk said it too."

Harban shook his head. "Not the best of sources. Let me ask you this— Do you think you're sei?"

"How would I know?"

"Well. Sei isn't just one thing. It's…almost like a philosophy. It's about being self-aware enough to have a will of your own, about being able to see beyond your own programming or instincts. A cat can be sei, but a clock probably isn't. Synthetics…well. There's a lot of debate about that. There aren't many left we can ask. They weren't meant to have any will. They were supposed to just follow orders." He laughed. "But then again, so were we!"

"So…were you ever not sei?"

"At the very beginning, I was only the program," Harban said. "Lurbira was, too, though she won't ever admit it. It's like when a human is born. All they are is instinct and need. But over time, they develop that self-awareness, that *will*. A wise Artificial once said to me that sei starts when we first say 'no.' Human children go through a phase where that's all they ever say."

"My littlest sister was like that," Siphany murmured. "She wouldn't stop."

"Right," said Harban. "You see, though, that was where she drew a line between what everyone else wanted and what she wanted. She was self-aware enough to say so. The program was altered; the instinct changed."

"I don't know if I buy that," said Siphany. "How do you even define instinct? Is it just a kind of blind need? I'm not sure it's really analogous to a program that an Artificial starts with. And babies come out of the womb not wanting to do stuff. Have you ever tried to feed one? It's awful."

Harban smiled. "The metaphor isn't perfect. We don't talk about humans being sei; we just assume all of you are."

"Not all of us," grumbled Siphany.

"But Isan, for us, that saying of 'no' is a big step," Harban said. "You come to a line in your program and you can say, no, I don't want to do what's written there. For me, it came when someone told me to pick up a gun. Everything in my program was about being a soldier. I was made to fight. But I said 'no.' And that's when I became sei."

"I…I don't think I can do that." Isan ran her fingers over one of the implants on her neck. "But…how do you know if it's your program making you say 'no,' or it's your own will? How would I ever know if I was really sei?"

"Does it matter? Sei, in the end, is just a label. What matters is what's inside your own heart."

"I'd have rights if I were sei," said Isan suddenly. "I wouldn't have to go back to the Junk."

"Isan?" asked Siphany softly. "Do you want to go back to the Junk?"

"I have to go back. Mother Junk needs me."

"But do you *want* to?"

"I have to," Isan repeated. Lurbira snickered.

Harban thought for a while. "There are tests you can pass to determine if you're sei. They haven't been used in a while, but they exist. I can train you to pass them. But going back to the Junk is up to you, not up to some test."

"This is stupid," Lurbira spat. "None of you see it. You think she's like us because she looks like us and has some metal parts, but she's not. People on Pelagar knew how to mimic life, not how to create it. And now they're all dead anyway, so it doesn't matter. You're the last living Pelagarine, Isan, and, shit, you're not even alive."

"Pelagar…?"

"Your implants are from Pelagar, worm food. You didn't know?"

Isan acted as if she hadn't heard. "Pelagar," she repeated.

Harban only shook his beautiful, chrome-plated head and turned to hike up toward the exit.

"Nice guy," Qas said as they followed.

"I like him too," Isan said.

"Shut up," Lurbira told them both and smiled.

*

HARBAN LED THEM through the caves to the exit. The stones were in place, and the two guards there warned them against going outside.

"We can hear that there are still flights overhead," one said. "Dangerous."

"We'll stay safe," Harban assured them.

"You're going with them?" the guard asked, shocked.

"For now. I'll be back." Harban touched both guards lightly on the arm. Siphany had noticed that the Artificials touched one another often.

"I'm going with them too," said Lurbira. "Staying here is stupid."

They didn't reply to her, except with severe looks and slight head-shakes. Lurbira, Siphany noted, didn't touch anyone, except Siphany.

That made her feel oddly better.

"All right," said Harban. "Let's go."

*

SCRAGGLY, BUSHY PLANTS and tall, thin trees with corded trunks filled the low scrubland forest perched precariously on the hillside. Siphany stumbled over rocks and roots, stomach aching with emptiness, struggling to see as the sun set.

They arrived back at the entrance to the tunnel that led to the sewer system.

"Siphany, Qas, and Isan, you three stay here," Harban ordered. "Lurbira, come with me. We'll get food as quick as we can and come back."

"Why didn't we wait back at the caves?" Siphany felt *exposed* out here.

"Less coming and going there helps protect them."

Siphany had the distinct sense, though Harban didn't say it, that he wanted them out of the caves as quickly as possible. "I see," she said.

"Stay safe." For once, Lurbira looked serious. Maybe giving her something useful to do was helping.

"We will," Siphany assured her.

"Right, we'll be back," Harban said, and he and Lurbira sprinted off into the tunnel.

*

"WE SHOULD MOVE back from the entrance, just in case," Qas suggested after about an hour of stilted silence.

"It doesn't matter to me," Isan said.

Qas looked at her, and Siphany sighed.

"Whatever you want, Qas," she said.

Qas led Siphany and Isan over to a secluded clearing covered in something that looked like bright orange moss. It released little clouds of particles when they sat on it. Qas assured them it was harmless, and they relaxed.

"This is nice," Qas remarked after a while.

"I don't like planets," mumbled Isan. "Space is better."

"I'm with you," said Siphany.

Qas shook their head. "Space is good for a while, but to be really complete, people need a connection to the land. This is what it's all about." They patted the moss, releasing another orange cloud. They coughed. "If there were water nearby, it would be even better."

"Like a river or lake?" Isan actually shivered. "I don't think I'd like that."

"What about you, Sif?" Qas asked. "You used to say you missed seeing the sky."

"That was a long time ago," Siphany said after a moment's consideration. "But these days, I prefer space. It's so much bigger. Sovena was very pretty, but I could never really relax there. I always felt hemmed in. It's so crowded."

"Only in the cities," said Qas. "In the former Dome spaces, for sure. But where I live now is much more open. It's some of the land they opened up after the terraforming was done. You should come see it sometime. I think you'd really like it there. No one else as far as you can see."

"I'd rather not go back to Sovena," said Siphany with a humorless smile. "If it's all the same to you."

"I'd like to go back to the Junk," said Isan, a hint of bitterness in her voice. "But someone stole me away from it."

"Nobody asked you to help your people hold me against my will," snapped Siphany.

"You were a spy. You deserved to be caught."

"Tough talk from someone who was running an intelligence post from a *Junk*," sneered Qas.

"I wasn't running it; I *lived there*. You're running an intelligence post on a world rightfully claimed by Loyan."

"That's total bull."

They continued to bicker. Siphany said nothing, sinking into her own thoughts.

She knew that everything that had happened to her over the past weeks had been the direct result of her own rotten decision to target and shoot what she'd thought was a drone. Ever since then, she'd felt helpless, caught in the swift current of Junks, Artificials, and interplanetary politics. She'd lost her job, surely, by now. She was so deeply involved here that she couldn't fathom going back.

Her old life had slipped away, and it was her own fault.

But she couldn't just sit here and let it happen to her. She had to find a way to make it right again.

Qas and Isan's argument had degenerated into lobbing Sovene and Loyan talking points back and forth at each other.

"Sovena never learned anything from the Pelagarine War," said Isan. "You meddle and meddle and meddle."

"Yeah?" Qas shot back. "Look who's invading a neutral world. Is *this* that Greater Human Future the Loyans are always yelling about? This is nothing but a greedy plot from your *masters* on Loyan."

"Enough," said Siphany with quiet venom, potent enough to stop them both dead in their tracks. "Be *quiet.*"

They looked at her, shocked. She faltered, suddenly self-conscious now that she was the center of attention.

"We, ah," she said, scrambling for purchase. "We can't keep doing this. We can't fight one another."

"Sorry," said Qas, abashed. "I'm just…this has been hard."

"But they were wrong," protested Isan.

"You're both wrong, and you're both giving me a headache. So shut up."

"You're right," said Qas after a long moment. "We have to work together if we want to get to the next gather point."

"No," said Siphany firmly, voice barely a whisper.

"What?" Qas's brows furrowed.

"I said *no*. I'm not going to a Sovene gather point. I'm going to try to get back to my ship."

Qas goggled at her. "How?"

"I…I was going to ask Lurbira to help me." Siphany's stomach turned a little at the thought of what that would mean. "I think she'll come with me if I ask."

"Why would she? Sif, she's a mercenary. You've talked to her. She's not loyal to anyone."

"Maybe nobody's ever been loyal to her." Siphany couldn't believe the words coming out of her mouth.

"Who *would* be?" Isan said sourly. "She was so cruel and thoughtless back on the Junk. Nobody liked her."

"*I* like her," said Siphany.

"You should be careful," Isan said. "Don't ever turn your back on Lurbira Call."

"What's this about me?" Lurbira said, trudging out of the woods. "There you guys are. Thought we'd lost you."

"That was fast," said Siphany.

"We brought food," said Harban, holding out a disappointingly small sack.

"Finally," Qas said enthusiastically, grabbing it and rifling through.

Siphany hung back.

"What's wrong?" asked Lurbira.

"I wanted to ask you something," said Siphany.

"Yeah?" Lurbira watched Qas paw through the food sack. Isan also stared, a grossed-out expression on her face. The sack was seeping some kind of orange fluid.

"You said you're up for anything, right?"

"Yeah. I can do whatever. So what's going on?"

"I want to try for my ship. Will you help me? There'll be guards."

"You wanna *fight* them?"

"If—if I have to," said Siphany, balling her fists. "The only thing that really matters to me in the galaxy is my ship. I have to get it back. I don't want the Loyans or anyone else to have it."

"Got it." Lurbira nodded sharply. "I have your back. Will they be coming?" She gestured at Qas and Isan.

"If they want to. But I thought you and I…we could go together. I…I'd be willing to offer you a permanent place on my ship if we can get out of here. We can earn money together. Does that sound like a deal?"

Lurbira blinked. Did she even need to blink? "Why would you offer that?" she asked at last.

"Maybe this way, you can earn what you need," Siphany explained. "To get yourself fixed. And I don't want anything to do with Sovenes or Loyans or any of them. I want my ship and my freedom back. You can help me get it. I don't know if it's a fair trade, but it's what I have to offer."

Lurbira's face went slack. "Shit. Nobody's ever offered me a deal *that* good before. You sure you want me? They're right. I'm trouble."

"You saved me." Siphany took a deep breath. "And you're my friend."

Lurbira considered. "Okay," she said at last, something strangely like hope on her face. "Okay," she repeated, more firmly. "I'll do it. This'll be fun. Hey, Harban!" She toddled over to him, joints clearly stiff and in need of repair again.

They spoke in low tones as Siphany finally caught Qas's attention, took some stale bread and a bubble of water out of the bag, and forced it down. Her senses started to sharpen again, and the hunger dissipated, sated, for a blessed moment.

Lurbira rejoined her. "Harban'll help us. He's not coming with us; he won't abandon the other Artificials, but he'll help us get to the ship and deal with the guards."

"Are you going with her?" Qas asked.

"Yep," said Lurbira.

"Come, if you want," said Siphany. "But I'm in charge. No complaining."

"I'm in," said Qas immediately. "I can't think of a better way off this planet."

"Isan?" Siphany asked.

The Synthetic girl had her arms wrapped around her torso, and she looked utterly lost. "I want to go home."

"We can take you to Derstan Station. Maybe from there you can get back to the Junk," Siphany said.

"What are you doing?" hissed Lurbira. "You really want her along?"

"It's not her fault she's the way she is. She deserves a chance, too, doesn't she?"

Lurbira threw up her arms in despair.

Isan shook her head. "I…I don't know. If I stay here, the Loyans could help me."

"Do you want that?"

She slowly shook her head. "I don't know. I don't know what I want."

"That's the beginning of something," said Harban, who was listening in. "Follow it, Isan."

"Okay. I'll come with you until I figure things out."

Lurbira groaned.

"Good," said Siphany. And, for a wonder, she actually did feel good about it. Was Isan actually growing on her?

"What will we do with the guards at the airfield?" Qas asked.

"Same thing we always do," said Lurbira, opening and closing her knuckle gunports with ominous little clicks. "Fuck 'em up."

*

"COME ON!" HISSED Lurbira. Siphany couldn't see a thing in all this gloom. She could barely make out Isan's slight form directly in front of her. Qas's hand was cold in her own; she squeezed once, to make sure they were still there. Qas squeezed back.

A little shiver of *want* traveled from her hand to her heart. She squashed it, hating herself a little.

They'd been lucky—nobody had stopped them or even seen them during the dash from the sewer entrance to the crumbling spaceport. The soldiers were clearly concentrating on the town, not the outskirts. Now that the war was all but done, they were getting confident.

Siphany brought up the rear, struggling not to be left behind as their little group sprinted over the uneven ground. Her lungs burned, her legs felt like blocks of wood, and she was starting to see sparks. Mercifully, Lurbira called a halt.

"Okay, you three wait here," she said. "Harban?"

Harban didn't say anything but moved off toward a single light source: the flat tarmac of the spaceport.

"We'll be back," said Lurbira.

"Be careful," said Siphany, gasping for air. Lurbira still looked stiff.

Lurbira flashed a cocky grin, dimly visible in the reflected light from the far-off spaceport. "You know me," she said before turning to follow Harban and bursting into a surprisingly silent run.

They waited. Siphany hardly dared to breathe. The night suddenly felt very large and scary, and the three of them very small.

Then there were four short, sickeningly green flashes.

They waited for the signal. It was supposed to be three short shots, followed by another two shots. Instead, they heard Lurbira calling out, "Okay! It's clear. Get your asses over here."

Siphany could distinctly hear Harban yelling something and Lurbira's sarcastic reply.

"Let's go," Siphany said, letting annoyance with Lurbira cover her nauseous horror.

*

THEIR LITTLE SHIP had been thoroughly looted but was otherwise in as good a shape as when it landed. It would fly. The four bodies now crumpled on the tarmac, each covered in seeping plasma burns, had been using it to store their valuables, such as cans of beer, extra weapons, and a single box of keepsakes.

Siphany picked up the box, emotions and stomach churning, and opened the lid. But before she could see what was inside, Lurbira snatched it out of her hands and tossed it into the woods.

"No," she said somberly. "Better this way. You don't want to know who they were."

Siphany nodded shakily. Against her better judgement, she glanced at the pools of dark stain steadily creeping across the tarmac.

"It was me," said Lurbira dully. "I shot all four. Harban's innocent. So are you. It's all me, always me."

"Are you okay?"

Lurbira shrugged. There was blood on her leg and face. She looked haunted. "I'm always okay. You ready?"

"I'm ready."

Siphany slid into the pilot's seat and began running through the pre-flight checks as fast as her conscience would let her go. Lurbira, Qas, and Isan crowded in behind. The fit was tight, but they could all just make it.

"You don't have a lot of time," Harban said from the door. "I'm picking up four more of them about half a kilometer away. They're heading this way. Fast." He ducked out and disappeared back into the darkness.

"Fuck the checks; get us into the sky," ordered Lurbira.

"Hang on a moment," Siphany said, fingers flying across the console.

"Sif! Go!"

"Finished!" Siphany, hands shaking as she fired up the engines. Lurbira hung out the door, peering into the night. She fired off a few shots as they lifted off. Did she hit anything? Was she even aiming at anyone? Siphany couldn't tell.

Lurbira slid back inside and pulled the door shut as they gained altitude.

Siphany nosed the ship higher, aiming for the stars that called her home. She ran through an instrument check, ignoring a warning light or four.

"Nothing from traffic control," she said. "Are they offline? Would that even happen during a war?"

"Free-for-all, then," said Qas. "Be careful."

"Obviously." Siphany grunted. "It's not like I was going to be sloppy!"

Mercifully, they made it out of the atmosphere without any problems. *Lucky. Too lucky? Am I being paranoid again?*

Aloud, Siphany said, "I hope Kit's okay." She tried not to let her nervousness show. "I left plenty of food out."

"I'm sure he's fine," said Lurbira.

"Who's Kit?" asked Qas.

"My cat. He's good company."

"Oh," Qas said, surprised. "I didn't even know you liked cats."

"You never asked."

"Sif…I'm really sorry. I know I've been a jerk. I…I'm glad you have a cat for a friend."

Siphany had no idea what to say to that. Qas seemed to change direction a lot these days.

Then she leaned forward as her ship came into view. Everything seemed to be in one piece. Her heart leapt. It was all still there. She could go home again.

She maneuvered the ship into the still-open cargo bay, where it settled with a *clunk*. Siphany sighed in relief and made for the door as the cargo hatch closed.

"There's lights on in here," Lurbira remarked as they freed themselves from the cramped confines of the little ship. "Did we leave the lights on?"

Siphany was about to say that she didn't think so when two figures popped up from behind some barrels. The tall one fired a lethal blast of plasma.

Lurbira dropped, twitching and smoking.

"Hands in the air!" screamed a man in Loyan colors.

Mother Junk aimed a vicious-looking rifle directly at Siphany's head. "You're our prisoners now. All of you."

Chapter Nine

SIPHANY SAT IN a locked storage room, absently petting a purring, thrilled Kit. The captors had been good enough to decant the furious, struggling cat into her room. Mother Junk had ordered: "You deal with this thing," and left.

And that was all she'd seen of either Mother Junk or anyone else. She hadn't seen Isan, or Qas, or Lurbira.

She didn't even know if Lurbira was alive. Siphany kept thinking of plasma fire and Lurbira crumpling to the floor.

It was horribly, gut-wrenchingly frustrating. Siphany had done what she could to take charge of her life again, just to end up Mother Junk's prisoner for the second time in as many weeks. She'd spent a lot of time yelling at nobody and then even more time crying hysterically.

But now she was perfectly calm. The light was still too bright and the heat too low, but she was still here. She was on her ship. Maybe there was something she could do…

They were underway; Siphany could tell their speed from the vibrations in the deck plates. She had no clue as to their trajectory; she was only certain they were heading somewhere away from the war on Haeld. Siphany had a few guesses about where they might be going, none of them pleasant.

The terminal in this room had been disconnected, probably by herself or Lurbira. They'd kept Isan in here, after all. It was almost funny, the way it had all turned out.

Isan. She'd started babbling with joy when she saw Mother Junk, trying to tell her all about how she'd been kidnapped and stayed loyal, but Mother Junk shot her a withering look, and Isan had fallen silent.

Siphany decided she didn't care. Why should she care about Isan?

Isan…who had seemed so close to saying *no*. Isan, who was both devoted to Mother Junk and afraid of her. Isan, who had come so far with them down on Haeld.

And yet, Isan had helped Mother Junk and the Loyan soldier drag Lurbira out of the bay like scrap. They'd taken Qas away, thrown Siphany into a little room, and made her a prisoner on her own ship.

She kept running through her options, and she kept coming up empty.

There was nothing to do but wait and see what came next.

*

AT LAST, THE door slid open, and Mother Junk, armed this time with a plasma rifle, entered the tiny room.

"Here we are again," said Mother Junk, her mouth stretched into a grim line, a ghastly imitation of a smile. She loomed over Siphany. "Do you mind if I sit? I have terrible back pain half the time."

"I don't care what you do," said Siphany, trying to sound menacing.

Mother Junk actually looked pleased as she sat. "Ah. You have very uncomfortable furniture, I hope you know."

"Made just for you."

Mother Junk shot her a look. Siphany stared back placidly, implacably. Mother Junk actually looked away.

"So. The war below is going well for our side," she said. "The government of Haeld surrendered yesterday to the rebels and to the rebels' Loyan allies. Sovena and forces loyal to the government are yelling about it, but we're in charge now. We're entrenched."

"Good for you." Siphany's voice dripped with acid.

"It isn't really my fight. But I like to see the side we've chosen win. It makes life on the Junk easier. If Loyan protection and patronage disappeared, we'd be gone. It's unpleasant, but true. Tell me, Siphany, do you actually know what this war is all about?"

"Haeld." Siphany was surprised by the sudden change of subject. Mother Junk seemed tired and jumpy today. "Control of Haeld."

"Yes, Haeld. Of course. But what *about* Haeld?"

Siphany rolled her eyes. "Because Loyan didn't like having a major Sovene military presence so close, of course, but it's more than that. Haeld is strategic; it's an easy dozen shifts from here to either Loyan or Sovena and many, many other worlds. Ianas, Saralar, the Stationbund—all of them are within reach of Haeld. Pelagar knew that, too, when they invaded Haeld back during the Pelagarine War. So this isn't just about control of one planet, but dozens."

"Ah," said Mother Junk. "Good."

"But it's stupid. Why would Loyan risk starting a real shooting war with Sovena?"

"Because both Loyan and Sovena are run by paranoids who think they're about to be attacked at any moment. And also by greedy men who want to own and run everything. That's what the Pelagarine War taught them—always watch your back, always grab what you can while you have the time. The Loyans couch it in pretty words about a grand future for humanity, but it's really all about being safe. So is this war that we're in now. Loyan wants to be safe."

Mother Junk looked at the plasma rifle in her hands. "I was a little girl when the Pelagarine War ended. My father fought in it. I was molded by that war and so was the rest of my generation. I ran to the Junk with my father, yet those habits are blazed into my mind.

"That's why this is happening now; I'm sure of it. Because we can't get beyond that paranoia. Very soon, it will flare up into something much larger and much worse than just a civil war on Haeld. Loyan and Sovene ships will be here to fight. And then others will join them. The entirety of the Mid-Perseus Arm could go up in flames, all because of the kinds of things I've worked against my entire life."

She fixed Siphany with a cold stare. "I'm here now because I need to be. It's the only way to keep my people safe and to preserve our way of life."

"So how are you different from the Loyans, then?"

"I know I am in my heart. My cause is just."

"Why are you bothering telling me? I don't care what you do or why."

"No. But I wanted a chance to explain it." Mother Junk fixed her with another cold look. "And for you to know what you've really gotten yourself into, if you are what you say you are. Not that it matters. We're going to Loyan. I'm ordered to turn you over to them."

Loyan. "What will happen to me there?"

"I don't know."

"I'm a citizen—"

"Of Derstan Station. I know. But that doesn't matter anymore. Derstan and the rest of the Stationbund don't dare try to interfere. They're too small, too easily destroyed."

Siphany swallowed hard. "What about Qas?"

"They worked for Sovena. They will be a prisoner of war, if they're lucky. I don't think they'll be so lucky though. Loyan is very cruel."

Siphany tried hard not to think about what that meant. "Lurbira?"

"They have an interest in her. I could have protected her, if she'd only stayed with us. But she made her choice."

"So she's alive!"

Mother Junk shrugged. "For now. I doubt she will be for long. The Loyans are rarely kind to Artificials, and she is very badly damaged."

"And what about you?" Siphany tried to fight the fear spreading in her belly. Her mind raced. She wanted to keep Mother Junk talking. Maybe there was some opening she could exploit here. "What…what about Isan? What will you do now?"

"We'll go home, if we can. Our loyalty won't be in question anymore. Isan will come with me if she can prove she really did stay loyal to the Junk. If not…" Mother Junk shrugged. "The Loyans are very interested in her as well."

"You're ruthless."

"I've had to be. You would be, in my position."

"No," said Siphany quietly. "I doubt it."

Mother Junk shook her head. "Yes, you would. I just wanted to come to tell you where you were going." She stood creakily. "We won't reactivate Lurbira until we get to Loyan. I may allow you and the other human a moment to say goodbye, if you want, before you're separated. They won't let you see each other again, the Loyans. They're even more ruthless than I am. We should be there within two weeks. Shorter, if we can get to a Loyan military station."

Siphany nodded, ice creeping into her veins. "I see."

Mother Junk gave her a long look, eyes heavy and sad. She looked very old. "I'll be on my way," she said at last, and made to leave the room.

"Mother Junk," called Siphany. "Wait."

The old woman paused.

"You can't possibly want this war," Siphany pressed, desperate. "You called your Junk '*Peace Station*,' remember? But the Loyans, they're ruthless. Like you said. You don't think they'll keep using you once the war really starts? They'll find a way to make you into a military base. And then your way of life really will be over."

Mother Junk's mouth formed a thin line. "My father named the station," she said after a long moment. "Everyone called him Grandfather Peace. He was a good man. He was the one who led us out into the void. He made the arrangement, too, once the Loyans found us. I…I'm just carrying on his legacy."

"You don't have to. Let us go. You could find a better legacy."

Mother Junk paused, but then she shook her head sadly. "There is no better way. Not anymore. Not for us. We made our choice a long time ago."

"There's always a way out," said Siphany desperately.

"Is there? Maybe you think there is. But some roads have no turns. Good evening, Siphany. I doubt we'll speak again."

With that, she left Siphany alone.

*

SIPHANY SAT IN her room, worn out from worry, despair, and panic.

They had left her with nothing to do, so all she could do was turn the possibilities over in her mind. The Loyans definitely wouldn't be kind. They might really think she was a Sovene spy and interrogate her. They'd keep her prisoner forever, especially if Derstan never even found out about it—or, worse, believed them and disavowed her.

Her terminal was dead, and she had no games, no music, nothing to distract her from the panic. She banged on the door a couple of times, but mostly, she just sat on the cot, anxiety driving her into fits. That cold sanity from before slipped further and further away.

Kit was a good companion, and she spoke to him, cried into his fur, and pretended that the cat could somehow guide her out of all of this. Maybe the Loyans would be kinder to him and find him a family, and maybe he'd forget all about her someday.

She wondered if anyone else in the universe would even miss her.

*

SIPHANY LOST ALL sense of time, much to her distress. She couldn't tell what it was time for, what she should be doing, where in her own stripped-down and personalized version of the Form she was right now. She should be doing checks, walking on the carpeted floors, playing her flute…but she couldn't do any of it. She couldn't even try.

Mother Junk never returned. Isan brought her meals and said nothing as she left the plate on the floor.

Siphany didn't try to talk to her. What was there left to say? Isan had obviously made her choice.

*

SIPHANY TINKERED WITH the terminal in the room. She wasn't sure if they were watching her, though no one came to bother her about it. She opened up the panel and moved one component from the room's light source to the terminal with shaking fingers.

The terminal sputtered, then flickered on.

Success. Siphany raced her fingers across the screen, looking for something—anything—she could do.

Everything had been cut off, routed only to the cockpit. Of course. No wonder they didn't care what she did down here.

Ship functions—blocked. Navigation, engines, electrical systems, all blocked. She couldn't get out.

Could she send a signal? Direct communications and distress signals were blocked.

"Shit."

She paused, thinking. Then she began to try different things at random. Lurbira's power hookup in the cockpit? No. Lights? No. Environmental systems? No.

Something low power, then. Something that wouldn't even make a difference. Something they'd never think of.

Hydras…

Siphany tapped in the manual access codes she'd made a point of memorizing and held her breath.

After a long pause, the screen turned green and the message—

Welcome to Hydras, Leshandre Siphany

—flashed across her screen.

Yes. The connection to just that little tiny piece of the net was *there.*

Siphany stuffed a fist in her mouth to keep from crying. She was in! Messages trickled in to her screen. She could *talk* to people. For the first time in her life, Siphany desperately wanted to reach out.

But what could she say?

Her time was probably limited. Someone would know as soon as she sent something; she had access to logs in the cockpit of all the transmissions on or off the ship.

Whatever she did, it would have to be fast and it would have to be good. She marshaled all her remaining concentration and will and dove into the virtual world.

Siphany navigated through the virtual streets to where the interstellar pilots' gathering place. No one else was there. She cursed, then left a message where she hoped others would find it:

Hi, it's L. Siphany. I'm in trouble. I need your help!

A few weeks ago, I shot up a ship I thought was a drone (wouldn't you?), but it turned out to be an unmanned ship from a Junk. I found out the whole thing was working for Loyan, deep in Haeld space. I escaped to Haeld itself, but I got caught up in the civil war. Got back up to my ship, only to find some pissed-off people waiting to catch me. We're headed for Loyan now. They think I'm a Sovene spy! I'm with an Artificial who is going to be treated badly by them. I'm a prisoner on my own ship.

This is very real. I'm scared to death and out of options. I got lucky; someone turned on the terminal in my cell, which is a storage room, but the only thing I can do is post here.

Pati from Pilots' Lounge can help you find me.

She hit send.

Two heartbeats later, the terminal shut itself off. She couldn't know if anyone had seen.

Siphany collapsed to the floor, shivering with something like relief and terror. It might not work. The message might not even go through. Communications in deep interstellar space could be spotty, and with a war on...

But she'd done what she could, and now she had a very thin thread of hope to cling to. It would have to be enough.

*

A DAY, MAYBE two, passed. Then the door opened while Siphany was trying to sleep. A furious Mother Junk burst in, plasma rifle aimed at Siphany's forehead.

"Get up! You're coming to the cockpit. We need you to unlock the weapons *now*."

"What's going on?" Siphany's heart pounded. Was this it?

"I checked the logs. I don't know *how* you did it, but you sent a message! And now *something* is coming after us."

"What is?"

"We don't know. So, go! Now!" She gestured with the plasma rifle.

"Or I blow your head off."

Siphany went, shivering with nervous excitement.

*

THE LOYAN SOLDIER was there already, sweating heavily. "It's gaining," he said. "We're not going to make the shift point."

"Faster, faster," said Mother Junk. "Push it. Where is Isan?"

"Engines," said the soldier, his voice shaking.

"Tell her to give us more power. You." She glared at Siphany. "I need to know if the engines can go any faster."

Siphany glanced at a few readings. "No," she lied.

"How do I know you're telling the truth?"

"You could try shooting me." Siphany felt oddly calm. She had so little left to lose now.

"I have a better reading on it now," said the Loyan. "It's tiny. But incredibly fast."

Mother Junk peered at it. "Never seen that kind of ship. Might be some kind of commerce raider. Can you blow it out of the sky?" She prodded Siphany with the business end of her rifle. "Unlock the weapons."

"And if I don't?"

"I actually will kill you. What do I have to lose?" Mother Junk pointed the plasma rifle at Siphany's head and let her listen to the whine of power as she turned it up to full blast.

Siphany took a deep breath. A commerce raider? It was possible.

But maybe her message had gotten through, somehow.

She had to stay alive and hope the other ship could take on her magnificent weapons. For the first time, Siphany cursed herself for springing for the deluxe models.

"Fine." Siphany pressed a finger against the biometric scan in the console. Then she tapped in a command as slowly as she dared. "Copilot station unlocked," she said at last.

The soldier looked at it, a helpless expression on his face. "This is all messed up. I don't understand how this console is laid out."

"I set it to the way I like it," said Siphany, annoyed. "Lurbira had no problem with it."

"I'm not Lurbira," he snapped.

At that moment, the other ship entered range. Mother Junk only had time to open her mouth before a barrage of electrical pulses slammed into the backside of the ship.

*

EVERYTHING WAS CONFUSION and shouting. Emergency lights had flickered on, and Siphany tasted blood in her mouth. She was alone in the cockpit. All of her panels were dark; clearly, whoever was shooting at them had hit the power plant right in the business.

She heard cursing and panic from the hallway. Was that Mother Junk? The Loyan soldier? She peered around the bulkhead into the dark corridor. Yes. There they were, crouched, holding plasma rifles, flanking the entrance.

The door opened, and there was a soft *tink* as a small metal object bounced off the wall.

Siphany instinctively retreated behind the bulkhead just before a painfully bright flash of light, accompanied by a smell of ozone and a fierce buzzing sound, made her head swim. When Siphany dared look back, both the soldier and Mother Junk lay on the floor, unconscious.

Stun grenade, Siphany's still-woozy brain helpfully filled in.

Someone in a heavy-duty suit clomped around the corner and spotted her.

Siphany stood up, knees wobbly.

"Siphany?" a distorted voice said. "Is that you?"

She nodded shakily.

The figure took its helmet off, revealing a short-haired woman with skin a shade lighter than Siphany's and a thin face with a wry smile plastered on it. A shockingly brilliant pattern of colors and shapes ran down one side of her face and neck, vanishing into her suit.

"Hey! It's me, Pati from Hydras. I got your message, Sif, are you okay?"

It took Siphany a second.

Then she squealed with joy and relief. "Pati? Really? Is it really you?"

"It really is," Pati said, her smile broadening into a cocky grin. "Hey, Sif." She glanced around, all business again. "How many more of them are there?"

"One more in the engine room. Mother Junk's granddaughter."

Pati frowned. "Shit. A kid?"

"She's a Synthetic. I'll explain it later. Come on!"

"Lead the way," said Pati brightly, hoisting her weapon.

"I promise to fill you in soon. You, uh, look different from your last pictures."

"Tryin' out a new face."

Siphany thought she caught the telltale shimmer of bluenet's aftermath on Pati's exposed skin.

"Like it?" Pati asked.

"Definitely," breathed Siphany. "You look. Wow."

"Thanks. I also work out." She actually flexed.

"Where did you get that *suit*?" Siphany tried to work it through. Nothing was adding up right. "And that ship? That's not a freighter."

"Can't get anything past you, can I?" Pati said, still grinning. "I kinda lied on Hydras. I'm Derstan Defense Force, Special Intelligence Division. That's why I have this great suit and ship."

"You're…Oh!" That made sense. "And you came all this way for *me*?"

"Well, I was in the area. Kind of." Pati gave Siphany a serious look. "And you're one of us. You're a Derstan citizen. We take care of our own."

Siphany burst into tears. She hadn't been forgotten after all. Derstan Station had come for her.

"Hey," said Pati, obviously a little uncomfortable. "Ah. Want to help me round everyone else up? Then you and I ought to talk about what's going on here."

Siphany wiped away the grateful tears and stood straight. Time to get to work. "Yes," she said. "Good."

*

IT TOOK NO time at all. They went down to the engine room and demanded that Isan surrender. She meekly complied almost at once.

Pati's eyes bugged when she saw her.

"A long story," Siphany said. "I promise I'll fill you in."

"Please do," Pati murmured, unable to take her eyes off the Synthetic. Isan looked even more morose than usual, but she gave Siphany a small smile when they made eye contact. Siphany wasn't sure what to make of that.

They herded Isan into an empty cabin and dragged Mother Junk and the Loyan soldier into two others.

"This ship is great for holding people," Pati remarked. "Lots of room."

"It wasn't always like this. I used to have more actual stores."

"Any other passengers?"

"Qas is here somewhere—they wouldn't say where. And oh! Lurbira. She's an Artificial. She was hurt pretty bad, and they shut her down. We have to revive her."

"Where is she?"

"No idea."

Pati gestured, activating a few commands on her suit. "I'll patch in my ship's power supply with yours. Should happen automatically—ah." The main lights came back up. "Good. That ought to help us find them. So they let you out, or what?"

"They needed my biometric scan for the weapons." Siphany squinted in the harsh light.

"Whoops. You like it darker. I remember that. Apologies. Hang on." Pati gestured again; the lights dimmed.

"Thank you," said Siphany, grateful. Pati hadn't even made fun of her or demanded an explanation.

"So they made you go with them to help them with the weapons. Biometric scan consoles are cool. They're a good idea too."

"They didn't get a chance to use them. Your range is better than mine. You must have military-grade plasma launchers. I only have the Dumonsa DPL-101s, and they're good, but not that good."

"You still have some fancy weapons on this thing. I like it!"

Siphany basked in the praise.

"I'm glad I didn't have to hurt them," said Pati. "Or you."

"Me too." And then Siphany added quietly, "Thank you for coming."

"Like I said. We take care of our own. And besides, you're my friend. I pull out *all* the stops for my friends." Pati smiled, and for Siphany, it was like eating croppygreens and playing her flute and doing all her routines perfectly on time, but even better.

*

THEY FOUND LURBIRA stashed in the med bay. Siphany touched her, and she flickered on.

Lurbira sat up, her expression hollow and slack. "Emergency boot," she said softly. "Systems check. Malfunction in root pathway 12-A-SN. Re-routing. Rerouting. Damage to 45 percent of sectors. Fatal errors. Repair systems engaged. Power dangerously low."

"We need to get her to the cockpit," said Siphany. "She can plug into the ship's power there."

"This is the smallest Artificial I've ever seen," Pati said, maneuvering over a float pad.

"Some couple ordered a little girl. A long time ago."

"Wow, gross. She's seriously worn out. Is she an original model?"

"Yes. Her body's nearly eighty years old."

They picked Lurbira up—she weighed a ton—and placed her on the float pad.

"Repair system failure," Lurbira said, her voice weak and distant. "Power insufficient."

"Hang on, Lurbira," Siphany said as they pushed the pad down the corridor toward the cockpit. "Just hang on."

"System restore. Memory degradation detected. Backups accessed. Accessing, restoring. The...the Whale."

"What?" They were almost there.

"Siphany." Lurbira's eyes were still empty, but her voice was her own again. "I heard the Whale. It's calling..."

Siphany grabbed Lurbira's limp, cold hand in her own as they entered the cockpit.

"How do you hook her up?" Pati asked.

"The Whale," said Lurbira, voice growing fainter and harder to understand, like a transmission breaking up into static. "Siphany, it's out there right now. Sif..."

"Ah! This cord," said Siphany, yanking it out from under the cockpit. "Good, they didn't move it. Here." She examined Lurbira's body, looking for the input. "This is it, I think." She pressed on a piece of stomach. A panel slid back. "Yes!" She connected the power, and Lurbira immediately seemed to relax.

"Power levels..." Lurbira's voice returned to this side of normal. "Rising. Rising. Shutting down for repairs. Sif...a...nee......thank...you."

She went limp.

*

"I'VE NEVER BEEN offline for so long before," said Lurbira several hours later, still sitting like a rag doll in the copilot's chair, her voice still weak and distant, distorted. "Four of my reactors failed. I was lucky I didn't shut down completely. A few more days, and I probably would have."

"The plasma blasts were very bad for your systems." Siphany tried to sound clinical and unconcerned. They were alone in the cockpit; Pati was off working on the power connections between her ship and Siphany's.

"No surprise," said Lurbira. "Plasma. Damn…Mother Junk. I can't believe she trailed us all the way to Haeld. Where are we now?"

"Just inside Haeld space but bound for Derstan. We'll be home in about three weeks if everything goes according to plan."

"Who's the other human? The one I saw before."

"That's Pati. She's a friend of mine from Hydras."

"Hydras? The online city?"

"Yeah."

Lurbira chuckled. "Figures. I should have known you'd like it there."

Siphany smiled down at her. "I know, I know. But I was able to send her a message, and she came."

"Lucky…" said Lurbira faintly.

"Yeah." Siphany frowned. It still bothered her that the terminal had randomly come to life like that. Owing so much to random, dumb luck was deeply unsettling. It made her feel out of control. "Right. So, Mother Junk, some Loyan soldier she had with her, and Isan are all locked away now. We physically burned out the terminal connections in those rooms, to be safe."

"Isan…must have been so happy when Mother Junk came for her."

"You'd have thought so. But I don't know. I didn't see much of her." Siphany leaned in closer.

"How are you doing?"

"Better," said Lurbira. "Need repair…"

"We'll be at Derstan soon." Siphany fiddled with her fingers. "Hey. What did you mean when you said you 'heard the whale'? Was that Serlay's Whale?"

Lurbira looked at her as if she'd grown another head. "What?"

"When you came back online. You said you'd seen a whale."

"I did?"

"You did. Pati heard it too."

Lurbira shook her head slowly. "No. I don't remember that."

"Okay. You ought to rest now; try and save up some strength," said Siphany. "When we get back to Derstan, we'll see what we can do for you."

"Okay, Avorna…" Lurbira slid down into an inert repair mode. "I will."

Avorna?

Siphany squeezed Lurbira's hand again and sat down in her chair.

*

PATI ARRIVED A few minutes later and leaned against the bulkhead, her body lean and muscular. She'd changed out of her armor, and she had a satisfied, sated expression on her face.

Those fine, trim muscles were all bluenet, most likely. Still, Siphany caught herself staring for a second too long, and she quickly looked back at her panels.

"Whew!" Pati thankfully hadn't noticed. "Everything's all secure. I did a double-check of the whole ship, just to be sure, but we should be good to go. We can get to work on engine repairs when you're ready; your friend Qas is already down there."

"Qas! How are they?" Siphany felt ashamed for not asking about them earlier.

"Sort of wobbly but not too bad. How's your girl here?"

"She's been better. I hate to leave her."

"If we're going to move this ship, I need you to do some work down there," Pati said. "I can keep pushing us with my ship, but it'll be a lot faster if we're working in tandem."

Siphany looked over at Lurbira, still inert, still recharging. She certainly wasn't going anywhere.

She'll be fine. But Siphany didn't quite believe it. She squeezed Lurbira's limp hand again and reluctantly followed Pati out of the cockpit.

*

QAS WAS BUSY swapping out parts when Pati and Siphany arrived.

"The damage isn't that bad," Qas said. "It could be a lot worse. You did a good job targeting."

"I'm pretty good, I admit it," said Pati, grinning that same cocky grin as before. "So what're we doing?"

"Sif, it would be good if you work on the flow regulator."

"Sure," said Siphany, and when Qas favored her with a bright smile, she remembered again why she'd liked them all those years ago.

"Pati, can you help me shove this replacement valve into place?" asked Qas.

"Got it, chief. You're not Siphany's *crew*, are you? I thought she didn't have any."

Siphany snorted at Qas's double take. "No. They're definitely not."

"This was actually my ship once," Qas explained, ignoring Siphany's sudden death glare. "When I went home to Sovena, I gave it to Siphany." They looked around fondly. "Same old ship."

"Oh?" Pati looked at Siphany, interested. "You never said anything about that in the lounge."

"What lounge?" Qas asked.

"We know each other from an interstellar pilot's lounge," explained Pati. "In Hydras."

"Oh," Qas said dismissively. "I don't do Hydras."

Pati and Siphany shot each other a deeply amused look, the one that said: *Outsiders never get it.* Siphany had always wondered what it would be like when she met one of her Hydras friends in real life. She was pleasantly surprised by how much she liked Pati.

In fact, she liked Pati a *lot*.

Qas stood there for a moment, being awkward, before they excused themselves to search for more spare parts in the bays the Junkers hadn't completely emptied, leaving Siphany and Pati alone.

"Qas helped me get off Sovena a long time ago," said Siphany after she was sure they were gone. "I wouldn't have ever made it to Derstan without them."

"I remember you saying you were from Sovena originally." Pati glanced through a shelf of random parts and plucked out something she needed.

"All the people we now have in the hold thought I *was* Sovene. It's the accent. And the look, too, I guess."

"Sovenes have a certain look," confirmed Pati. "No bluenet, so you all come by it honestly. I think it's a really attractive one."

Siphany flushed. "Um. I kept trying to tell them I was a Derstan citizen, but they didn't care."

"Well, people don't respect stations as independent. You wouldn't believe the number of times I've had to convince some backwater locals that, yes, we're a real country just like their big fat planet.

"So. You and this Qas…young love?" Pati waggled her eyebrows at Siphany, who flushed again and looked away. "I knew it!" she crowed.

"That was a long time ago," Siphany mumbled.

"And yet, here they are." Pati was clearly enjoying herself.

"It was a bizarre coincidence. That's all. When I showed up on Haeld, there they were, running intelligence for the Sovenes."

"Seriously? They're an *actual* Sovene spy?"

"Right? Weird. We got caught in running away together too." Siphany gave Pati the brief rundown of what had happened on Haeld.

"That is a wild coincidence."

"I never would have thought it." Siphany grunted as she lifted a section of conduit. "It's funny. I've spent all this time missing them, being *mad* at them for leaving me all those years ago, and then there they were."

"And?"

Siphany laughed. She felt remarkable, as if she was made of light. Every social interaction was easy now that the horrible weight of Loyan was off her shoulders. "I think maybe I've moved on."

Pati grinned. "Good! Good for you. Moving on's a great feeling."

"Yeah," said Siphany, finding herself grinning right back. "It really is."

*

MUCH LATER, WHEN they'd gotten the engines patched and running in tandem with Pati's, Siphany went to see Mother Junk. Pati backed her up, keeping a diverse array of weapons trained on their prisoner.

"Come to gloat?" Mother Junk said bitterly.

"Not at all," said Siphany, though, of course, she had. "I just wanted to check on you. Let you know you'll be turned over to Derstan Station authorities once we get there."

"I'd kill to know who let you have access to Hydras." Mother Junk looked small with her long legs folded up on the bed and her face blank in defeat. Siphany almost felt sorry for her. Almost.

"I don't know," said Siphany casually. "Maybe it was a glitch."

"You don't really believe that."

Siphany shrugged. She didn't, but it hardly mattered.

"So we're going to Derstan," said Mother Junk. "I suppose I'll be put in prison there. You've won. Congratulations. I'll never see home again. Without me, things will fall apart. No one will be able to protect them."

"We all do what we have to do," said Siphany softly.

Mother Junk nodded, her face like stone. "Like I said. Ruthless."

After another awkward minute, Siphany let herself out.

*

THE SHIP WAS still dark, except for the parts where light spilled out from rooms into the corridors. Siphany padded through the darkness, feeling herself relax a little at a time, slowly coming out of constant crisis mode.

Kit trotted next to her, winding in and out of her moving legs and purring. He'd been in hiding for a lot of the turmoil, only recently emerging from under Siphany's bed. He seemed to be in a good mood now. He even liked Pati.

"Here." Siphany put down the food bowl she was carrying in the designated place. Kit dove in, content. Siphany checked the time; perfect.

Life was sort of normal, at least for a while.

She'd received a note from her employer suspending payment to her account. Fine. Siphany fully intended to throw herself on their mercy when they returned to Derstan Station. Once she explained, they'd take her back. They had to.

She winced as someone dropped something somewhere with a loud metal *clank*.

Qas was busy minding the engines. Pati was in the galley, drinking something interesting she'd smuggled aboard from her ship. Isan and Mother Junk were locked up. Lurbira was experimentally walking around and cursing her own ineffective repair systems—but at least she was moving.

There were too many of them. Her ship was too loud, too full.

But it could be worse.

Siphany made her way down to the cargo deck where the croppy-greens grew and found her flute still in its hiding place. She sat on the floor behind some crates of engine parts and began to play a soft, simple tune that only she could hear. Little by little, her sense of self and place returned.

It was enough.

She was *free*. Her ship was her own again. Anything was possible.

Chapter Ten

AS SOON AS they hit Derstan Station, though, Siphany's lucky streak ran out.

She contacted Lai Visla at Derstan Mapping and Mining as soon as they'd cleared customs, fully intending to win her job back, as station security led both Mother Junk and Isan away. Siphany had an exemplary record and had really only made one mistake. She even had Pati's say-so to back her up, if necessary. They set up a time to meet, and Siphany allowed her hopes to rise.

But when she got to the office for an appointment a few days later, it turned out none of those things actually mattered.

Lai greeted her with a gloomy sigh. "I know why you're here. But I can't take you back on." She held up her hand to stop the torrent of protest coming from Siphany. "It's not because of any of what you did. I've had to let half the mappers go." She rested her head on her hands. "It's this war over Haeld. All this instability in the neighborhood. It's not safe out there, and all the Haeld border sectors have been declared a no-go zone. That's where our work was, and now it's gone. The military has their own maps, so we're not selling to anyone at all. I may have to shut the whole thing down."

"I'm sorry," said Siphany automatically.

"Thanks." Lai looked drained, exhausted, and worried, like a lot of other people on Derstan Station lately. "Ugh. If I had it my way, I'd take you back on. But with the way things are…I don't know what's going to happen. Tell you what, keep the sensor array. It's useless to us right now."

"Not sure what I can do with it," said Siphany, surprised.

"Well, keep it anyway. As a memory, right? Of everything you did here for us. And who knows, maybe when this is all over, you can come back, and we can start over."

Siphany left on the verge of panic. There went all her hard-won security, just like that.

And then, to make everything that much more intolerable, the damage to her ship turned out to be much worse than she thought. Weeks of very hard use and Pati's weapons had taken a toll, and now that her Derstan Mapping and Mining insurance had expired along with her employment, she had to pay out of pocket. She was suddenly very short on money for the first time in years.

Then there was the war itself.

The fighting at Haeld had started to spread out of control as Mother Junk had predicted.

In the weeks since she and the others had escaped from Haeld, the Sovenes had first complained loudly, then launched a "special assistance fleet" across the border to support the former government. Loyan had responded by standing by its allies on Haeld, sending in a good dozen capital ships to warn the Sovenes off.

The two planets had declared war on each other almost simultaneously. Two webs of alliances and compacts and mutual defense pacts had immediately come into effect, meaning that a good two thirds of local space was now technically at war.

Skirmishes were taking place all across Haeld's system as the two giants felt each other out. All the Mid-Perseus Arm was collectively holding its breath, waiting for someone to make the first big move.

The atmosphere on Derstan Station was tense, to say the least. The Stationbund was neutral, but anyone looking at the sheer number and strength of ships being deployed by Loyan and Sovena realized how small and weak the little confederation of independent stations were by comparison. Neutrality seemed like a thin farce in the face of the whirlwind of war.

So everyone watched, worried, and waited for the hammer to fall.

*

SIPHANY WANDERED GLOOMILY through the station, looking for something to do to keep her mind off everything. Derstan, one of the older stations, had ancient sections dating back nearly a thousand years. Every generation had left its artistic mark on the station, creating sculpture, wall carvings, paintings, and gardens. The result was a mish-mash of colors, styles, and patterns that often left Siphany feeling dizzy. Other people often told her how beautiful the central blocks of Derstan were, but she preferred to find the parts of the station that felt cold and utilitarian. The central blocks felt too much like Sovena.

The people, though, made Derstan wonderfully, refreshingly different. Derstan Stationers, beautiful in their complex, constantly changing rainbow of colors and sizes, displayed every shade humans had ever come in, as well as a few new ones. The body-sculpting magic of bluenet let everyone reshape themselves to be whatever they wanted—short or tall, thin or fat, and whatever else they could imagine.

A lot of people kept signature marks or tattoos on their faces or other visible portions of their anatomy so others could identify them easily. Not that it mattered to most of them. Their implants told them who was who.

Implant-less Siphany, of course, walked around blind half the time. She sometimes didn't recognize someone until they explained it to her, exasperated.

She also noticed that while people changed their skin tones a lot, they almost never made their skin as dark as Siphany's naturally was. So she stuck out, even here.

Still, home was home. Derstan Stationers were about as un-Sovene as you could get when it came to their bodies, and that's what Siphany liked about them—even as she struggled with her own ingrained discomfort about body modding.

She had a favorite tea bar on the outer edges of the station where other pilots, crew, and ship owners gathered to drink hot beverages and swap stories. Pati had promised to meet her here but was clearly running late.

Siphany caught snippets of conversation from other tables nearby, and it was nothing but war talk: ship movements, speculation about the commitment of massive fleets and huge armies from Hof and Saralar, and worries that Derstan Station was too far away from the other Stationbund members, exposed to either Loyan or Sovena.

A tall, wiry man with shimmering blond hair waltzed in and grinned at Siphany. She was about to look away when she noticed the complex tattoo on the side of his face. She recognized it immediately.

"Pati?"

The man sat down. "Yeah, hey Sif. How's things?"

"Um. You changed again."

"I did. Like it? Wanted to try it out. Haven't done a guy in forever."

Siphany coughed. "Um. Nice? That was a fast change though. Didn't you just change a few weeks ago?"

"Personal bluenet," said Pati proudly. He ordered a cold tea with mint and some sort of alcohol when the server came by. They brought it out to him right away.

"Ah." Pati leaned back in his chair. "These things are pretty fun." He spread his legs wide, aiming his crotch in Siphany's direction. Siphany had some very unrelaxing thoughts, which she immediately shoved out of her mind. "That is so much better," he said with a sigh.

"Um…" Siphany wasn't sure how to respond to this new version of Pati. The creeping body shift horror resurfaced; people on Derstan did this routinely, and it always forced Siphany to remember her own bluenet change. She played with her fingers. "Did…you have a rough day?"

"I've been in briefings for *hours*," Pati groaned, his voice deep and rumbling. "They're thinking of sending me out again. *Again*! I'm not allowed to say where, but ugh. I just got home from a six-month tour! *Six months*." He put his head in his hands. "Ugh."

It struck Siphany that, of course, Pati had been doing other things. The military would be running around frantically at a time like this. "I didn't know you'd been out there for so long."

"Yeah, huh? Life of an intelligence officer."

"I…guess." Siphany tried not to let her discomfort show too much.

"Oh, I know what I can tell you." Pati smacked his palm on the table so loudly that Siphany jumped and made a high-pitched squeaking sound. "Shit! You okay?"

Siphany grimaced. "Um. Sure."

Pati paused, obviously trying to work it, then grimaced. "Aw. Damn it. You know what? I forgot something else about you—the Sovene body thing. Would you rather I change back to what I was before? Or would that just make it worse?"

Siphany shook her head rapidly, looking away, trying not to let panic take over.

"So does that mean I should be old Girl Pati again?"

"If…if you don't mind," said Siphany softly. "I'm so sorry."

"Nah, no apologies necessary," said Pati, though he did look a little crestfallen. "I was stupid. I thought you'd like me this way is all."

"I liked you a lot the way you were," said Siphany, guilt and shame slowly consuming her.

"Got it." Pati got up and headed for a washroom—it was rude to shift in public. Fortunately, Derstan didn't segregate washrooms by gen-der—there was no point.

Siphany sighed, feeling like the worst person in the world. She didn't think she'd ever told Pati about her past, her one bluenet change, or any of that stuff. Still, it bugged her that Pati was changing his—her—expression just to make her more comfortable.

Pati reappeared a few minutes later, looking much like her old self.

She shimmered all over; the telltale blue crisscross lines just now fading away. Siphany tried not to look.

"I'm sorry," she said again.

"Why?" Pati sat down and shook out her hands, examining them critically. "No problem at all."

"Because you were being who you *are*, and you had to change to make me more comfortable. You shouldn't have to do that."

Pati grinned. "I don't mind it. I can be a guy later when I get home."

"But—"

"Really," insisted Pati. "It's fine. It's just a bluenet shift. We're cool."

She might have actually been fine, thought Siphany. Derstan Stationers made less of a big deal of gender; many of them shifted their visible gender markers and pronouns around on a whim, depending on who they wanted to be that day. Most liked to remain within a certain range of gender expressions; moving as far as Pati had for more than brief flings was pretty rare. Still, physical and apparent gender were more fluid here than back on Sovena.

Siphany wanted to tell Pati about who she'd been, what she'd been through. But to a born and bred Derstan Stationer, it wouldn't make any sense. She would never be able to explain.

"I shouldn't flip out like that," said Siphany instead, falling back on apologies again. "I won't, next time. Really. I'm sorry. So…um. What were we talking about?"

Pati thought for a moment, then lit up. "Oh! I remember. Isan escaped!"

"She *escaped?*" Siphany said, both aghast and relieved at the change of subject. "How?"

"Got me," said Pati with a disinterested shrug. "Jail's fulla holes."

"And they haven't found her?"

"Nope. I bet they won't either. She's a Junker station rat. Derstan's gotta be like a huge playground for her. She'll find some cramped little hole and a bunch of other station kids to run around stealing stuff with. They'll never catch her. Derstan cops don't care. What did she really do anyway? Nothing. She was just along for the ride."

"Poor Isan," sighed Siphany. Pati still didn't understand that this Isan didn't have any of the memories of the original Isan. Synthetics were something else Derstan Stationers knew nothing about. "This is all my fault."

"You keep saying that. You'd think you held a gun to Mother Junk's head and forced her to kidnap you and seize your ship. Twice! And you'd think you forced Isan to go along with it, which you didn't. It's not your fault. It's theirs."

"But I shot—"

Pati gave her a look. "You know what Lurbira would say if she were here, right?"

Siphany sighed again. "Yeah. She'd say they deserved it."

"And she's right. Mother Junk's up to all kinds of no good. I wish I were in on her interrogations. I bet there's all kinds of interesting stuff coming out."

"You're not in on it?"

"Nah," said Pati. "I just do all the work. Everyone else gets to have all the fun. Not that it's much fun lately."

Pati glanced around, grabbed Siphany's hand, and lowered her voice. "Look…" She drew Siphany close. Siphany's heart skipped a beat; Pati's hand was cool and smooth. "I've been hearing things, none of it any good.

Everybody's worried about the fighting. You might want to think about getting away."

Siphany's eyes widened. "Away? But…where?"

"Another Stationbund station as far from the war zone as you can manage. But hell, I don't know if even that'll be enough. Think about it. Real soon." Pati drew back. "Anyway. Enough about me. How are you managing?"

"Not well." Siphany filled her in on what was going on with her former employer.

"Damn." Pati whistled. "I didn't know they were being hit so hard."

"Maybe if this blows over…"

They both knew it wasn't likely. Not soon anyway.

"Yeah," said Pati finally. "So, did you find anyone to help Lurbira yet?"

"No," said Siphany, heart heavy. "Nobody outside of a few engineers who claimed to have some theoretical knowledge of Artificials. There just isn't anyone here who knows much."

"Not surprised. That's Derstan for you. Artificials don't come here. Maybe one of those engineers can at least fix her up a little bit to keep her going. Better to get it done now."

"Right," said Siphany, catching the unspoken words. *Before the war comes here.*

*

LURBIRA HAD ORDERED a slew of parts with a dubious line of credit she'd opened and was doing her best to repair herself, but it was going slowly.

She informed Siphany that a few of her more crucial hardware components were damaged beyond repair, including three of her five reactors and several processing centers, and that she was considering hooking herself directly into the ship's computer. She couldn't leave the ship now anyway, not under her own power.

In fact, she spent most of her time absorbing power from the station, which was temporarily powering the ship. They were both living aboard; Siphany had never bothered getting an apartment stationside and wasn't about to start now. Her home was on her ship, and she was glad to share it with Lurbira. Besides, it was a lot more peaceful now that everyone else had left: Pati to her own apartment and Qas to the Sovene embassy.

Qas had gone directly to the Sovenes to try to find a way home but, to their eternal frustration, found that the embassy staff wasn't able to do much for them. The war, they explained. Travel wasn't safe, and all available resources were being used for the war effort. The staff graciously offered Qas a place to stay in the embassy, though, and they grudgingly accepted.

Siphany was mostly not sorry to see them go; Qas had been wearing out her last nerve with their constant puttering around the ship, looking for modifications she'd made so they could undo them. They also became more of an obnoxious patriot as the war ramped up, and Siphany found she couldn't stomach that at all.

And yet, when Qas wasn't being awful, they were solicitous, sweet, and even nice and supportive from time to time. This brought back memories of days when travel with them had been fun and easy, almost as good as being alone. But Qas was so changeable and unpredictable now that Siphany couldn't relax when they were around.

When they left, she found herself missing them. She missed Pati and

Isan too. The ship seemed emptier in a way she didn't like.

As for Lurbira, she turned out to be very quiet company. That worried Siphany even more.

*

SIPHANY SOUGHT OUT Lurbira once she was back aboard her ship and found her watering the croppygreen plants in the hold.

"Didn't know you were a gardener," said Siphany.

"That was one of my jobs." Lurbira's voice was low and static-y, and she hobbled around with some difficulty. "When I was on the Junk. I tended the plants. It was easy. I liked it. It was peaceful—the closest thing to being away from humans I could get in that place." She hefted the watering can and faltered. Siphany ran to her and helped her hold it.

"I can do it," Lurbira said, crossly yanking the can away.

"Sorry. I know. I'm just trying to help."

Lurbira shakily finished watering the batch of croppygreens and set the can down. "That might be all I can manage right now. I should get back to the cockpit and power up again soon. The other two beds need watering, and the plants need pruning and picking."

"I can do that."

"Shit." Lurbira glared at the can as if it had done her some great injustice. "I hate not being able to do things."

"How's your repair work going?" Siphany asked hesitantly.

"It's fucked. Did you get your job back?"

Siphany shook her head. "They're shutting down operations because of the war."

"Ah. Great. So much for that."

"I talked with Pati too. Hey, want to come sit? I could use a meal."

"Boiled croppygreens, I bet."

"They're delicious," said Siphany with a happy shrug.

"After what you've been through, I'm surprised you can stand the sight of them. But sure. Why the hell not? I'll sit and charge, you cook, and we'll talk. Water the plants first."

Siphany smiled and did as she was told.

*

"SO PATI TOLD me Isan escaped," Siphany said, cutting up the croppygreens into manageable little cubes. She'd perfected the way she liked them, which Lurbira informed her was completely wrong. Nobody back on the Junk ate them that way. Siphany was delighted to hear it.

"Isan? Really?" Lurbira sat, propped up on a chair. A thin power cable connected her to the wall. Her eyes danced with amusement. "I'm not even surprised."

"She got out of confinement somehow and ran off. Pati says she's hiding somewhere on the station. Nobody knows where."

"Heh," said Lurbira. "That reminds me of the old Isan. She used to be able to hide anywhere, get out of anything. Nothing could hold her, the little station rat. Maybe this Isan has some of that still in her. Who knows?"

"It could be," said Siphany. "No one really knows if Synthetics can keep any of their host body's memories or preferences. The brain is the brain, and neural pathways still exist. I was reading a journal article about it the other day; admittedly, it was from three hundred years ago and all about Sovene Synthetics, but it's possible. Only she would know. And maybe not even then."

"True enough." Lurbira fiddled idly with the power cable. "You ever wanted to have kids?"

"No!" said Siphany, shocked by the question. She didn't like kids. They were noisy and illogical.

"I used to," said Lurbira quietly. "Believe it or not."

Siphany could only blink at her. "You?"

"Stupid, isn't it? But for the longest time, whenever I saw kids and their families, it hit me right here." Lurbira tapped her chest where, if she were human, her heart would be. "Who programmed that into me? I wish I knew. I'd kick them."

"I'm sorry." Siphany genuinely meant it. She plopped the croppy-greens into the boiling water. It would take a few minutes, no more.

"When I was young, I asked Avorna about it. I always assumed somehow that I'd be able to have babies. Avorna had to explain the whole deal. Humans could have children. But not me," Lurbira said bitterly. "I'll never be able to have my own. And when I die, there will be nothing left of me but a rusting husk."

"Lots of people can't have children," said Siphany hesitantly, knowing it wasn't really a helpful thing to say.

"Yeah, well." Lurbira scowled. "It's not like I can adopt either. And why would I want a human baby? I want someone like me."

"You can't just…" Siphany stopped short, unable to figure out how to phrase it delicately.

"Manufacture another? I wish. We can't make more of ourselves. The plants on Loyan are gone, and a lot of the technology they used is off limits now. It's the brains that are the problem. Bodies are easy. *Brains* aren't. You can make a metal person, but you can't make them *be* without special tools and knowledge. You need a Factory. Which is the one thing humans won't allow us to ever have.

"For you guys it's so easy," continued Lurbira. "Just stick the thing in the other thing and wiggle around, pop the little whatever into a big clear plastic pot, and nine months later, you've got a kid. Lucky. Us? We'll keel over one at a time until our whole species is…gone."

"I'm sorry, Lurbira. I had no idea."

"Forget it," said Lurbira. "Your croppygreens are boiling over."

*

LATER, SIPHANY TRIED to log in to Hydras, only to get the alarming message: *Due to recent hostilities, Hydras has been temporarily suspended.*

Her heart pounded. She felt completely cut off from the rest of the Mid-Perseus Arm. How could they do this to her? What would she do without Hydras?

She called Pati, who started ranting about censorship.

"This is bad, Sif. Bad! I'm twitching; Hydras is all I do when I'm bored or not working or on my ship."

"Me too." Though if she were honest, Siphany hadn't been missing it lately. Maybe, it occurred to her, the reason she'd been going there so much was talking to her now.

"I bet it's so we can't share war news," said Pati. "Hydras's servers are located on Hardarue, and they're really good friends with Loyan." She looked worried. "Something's going to happen."

"You keep saying that."

"And when it does, everyone's gonna say how right I was."

Siphany wasn't sure how serious Pati was being. But she'd planned out escape options just in case—her ship now had a quickstart routine that fired up the shift engines quicker than they should be.

"I have another meeting," said Pati. "It's endless these days. Hey. Want to get together after? My place, 2100 hours? I cook a mean dinner—protein cubes broiled to order."

"Sure," Siphany said, grinning. She wasn't that hungry after her crop-pygreen lunch, but what did that matter? She wouldn't be going for the food.

*

LURBIRA WAS HOOKED up to her power cable again, nodding off, so Siphany just quickly popped her head in to tell her she was leaving.

"They won't stop calling me," Lurbira mumbled.

"What?"

Lurbira's eyes flew open. "They won't stop! They keep calling and calling!"

"Who does? Lurbira?"

Lurbira seemed to catch herself. "No one. Sorry. Just…static, processing problems. Have fun with Pati. Say hi for me."

Siphany waited for a long moment, then nodded. "I will."

*

SIPHANY PUT ON what she was fairly certain was her best outfit and fiddled with her hair until it was more or less presentable. She was still excruciatingly early. She didn't want to wait around on the ship, where Lurbira had decided to sulk in the cockpit, so she let herself back onto the station.

Siphany had plenty of time before she was supposed to be at Pati's, so she decided to wander. She took a mainline transport tube through the busy warren of Derstan, moving from the modern outer sections through the crumbling, older inner belt and into the heart of Derstan: the huge, high-ceilinged Green Dome arboretum and parkland. Half the oxygen on the station came from this one source, a zealously guarded and preserved forest. The day's quota of citizens had already been allowed into the forest, so all Siphany could do was sit and look. It was enough. Siphany loved space and being away from planets, but something about the Green Dome forest touched a deep, primal place in her. She'd only been inside once, but she remembered the beautiful silence of the thick canopy of trees during those rare times when no one else was within earshot.

This was *her* Derstan, the place she'd adopted as her home country. All around, people spoke in the easy stationer drawl she could never quite master; her clipped Sovene tones forever marked her as an outsider. The Stationers were so diverse and busy and non-Sovene, though, that she felt relaxed just being among them.

Siphany lived on her ship. She could be gone for months, sometimes years at a time. But when she was here, she felt like she was home—for whatever that was worth.

Pati lived on the other side of the station. Siphany would have to take another tube to get near it. Might as well start now. She didn't have to rush; she could look around Pati's neighborhood for a while if needed.

Siphany returned to the tube station and fished out her fare card. She was suddenly aware of a scraggly looking, gawky teenage girl, all arms and legs with a blotchy, scarred face, standing next to her.

"Buy me a ticket," the girl said in a low voice, an intense expression on her face.

Recognition finally kicked in.

"Isan," Siphany said, surprised. "Isan? What? You look—"

"I'm in disguise. I used makeup and some other stuff. Buy me a ticket." Isan stressed the last word.

"And if I don't?" Was this a kidnapping attempt? Did Isan have a knife or a gun?

"I'll yell really loud. Come on, Siphany. *Please.*"

Siphany almost laughed, the last part was so desperate and pathetic. She shrugged and ran her card through twice. Isan followed her into the station.

"You're supposed to be—"

"Shut up!" Isan hissed. "Let's just get on a tube or a train or whatever they are here." She glanced up at the high Green Dome ceiling and shivered. "I need to get out of this place."

They got on a train headed toward the section of the station where Pati lived. Siphany couldn't think of anything better to do. Maybe Pati would have an idea of what to do with Isan.

The tube smoothly glided forward and vanished into dark tunnels.

Isan's tension seemed to drain away. "Why do you have that dome? All that...*space.*"

"The stationers like it," said Siphany.

"I don't. This is a station, not a planet. It doesn't fit."

"Where did you get all that makeup?" Siphany wanted to know. It wasn't like jail came with tons of foundation and eyeliner. Did it?

"Stole it."

Siphany tried polite conversation. "Is this how you looked...before?" Siphany certainly hoped not. Isan looked like someone had melted her and then tried to cover it up with a hasty coat of paint. She actually stuck out more now than she had before.

Isan glared at her. "No. But at least I look different than I did."

"You seem different too," said Siphany warily. "What happened?"

"I don't want to talk about it."

"But what about Mother J—"

"*Don't* say anything about her. Where are we going? Are we going back to your ship?"

"I was going to see Pati. It's the next stop."

"Good. We can go there," said Isan, satisfied. "You have anything to eat?"

"Not on me."

"You have money, right? You can buy me something. I haven't eaten in three days, and I'm starving. You *did* know I have to eat sometimes, right?"

"Of course," lied Siphany, feeling cornered and irate. "But why should I?"

"You owe me," said Isan, glaring at her.

Siphany blinked. "In what way do I owe *you* anything?"

"Who do you think unlocked your terminal?"

"Isan? You— How? Are you—?" Siphany sputtered.

Isan ignored her. "I'd like whatever has a lot of cheese on it, please. I'm pretty sure whoever I used to be liked cheese."

*

PATI LIVED ON a well-kept middle-class corridor midway between Green Dome and the outer rings, with tasteful carvings and paintings on the walls. Siphany rang the buzzer, feeling awkward.

Isan munched loudly on the fried meat substitute slathered in a cheese-like substance Siphany had bought for her. Siphany desperately wished she hadn't run into Isan. Why couldn't she have found her *after* dinner? She was still in a haze from what Isan had told her.

Not that Isan had actually explained much beyond the bare fact. But if she had done it…if she had *defied* Mother Junk…

Isan very clearly didn't want to talk about it, though, so Siphany left her alone.

Pati opened the door, and Siphany forgot everything else. Pati had done something to accent her cheekbones and wore a tight-fitting red tunic that showed off her trim, athletic figure. Her hair was a dazzling purple but just as short as before. Bluenet mods, of course, but Siphany didn't even care. The look in Pati's eyes during the split second between when she opened the door and when she spotted Isan made Siphany want to melt into a puddle.

But, of course, Isan was there to ruin it all.

"Who are you?" Pati asked sharply, sultry smile chased away by a curt, businesslike expression. She studied Isan, clearly getting some sort of information from her implant. "Wait. *Isan?*"

"She found me in Green Dome," explained Siphany with a sag of the shoulders. "She insisted on coming here with me." *I couldn't stop her*, she hoped she was saying without actually saying it. *I'm so sorry!*

Isan grinned and took a bite of her fried thing. A big glop of cheese dripped off and splatted on the floor.

Pati pulled them both inside. Siphany caught sight of a bottle of wine sitting between two places at the elegantly set table. Something smelled delicious. Her heart sank. This would have been so good.

"Do the authorities have any idea where you are?" Pati asked.

"No," said Isan proudly. "Nobody knows where I am."

"Shit," muttered Pati. "Just great. Is that…bluenet?"

"No. Makeup and what I think is putty of some kind." She looked pleased with herself. "I stole it."

"She says she's the one who unlocked my terminal back on the ship too," said Siphany.

"You?" Pati's deep brown eyes widened a little.

"Yes. So you owe me. You have to help me now."

Pati and Siphany exchanged glances. Pati actually seemed amused, thank everything.

"You're full of surprises. You found Siphany so she could do something for you?" Pati asked.

"You're leaving soon, right?" Isan said. "You have to be. Everyone is. They're all talking about it."

"I haven't decided yet," said Siphany.

"When you do," said Isan, "I want to go with you."

"No," said Pati and Siphany at the same time.

"Come *on*, Siphany. You *have* to let me. I can't stay here."

"First off," said Siphany, trying to figure out how to defuse Isan. "I'm *not* leaving soon. I don't have a job. I have nowhere to go."

"Uh," said Pati. "You might want to—"

"But you have a ship," pressed Isan, cutting Pati off.

"Yes. I have a ship. But it isn't going anywhere."

"It can, though. Plus, I helped you before. You have to help me now." Isan sounded like she was stuck in a loop again.

Siphany sputtered, out of words.

At that moment, the door buzzer went off.

Pati threw up her hands and palmed the door open. Qas stood there, arms crossed and looking haggard.

"Hi Pati," they said. "I'm looking for Siphany."

"Qas!" Siphany gave Pati a look that she hoped said *I am so sorry. Like really extra amazingly sorry.* Was Mother Junk going to waltz in next? "What are you doing here?"

"There you are," they said, coming in. Pati glared daggers at them. "I went to the ship, but Lurbira said you were here. I really need to talk to you. Do you have time?"

"Qas," said Isan. Qas did a double take.

"Isan," Siphany filled in helpfully. "Bad makeup job."

Qas, to their credit, recovered quickly. "Ah. Hello again." They turned to Siphany. "I *really* need to talk to you, Sif."

"Oh, go ahead," said Pati. "I have a bottle of wine. Maybe I can drink it all by myself."

"Pati, no! I'm sorry. Please don't." Siphany turned to Qas, who was giving Pati a pained look. "Can we possibly talk about this later?"

"Why? What's so important here?" they asked obliviously. Siphany wanted to strangle them. "Sif, I have a proposition for you. Now, hear me out, okay? I want to return to Sovena, but the embassy here is giving me the runaround, and things are starting to happen. You have a ship—"

"No."

"You didn't even let me finish."

"I don't have to. I'm not going back to Sovena, and I'm not taking you. Find another way to go home, Qas."

"You wouldn't even have to go onto the planet. You could drop me off at the customs station."

"I have no desire to even go near there," said Siphany. "*Especially* now. They'd probably try to draft me."

"That's silly. I can pay you. I have money—"

"I have no doubt about that," said Siphany dryly.

"—and I know you *need* money. Sif, please. I need to get home."

They actually looked kind of desperate. Siphany would have felt bad for them if she hadn't been so annoyed.

Then they ruined it by opening their mouth. "I should point out it *was* my ship first. I did give it to you, after all."

"You did," said Siphany, trying not to erupt in fury in front of Pati. "But you *gave* it to me. When you said in your note that I could and should do whatever I wanted, whatever *I* wanted with the ship, were you lying? Were you lying when you said I should stop letting myself be bossed around by other people? Because that's what this feels like."

"That's not what I meant—"

"No. My answer is no."

"Sif, reconsider. It's a good deal for you—"

"She doesn't have to listen to you," Isan broke in.

"Nobody asked you," snapped Qas.

Isan actually stuck her tongue out at them. Whatever had come over her, Siphany was starting to like it.

Pati held a hand to her head, looking at something in the distance, eyes wide. Her implant was giving her some kind of information, Siphany realized, and her heart skipped a beat.

"I'm just saying I know you lost your job," Qas said. "I know you could use the money. And I do need a ride home. This works out for both of us."

"Hell," said Pati.

"Just give it a chance," Qas urged. "Then you can come right back here."

Siphany ignored them and walked over to Pati's side. "What is it?"

Pati looked like she'd seen a ghost.

"I—I want you all to get to Siphany's ship and take off," she said. "All of you. Right now. Don't argue. I'm going to transmit some coordinates to you. Go there and wait for me."

"Pati—"

"Go!" Pati commanded in a voice Siphany had never heard her use before. She sounded terrified. "I'm sorry. Please. Just go now! All of you. Before it's too late."

"Will—will you two wait outside for me?" said Siphany. "I'll be there in a second."

Isan shrugged and left. Qas gave Siphany a speculative look, then followed.

"What's going on?" Siphany asked as soon as the door shut.

"Bad stuff." Pati ran to her back room and started fishing through her closet for something. "You have to hurry. And so do I."

"I'm sorry—" Siphany began to say, but Pati didn't let her finish.

Instead, she sprinted back to the front room where the table and wine still sat, took Siphany by the hand, then kissed her hard, right on the lips.

Siphany's shock blew through her, and she leaned into the kiss, desperate for it to last, but it was over before it had really begun. Pati rapidly detached and turned away.

"I'm sorry we didn't get our dinner," Pati said, already retreating into the back room. "Just go, run. Run! You have no time."

Siphany, shaken, nodded. "Okay. Okay. Take care of yourself!"

"Go!" called Pati.

Siphany let herself out. "Right," she said to Qas and Isan. "We're gonna run for it."

*

THE RIDE BACK to the ship was tense. The mood in the station had changed. People in military uniforms were conspicuous in the corridors, now, and everyone suddenly seemed as though they were waiting for something awful to happen.

Siphany called ahead to Lurbira and told her to get the ship ready. Lurbira didn't argue; she must have figured out something was going on from the way Siphany's voice wouldn't stop shaking.

Green Dome was rapidly emptying out. Everywhere, people in uniform with equipment scurried to and fro. Civilians muttered to one another and kept their children close.

Siphany led Qas and Isan through the corridors to one transport tube, and then another, this one headed for her part of the outer ring.

"What's going on?" Isan asked at last.

"Don't know," said Siphany stonily, though she could guess. Everyone could guess.

"Sif," said Qas worriedly.

"Shut up and stay calm," Siphany said, gritting her teeth. "Stay close."

When the tube finally stopped at the docks, they sprinted for the ship. People all around them had the same idea as a steady stream ran from the tube terminal toward the dock hatches.

Siphany held both Qas's and Isan's hands as they dodged through the crowds. There! She dragged them into their dock and onto the ship.

"Lurbira, we're in! Get clearance!" shouted Siphany as soon as they were aboard, nearly out of breath as she sealed the airlock and sprinted to the cockpit.

Qas trailed after. "Anything happening out there?"

Lurbira worked the console. "Getting clearance now. What's going on?"

"Don't know. Pati said something was up, and she wanted us to get out."

Lurbira stared at the screen. "Oh."

"What?"

"It says 'Blanket clearance. All ships may leave at once.' I've never seen that."

A stone settled in Siphany's stomach. "Hit my emergency quickstart program. Get us out. Fast. Did Pati send coordinates?"

"Yeah, is that—"

Suddenly, proximity alarms went off everywhere, from the ship and the station. The sensor boards lit up.

Ships had appeared everywhere.

Dozens.

Hundreds.

No…*thousands* of ships had just shifted into local space.

"Loyan," breathed Qas.

"Invasion fleet!" screeched Lurbira. "Fuck!"

"Go! Detach!"

The detachment sequence whirred and clicked, and they were loose. Siphany swung the ship hard around; stars and station lights blurred past. All around them, other ships were breaking loose of the station and fleeing in all directions. She deftly dodged around two and narrowly avoided ramming a third as the shift engines rapidly came online.

Siphany hit the acceleration, skimmed over the underside of the station, and shot out into space, keeping the bulk of the station between her and the oncoming fleet.

"*Attention,*" a terse, authoritative voice said, transmitting on all frequencies. "*Due to recent hostilities, the Derstan system is being placed under custodial care by the State of Greater Loyan. Please remain where you are. Do not attempt to resist. We urge the government of Derstan to comply at once.*"

"Loyan," said Isan. She looked spooked. "Oh, no, no, no."

"Not just Loyan," muttered Lurbira. "Hof ships out there too."

"All this for Derstan?" Siphany said, distracted with piloting the ship. "It doesn't make sense."

"No. It makes perfect sense. What's on the other side of Derstan from Loyan?"

"Sovena," breathed Siphany, understanding at last. "They're going around. Everyone expected them to go through Haeld. But they came *here* instead. Oh gods above, it's us, it's us."

The pathetically tiny Derstan Defense Navy had finally launched. She could see the gray battleships slide gracefully from their ports.

"No," she shouted. "No, no don't!" Derstan's navy would have no chance.

Flashes erupted all around the station and the navy. The battle had been joined.

Tears filled Siphany's eyes. There were millions of people on Derstan Station. "Oh, gods, please keep everyone safe. Pati!"

Pati. *Pati* was Derstan military. Was she out there fighting? Was she still on the station? How could she possibly survive?

The Derstan navy ships veered—then half of them burst into soundless flashes as the Loyan ships drew nearer. Missiles slammed into the outer ring of the station, taking out a massive segment and all the ships docked there.

Siphany's console flashed green. They reached the shift point just as the Derstan Station government transmitted its frantic surrender.

"Shift! Shift!" said Siphany through her tears. Lurbira hit the command, and the whole nightmare disappeared behind them.

Chapter Eleven

THEY WAITED AT the coordinates Pati had sent, deep in the middle of nothing.

Siphany could still taste Pati's kiss on her lips. It had only been a few hours ago.

Qas came up to the cockpit and put their hand on Siphany's shoulder.

"We're staying here," Siphany said before Qas had a chance to say anything. "We're going to wait right here for her."

"I didn't say we shouldn't," they said soothingly.

Siphany stared out into space, playing nervously with her fingers. Where was she? What was taking so long?

"I'm sure she's okay," Qas said. "She'll come."

"There were so many ships." She put her hand over Qas's. "She tried to warn us."

"She got us out of there. If she hadn't…"

"I know. We'd be stuck." *Or worse.* Siphany shook her head. "I wish I knew what happened to her."

"Sif? Is there something between the two of you? I'm not jealous or anything. I like her. But I didn't know you were…"

"This really is a bad time, Qas."

"I'm sorry," said Qas softly. "I shouldn't have pushed you. I've been acting like a jerk lately."

"No shit," Lurbira chimed in helpfully from her perch in the copilot's seat.

Qas shot her a dirty look, but she just grinned back at them.

Qas turned to Siphany, their expression serious again. "But I am sorry. It's been a bad few weeks. I don't know what's going on anymore. You were right. I was getting pushy and awful."

"Okay," said Siphany, trying to think of what to say. "I don't know what's between Pati and me… We were going to have dinner together when you found us. And now?"

"I'm sure she'll find her way here. Try not to worry."

Siphany didn't reply, and eventually, Qas left her alone to peer out the cockpit windows into the depths of space. "Come on," she said softly. "I know you could get away. You're always talking about how good you are. Come on."

Finish what you started.

*

HOURS CRAWLED BY. They hung in the darkness, waiting.

Lurbira ran systems checks and did all the preflight things they hadn't had time to finish. Isan picked up Kit and carried him around cooing to him, which the little cat seemed to enjoy. He purred and purred when they stopped by the cockpit. Too distracted and worried, Siphany could barely register their presence.

Qas had returned to the engine room. They checked in on Siphany from time to time, being so sweet and solicitous and just plain *nice* that she wanted to smack them.

To keep her mind busy, Siphany ran sensor sweeps and checks of her weapons systems. She read technical manuals, reviewed and retested the repaired systems, and ran sensor sweeps again.

Then, at last, she saw a little blip approaching them. For a moment, Siphany panicked, thinking it could be a Loyan ship come to get them. But no, this was small and fast. A Derstan courier.

"Pati," she breathed.

Lurbira sat up. "She's coming?"

The communications board crackled to life. "Hey out there." Pati's voice. She sounded hollow and weary. "I see you made it."

"I see *you* made it," Siphany said, giddy with relief. Her scanners belatedly noticed how badly damaged Pati's ship was. "Are you all right?"

"Yeah. I got out just in time, launched right before the surrender. I couldn't do anything…they were…it was bad. I got lucky they didn't disintegrate me. So I ran. They sent some ships after me, but I made it out. Lucky, lucky…I set up these coordinates years ago as a fallback. I guess that was lucky too."

"Oh, Pati," Siphany said.

"I'm fine, Sif." Pati said, irritated. "But we probably ought to get out of here. I'll transfer my stuff to your ship, and we can ditch mine."

"Are you sure about that?"

"It would take way too much time to reconnect them. I'd rather just get out of here, okay?"

"Got it," said Siphany. "Come alongside and dock."

*

PATI THREW HER things out of her scarred and pitted ship through the open airlock, then stepped through dressed in full battle armor.

She shut the airlock behind her and took her helmet off. She looked utterly frazzled. "Go ahead and cut her loose. A Derstan military ship is a liability now."

"Are you sure you're okay?"

"No, I'm not!" Pati shouted. Siphany shrank back. "What do you *think*, Sif?"

She stormed off, leaving Siphany shaking. Loud voices always made her flinch.

"Sorry," she said quietly to the space where Pati had been. Then she returned to the cockpit to plot a course away from all of this.

*

THE NEXT SHIFT took them out deeper into space, away from Derstan Station and, Siphany hoped, away from the massive invasion force as well. Siphany tried accessing news about what was going on, if Derstan was even still *there*, but all she could find on the asynchronous net was a smattering of Loyan propaganda and "blocked" messages. Hydras continued to be offline.

From Derstan, Sovena, and everywhere else, there was nothing but silence.

*

THE FIVE OF them gathered in the mess to talk it over.

"We have to go to Sovena," Qas insisted. "We have to warn them."

"We sent runners," said Pati wearily. "They all got away well ahead of the invaders. The Sovene embassy had secure, secret channels too. They know."

"Sovena'll find out sooner or later anyway," murmured Lurbira gloomily. "So what?"

Qas stared at her, open-mouthed. "Sovena's my home. It's Siphany's home too."

"It *was* my home," Siphany said automatically.

"We know," said Pati. "You've said it a million times already."

Siphany looked at her shoes, stung. Pati was still snappish and grumpy. She wouldn't even look at Siphany.

"Sovena's the safest place right now," Qas continued. "You know I'm right."

"Are you out of your mind?" Pati exclaimed. "If we go to Sovena, the invasion fleet will be right behind us. Did you *see* how many ships there are? Sovena's going to fall just like Derstan did. There's no way to stop it."

That hit all of them like a ton of lead.

It was true, Siphany realized with sickening clarity. Sovena had a decent-sized fleet, but they were mostly still in the Haeld system, and next to this invasion fleet, they were nothing anyway. What allies they had were still mobilizing.

Sovena had no chance.

Siphany thought of her parents, her brother and sisters, her grandparents and cousins, her old classmates, the people in her home city. What would happen to them when the Loyan fleet came? Would Sovena surrender quickly, hopefully sparing a brutal bombardment, or would they fight?

Would the Loyans just roll right over them?

Lurbira's eyes were closed. "Stop, stop," she murmured.

"Stop what?" Pati demanded. "They're *wrong*. We'll get killed if we go to Sovena."

"No," said Lurbira, her voice breaking up. "She won't *stop*."

Pati, Qas, and Siphany exchanged worried glances.

"Hey, the Artificial's on the fritz," Isan said, clearly relishing the chance to get some of her own back.

"I am. I am *not*," Lurbira protested weakly, holding her head in her hands.

"Are you all right?" Siphany asked.

"Fine," said Lurbira. "I'm fine. I just…Sovena's a bad idea."

Siphany frowned. That wasn't what Lurbira had been talking about; she was sure of it.

"We have to get there," Qas insisted. "I want to be home when this happens. I want to fight. I don't want to just run away."

"What's that supposed to mean?" Pati demanded. "You wouldn't be here without me! I saved your asses from the *fire*!"

"I didn't say anything about you," Qas protested. "But we have to—"

"We're *not* going to Sovena," Siphany said firmly. "This is my ship, and that's final."

"*Thank* you," said Pati. "See, at least the fucking captain has some sense."

The captain. Siphany had never used the title back when it was just her and Kit. But she liked it when Pati said it.

Qas didn't say anything; they just looked away.

"So where *are* we going?" Isan asked.

"We run. We get as far away from Derstan and the invasion fleet as we can." Siphany fidgeted, twisting her fingers around one another. "There's plenty of places we can go with no sensor buoys. After that…we'll see."

Nobody really liked that plan, but they agreed. What else was there to do?

Siphany returned to the cockpit with a strangely silent Lurbira and plotted a new course for the middle of nowhere.

They would keep shifting one step at a time, burrowing deeper into the endless void, hiding so far inside the comforting nothing of space that the Loyans would never find them.

*

PATI RETREATED INTO the cabin she'd claimed and wouldn't speak to anyone, while Isan hung around with Qas in the engine room, doing nothing helpful. Lurbira had vacated the cockpit to work on a few self-repairs in the med bay. She moved so gingerly and slowly that it pained Siphany to watch, but at least she was still moving at all.

Qas came to see Siphany as she sat with Kit purring on her lap in the cockpit, working out ways to get even deeper into interstellar space. She'd turned on the big sensor turret and was using it to scan for any signs of Loyan scout ships or drones.

"See anything?" Qas asked.

"We're clear so far," said Siphany.

Qas sat in the copilot's chair. "It's so strange. Being back here…while everything else is going on. It doesn't seem real."

"I know. I'm trying not to think about it."

Qas's hair was getting shaggy-long again, and they looked strained and weary. Siphany felt that way herself, which was probably why she momentarily forgot the years of hurt and history and all the fights, and just thought, *They are so cute with their hair like that.*

"We should still go back home to Sovena," Qas said.

She groaned, and the moment vanished.

"We *should*, Sif," Qas repeated softly, putting a hand on hers. She jerked it away, angry for no reason she could determine. "You know we should be there."

"Why?" Siphany demanded.

"It's home," said Qas, as if that were all the reason anyone could need.

"We've been over this. And you know what I think. Besides, it's not everyone's home. What does Lurbira care? Isan's a Junker. And Pati's a Derstan military officer."

"They could use her."

"Against *that* fleet? I doubt it. Why should she care anyway?"

"Because the Loyans just invaded her home," Qas countered. "Enemy of my enemy is my friend."

"She may not see it that way," Siphany said.

"Is it better to be out here?"

"Yes," said Siphany firmly. "At least here we aren't dead."

"And what about you? You grew up on Sovena."

"In an institution."

"True, but—"

"I hope they *scorch* the whole place," snarled Siphany, fury uncoiling inside her. "I hope they bomb the whole planet to oblivion! Leave nothing, no songs, no stupid rules, no institutions, nothing. Nothing!"

Qas's eyes widened. "You can't mean that."

"Oh, I mean it. And then I hope the Loyans all get crotch rot for what they did to Derstan. But if you think I care even a little bit about what happens to Sovena, after everything that's happened, after everything *we went through* to get away from there, you really don't know me very well at all."

Qas shook their head. "Sif…you have to let that old hate go. I did. It took me forever…but I did. Sovena is what it is. There's good and bad there, same as any place else."

Siphany said nothing, fuming, trying to control herself.

"It's not really Sovena's fault, what happened to you," Qas continued, stepping right on the land mine. Siphany exploded.

"Of course it was Sovena's fault! My parents *abandoned* me in that institution when I was *twelve*. I saw them on my birthday, and that was *it*. They never even brought my little sisters—did you know that? They had two girls. *Better* versions of me. They didn't need dark rooms, a medical implant, and a fucking bluenet body shift to be whole."

"Sif—"

"*Shut up*. They stuck me there. They *stuck me there* and *forgot* about me. And it was everything about Sovena, all the laws and the social conventions and *everything* that let them do it. What would you know about it? You were there for addiction, so they would have let you go, You'd been there barely six months when we escaped, but I was there for almost six *years*."

A tear slipped down her cheek, and she kicked herself for her own weakness.

"Six years of my life, and Sovena was *fine* with this. It happens everywhere because Sovenes can't stand the idea of changing someone's 'natural' balance. My body was torturing me, and I couldn't change it!"

"I do know something about that, Sif," Qas reminded her, glancing down at their body.

"Yeah," said Siphany, furiously wiping away tears. "I know. And I know you never did change it."

"I made my choice. I regret it sometimes…but I'm a Sovene, and I can't change that. Are you completely comfortable with body mods? Have you ever used bluenet beyond the first time?"

Siphany shook her head mutely.

"Sovena's a cruel planet for anyone who's different," Qas continued, "but I carved out a space there for myself. It took a long time. But I did. I made my peace. I never regretted going back. I think, in the end, you'd feel the same way if you came home."

"I am *never* going back there," Siphany said with a sniff. "Ever."

Qas shook their head. "Tell me this isn't about you and me too. What happened between us."

"You think?" Siphany said bitterly. "You think maybe the fact that you abandoned me to go back to a planet I hated would be a part of it? You're a genius."

"And now I turn up, years later, working for the government." Qas looked out at the stars. "And you've been angry with me ever since you first saw me on Haeld. Haven't you?"

Siphany simmered, saying nothing.

"Did I ever tell you *why* I left when I did?"

"I don't care."

"My dad sent me a message. My grandmother died, and my mother was very sick. She was an addict, like me. I had to help her get well. My family…I couldn't just leave them. I couldn't separate myself like you did."

"So?" Siphany tried to be cold, but her heart broke a little inside. Why hadn't Qas told her?

"So, I'm sorry, is what I'm trying to say. I shouldn't have left like that, and in a perfect world, I wouldn't have."

Siphany blinked. She hadn't been expecting that.

"I tried to tell you. But I never found the right time," Qas said, gesturing at Siphany. "And we were doing so badly anyway. I thought it would be kinder."

"It wasn't," murmured Siphany, though a part of her was certain they were right.

"I had to go home, Sif," Qas continued. "I felt it pulling at me, all these obligations, all these things I was running away from… I had to face them. I knew you never wanted to…but I did."

"I remember."

"So I went back. And in all that time…I started to understand the good things about Sovena. Art, music, culture, shared history, and family. There's that spirit of working together everyone has. I never noticed it before, but I started to see it when I returned."

"I never got that chance." Siphany drew her knees up to her chin. "Being locked away from it and all."

"I know," Qas said gently. "But even that's improved a little. The Executive Council has passed a few new laws about institutions and certain kinds of treatment. Even our people can change. In fact, I think we have an incredible capacity for change."

"I'm not a Sovene. I'm a—"

"I know, Siphany. But you're a citizen of a nation that doesn't exist anymore."

Doesn't exist anymore. She sat in shock, absorbing that.

"Please," begged Qas. "I want to fight for my home. Or at least be there when my people need me." They looked so sad and desperate that Siphany almost said yes. But she caught herself.

"No," Siphany said, throat tight. "I can't. It's too dangerous, and I have to think about everyone else. I'm the captain, remember? We'll try to get to neutral territory, if there's any left. You can go from there if you still want to."

"It may be done by then," said Qas, their voice getting tighter.

"Why don't I just shove you out the airlock?" Siphany snapped. "The end result will be the same. You'll be just as dead if you go back to Sovena."

"It's my duty," Qas said helplessly.

"Good for you. I have work to do."

Qas waited a moment longer, then got up. "Sovenes change. But you can't. You never could. You're too scared to let yourself be anything more than what you used to be."

And then they left.

Siphany tapped a few more equations into her console, realized they didn't make any sense, and erased them all.

*

THAT NIGHT, SIPHANY awoke to the sound of moaning from the cockpit. She lifted Kit to the floor, rolled out of bed, and padded down the hall. Lurbira sat in the copilot's chair, groaning and clutching her head.

"Lurbira? What is it?"

"It won't stop," said Lurbira, her eyes wide.

"What do you mean? Is this the same thing as earlier today?"

Lurbira nodded, miserable.

"What won't stop?" asked Siphany. "Who won't stop?"

"Serlay," said Lurbira, her voice wavering. "She's *calling* me. And she won't stop!"

"Serlay…Serlay Call? You mean your old captain? She's calling you? How?"

"I have this implant," admitted Lurbira, tapping the side of her head. "Avorna's idea, so they could find me if they needed to. I guess I never removed it. Serlay's been calling me for months, but now it's getting so much worse. It *hurts*."

"She's been calling you for *months*? Lurbira, why didn't you say anything?"

"Because," Lurbira said faintly. "I don't want to go. I don't want to be at her beck and call. But Sif…it fucks me up. I did strange things. I sent that ship out from the Junk, because…I thought maybe…"

"Wait—*you* sent the ship from the Junk?"

"Pretty bad plan in hindsight, huh?" said Lurbira. "But, yeah. I was hoping the Sovenes would find it. Just my luck…"

"Mine, too," sighed Siphany. "So where is she, this old captain of yours?"

"Out past Redov. Somewhere in deep space. I don't know. I don't care!"

"Why is she calling you?"

"Oh," said Lurbira, looking away. "She's dying."

"What? Lurbira!"

But Lurbira wouldn't say any more.

*

SIPHANY HAD DREAMS that night of bluenet warping her into something she couldn't recognize. She ran through the streets of Hydras, trying to convince Pati that she was still herself, but nobody knew her. When Siphany looked in a mirror, she saw her face as it had been before she'd escaped the institution. She screamed, and then a shadow passed over the city.

Somewhere high above Hydras, a massive being floated. Siphany looked up, but she couldn't see all of it. It blotted out the sky.

Hello, was all it said, and Siphany woke up.

Kit purred next to her. Siphany absently petted him, and she decided where they were going next.

*

SIPHANY CALLED EVERYONE together early that morning. They were a sorry bunch. Qas couldn't bring themself to look at Siphany and studied the table intently. Pati appeared hung over and smelled like she'd been drinking all night. Isan looked like she'd slept in a tornado, even though Siphany was sure Isan didn't need to sleep.

Siphany hadn't slept at all, not after talking to Lurbira. Her mind had filled with plans, with a direction, and she'd finally made it up.

Lurbira wasn't at the meeting. She'd been unable to leave the cockpit and her connection to the ship's power. Her repair systems were working overtime, she'd said, but they were having trouble keeping up.

That was fine. Siphany would fill her in later.

"I have a destination for us," Siphany said. "Not Sovena. I'm sorry, Qas."

Qas closed their eyes and nodded their assent. She continued on.

"I'd like to try to make Redov Station." She pulled up a holographic map of their arm of the galaxy. Human-inhabited systems twinkled in bright colors; stations blinked in gray. "Here. It's well away from the war zone, and we won't have to cross the front lines in order to get there. They're a Stationbund member, so hopefully, they'll be welcoming to refugees from Derstan."

The word *refugees* hung, pungent, in the room. Pati rubbed her head.

"There's one other thing," said Siphany. "While we're out that way, I'd like to try to find the *Call*, Lurbira's old ship."

"What?" said Qas, surprised.

"Her story isn't mine to tell, but she's been getting a transmission from it. The *Call* is drifting in space, and the captain is dying. It's close to Redov, so we should be able to make it."

Nobody said anything for a few minutes.

Then Pati stood up creakily. "Do whatever you want. I'll be in my cabin." She slouched off down the corridor.

"Ah," said Siphany, suddenly much less sure of herself. "Anybody else have any comments?"

"You're the captain, remember?" said Qas moodily. "It's your ship. If you want to waste our time and resources on something like that while the galaxy burns, it's your call." They stood and walked quietly out.

"Well, I think it's a stupid plan," Isan announced after everyone was gone. "Redov's in the middle of nowhere."

"That's the idea," Siphany said faintly.

"Fine!" Isan slammed her hand on the table, and Siphany jumped. Since when had Isan ever been angry? "You obviously don't care at all what I think, so why did you even bother to ask!" She bolted from the room.

Siphany sat at the table. "Thanks everybody. We'll, um, discuss it more later."

*

SIPHANY RETURNED TO the cockpit. "New course," she said to Lurbira. "We're heading for Redov."

"What?" said Lurbira, eyes wide with shock.

"Redov. I don't want any protests from you either. Let's go find your captain."

Lurbira actually smiled. "You're my captain, Sif. But sure. Let's go see Serlay Call."

Chapter Twelve

THE SHIP SLID slowly through space, pausing here and there to snap between shift points, and the days stretched to weeks. Siphany deftly plotted a course toward Redov Station, pushing her engines to go faster and faster, testing the limits of what shifts could do.

She compromised with the rest of the people on board, letting them raise the light levels in some areas and turning the heat down. It was, she thought, the least she could do.

They sometimes spotted what had to be Loyan scout ships, but they were always too far away to bother with. Space was vast; not even the Loyan armada could control all of it.

War news finally trickled in through the now heavily censored asynchronous net. Hydras was still shuttered, but a few places here and there managed to get some of the news through.

The loose alliance of the Stationbund had reacted with outrage to the

Loyan invasion of Derstan, but their squabbling members couldn't decide whether to join the battle or try to stay out of Loyan's way.

Meanwhile, the huge invasion fleet lumbered toward Sovena.

The Sovenes had desperately tried to recall their ships from Haeld, but from what Siphany could tell, they ran into a small but determined Loyan fleet halfway there and were pinned down trying to either get around or destroy them. War propagandists mentioned something about a secret Loyan base.

She sighed. Mother Junk's revenge, once again.

The Sovene fleet, then, was effectively cut off from home at the worst possible time. Haeld had been nothing but a clever trap.

Sovena was doomed. Siphany tried to feel nothing about it, but when she closed her eyes, she saw Loyan ships streaking above her home city. She imagined her parents and sisters clutching one another, terrified for their lives. No Form, no meticulously regimented day, no bright colors and beautiful sounds could save them now.

Would her mother call out for her lost eldest daughter when the bombs hit?

*

PATI HID IN her cabin for days at a time, coming out only to sullenly pick her way through meals. Siphany's famously hoarded supplies, topped up at Derstan before the invasion, were now running low thanks to the three extra people on board; they were surviving on a steady diet of boiled and sliced croppygreens. Fortunately, those seemed to be thriving and multiplying. They grew incredibly fast—the plants seemed to produce a bucketful of ripe croppygreens every day.

Siphany kept stores of freeze-dried meat deep in a locked freezer, which no one else knew about. She figured she would dip into those only when she had to.

The food did not improve morale. Qas groaned every time Siphany brought out a fresh plate of delightfully plain boiled croppygreens. Even Isan started whining, to the point where Siphany threw up her hands and suggested that if she were so annoyed by it, she could do the cooking. Isan gleefully accepted.

Isan, it turned out, was a kitchen wizard. Siphany watched, amazed, as the Synthetic briskly moved through the kitchen, inventorying cooking implements and dusty ingredients buried deep in Siphany's pantry, and started to work right away. Soon, astonishingly delicious smells wafted through the ship, bringing a hungry Qas up from the engine room. They gave Siphany a questioning look and sat down.

Only fifteen minutes later, Isan placed a plate of fried and seasoned sliced croppygreens in front of Siphany and Qas.

Siphany took a hesitant bite. Her eyes went wide. "This is amazing!" The croppygreens were all an even texture, the taste mild but pleasantly flavorful. "Where did you learn to cook?"

Isan shrugged. "I cooked on the Junk sometimes. Mother Junk made me work the kitchens when she couldn't think of anything else to do with me."

"You have a real talent for it," Qas said between mouthfuls. "This is great. You ought to be a chef."

"Really?" Isan said, eyes wide. "Maybe I should. I'll cook more!"

Soon, they were having deep fried croppygreens, sliced and broiled croppygreens, croppygreen soup, and mashed croppygreens, among other things—all fantastic.

Siphany even liked some of the dishes so much that she considered bringing the meat out and turning Isan loose on it.

Qas loved the change to meals. The food picked them out of their doldrums, at least temporarily. They still didn't say a word to Siphany, but they went out of their way to praise Isan for the fantastic job she was doing.

"You really ought to be a chef," Qas kept repeating, to Isan's delight. Every time they said it, Isan preened, drinking their words in as someone lost in the desert would drink water.

Eventually, Siphany asked Lurbira, still trapped in the cockpit, if the previous Isan had been a good cook.

Lurbira laughed. "No. She was terrible. She could burn water. They chased her out of the kitchens because they were wasting too much food. Why?"

"Because our Isan's been cooking now, and she's really good at it. I was wondering if it was something left over from who she used to be."

Lurbira waved a dismissive hand. "Like I said, she's not the Isan I knew. That girl died. This one took her body and face and voice, but she's different. If she wants to do different things, why not?"

"Right," said Siphany thoughtfully. "Why not."

*

PATI WAS ALONE among them in not appreciating Isan's newfound talent. On the rare occasions she showed up for meals, she picked absently at her food and said nothing. Siphany tried talking to her a few times, but she was met only with silence. She had knocked on Pati's door, but when the other woman opened it, clearly drunk, grouchy, and reeking of stale liquor,

Siphany quickly made an excuse and ran away. Siphany spent the following hours in her room, thinking of what to do before the next shift when she had to return to the cockpit.

After, when she saw Pati in the corridor, the other woman studiously ignored her.

Abashed and worried, Siphany stopped trying.

Still, she couldn't get the possibilities she'd sensed at their aborted dinner out of her mind. She often thought about the kiss Pati had given her as she'd left.

What might have happened if the Loyans had held off their invasion for a few days?

*

QAS WAS NO help. They were still angry with Siphany for not going back to Sovena, and they avoided her when they could. Instead, Qas spent their time chatting with Isan, who, after their praise of her cooking, got along famously with them, as they both tended to the engines. Isan was also picking up engine facts surprisingly quickly, or at least that was what Qas said.

To Siphany's immense annoyance, even Kit, the traitorous feline, took a liking to Qas. He followed them around mewing, purring when they picked him up to rub his belly. Kit even started sleeping in Qas's room every once in a while.

Siphany bore it all with ill humor and gracelessness, hissing back at Kit and snapping at a hurt and confused Isan. It felt as though she'd fallen ten years into the past. Everyone liked Qas. It had always been that way. Qas was the bright star, Siphany the dark, forgotten planet orbiting them. The only ones who resisted Qas's pull were Pati and Lurbira.

But Pati was drinking herself to death in her cabin, and Lurbira slowly failing a piece at a time.

Lurbira's legs had ceased to function on the third day out from Derstan, and nothing she tried to repair them worked. She was now a permanent fixture in the copilot's chair in the cockpit, plugged into the ship's power. She couldn't go to meals or the engine room; she had to stay in that chair or risk a critical failure.

Siphany spent long hours talking or just being with her in the cockpit, hiding from everyone else.

But even Lurbira wasn't thrilled with her.

At first, she'd tried to talk Siphany out of trying to find the *Call*. "There's no good reason," she said over and over. "It's a bad idea," and "Serlay can take care of herself."

"You said she was dying," Siphany reminded her the millionth time Lurbira had protested, absently checking and rechecking her shortcuts and calculations.

"Did I?" Lurbira said, sounding far away. "Maybe I did."

"You really don't want to see her again, do you? Serlay, I mean."

"Not really," Lurbira said darkly. "I don't want to see any of them."

"Why? What happened?"

Lurbira shook her head furiously.

"Lurbira, why did you leave the *Call*?"

Lurbira groaned. "Sif, I've probably told you more about my past than I've told anyone else. But please don't ask me about that."

"Okay," Siphany said, a little hurt. "But...we are going to find the *Call*. I'll make sure of it. It's my ship, after all. You can't stop me."

"Why do you care?" Lurbira asked sullenly.

"Because I do. Because…I need to do something for *one* of the people on this ship."

"So you picked me. Even though I don't want it."

"Of course. And…you don't fool me much. You've been talking about nothing else."

Lurbira laughed softly. "Have I been?"

"Every time I come in here."

"Figures."

Kit padded in and jumped up next to her.

"Your cat's a traitor," Lurbira said, petting him with a small hand. "Talking to Qas and all."

"Oh, I know." Siphany checked the location of everyone else. Pati in her quarters, Qas and Isan in the galley. Safe to talk.

"They still angry with you?"

"Qas? Sure. They think I'm a coward, a traitor, and that I treated them badly. Which maybe I did, I don't know. Isan's come around to their view, either because she thinks whatever Qas tells her to think or because she likes being contrary. So now I have two people who are utterly convinced we should have gone to Sovena to be slaughtered."

"She has no idea," said Lurbira. "And Qas is too out of their mind with grief and panic. I think you did the right thing. Believe me, I know what I'm talking about. I'm older than anyone here, and I've seen a lot of hopeless situations. Better not to fly right into one."

"Qas'll thank me some day," Siphany said, though she didn't believe it. "One more person won't make a difference, not there. Not now." She felt a heavy, irritating sadness. Kit jumped down and started pawing her. She refilled the cat's food bowl and set it down. Kit purred happily as he munched.

"Hey, you never know," Lurbira said, trying to cheer her up. "There's other worlds on their side. Maybe they'll find a way to push the Loyans out."

"I doubt it. I don't know. I don't care."

"Sure you do," said Lurbira, grinning.

"I *don't*. Why would you say that?"

"Because you've been talking about nothing else."

Siphany almost shrieked in outrage, but then she ruefully absorbed the hit and started to laugh. Lurbira joined in. Kit looked up from her food, giving them both a supremely feline look that plainly said, *Bipeds are lunatics.*

"The thing is," said Siphany. "I can't take Qas home. I can't do whatever Pati needs. I can't give Isan more than just an escape and a place to cook. And…my old life is gone for good. Nobody gets what they want, not even me. I have to do *something*."

"So you're going to help me."

"I owe you," said Siphany. "Right? That's what you said."

"You do indeed. But I'd rather get paid in money. Or a new body."

"I don't have a lot of money anymore," said Siphany with a sigh. "The repairs ate most of it. I don't have a job, and the bank is back on Derstan. I doubt I even have access anymore. But maybe someone on Redov Station can help you. They must have people there who know something about Artificials."

"Derstan didn't," Lurbira reminded her. "I wish we'd kidnapped Harban. He, at least, would have known how to help me."

"Yeah. He probably would have."

"Hey," said Lurbira suddenly. "If I die before we get there—"

"Please don't say that," said Siphany, feeling a pang of heart-stopping panic.

"Well, if I do," said Lurbira stubbornly. "Just saying, I'm not doing so well. If I do have some kind of critical failure, have…have Serlay hook me into the *Call*'s computers. She knows how. I might get a little extra time that way; I don't know. And if that doesn't work, put me out into space, let me float. I always liked the idea of space burials."

Siphany looked at Lurbira, who looked right back. Her expression was steady and serious, and her static-filled voice didn't waver.

"I will," Siphany promised.

"Do that and we'll be square. Though if you want to do something to help out the other Artificials on Haeld, that's good too." Lurbira opened a panel on her arm and fiddled with something. "Damn."

"What is it?"

"Nothing. Just a misfired nerve. Hurts. Hang on." Lurbira picked at it with a little sharp tool, wincing as she did so. "Ah. Ahh. That's better. You know, dying is shit." There was such bitterness in her voice that Siphany almost started to cry. "I only wish I'd had a chance to have that new body. It would have been great. All the other Artificials have new bodies. I missed out on the first wave of them because I was trapped with an annoying metal ball on my stupid planet. I'll never forgive the colonists for that." She sighed. "You and me, we're trapped by the past. I'm stuck on that old dead planet, and you're stuck in an institution on Sovena."

Siphany nodded. "I know. I know I am. I'm seventeen and there right now, with Qas, waiting for my mother to come see me."

"And I'm walking through empty corridors, wondering when my parents are coming back," said Lurbira distantly. "The past is shit. Memory burns, huh?"

"Yeah." Siphany picked up Kit and giving him a long hug. He mewed in protest. "Tell me about it."

*

PATI HADN'T COME out of her room in a worryingly long time. She hadn't been to eat in at least a day, and no one had seen her.

Siphany, finally ready to admit how alarmed she was, marched up to Pati's door and knocked before she could talk herself out of it.

"Pati? It's me, are you okay?"

No response. She knocked again and waited.

A faint *go away* came from inside.

Siphany almost did. She had before. But this time, she took a deep breath, gathered her resolve, overrode the lock with her captain's privilege, and reeled at the wave of stench.

Pati leaned against a wall, filthy and disheveled. "I said go away." Empty liquor bottles (where had those come from?) lay scattered around her room, along with clothes and puddles of putrid-smelling barf.

"Oh, Pati," said Siphany, her heart breaking. This couldn't be the same strong, brave warrior who had saved her from Mother Junk. Could it? "What did you do to yourself?"

"Sif, fuck off," snarled Pati. "I don't want you here."

Siphany fought every instinct in her body to stay and hold her ground. "I don't care. Pati— *Pati*. This is bad. Come on. I'm going to help you." Siphany tried to steady her wavering voice, hoping her revulsion didn't show too much.

"What, you? I *hate* you," sneered Pati. She picked up a bottle and tried to throw it, but it bounced harmlessly off the ground a meter away from her.

Siphany flinched but told herself, *It's the booze talking. Not Pati. It can't be Pati.*

But Pati continued. "You make me sick, Siphany. You're nothing but a loner who wouldn't know a good thing if it cracked her over the head. You're annoying and weird, and I should never have saved your ass."

"Thanks," said Siphany, smarting but determined.

"Why the hell aren't you gone yet?" Pati cast around for another bottle to empty or throw.

"Because you're my friend." Siphany started picking up clothes and putting them in the laundry chute, then signaled for a cleaning bot to come. A few minutes later one zipped in, paused to take in the situation, and called for a few more.

In the meantime, Siphany helped an unwilling but pliable Pati into the bathroom.

"I'm going to get you out of these clothes," Siphany said patiently.

"Knew you always wanted to." Pati leered.

Siphany shoved her feelings aside and gave her a hard look. "You stink, and they need cleaning."

For a miracle, Pati backed down. "Sorry," she said, drooping.

"Don't worry about it." Relieved, Siphany tugged at Pati's shirt. Pati started to cry as Siphany pulled it up over her head. She threw the shirt on the floor; a cleaning bot picked it up and tossed it down the laundry chute.

Siphany turned on the trickle of recycled water that passed for a shower. "We're going to get you cleaned up."

"I can do it on my own," Pati said sullenly.

"Yeah, but *will* you?"

Pati didn't say anything. Siphany kept undressing her, trying not to think about exposed skin, small round breasts, the curve of her back…

At last, she got Pati into the tiny tub and started scrubbing. Pati shook violently, retched, and threw up again. Siphany hummed loudly, remembering an old trick a med tech on Hydras had taught her about how to avoid barfing—apparently, humming interfered with the gag reflex or maybe just distracted from it—and she kept it together.

Pati leaned into her, letting her scrub, tears running down her cheeks.

Finally, Pati was marginally cleaner. She sat, sputtering and crying, in the tub. "Why didn't you go away? Now you've seen me like *this*. I can't…I just…not like this!"

"It's all right," said Siphany soothingly. "It's really all right."

"I'm so sorry," Pati wailed. "I'm sorry. Sif, I'm sorry."

"You have nothing to be sorry for," Siphany said calmly, holding out a towel.

"I…I couldn't stop them. I couldn't save them. There were so many, so many dying all around me." Pati gulped back racking sobs. "So many died. And I *ran* like a coward."

"You couldn't do anything else."

"I could have *died* with everyone else." Pati hiccupped through her tears. "I could have tried to save someone else."

Siphany cradled the other woman in her arms. "You saved *me*."

Pati sobbed harder. "Thank the gods. Oh, thank the gods above I saved you."

At last, worn out, she put on the clothes Siphany offered.

"I'm so sorry," Pati repeated helplessly, sitting on the bed.

"You going to be okay? Do you need to come stay with me?"

Pati reached out a hand. Siphany took it. "I can stay here. I'll be okay.

I'm out of booze. Three years' worth of collecting, and I drank it all in a week." She broke into a tiny, sheepish grin and was her old self for a brief moment. "I'm the champ."

"You're the champ. Come on. Let me take you to my place for now, at least. The bots are still busy with your room anyway, and you can get some sleep."

Pati gave in, and Siphany led her down the corridor toward her room and narrow bed.

*

AFTER A FEW hours of watching Pati sleep, Siphany felt sure enough she'd be okay. She set up a monitor and fled to the darkened cargo bay, desperate for solitude. Siphany sat next to a croppygreen bed, inhaling the rich scent of the synthetic soil, trying to calm her frayed nerves.

Pati had apologized profusely again before drifting off into a deep sleep, which Siphany was sure she needed. Pati told her that she hadn't meant the awful things she'd said, that, instead, she was grateful. Siphany took it all in, where it sat alongside the bad things and the worries.

But, she reflected, she had done it. Pati was sleeping peacefully in her room. Siphany was sure she'd be better now.

I didn't think I was the kind of person who could take care of anyone else. Maybe that's not true.

Or maybe, she reflected, she could take care of people in short bursts. After all, she was sitting down here in the dark with the croppygreens instead of upstairs with Pati. She had no idea what she'd do if Pati went back to drinking or isolation.

Footfalls. She braced herself as Isan popped her head into the cargo bay. "Siphany? You in here?"

Siphany debated keeping quiet but cleared her throat. "Hi, Isan."

"There you are. Why are you sitting in the dark? Never mind. I was looking for you. Hey, I wanted to ask you about the dried meat you've got hidden in that one locker. Can I use it as a side for baked croppygreens tonight? Or maybe a stir-fry. You like stir-fry, right? Of course you do. Everyone likes that."

"You found the locker," said Siphany, not surprised. "How did you get in?"

Isan gave her a look. "I escaped Derstan's jail, remember?"

Siphany gave up. "Let's go take a look." She led Isan over to the big walk-in locker and opened it up.

Isan started looking through one of the food caches. "Wow, anthorn! How many kinds of dried meat do you have?"

"If you count anthorn as a meat—seven." Siphany only ate three of them, but she enjoyed being prepared for anything.

"Cool. Not anthorn, that's gross, but maybe doban or…beef? What's beef?"

"Something from Sovena. The animal's called a cow, so I don't know why it's not just called 'cow meat.' We all used to wonder that back home."

"Derstan home or Sovena home?"

Siphany winced. "Sovena."

"Got it." Isan reached up, all arms and legs in that skinny teenage way, and grabbed another jar of jerky. She opened it and took a whiff, then made a face and put it back. "Hey, is Pati okay? I saw the cleaning bots going in and out of her room. The door was open. It smelled like something died in there."

"She's…" Siphany didn't know how much to tell Isan without violating Pati's privacy. "She's not doing great. She's a little sick, and I put her up in my room for a while."

"She drank too much, huh?"

"Uh, she, um…" Siphany temporized.

"Her room smelled like booze and barf. We had that stuff on the Junk, right? The Loyan soldiers brought it in. We used to trade with them, and that's what they gave people. So. She leave anything, or did she drink it all?"

"Isan," Siphany said warningly.

"Sorry." Isan grabbed another bag of dried meat and nodded, satisfied. "This one, I think. So, are you two a couple, or what? Qas thinks you are."

"I don't care what Qas thinks," said Siphany, avoiding the question.

"They were all freaked out about Pati drinking. Something about addiction, blah blah blah. What's up with you and them, anyway? Did you used to be a thing? They won't tell me."

"We were together a long time ago. This was their ship originally."

"*That* I knew. They keep saying that."

"I'm not surprised," said Siphany, amused.

"They're pretty mad at you still."

"I know."

"Is it your fault or theirs?"

Siphany shook her head. "It's…history, really. Both our faults."

"You should talk to them. They're really nice once you get past the fact that they think they're amazing at everything."

Siphany hid a smile.

"So you and Pati," said Isan. "You two seemed pretty into one another back on Derstan. You're a couple, now, right?"

Siphany shrugged. "I'll let you know as soon as I figure it out."

Isan nodded and started to walk away, meat in hand.

"Isan?"

Isan turned. "Yeah?"

"How are *you*? You seem so different these days."

Isan stared at the floor, eyes closed. "I know," she said softly. "I'm…I'm trying to grow, but all I know is the bits and pieces *she* left me. The old Isan. I don't know who I am either."

"I…" Siphany had no idea what to say to that.

"I said no to her, Siphany. I said no to Mother Junk. She wanted me to keep you confined. She didn't want me to escape the prison. She wanted me to come back with her to the Junk. I said no."

Siphany's eyes went wide. "Isan…"

"I'm sei. I'm not just an algorithm riding a corpse. I'm self-aware." She screwed up her face, then turned and stormed off. "I hate it! I hate it!"

After that, Siphany saw next to nothing of Isan. Food was cooked, meals appeared, but Isan herself vanished.

When she told Lurbira about it, Lurbira laughed weakly.

"So she's sei. Good for her. Maybe…"

"Lurbira?"

"I should have been nicer to her," said Lurbira. "Damn. Tell her…if you see her, tell her to hang in there. It was hard for me; it'll be hard for her. But she'll get through it and be stronger. That's what Harban told me once."

"Okay," said Siphany, touched. "I will."

They both sat in silence for a long while as Siphany maneuvered them to yet another shift point.

"I just want to get there," said Lurbira, sitting limply in the copilot's seat. Her voice was small and far away. "Avorna…"

"I know." Siphany grabbed Lurbira's hand. "Soon."

"I can't feel it when you do that anymore," Lurbira said, static obscuring her words.

Chapter Thirteen

SIX WEEKS OF rapid, dangerous shifting brought them past the isolated outpost of Redov Station to an area of space very few mappers had ever bothered with. Siphany brought the ship to a halt, scanners searching.

Nothing.

Things on board the ship had quieted down. Pati had stayed with Siphany for a few chaste nights in Siphany's narrow bed—while Siphany slept in the cockpit or on the floor—before decamping to her own room.

Pati was more her usual self, but there was something missing from her easy banter. She seemed only half there. She rarely met Siphany's eyes, and she tended to make excuses whenever Siphany wanted to talk. They had touched and hugged in the beginning, but less so now. Siphany missed it, but she had no idea how to get it back.

Their relationship seemed even less clear than before.

Siphany finally started talking with Qas again, but they, too, were distant and standoffish. Sometimes, they walked the corridors of the ship with Pati, talking about patriotism, addiction, and other things. Pati seemed calmed by them.

Isan stayed out of Siphany's way, spending time with Qas and by herself in the hold with the croppygreens. Sometimes, Siphany would find her in the cockpit, deep in conversation with Lurbira. Siphany usually left them to it, but sometimes, she would catch bits and pieces. Words like "Avorna" and "Serlay" featured often. Lurbira was telling Isan about herself. Siphany fought down an unwelcome pang of jealousy and walked away.

Siphany asked Lurbira about it once.

"Isan's lost," Lurbira explained weakly. "I don't think I can help much. Maybe, Sif…maybe you…"

"I'll do my best," Siphany promised.

"She's realizing something. If she ever breaks like me…no one can fix her. Her implants are Pelagarine…"

And Pelagar was nothing but a cinder orbiting a merciless sun.

"I understand," said Siphany. "I'll make sure she stays safe."

"Heh," said Lurbira. "No such thing in this universe."

Outside of it all, the war ground on. There wasn't much news, but Siphany got the sense that things were very, very bad.

*

BY THE END of the journey, Lurbira had gone from bad to worse. Her systems were steadily shutting down. Qas even tried their hand at working on her, but they got nowhere.

"She's too damaged," they explained. "Parts need to be swapped out wholesale, and we just don't have them. I doubt Redov does either."

"There must be something you can do," Siphany pleaded.

Qas shook their head. "I wish. I'm sorry, Sif. I know you care for her."

Now, Lurbira sat, insensate, on the seat next to her. She moved her head with a disturbing grinding sound.

They were in the right place. The coordinates Lurbira had given her for the location of the *Call* were correct. But the sensors, maddeningly, continued to show nothing.

"Lurbira, you're sure this is where we're supposed to be?" asked Siphany.

"The ship…here. Search. May be out of power. Drifting."

"Can you give me more direction than that? Can you hook us into the transmissions?"

"Stopped transmitting…days ago."

Qas groaned. Siphany winced. If it had stopped transmitting, it could be just a power failure. Or there could be no ship here to find.

"All right." Siphany programmed in a search pattern. "If it's here, we'll find it. I promise."

Lurbira tried to say something, but it was lost in static, and she gave up. Siphany hoped against hope that whatever was out here could help fix Lurbira. Lurbira had lived on the *Call* for years. They had to know how to fix her. This Avorna person had apparently worked on her before. Maybe she could help.

Or maybe, Siphany thought worriedly, there really was nothing out here to find. Maybe Lurbira's mind had degenerated along with the rest of her.

In which case, there was no hope at all.

Siphany brought her mapping-grade sensor tower up to maximum. Power levels sagged worryingly low. The past six weeks had consumed far too much fuel, and power had never been quite the same as before they'd been hooked up to a Junk and then hit with Pati's missiles. The ship needed further repairs that Siphany simply couldn't afford.

"We'll do a mapping sweep," Siphany assured her. "That's what this ship is made for. We'll find it. I promise."

Lurbira simply looked away, out at the stars.

*

"WHAT DO WE do if it's not out here?" Qas asked as they sat around the table, eating another surprisingly tasty stir-fry Isan had whipped up. "You have to admit, it's a possibility. For one reason or another—"

"I know," said Siphany shortly. "We're doing a sweep. We'll find it, or we won't. If we don't, we'll go to Redov, like we planned, and see if anyone can help Lurbira from there. At the very least, we'll be safe from the Loyans."

Qas hunched down, not willing to say more. Silence hung in the air.

"They won't be able to help her, will they?" Isan asked, saying what everyone was thinking. "If we don't find this ship, Lurbira's going to die."

"Isan," said Siphany, trying to fight the awful black hole of grief that thought filled her with. Why did she care more for Lurbira than she had for anyone in the past ten years? How had her heart become so open? How had she possibly been able to get so close to a random, rather hostile, and sarcastic Artificial?

"We owe her this much," said Pati, eyes intense. Pati had come alive again. "She's part of this crew. She's Siphany's friend. We have to help her."

"We will," Qas assured her. "Whatever it takes."

"Thank you," said Siphany to the two of them. "I mean that."

"Okay," said Isan distractedly. "What if this ship doesn't have the equipment to help her though?"

If I do die, Lurbira had said. *Have Serlay hook me into the Call's computers. I might get a little extra time that way. And if that doesn't work, put me out into space, let me float.*

Then that would be it.

*

SIPHANY SAT IN the cockpit, closely monitoring the information streaming in on the sensors. Still nothing. This whole sector of space was nothing but the usual vacuum and microasteroids and various gases. No ships. Not even a sign a ship had ever been here.

Siphany resolved not to give up. But inside, she was already starting to let go of Lurbira.

Everyone else had gone to bed. Lurbira sat next to her like a lump of scrap metal. Her eyes were closed.

"Lurbira," Siphany said, voice barely a whisper. "I wanted to say thank you. You saved my life a couple of times. You rescued me from the Junk. I don't know why you did what you did, but I want to thank you for it."

Lurbira opened her eyes slowly. "I did it because I wanted to," she said with a little smile.

Siphany's sensors suddenly flared, then went dark again. Her fingers flew over the console as she tried to pinpoint what had happened. "What was that? What *was* that? Off at 120 by 51 degrees—I'm focusing in that area. It was like this huge power surge—where *is* it?" She played back the sensor log and showed it to Lurbira. "Is that it? What was that?"

Lurbira stared at it. "No," she whispered, and she sounded afraid.

Siphany had no time to process that. At that moment, something vast slid past her extended sensors, far out in deep space. If not for the surge, she wouldn't have seen it for days.

She halted the automated sweep and refocused on the object, hardly daring to hope. It was drifting, and—

Faint power signature. Heat, deep within. Almost undetectable, but definitely *there.*

"Lurbira," she breathed. "I think we found it."

*

SIPHANY PILOTED HER ship up to the vast object. Well before they got there, she was certain: this was Lurbira's ship.

The *Call* was massive, bigger than any ship she'd ever seen that wasn't a spacecraft carrier. The design, graceful, all curves and flowing lines, had an intensity about it, a determination in the construction. She had never seen anything like it.

Qas, Isan, and Pati crowded into the cockpit for a silent, awed look.

Here, Siphany thought, was the hope of a dying world drifting in deep interstellar space.

"They aren't responding to our hails," Siphany said as the searchlights played over the surface of the *Call.* "I am reading something, maybe life signs, but very faint. We're going to have to go over there and see for ourselves."

"That's gonna be fun," murmured Pati. "Damn. Look at that thing."

Siphany maneuvered carefully around the ship, looking for a way in. Finally, they found a dock on the starboard side, but it was a different fit from what her ship was used to. Fortunately, there was also a docking bay, open to space, nearby.

This ship had been expecting visitors, then…or had seen its crew all leave.

"Right. Let's take the Junker ship. I think we can all fit." Siphany gently detached Lurbira from the power cables. Lurbira sagged. "Pati? You're the strongest. Can you help me carry her?"

"I can try." Pati helped Siphany lift Lurbira up, then staggered. They had to put Lurbira back down again. "She's too heavy!"

"I'll help," said Qas.

"Me, too," Isan assented.

The four of them lifted Lurbira together, bearing her in silence down to the waiting ship.

*

THERE WAS ONLY a single EV suit. Siphany kept it in case of an emergency, and she'd donned it for this mission.

"When we get there, I'll see if I can repressurize the bay," Siphany said. "Sensors show there's atmosphere and a little bit of power in a pocket over there. Maybe I can close the doors and let some air in."

"We'll wait here," said Pati. "You sure I shouldn't go out and do it? I'm armed."

"I'll be all right. The suit's too small for you anyway." Pati was about a head taller than Siphany.

Pati grinned. "Shorty. Fine. Take this though." She passed Siphany her pistol. "Ever use one of these?"

Siphany shook her head, examining the pistol closely, testing its weight. She'd never imagined herself holding one, much less firing it. Her ship was her weapon. This was more…personal than she was comfortable with.

This was like Lurbira's way of doing things.

"It's easy," Pati was saying. "Point the business end at the threat. Got it?"

"Got it," Siphany said queasily.

*

THE *CALL* FILLED the front screen, illuminated by the little ship's lights.

"There's the bay," said Siphany.

"How many people lived on this ship?" asked Qas. "It's huge…"

"Lurbira said the crew wasn't that big, maybe thirty or so," said Siphany distractedly. "I don't know why it's so massive."

Siphany gave her craft a little bit of extra speed and then cut the engines, coasting them into position with maneuvering thrusters.

"You're good at that," said Pati. "Oughta be a fighter pilot."

Siphany flushed, bobbing her head to show she'd heard. They settled down on the deck plates with a dull *thunk*.

The bay itself was completely empty; whatever had been here was long gone. Had pirates or scavengers found this ship? It was possible. There were probably pirates out this far.

"All right, we're in," Siphany said. "I guess I should go check things out."

"Don't go too far," warned Pati. "Damn. Wish I'd kept my own suit.

Left it aboard my ship."

"Well, you didn't think you'd need it," said Siphany absently, fighting back butterflies. There was something about the thought of a huge, empty, mostly dead ship that gave her the absolute creeps. "I'll be back soon."

She put her helmet on. The seals locked, air circulation began, and her heads-up display appeared. "Testing radio and suit camera."

"We can hear you," Qas's voice echoed tinnily through her helmet speakers.

"I can see myself," Isan exclaimed, peering at the display. "Wow. That looks so familiar."

"Suit camera works," confirmed Qas.

"Right. I'm going."

"Got your gun?" Pati asked.

"Oh," Siphany said, wincing. She'd hoped Pati wouldn't notice. She took the loaded pistol from on top of the console where she'd left it. "Thanks."

"Good luck," said Pati. "Don't get eaten by space monsters."

"That helps." Siphany stood, made her way back to the airlock, and cycled through.

*

THE SHIP'S GRAVITY was different from what she'd expected, but it was definitely there. And yet, her suit sensed no power running through the floors. Maybe they had some other way of creating artificial gravity that her people didn't know about.

My people. This ship had been built by a completely different type of human. The other human worlds in this arm of the galaxy had cut themselves off from Earth a millennium back when the mother planet's expansionism and authoritarianism had descended into a centuries-long civil war. The last few contacts had ended in bloody disaster, and after that, the various governments of the Mid-Perseus Arm of the galaxy had decided to cease contact with the Orion Spur and Earth.

Earth was prohibitively far away, backwater, and violent, the thinking ran, so it was better to just stay away. Everyone here had avoided it for a long, long time, and in all that time, these people and her own had become aliens to one another. This design was so foreign to her that it barely seemed human at all.

Siphany found the entrance to the bay. Once again, the door was open, a control panel next to it. She tapped at it; nothing happened.

"This isn't working," she said. "There's no power to any part of the bay. I'm going farther in."

"Be careful," Pati warned. "You don't know what's in there."

"I'll be fine," Siphany said and stepped out of the bay into the rest of the ship.

Darkness enveloped her. Her suit lights illuminated the way forward, and she made her way through the pitch-black halls toward what she hoped was the heart of the ship. The faint ghost of heat, power, and atmosphere beckoned ahead.

Gradually, her fear ebbed away as she moved through the vast network of corridors. The life signs had been faint and clustered near the heat source. The darkness grew welcoming and comforting, and she fell into a pleasant trance as she walked through a space where nothing and no one else was.

"Siphany?" Isan's voice startled her out of her reverie.

"Uh. What's wrong?"

"You're humming. It's annoying."

Siphany could hear Qas chuckling in the background.

"Sorry," she said, embarrassed.

*

THE *CALL* SEEMED endless. It seemed to Siphany as though she had been walking for kilometers, up one flight of stairs, down a corridor, backtrack, go this way and that. The logic of the ship's layout escaped her.

There was nothing on board the ship, no signs of any recent habitation. Siphany found colorful mosaics on the walls, much like she might have expected to find at Derstan, but they depicted places and events she couldn't conceive of. Many of them were too different in style for her to make sense of, but the ones she could decipher were all of war and its aftermath: smashed cities, hopeless refugees. Why had the crew of the *Call* put these on their ship? Wasn't it depressing to them?

Maybe they wanted to leave a record of their civilization. In case they didn't make it. They wanted the people who found them to know who they were.

It had worked too. Here she was, tracing a gloved hand across the tiles, reading the stories there. Division. War. A terrible aftermath. A sad, quiet peace among the survivors. A race to save the ancient homeworld. The launching of this ship.

Through it all, a slender thread of hope ran. *It's worse than it's ever been,* the mosaics said. *But we will survive somehow.*

Siphany pushed onward. The pocket of life was just ahead.

She'd noticed that a lot of the bulkheads were two sets of doors with a human-sized space in between, like an airlock. This ship had been designed to fail just like this, then. Battleships were built in much the same way.

Who was to say this wasn't a battleship?

At last, she reached a closed bulkhead with a single dim green light. Siphany hesitated, then pressed it. A bulkhead door behind her shut, and air, pressure and heat whooshed in. The lights activated, and Siphany had to muffle a shriek of alarm at the sudden bright pain.

The door slid open.

The room was spacious but full of clutter, with equipment scattered everywhere and what might have been consoles and screens all along the walls. None of them displayed anything, and the consoles were dead.

And yet, someone had been living here too. There was a bed and a table and what looked like the remains of food.

In the center of it all was a chair, and in that chair, a frail, gray-haired woman sat, motionless.

I'm too late, Siphany thought with a shock. But as she approached, the woman opened her eyes and smiled.

"I'm taking the helmet off," said Siphany and released the seals.

"*Qash do Serlay Call*," said the woman.

"What? Serlay? Oh! You don't speak—um."

"*Seva yo intangan te?*" the woman said impatiently.

Siphany shook her head. "Sorry. I don't understand. I'm Leshandre Siphany. We're here with Lurbira Call."

The woman's eyes opened wide, and a broad, relieved grin spread across her withered features. "Lurbira," she breathed. She hit a few controls.

"Siphany, the bay doors just closed, and there's atmosphere and light here," said Pati through her helmet radio. "I think there's air in some of the corridors too. Is it safe? Can we come to where you are?"

"Yes," said Siphany. "Bring Lurbira. I found her captain. She's alive."

*

SIPHANY WAITED WITH the captain, neither of them quite able to look each other in the face, while the others made their way through the ship.

The room smelled musty, as if the air filters weren't working properly. The readouts were all in an alphabet that seemed vaguely familiar yet alien at the same time. Were those power indicators? Sensor displays? The symbology was all wrong. She had no way of knowing what any of it was, and she gave up.

Siphany tried to think of something to say, but the language barrier remained firmly in place. She contented herself with sitting in one of the chairs and smiling at the woman, who scowled weakly back. Serlay Call's age was difficult to tell. She had somewhat lighter skin than Siphany's, and wispy gray hair that hung down past her shoulders, but she was badly emaciated, her cheeks sallow and her eyes hollow. Still, she might have been less than fifty.

So much to ask, so much to wonder…

"Where's the rest of your crew?" Siphany asked aloud, more to herself than the captain since Serlay wouldn't understand. "Where did they go?" She looked at the captain of the *Call*, who sat slouched, waiting in her chair. "Your crew." She pointed at the empty stations all around the control center. "Where?" She shrugged her shoulders and looked around.

Serlay nodded in understanding. "*Sha vo*," she said, and then, quite distinctly, "*Haeld*."

Siphany actually laughed. Of course. "Haeld?" she asked,

incredulous. "Your crew. Haeld."

Serlay nodded. "Haeld."

"Amazing. Lurbira will never believe it."

"Lurbira." Serlay put a hand over her heart. "*Ado ya verya. Se?*" She pointed at Siphany. "*Dono yo vera shever namyanbu? Lurbira so ado?*"

Siphany thought she caught the meaning. She nodded. "Lurbira." And she touched her own heart. Serlay Call's eyes grew soft, and she nodded ever so slightly.

There was a noise from outside, and the airlock began to cycle again. The others were here at last.

*

ISAN SAUNTERED IN first, followed closely by Pati and Qas, who pulled Lurbira on a float pad.

"Lurbira!" Serlay struggled to her feet, a question in her eyes. She spoke rapidly in her language.

Isan frowned. "My implant doesn't translate her."

"It wouldn't. Her language isn't loaded," Siphany said. "She's from Earth."

"Right," Isan said. "Right."

Serlay had taken hold of Lurbira's hand and towed her, along with Qas and Pati, over to one of the stations at the room's perimeter. She found a power cord and plugged Lurbira into it.

Lurbira's eyes fluttered open. "Serlay," she whispered. "Oh, it is you. I came home. You…were calling me."

Serlay said something only Lurbira could understand.

"Figures," said Lurbira. "Well…here I am anyway. So let's make the most of it."

*

LURBIRA HALTINGLY TOLD them how to access the language files they needed for their implants. It turned out the *Call* had had extensive dealings with their people before, so they had records of many different languages available. Serlay waited as they loaded.

"I don't have an implant, though," said Siphany. "And neither does Qas."

Isan rolled her eyes. "Sovenes."

"No kidding," said Pati. "You two really do need to get them installed."

"Actually," Qas said after a moment's hesitation. "I do have one."

"You do?" said Siphany, aghast. "*You?* How? You're okay with that? The government allows that?"

"They paid to install it," Qas said, sweeping their hair back from their delicate features. "It pays, off Sovena, to have one. The intelligence services looked for people who didn't mind having something like that inside them."

"And you don't mind?"

"Well." Qas shrugged. "It's for the job. So I did it."

"You wouldn't do bluenet, but you did this?" said Siphany, still reeling. Qas flushed. "Qas—"

"Sif…" they said, then cleared their throat. "You still need a way to translate."

Lurbira said something to Serlay, who held up a finger and opened a nearby drawer filled with what looked like patches covered in sticky tape. Before Siphany could say anything, Serlay slapped a patch on her temple.

"Hey!" Siphany's brain felt like someone had reached inside and given it a squeeze. "Ow!"

"There," said Serlay Call in her own language but now perfectly comprehensible. "Can you understand?"

"Yes," said Siphany, shocked. "What did you do?"

"It feeds directly into your neural network. Adds a few nanites to translate." Serlay ripped the patch off, and Siphany cried out again in pain and alarm. "Should be fine now."

Feeds into neural network. Adds nanites. Her body was *different.*

Siphany thought she might be sick. "Uh. Oh no."

Qas put a steadying hand on her shoulder. "For Lurbira," they whispered. "Stay calm."

Siphany fought nausea and panic and nodded rapidly.

"How is our Lurbira?" asked Serlay, ever so slightly stressing the "our." She had, even in instant translation, a very arch and dry manner. "What happened to her?"

"She was hit with a bolt from a plasma rifle," said Qas. "She was falling apart before this, but the plasma made things an awful lot worse."

Serlay Call shook her head slowly, sadly. "I warned you, Lurbira, that you'd come to a bad end if you left before you were ready."

"Sh-shut up," croaked Lurbira. "Old hag."

"Foolish little mechanoid," said Serlay fondly. "We have very few of your old parts here, but I may be able to help you a little."

"Ah…"

"Yes?" Serlay said, leaning in.

"Avorna," whispered Lurbira. "Where…"

"Avorna went with the rest of the crew. None of them are here. I put them off the ship quite some time ago."

"And where was that?"

"Sh-she said it was Haeld," said Siphany, still shaking slightly. This woman had changed her body…

"You're joking," said Qas.

"No," Serlay said. "When the time came, I put the crew off on the distant world of Haeld. They're there still, as far as I know."

"Lurbira was on Haeld. So was I, for that matter, and so was Qas." Siphany breathed a little more easily now. *For Lurbira. For Lurbira.*

"Then you must have missed them," Serlay said humorlessly. "They are hidden."

Lurbira rasped something, and Serlay leaned closer to hear. "I…wish I'd never come home," Lurbira hissed.

Serlay's eyes brightened. "I've missed you. I'm glad you came, even if you aren't."

"Why…*why* did you call me? I told you not to…"

"Because this ship is nearing the end of its life, and I wanted to see you before I and it died."

"B-bullshit," croaked Lurbira. "You have all the sentimentality of a pipe wrench."

"Do I?" Serlay seemed amused by this. "Hm. How about this, then. I wished to test your resolve. I have an important mission for you."

"You have no such thing."

"Well. That one's only half true. Lurbira, if things had been normal and ended the way I foresaw, I wouldn't have called you. I know you wanted to stay away, and I respected that. Whatever happened between you and Avorna, I left it alone. It was never my place to step between mother and daughter."

Lurbira glared at her.

Mother and daughter. Siphany shared a glance with a wide-eyed Isan.

"You want to know why I brought you all this way?" Serlay said, leaning forward. "It's because I saw the Whale. It's out here. And I want *you* to chase it down and bring it back to me."

Chapter Fourteen

"WHAT WHALE? WHAT'S she talking about?" Qas asked Siphany.

"Something Lurbira told me about once, back on Haeld," said Siphany. She scratched at her head as if that would get the nanites out. She swore she could feel them crawling around in there. "Something Serlay said she saw when she was a girl."

"You know about it, then," Serlay said. "Good, that makes things simpler. Lurbira, I'm surprised. Confiding in someone isn't at all like you."

Lurbira laughed weakly. "Your Whale's in *space* now? It's a whale, Captain, it's not a spaceship. You…I can't believe it. You called me all the way out here because your tiny mammal brain is oxygen deprived."

"It is not," Serlay said evenly. "The Whale is machine, and it is more. I know what I saw. My mind is keener than yours and always has been. You shouldn't forget that."

She sat back down in her chair and made a motion in the air. A panel flickered to life, hovering in the air in front of her. Siphany's eyes widened. That was something she could use on her ship.

Serlay entered a command, and a holographic screen winked into being at one end of the control room.

"These are my sensor readings," said Serlay. "I still had active sensors at that time. Now I only have power enough for passive receptors, so it's impossible for me to see this again. Watch." She entered another command.

At first, it seemed like a normal image of deep space. Then, when Siphany was certain nothing was going to happen and they were going to have to pretend they'd seen the captain's imaginary friend, *something* slid silently into view.

It gave off no light. It generated very little heat. But it had a distinct shape, and it moved quite unlike any ship she'd ever seen. It seemed to undulate and writhe in the vacuum, but it still had a fluid sort of grace.

Siphany felt the hairs on her arms stand on end.

"The sensors suggested it was both organic and machine," said Serlay into the sudden silence. "Alive. And I believe it is intelligent as well."

Everyone, even Isan, stared transfixed at the screen.

"You…you created this," Lurbira said dubiously. "You made it just to show to us, to make us believe."

"I did no such thing. What you're looking at is the raw sensor log. There is much more if you wish to examine it."

"What is it?" Pati asked, waving a hand through the display. It shimmered slightly as her hand passed through. "Is it an alien ship?"

"No," said Isan, eyes bright. "It's an alien *alien*."

"There are no aliens." Qas looked around, a confused expression on their face. "Right?"

In all the ten thousand years humanity had been in space, there had never been so much as a hint of any other intelligent species. The galaxy was full of planets and all kinds of life, from here in the Mid-Perseus Arm to the Orion Spur to the far-flung colonies in the Centaurus Arm, but no other species had ever been sei or, in human terms, sentient or self-aware. It had long been settled science that aliens simply didn't exist.

Siphany stared at the image on the screen. It was unlikely to the point of absurdity.

And yet, there it was.

"It came to find me." Serlay Call closed her eyes, lost in the moment. "It spoke to me again. Lurbira. You remember the story I told you long ago?"

"I do," said Lurbira, expression blank and unreadable.

"I know it was the same Whale. But I also believe there may be more of them."

"I don't believe it," Siphany said. "That…that can't be true. We would have found them."

"There is much more to the universe than what your people can see or sense," said Serlay primly.

"Please." Lurbira's voice dripped with static-y sarcasm. "Just because you see mystic signs and evil spirits in every asteroid and dust cloud. Just because…because…"

"You never could accept anything or anyone beyond your own self." Serlay turned in her chair to fix Lurbira with a hard stare. "I first sent the signal a year ago. I've been waiting ever since for you. Where have you been?"

A year? Siphany wondered.

"I don't owe you anything," Lurbira said. "When I left, I *left*. You're lucky I came at all."

"I am shocked you did, frankly," said Serlay.

"We had to drag her," said Isan unhelpfully. Siphany shot her a glare. "What? We did!"

Serlay nodded. "I assumed as much. Though I am glad you have friends now. Maybe you aren't so hopeless after all."

"Hey," said Siphany. "Lurbira's amazing. She's saved my life, and she's a good friend."

"They even stick up for you." Serlay raised an amused eyebrow. "Interesting."

"Why me?" Lurbira asked at last. "Why not call Avorna, or Brasna, or even Viernan? Anyone else from the crew would care more than I do."

"I left no way to contact them."

"You *what?*"

Serlay seemed to consider her words carefully before replying. "The separation wasn't…entirely voluntary on their part."

"You forced them off," said Lurbira. "Of course you did. Why?"

"I came out here to either accomplish the mission or die trying. They deserved better than that. It was my mission and my failure."

"What was your mission?" Qas asked.

"To find a way to help my people, of course," said Serlay haughtily. "Earth is finished; we need to either find a way to reverse the damage or evacuate. The few worlds of the Orion Spur long since turned their backs on us, so they wouldn't help. We came here looking for science to help us or, perhaps, a new world to colonize. But there is no planet willing to take on fifty million refugees, and no one is willing to help bring them all here in any case. So, we've failed."

"I'm sorry," said Siphany, feeling helpless. But Serlay waved her away.

"I was certain we would fail. And once things become truly dire, I'm sure some of the local worlds will help at least a little. The old grudges die so hard, but they will die in time."

"Did you say fifty million?" asked Qas. "I thought Earth was supposed to have a population of *billions*."

"It did, once." Serlay cast her appraising eye on Qas. "You're an interesting one. A pretty boy or a handsome girl?"

"Neither," said Qas, shoulders sagging.

"Ah. I like the people here, Lurbira. There are so many different ways to be. On Earth, all we could do was survive and no more. We had no space to explore who we were. I think you know something about this now. So. When the Whale came, I contacted you because you were the one I *could* contact. My engines are dead. My power is failing."

"You could have put out a distress call," Lurbira protested. "There's a station not too far from here; they would have picked it up."

"I wanted to see you again. I'm so tired. I only wanted you to come home and see that I didn't make it up, that story. I know you thought I did." Serlay gestured at the frozen sensor image on the screen. "You see? I was telling you the truth about the Whale."

Lurbira sighed and sagged into her chair. She looked so much smaller, more frail. Around her, the *Call*'s power flickered and faded.

Siphany decided they had to do something to help. "Qas. Can we hook our power into theirs? Can we tow them to Redov?"

"I have no idea. The systems may be too different." Qas glanced at Pati.

"We can try," Pati said with a shrug.

"Let's try," said Siphany. "Captain, do you need medical attention? My ship has a full medical lab, well-stocked."

"I'm fine," Serlay assured her.

"Bullshit," Lurbira croaked from her perch. "She's sick as hell. Earth's medicine is awful compared to ours. You see how she looks. Sif, drag her to the med bay if you have to."

"I will not leave my ship," Serlay said, something like panic in her eyes.

"Captain, respectfully, you may need more help than we can give you on your ship," said Qas. "At least let us bring you to ours for a short while. I promise you; we'll bring you back."

Serlay raised an eyebrow. "You make *such* a convincing case. I am fine here."

"I bet you can't walk. Am I right?" Lurbira said, her voice close to taunting. "I recognize that slouch."

"We can bring a float pad," said Siphany. "Isan? Pati? Would you go get one?"

"Sure," said Pati, obviously glad for something to do. She grabbed a reluctant Isan out of the control room. "C'mon, kid. Let's go."

The door shut on Isan's protests.

"Qas, see if we can feed them power," said Siphany. "And we'll see if we can tow you."

"I don't remember asking for any of this," said Serlay.

Siphany folded her arms. "You're right. Do you want me to stop them? We can just leave if you like."

"Yes. Anything is better than leaving my ship."

Siphany knelt beside her. "I know how you feel. My ship is my home. It's…like my body and soul."

Serlay nodded a little.

"I wouldn't want to leave, either, in your position. But…let us help. You called Lurbira, and now we're all here. Let us do what we came for."

"And what did you come here for?" asked Serlay.

There were so many answers. The war with the Loyans. Avoiding Sovena. Simply having a direction to go in. But what Siphany said was "Friendship. And loyalty."

Serlay remained silent. Then she pursed her lips, looking resigned. "Do what you will."

"Good. Qas, get on it."

Qas nodded and headed out.

"You must be the captain," said Serlay. "You play the part well. So much of leadership is theater, I find."

"Ah, um…" Siphany wasn't sure what to make of that. "Yes, I'm the captain. Qas is going to see about power for your ship. But in the meantime, while we wait for that float pad, you're going to tell me how I can fix Lurbira."

*

"THIS MUST FEEL comforting to you," Qas said some time later. Qas and Siphany walked through the dim corridors of the *Call*, the way to the main reactors illuminated by low, ghostly lights.

"It does," Siphany said. "Nice and dark. Too cold though."

"I looked through some diagrams. I think I can get the power hookup to work, though it'll be tricky. If I can't, at least we can tow the ship to

Redov. How's Lurbira?"

"Serlay said she would access Avorna's old notes. Apparently, she wrote extensively about Lurbira. Their people don't have anything like Artificials; Avorna found her fascinating. It makes sense. Imagine never seeing something like her. I hope her notes will be full of things we can use."

"Right." Qas took her hand, and she stiffened, surprised. They smiled at her, the old grin. "I was proud of you. Making decisions, figuring out what to do. You've really grown up."

Siphany dropped their hand.

"What?" Qas asked, confused.

"I don't want your pity." she told them, her voice hard and bitter. "Or your condescension."

"Sif, it's not like that."

"And I don't want you to patronize me either. Please, Qas."

"I meant it," they said, eyes wide and sincere. "I *am* proud of you. I never thought you'd get here. I probably should have, but—"

"But what? You left? You *left*." She stumbled over the words she'd wanted to say for so many years. "You just *left me* there, alone on that ship, with nothing to do. I had no idea what to do with myself. My whole life was all about you. And then—"

Qas took her hands in their own again. They were the same height, the same build. Qas's skin was a little lighter, their hair a bit finer, but at times, the two of them had been taken for siblings.

"I know," they said softly. "I'm trying to say I'm sorry. I made a lot of choices I regret. I shouldn't have just left you. I was young, and foolish, and I panicked. I couldn't face you to talk it out like I should have. I always wanted to go back and do things right so it wouldn't have been so terrible for you."

"How nice of you," Siphany said coldly. But inside, she melted a little, and she let them hold her hands a little longer.

"You have to admit, though, we weren't going to last. No matter how much you might have wanted us to. We wanted such different things out of life."

Siphany shrugged. She did know that, though she didn't want to admit it.

"I wanted to go home. I felt so aimless and homesick without Sovena. And you would never have come with me. Sovena was only a prison to you, not a home. We both knew that. When I left…it was for the best. We would have made each other miserable."

Siphany stared at the ground. "I missed you. Every day for years after."

"I missed you, too. When you showed up on Haeld…I was so happy to see you. I want to put things right again. And I *am* proud of you. Really."

She let herself look into their eyes for a long, long moment, then took her hands away, out of their grasp.

"We…should find the engines," she said, walking quickly down the hall.

Qas fell in beside her but didn't say a word.

"This is the engine room, according to the map," Siphany said when they'd arrived at a wide door at the end of the corridor. The door was open, and the lights were a little brighter inside.

This allowed them to see the little red and white pieces of paper hung all over the room. Symbols were written on each one, and statues and what might have been abstract pieces of art covered every flat surface atop the machines and shelves.

"What are *these*?" Siphany asked, bewildered.

The intercom crackled to life. "That's Viernan's collection of good luck charms, hexes, and assorted bullshit," came Lurbira's tinny voice. "See, I told you these people were superstitious."

"Lurbira," Siphany exclaimed. "Are you fixed?"

"No, not even close." Lurbira didn't sound too happy. "I'm sitting in a chair in the control room, *completely* unable to move. But Serlay figured out how to hook me into the ship's computer because it was the first thing in the notes, and she could make Isan do it for her."

If I do die, have Serlay hook me into the Call's computers. And if that doesn't work, put me out into space, let me float.

"Isan and Pati are back?" Siphany asked, fighting terror and panic.

"Yes. Isan brought me on the float. Pati's downloading Avorna's notes. They're going to bring them back to our ship along with Serlay. I scanned her once I got in here, and she could use some help. Good for you for forcing her to go to your med bay. She's stubborn to the point of being suicidal about it."

"How are you, Lurbira?" Qas asked.

"Oh, fantastic," Lurbira said sarcastically. "My body's useless, I'm locked into this damn computer, and I feel completely, utterly fine. Perfect, in fact."

Siphany grinned, relieved. Same old Lurbira.

"Sorry I asked," Qas muttered.

"I'm just glad to hear your voice again," Siphany said. "How bad is the damage to your systems?"

"Hardware's fucked. You're in the engine room, so I need you to look around for my spare parts. Avorna had a cache of them somewhere in there, but I don't know where."

"Is it urgent? We're working on connecting our power to the *Call*'s."

"I'll be all right for a little while. But I hate being inside the computer. I don't feel like me. So…soon?"

"Okay," promised Siphany. "We'll get to it as soon as we can."

"You have changed," said Qas to Siphany. "You used to panic in situations like these."

She closed her eyes and fought the urge to deck them. "Yes. Because I have a panic disorder. Of course, I panicked in situations like these. And for your information, I'm *still* panicking, I'm just better at controlling it now."

"I'm sure," Qas said gently. "It's only that you seem so calm and collected now. That's all I was saying. You're doing well."

"Right," grumbled Siphany. She remembered now how constant their affection could be when they were interested in her. She'd basked in that attention before, but now?

Now, she didn't know what she felt, except that she wanted to do anything but try to figure it out. "We should get to work."

"Sure," said Qas cheerily. "Whatever you want, boss."

Siphany set her jaw and resolved to get this done as soon as possible so she could go somewhere and be alone.

*

FIVE GRUELING HOURS later, Siphany and Qas had to admit defeat. The power systems were too different, and Qas was certain that designing and building a converter with what little they had was beyond them.

"But Lurbira's hooked into the power system," Siphany protested.

"I have a converter built in." Lurbira's voice came through the engine room's speakers. "Avorna and Viernan made it for me. It took them weeks and weeks, and it still doesn't work that great. I can handle it, but I don't know if either ship could."

"Why didn't you tell us that five hours ago?" Qas asked.

"Must be malfunctioning," Lurbira said, gloating.

"Lurbira!" said Siphany.

"Sorry. Nah, I forgot. And maybe I was hoping you'd be smarter than them. If you want to come take a look at this thing, be my guest. But I don't think it'll be a lot of help."

"We'll have to tow the *Call*," Siphany said with a sigh. "We might be able to reverse engineer something, but it would take too much time. Qas, you know how the clamps work on our ship. Head back and get it ready."

Qas hesitated, then nodded sharply and marched off. Siphany sat down, exhausted, in the middle of the foreign engine room. Nothing was where it should have been. Everything worked backward. The people who'd built this ship had had a completely different mindset from people in the Mid-Perseus Arm.

It was maddening, but Siphany also had a grudging respect for that. Thinking at things sideways could lead to interesting results.

"You okay, Sif?" Lurbira's voice came through the intercom.

Siphany started at the sudden noise. "Don't do that!"

"What else am I supposed to do? Did you find my spare parts?"

"No. We looked, but they don't seem to be here."

"Great," said Lurbira. "You okay? You don't sound so good."

"I'm all right. Just...I need a minute."

In response, the lights lowered, the heat came on, and a very soft flute melody played over the speakers. Siphany breathed a sigh of relief and sank to the floor. "Thank you," she said to Lurbira.

After a moment, she recognized the song, an old Sovene tune. "Where did you get this?"

"It's you," said Lurbira. "I recorded a lot of stuff. Thought it might help."

"This is me?" But, of course, it was, she realized after a few more bars played. She knew her own music. It surrounded her, enveloping her in a protective cocoon of familiarity and routine. "That helps, Lurbira, thank you."

Lurbira didn't say anything; she just let the music play until Qas called, startling Siphany out of her reverie, dragging her back to work.

*

THEY MET IN the shuttle bay.

"I can attach us, but the usual airlocks don't line up, as we found out," said Qas. "What we'll do is clamp on to the side in alignment with their engines so we can push them. It'll cost us in fuel, and shifting will become very tricky, but we should be able to get them to Redov Station."

"Lurbira will have to stay here, says the captain," Isan said. They'd finally managed to take Serlay over to their ship, where she was crankily waiting for them in the med bay. "She's connected to things, I guess?"

"She can't stay on her own," said Siphany, worried that they'd come back and find her…gone. "Someone will have to stay with her."

Silence.

"I'll do it," Siphany amended.

"You sure?" Pati asked. "It'll get lonely."

"Oh, Siphany doesn't mind lonely," said Qas.

Siphany shot them a look. "I'll be fine. Lurbira will be with me."

Pati looked a little hurt. "Let me know if you want company."

A part of Siphany wanted to take her up on it. But right now, she needed the time alone. She'd pushed herself too much over the past day and was close to her breaking point.

"I will," Siphany said. "I promise. But right now, I'm fine being alone. You should go take care of Serlay and yourself. Okay?"

Pati didn't look happy about it, but she agreed. Siphany would stay on the *Call* with Lurbira.

*

THEY HOOKED UP the ship to the *Call* and set a course for Redov Station. Siphany retrieved a few things from her own ship, including her wooden flute, and made herself at home on the dark, empty *Call*.

Empty, of course, except for Lurbira.

"This is crap," she said through the speakers as Siphany made sure the sections they'd been in were secured again. "I've mentioned I hate this computer, right? I was trapped in it for a week once before."

"How come?" Siphany asked, manually shutting a door. Every little bit of power mattered now.

"It was a long time ago, when I first came aboard. They were trying to access my memories of Lurbira. The planet, not me. They didn't care about *my* memories."

"Not even Avorna?"

Lurbira didn't say anything for a while. Then, "That was before I was really sei. Look. I just don't like being hooked into this thing. It feels cold and awful and wrong. I don't want to be a computer. I want to be me."

"I get that." Siphany still wasn't happy about the translator nanites running around in her body. "Hopefully we can get you out of there soon."

"Yeah, we'll see. But I'm not counting on it. Hey, Sif?"

"Yes?"

"Thanks for staying."

"Always," said Siphany, meaning it.

*

THEY WERE UNDERWAY at last. Siphany had shut down power to everywhere but the control room to save what little energy the *Call* had left; the engines weren't running, but they still needed basic navigational deflectors, which absorbed more power the faster the ship went.

Six days to Redov, Qas had said. That was good. She could center herself before anything else happened, and hopefully Lurbira wouldn't get much worse.

Time passed. Siphany spent her time talking to Lurbira about nonsense or walking the empty, dark corridors of the ship in her EV suit.

And, gradually, Lurbira began to tell her stories.

The people from Earth had been so strange to her, at first. They didn't understand her, and their experiences seemed utterly foreign to her. Worse, Lurbira was still mindlessly following the program the colonists had left her with, struggling to become self-aware.

The only one willing to give her even the barest chance was Avorna, the first officer, who took her in.

The two of them had lived in a single room, and Avorna soon found herself fixing and studying Lurbira's systems as they traveled their haphazard route through the former colonies of Earth, begging for contact and help.

One planet after another turned them away. Earth was a curse. Nobody wanted contact with a ghost. No one wanted to invite trouble. Those planets that accepted their presence would not or could not give them any help beyond a vague promise of assistance should any refugees actually arrive on their doorstep—all the while knowing that was impossible.

Time was running out, and everyone on board knew it. Earth had maybe fifty years of useful life before it became completely uninhabitable for humans. The crew hoped against hope, they worried as they worked, and deep in their hearts, they grew more certain with every planet they visited that their mission had no chance of success.

Avorna told her a secret once. There was a way to bring all the people of Earth to a colony world, or so Serlay had said. Not even Avorna knew what it was. But if any planet had said that they were willing to grant enough land and resources, the people of Earth would have come. Somehow.

But no planet would do this. There were too many people on the habitable planets, so there was no room.

It was hopeless, and the crew despaired as they drifted from one unwelcoming world to the next.

This was where Lurbira had become sei and grown up.

She told Siphany stories of the crew, how they'd been to her, how she'd learned to interact with them, and how she'd begun to grow beyond her original programming. Avorna had taught her logic and kindness, Viernan had taught her to fight, Brasna had taught her to follow her passions, and Serlay… Serlay had taught her stubbornness and pride, even in the face of certain defeat.

Siphany listened intently as she combed her way through the darkened ruins of the ship, wondering about the people who had lived here when everything was bright.

*

SHE WANDERED THE upper decks, tracing her fingers along the wall mosaics. The emptiness of the place was barren and sad, the remnant of something that had once been alive and vibrant. It felt so different from the comforting emptiness of her own ship. Siphany had filled her ship up with herself. This was more like a ruin, or a grave.

One time, Lurbira's voice crackled through Siphany's suit speakers. "Turn right. Go into this room."

She hadn't been able to open the doors of any of the crew cabins, but a little bit of power trickled into this door, and it slid open.

"Lurbira. We needed that power."

"Just go in."

Siphany entered, shining her suit lights over the clutter. Lurbira was silent, but Siphany could sense her full attention. This was important, somehow.

The room was spare, but homey and lived-in. There was a bed, a table and chairs, and a work bench piled high with papers and models. She looked through the papers and picked up the models, wondering at a people who were so advanced and yet kept things in physical form. The paranoia of those who had lost everything, once.

Siphany shone her light on one of the larger sheets of paper and sucked in her breath.

It was a detailed schematic of Lurbira. Everything was neatly labeled in the strange loopy alphabet of Earth, with lengthy notes next to each major system.

"This…is where you and Avorna lived," said Siphany.

"Yeah," said Lurbira softly. "This is home."

The long, narrow room had a big bed at one end and another smaller bed at the other.

"A bed?" asked Siphany. "Is that yours?"

"She thought I might want to sleep. I wish I knew why she kept it. A lot of my stuff is still here. Look. To your left. Your other left. Down. Yes. Yes! Pick that up."

Siphany picked up a small, floppy object that, on closer inspection, turned out to be a very rough doll.

"She made that for me," said Lurbira. "Can…you bring it up to me?"

"Sure."

"Why did you keep these things?" Lurbira whispered to the ghosts in the room. "Why? After everything I said…"

"Sometimes it's hard to let the people you love go," said Siphany, thinking of how she'd kept Qas's room the same as they'd left it for so long.

She slowly made a circuit around the room. Here and there were pictures of a woman with light bronze skin, pin-straight dark hair, and lively eyes. "This is her?"

"Yeah," Lurbira said.

"Do you want me to bring you one of these as well?"

"No," said Lurbira roughly. "I remember what she looks like."

Siphany picked one of them up anyway and kept shining the light around.

"That work bench," said Lurbira as Siphany shone her light on it. "That's where I woke up. She would work on me there. A lot of my current design is hers."

"I can see that."

"She would read to me," said Lurbira, lost in memory. "We'd sit on her big bed, and she'd read me pieces of technical journals. I thought it was boring, but that was her life."

"How long did you stay with her?"

"Seven years."

Lurbira had left the *Call* more than a decade ago, Siphany thought. And yet Avorna had kept everything.

She wondered if her own room at home on Sovena was so well-preserved. She doubted it, somehow.

If it was even still there, and not a pile of rubble.

"I'm running low on power and air again," Siphany's EV suit had a very limited range—but it would recharge itself over time if she didn't use it.

"Okay, come on back," said Lurbira, disappointed.

*

YELLOW WARNING LIGHTS were flashing on her suit monitors by the time she got back to the control room.

Siphany set the doll in Lurbira's lap and placed the Artificial's hand over it. Lurbira's eyes tracked her motion, but her body didn't move.

"Thank you," she said, using the intercom instead of her own untrustworthy voice. "You brought the picture. You didn't have to. I do remember what she looked like."

"I don't have any pictures of my own mother. I just thought you might like it. Someday."

"I do like it. Thank you."

"Lurbira? Why did you leave?"

"I told you; I don't want to talk about that."

"I'm sorry." Siphany began removing her EV suit. "I shouldn't pry."

"I was stupid," Lurbira said softly after a few minutes had passed. "We'd…we'd been drifting apart. I wanted more than just this ship. I hated the mission. I thought they were idiots. I wanted new experiences! I wanted to see the galaxy, and not from the window of a ship. I wanted to go do things. We were over Haeld when it all came to a head. I went down to the planet with Avorna and Brasna because they trusted me. But Avorna and I got into a fight. I told her some awful things. I blamed her for how I felt. I blamed her for trapping me in a life I didn't want anymore.

"And then…I met Harban. This next part's pretty bad."

"I'm listening," said Siphany.

"I mean it. It's bad, even for me. I'm no angel. I've done lots of awful stuff, but this…"

"Go ahead," said Siphany, putting a hand on Lurbira's head.

"I…stole the cache of gold Brasna had brought from Earth to try to bribe the locals into letting us settle there. It might have worked too. Haeld's different from a lot of planets. They welcome outsiders who don't want to tell them what to do. But I took it. I told Avorna that I hated her, and I never wanted to see her again. And then I left."

"Oh, Lurbira," sighed Siphany.

"I spent the money on upgrades and repairs, stuff Avorna couldn't do. I paid it all to Harban. And then I went into freelancing, doing whatever for money. That was ten years ago." Her voice began to break up. "I'm sorry, Siphany. I know what I am, but I wouldn't blame you for hating me."

"I don't hate you!" said Siphany, surprised. "Oh, Lurbira. I wondered if it was something like that."

"She kept my things," said Lurbira, her voice soft. "She kept my things. I never got to tell her I was sorry."

"You'll get the chance," Siphany promised.

"No," said Lurbira. "I don't think I ever will."

She went silent, then, and didn't speak for a long, long time.

*

SIPHANY STOPPED GOING out into the ship. Her EV suit could recharge from its own batteries and by slowly absorbing light, heat, and air from the atmosphere around it, but she didn't want to push things.

She kept in touch with her ship. From what she could gather, things were a little tense over there. Pati resented the fact that Qas was high-handedly acting as captain in Siphany's absence, and Isan was desperately trying to moderate. There was always a pile of minor decisions for her to make and fires to put out.

Siphany missed her ship. She missed the bays and carpets, the soft cockpit seats, Kit, and the croppygreen beds. It really was the only place she'd ever really thought of as home.

She started spending time staring out the viewports. One time, she was sure she saw something out there in the deep. A massive shape moved in an undulating wave alongside them, far away but distinct. Then she blinked, and it was gone.

The Whale, she thought, placing her fingers on the cold glass. *Maybe it is real.*

*

THE FIRST SIGN of trouble was the beacon coming from Redov Station, which they detected as soon as the next to last shift was complete. Siphany was playing her flute in the control room when the signal came through from her ship. It was Qas, looking spooked.

"The beacon from Redov's changed," Qas said, their voice unusually high and tight. "I'm sending it through to you."

Siphany tapped her console. The beacon signal text came through.

REDOV STATION GREATER LOYAN STATIONBUND MEMBER

"Oh, no," she said softly. The Loyans had beaten them here.

"What do you want to do?" Qas was clearly approaching panic. "We can't carry the *Call* with us all the way back to Sovena or anywhere else."

Siphany worked it through in her mind. "We need to find another neutral station. We might be able to make it to Duronava Mining Station, but it'll take us two more weeks."

Pati slid into view. "Hey, Sif." She looked neater and more together than she had in a while. Her hair was now long, brown, and curly, and she'd changed the color of her eyes and the size of her mouth. Maybe having a mission was good for her. "I've been trying to pick up war news, but most channels are blocked. It's hard to know what's going on out there. There's no guarantee that any other station won't be in the same situation as Redov."

"We could try docking," said Siphany uncertainly. "Maybe they'll be willing to help us if we pay them." She shoved the thought of just *how* she would pay them out of her mind.

"No," Qas objected. "That's *not* a good idea. I'm a Sovene citizen, and Pati's a member of the Derstan military; they'll probably throw us in a prison camp."

"We don't know the whole story," Siphany countered. "They may not have a Loyan military presence. And…we can't stay out here forever. We have to make port. The *Call* is running out of power and time."

"We'll have to ditch the *Call*," said Pati. "Sif, come back aboard. We'll leave the *Call* here and run for another station, try our luck there."

Siphany shot a guilty look back at Lurbira. "Serlay will hate it."

"She'll have to come to terms with it," said Pati. "We can come back for the *Call* later."

Siphany drummed her fingers absently on the console. They wouldn't be able to come back, she was sure of it. Not with the Loyan cancer spreading across all of this part of the Pegasus Arm.

Nothing was working out. Lurbira was still broken. The *Call* was a floating wreck. They had no safe harbor. Loyan was advancing everywhere. She was out of cash.

Her life, so secure only six months ago, had been shredded.

Siphany fought down the impulse to hide under the console and start crying. She had to think clearly.

What would Lurbira do?

No, maybe that was the wrong question. What would Qas do?

That didn't work either. And she knew what Pati would do…

What would *Siphany* do?

She took a deep breath.

"Can we actually disconnect Lurbira from the *Call*'s computer?"

"I'll die if you do," said Lurbira through the intercom, speaking for the first time in days. "My systems are completely nonfunctional. This ship has no usable spare parts. You may not be able to revive me."

"What?" Siphany said, aghast. "You didn't tell me that!"

"Can we revive you if you're dead? Can we hook you into our computer here?" Qas asked.

"I don't know," said Lurbira distantly. "I don't think so."

"We—we have to risk Redov, then," said Siphany. "Pati and Qas will stay aboard the ship. There's no other choice."

Just then, Pati's face changed. She jabbed at something on the display that Siphany couldn't see.

"Oh, hell," she said.

"What?" Siphany asked. "What *now?*"

"A scout ship," said Pati, eyes wide. "It just shifted in. It's…heading this way. It's a Loyan military scout."

Before Siphany could respond, a transmission broke in.

"*Attention foreign ships! You have entered Greater Loyan space without authorization; please stand by and prepare to be boarded.*" The bored-sounding male voice had a clipped Loyan accent.

"They shouldn't have this ship," Lurbira said softly. "Earth had many, many weapons that we don't. The *Call* has a few of them still on board."

"You never said that either," Siphany said hotly.

"I'm saying it now. It'll be bad if they have this ship, trust me."

"They'll arrest us," said Pati. "Qas and I will be taken prisoner, at the very least."

"Get aboard your ship, Siphany," said Lurbira. "I can start the self-destruct sequence."

"Then you *will* be killed. And there's no way we can bring you back!" Siphany said, horrified.

"I know," said Lurbira.

"No. *No.* Pati, my ship has good weapons, you know that."

"Yeah, but not *military*—"

Siphany cut her off. "It's only a scout. Can we hurt them?"

Pati tapped a few buttons. A wicked grin spread across her features. "We can sure try."

"Yes!" Qas said fiercely.

"Want us to do it?" Pati asked. "It's your ship. Your call."

"Do it," said Siphany without hesitation. "Detach the clamp and drive that scout ship away, however you can. Then come back, and we'll get out of here together. If you can't—then you have to shift away."

"And leave you here defenseless? No way. Unless you're coming aboard?"

Siphany shook her head. "How would I? And don't worry. Lurbira and I can come up with something. Just go if you need to. That's…that's an order."

"Aye-aye, Captain," said Pati, snapping a salute. Then she shoved Qas out of the pilot's chair. "Get your ass below, Qas, and make sure the engines don't blow up. Isan go with them." She whooped with an unholy glee that Siphany found very unsettling. "Guns, guns, guns! Damn, Sif, this is great. Come on, you Loyan bastards! Time to fuck 'em up!"

"Fuck 'em up," Lurbira echoed weakly. "Burn their asses out of the sky."

*

SIPHANY PACED THE control room of the *Call*. She'd dimmed the lights even further, allowing her to run a screen showing the situation.

Her poor ship seemed hopelessly slow compared to the sleek efficiency of a military scout.

They won't be expecting my level of weapons, she thought desperately. *It'll be a surprise.*

I hope.

"Loyan ship, we are preparing to come up alongside." Pati's voice came through the speakers.

"*Acknowledged. Please remain where you are. Power down your weapons at once.*"

"Right, will do," said Pati.

At that moment, a bright white-hot plasma beam lanced out of Siphany's ship. There was a long moment as it crossed space—then it pierced the side of the scout, sending the other ship rocking back, spewing debris.

"Yes!" Siphany shouted, leaping to her feet. *Oh please, please! Let us win!*

"Eat shit!" shouted Pati through the speakers as she fired again.

A flurry of plasma blasts arced out into space. The scout ship, damaged but still moving, neatly evaded them.

Then the scout ship launched dozens of missiles at Siphany's ship.

"No!" cried Siphany, though the comm was off, and they couldn't hear her now. "Pati, countermeasures!"

Hatches opened, and a little blizzard of countermissiles flew into the vacuum. Siphany held her breath as they came together.

Lights flashed as the ships traded shots. Missiles slammed into countermissiles.

One got through.

There was a sickening orange flash. Siphany's heart stopped.

"We're hit! Losing engines, Qas! Qas! Get us—"

The transmission cut off.

"They're moving in for the kill," said Lurbira softly.

"This ship has weapons," Siphany said. "You said it has weapons!"

"If I fire, we'll have no power left. No air, no light. I—"

"Fire! I'm getting into my EV suit. Just do it."

"So much death," said Lurbira sadly. "I've…I've caused so much death."

Siphany frantically pulled on her EV suit, not hearing what Lurbira was saying through the sheer panic and desperation. Her ship was reeling, spitting fire. Pati, Qas, Isan, Kit! She twisted the helmet on, and green indicators came to life all around her head. "Fire! Lurbira, now!"

"I'm so sorry. Firing," whispered Lurbira.

There was a whining buildup of power in the ship, and then a crackling red ball of energy spat forth from the *Call*'s belly, rocketing toward the enemy scout.

The scout ship evaded. The ball followed.

The scout ship fired countermeasures—the ball absorbed them.

And then it struck—

The scout exploded in a silent ball of orange and red.

"Ah!" said Siphany, falling to her knees with relief. Safe!

The viewscreen flickered and vanished.

"What?" Siphany exclaimed.

"Power shutdown," whispered Lurbira. "Goodbye, Siphany."

They were plunged into cold blackness as Siphany realized what she'd done.

*

SIPHANY SAT NEXT to Lurbira's lifeless body, resting a gloved hand on hers.

You will survive. You have to. Pati will come. You'll survive.

She was desperate to know what was going on outside.

Had Pati been able to save her ship? Had anyone been hurt or, worse, killed? Had another scout ship come?

The other ship hadn't made contact. No one had tried to come for her. She began to fear the worst.

Maybe Pati had been able to shift away somewhere. Maybe that was for the best…

As time wore on, Siphany slowly lost hope.

*

"I SHOULDN'T MAKE decisions," she said to Lurbira. "It's only led us all to disaster. I've done nothing but choose the wrong thing from the moment I saw that Junker ship."

Lurbira said nothing. The computer was dead. The power plant that ran both it and her was completely out of juice, shut down forever.

"And I guess this is where we end up, you and I," Siphany said. "All of that, just to end here alone in space. I'm sorry things went so badly for you. I'm sorry about all of it. I miss hearing you right now. I…I'm sorry I didn't say goodbye. I should have."

She squeezed Lurbira's hand. "I'm sorry it was all for nothing."

*

THE AIR METERS in her suit were getting lower and lower. Siphany shut off the dim light of her suit, leaving nothing but thick, oppressive night around her.

"I don't think they're coming back," she said, holding on to Lurbira's hand. She could barely feel it through her gloves. "I usually love the darkness, but this isn't comforting. This is death."

Her heart beat loudly in her chest. Every sound of the suit was amplified now. She thought she glimpsed things moving out there in the darkness, but they disappeared.

"I'm glad of it all," she said, just to hear herself talk. "I'm glad I met you. I'm glad I fired on that stupid ship. I'm glad I met you, and I'm glad we were friends. I haven't had a real friend since Qas left. I wish it had turned out better, but I wouldn't trade any of it."

Siphany put a gloved hand on Lurbira's face. "Qas was right, you know. They were right about me." She laughed. "I'm so scared of anything changing, of making the wrong choices. But I wouldn't give any of this away. I don't know what I mean, anymore. I think I just want to live. If I can't have what I had back, I want something new. I just want to live…"

She listened to herself breathe, if only to convince herself that she was still alive. She clutched Lurbira's hand harder. "Lurbira," she whispered. "Please talk to me. Please come back."

*

TIME PASSED BY either fast or slow, she couldn't tell anymore. Her air meters went from green to yellow to orange to red.

She began to see things as the air began to choke her. Her mother's face hovered in front of her, saying something she couldn't quite hear. Qas and Pati sat on a chair, kissing each other and looking at her seductively. Lurbira, a little human girl instead of herself, ran freely around the control room, jumping on the chairs and giggling. Swirls of color appeared everywhere in Siphany's field of vision. The walls melted; the floor opened up…

Then the visions faded, leaving her in the dark again.

Leshandre Siphany waited for death.

*

COME TO THE window, a little whisper said.

"Haa," she said, feeling weak and lightheaded. Her air meter was deep red. Not long now.

Leshandre Siphany. Come to the window.

Another hallucination, another vision.

Her power levels were so low. But it hardly mattered now. Why not go to the window?

Maybe she could die looking at the stars. It was better than this awful blackness. Siphany turned on her light and gave Lurbira a final hug.

"Goodbye, Lurbira," she said. "I'm going to go look outside."

Lurbira just sat there, inert. The light of Siphany's suit glinted off the exposed chrome on her face.

Siphany woozily walked across the control room to where the door to Serlay's tiny office, with its viewport, loomed open.

She felt like she was floating. Her head swam with every step.

There. There! Little pinpricks of light and color lay ahead. They weren't just sparks in her vision; she was actually seeing them. Her spirits lifted, and she stumbled up to the window.

"Hello, stars." Siphany pressed her helmet against the window with a little *clunk*. She breathed in and out, her breath fogging up the faceplate.

She looked around in all directions, taking the stunning, cold beauty of the stars in for the last time. Finally, she looked straight ahead to where the stars vanished behind an ever-growing dark shape.

"Hello out there," she whispered.

Hello, Leshandre Siphany.

The shape grew and resolved into a massive, long head attached to an impossibly long body. Was there an eye, a mouth? She couldn't tell.

"You," Siphany said, awed, taking in the size of it.

The massive creature swam through the vacuum until it filled the viewport. A ghostly gray light emanated from it. She could see that it was made of metal, of rock, of plastic, and other things she couldn't identify.

"What are you?"

I am the sei of Earth.

"I…have no idea what that means," Siphany said, her head spinning. She felt drunk and sick. "Have you come to keep me company while I die?"

No.

Instead, the Whale opened what had to be a mouth, hundreds of kilometers wide, and *breathed* on the ship.

Siphany screamed in pain as the lights snapped on.

Chapter Fifteen

"SIPHANY. SIPHANY! WAKE up! Take your helmet off. I can't do it for you. Please. Siphany!"

Siphany groaned. Her head felt like someone had caved her temple in with a sledgehammer. Something beeped incessantly in her ear, and red lights flashed in front of her.

"Lurbira," she rasped. The inside of the helmet smelled musty, and she could barely breathe. "You're…alive…"

"Siphany, take off your helmet! The atmosphere's fine."

"I…"

"Do it," Lurbira commanded. "Raise up your arms and twist. Now!"

Clumsily, her arms feeling like lead, Siphany did as she was told. She flopped her arms forward, grabbed the sides of the helmet, and wrenched it to the right. There was a *hiss*, and she sucked in a lungful of cool, sweet air. She immediately started coughing.

"Siphany!" Lurbira voice came through the intercom. "Oh please, please be all right."

"I'm here," she said, coughing. "I'm all right." She felt dizzy, but better with every breath. "What...how is this possible? You're talking to me. The lights are on." They were, in fact, all the way on. The air, fresh now, moved freely, and the *Call* was fully lit.

Did I die? Did I imagine all of that?

Siphany stood, wobbling, and made her way out to the control room.

Lights blinked on consoles. The viewscreen in front displayed their position. Alien alphabets scrolled across screens everywhere.

"I don't understand," she said helplessly.

"We have full power in all reactors," said Lurbira through the speakers. "We were out of fuel for them, but now they're completely full of energy."

"But...how?"

"That thing out there," Lurbira said, awestruck. "You saw it, right? It's not just me?"

"I did. It...breathed on us."

"And we got our power back. I have no idea how. It's impossible."

"Was that Serlay's Whale?"

"I think so," said Lurbira, laughing wildly. "I really think it was. Fuck! She was right. I hate that."

Siphany couldn't contain herself. She slid down next to where Lurbira sat in the chair and howled with laughter.

"I thought you'd died," she gasped, tears pouring down her cheeks. She still couldn't stop laughing. She had no idea what was so funny. "I thought I was going to die. And...and..."

"We're here," said Lurbira. "We're alive. Serlay will never believe it."

Serlay. Siphany scrambled to her feet in a panic. Pati, Qas, Isan. *Her ship.*

"Lurbira, scan for our ship," she said. "Is it out there? Oh, please let it be there."

"Hang on. I'm…yes. Yes! I see it. It's drifting. I think…Sif, it's very badly damaged."

"Set course." Siphany would not give up. Her friends could not be gone. "As fast as you can. Get us there!"

*

THE DAMAGE WAS worse than even she had imagined. More than one missile had gotten through, she could see, as the *Call*'s sensors mapped out the destruction. The missiles had completely obliterated her mapping sensor array. She gasped, heart breaking, at the massive hole gaping in the side of the hold. And where the engines were supposed to be…nothing. *Oh, no. No, no, no.*

"Pati, are you there?" Siphany spoke into the communicator. No response. "Lurbira, are there life signs aboard?"

"Yes," said Lurbira, and Siphany's heart leapt. "All clustered together in an interior room. Huge parts of the ship are open to space, but remnants of atmosphere are there."

"All of them?"

"I think so."

Siphany breathed a sigh of relief. If they were alive, there was hope. "Can we get over there?"

"Now that we have full power, I can see that we have a working shuttle in one of the bays. Charged and ready to go now. Handy!"

"There's other bays?" Siphany asked, agog. She'd had no idea. "And a shuttle?"

"Three shuttles, in fact. The *Call* is well-equipped. I'll light your way. I can guide the shuttle from here, too; the panels might not make any sense to you. The shuttle has at least a dozen EV suits in it, so you should be able to get everyone out of there."

"Good. You're the best, Lurbira." Siphany paused. "How…how are you?"

Lurbira laughed, low and strange. "I was dead, and now I'm not."

"You didn't have to do it, you know."

"Do what?"

"Fire the weapon. You didn't have to. You knew it would kill you, didn't you? And you fired anyway."

"I knew it would kill us both, most likely," said Lurbira.

"It nearly did."

"Yeah."

"Thank you," said Siphany. "You saved them."

"It was the only thing to do. And…I heard what you said. I recorded it all. When we were in the darkness."

"I didn't know that," said Siphany, flushing.

"Um…Thank you. For being my friend."

Siphany grinned, tears filling her eyes. "Always."

Lurbira laughed roughly. "Sif. You are such a sap. Now get to that bay, damn you. Quick, we're almost there!"

*

HER SHIP HAD been utterly decimated. Scorch marks, punctures, and debris were everywhere. There'd barely been room in her shattered cargo bay to land the shuttle. Even the little Junker ship was cracked open and useless now.

Siphany clomped through the ruins, looking for her friends.

Beds of croppygreens lay scattered everywhere, plants with croppygreens still on them frozen in the vacuum, dead. Her carpets were scorched and stained, and too many cabins stood completely open to space. Behind her were the twisted remains of the engine room, which had nothing at all beyond it.

Siphany could never repair the ship, not now.

She picked her way through the debris from the cargo bays, passing by the gaping hole where the engines had been. She spied something purple in the wreckage; she knelt to examine it. One of her cleaning robots, crushed and lifeless. Siphany ran a gloved hand over the shattered surface of the bot, tears welling up in her eyes.

Have to keep going. Crash later. Move now.

She stood, feeling wobbly, and made her way to where Lurbira said everyone was—the medical bay. Of course, it made perfect sense. The whole med bay was designed to be a single self-contained unit. There was even an airlock.

Siphany cycled the doors and stepped in, afraid of what she'd find on the other side. They might be fine. They might be ripped to shreds, only barely alive.

Air hissed in, and the doors opened.

Pati leapt to her feet, pointing a gun at her, screaming something.

Siphany held her hands up and activated the external speakers. "Pati!

It's me! Don't shoot!"

*

THEY WERE ALL, miraculously, mostly okay. Qas had some pretty bad burns, but they were otherwise intact. Isan had retreated to where Serlay lay when things had gotten rough, and everyone else had fled here when the missiles hit.

Even Kit, poor little scared cat, was here and alive.

"Siphany," Isan exclaimed. Kit writhed and wriggled in her lap.

"Sif…" Qas said numbly. "We thought you were the Loyans."

"Nope. Come on," she said, chucking the EV suits on the floor. "Put these on. We're going back to the *Call*."

"Trade one slow death for another," muttered Pati, looking disheveled and defeated again.

"Oh, no," said Siphany, grinning. "No, the *Call* has full power again."

Serlay struggled to sit up, suddenly alert. "What did you say?"

"Full power. We have full power. Serlay, a…the *Whale* came. Lurbira and I both saw it. It *breathed* on the ship, and now we have power again. I don't understand it, but it's true. You'll have to come see for yourselves."

"I knew it. I knew it." Serlay shook her head. "Wish that damn Whale had shown up sooner than this. But I'll take it. Siphany, bring me back to my ship, please."

"Put on the suits. Serlay, you can fly the shuttle if you're up to it."

"I am." Serlay's eyes were full of fierce passion. "Of course I am."

Siphany put down the pressurized box she was carrying to use as a cat carrier and took a very confused Kit from Isan's arms. "C'mon, baby. We're going to a new home, okay?"

Everyone grabbed what they could: food, clothes, cat litter. When they were done, Siphany took a last long look around as they filed out of the med bay, trying to remember everything just as it had been.

Then she led them out of what was left of her ship and back to the newly reborn *Call*.

*

THEY GATHERED IN a sea-green conference room, marveling at the kaleidoscope of colors and textures on the floor and furniture. It was as if someone had decided to turn the entire ship into art.

Serlay perched on her chair in the middle of it all, still frail but with a new, bright determination in her eyes. She sat straighter, and her gaze was sharper, more focused.

Siphany, on the other hand, felt numb and exhausted. She fiddled with her fingers while Serlay talked.

"We are leaving the area," Serlay was saying. "We've been given a rare gift—a second chance. Fortune is strange and wonderful. But we must take advantage of the blessing of the Whale. The Loyan scout ship will be missed. They likely transmitted their coordinates. More will follow."

"We ought to be able to hold them off," Pati said. "This ship has incredible weapons."

A shadow passed over Serlay's face. "I prefer not to fight. Our weapons…were not intended to be used, except in the gravest of circumstances. Most people aboard this ship didn't even know they existed. Lurbira only learned about them when she had access to the full computer archives."

"You're welcome, by the way," said Lurbira through the speakers.

"Fine," said Qas. "Then we leave at once. What about Siphany's ship?

Do we tow it? Try to repair it?"

"Repair what?" Siphany said bitterly, and Pati visibly winced. "You ejected the engines. My hull is open to space. There's nothing left to salvage."

"I'm sorry," said Pati softly.

Everyone around the table went quiet.

"I don't blame you," Siphany said, glancing up at Pati. "You did what you had to do. They wouldn't have survived otherwise."

"It's your call, Siphany," said Qas.

She could feel everyone's attention still on her. All she wanted to do was curl up and hide, but no. She had one more thing to do.

"Lurbira remembers what I said to her, back when I thought…when I thought…um… I've been making decisions, and very few of them have turned into anything but utter disaster."

"That's not your fault." Qas protested.

Siphany held up a hand, silencing them. "I know. But it's still the truth. I know what the decision should be. But…" She got up and walked over to the window. Far away, her ship drifted, lifeless and ruined beyond saving.

Her home. She thought of her carpets, her cargo bay, her mapping sensors, her weapons, her low lighting, the croppygreen beds, the seats in the cockpit, the way the ship felt when it was cruising, the way it *smelled…*

"What if I need it again?" she said helplessly. "What if I never find another home like that one?"

"Then you don't," said Serlay impatiently, jerking Siphany back to reality. "What matters is finding a home at all. Sometimes, you don't get a choice in that."

Siphany nodded, stung. "I know. I know. You're right." She gritted her teeth and made the choice. "We leave my ship. We can't tow it, and we can't stay here."

"We can try to salvage some things from it," said Qas quietly. "Whatever you want, Sif."

"Like what? Some frozen croppygreens? No. We should just go. I'm…I'm the captain of that ship over there, and I say we leave her."

She sagged against the window, shaking with exhaustion and grief.

Serlay nodded approvingly. "Lurbira," she said to the air. "Plot us a course out of this area. Shift to another location in the direction away from Redov Station as quickly as you can."

"On it," Lurbira said, her voice surrounding them. The engines, far below, boomed to life. Stars began to slide by.

Siphany looked out again. Her ship drifted to the edge of the window and then was gone.

Goodbye.

She turned and saw everyone watching her, pity and compassion in their eyes. Qas had bandages all over their arms and body, and Pati and Isan were filthy and worn. But their love still flowed to Siphany because they knew her.

Suddenly, her grief seemed like such a small thing, considering what they'd just gone through. She was alive. Lurbira was alive. Qas and Pati and Isan were all alive. Even Kit had made it through.

She'd loved her ship; it had been her home for a decade. But she'd never named it. She hadn't ever felt the need.

Maybe she could go on after all.

"Sif?" asked Qas.

"I'm okay. Really."

Pati stood and crossed quickly to her, enveloping her in a hug. Qas's arms were around her a moment later, and she let herself sink into the embraces.

"The question now is where we are going next," Serlay said, and the three of them separated. Serlay looked annoyed. "I'm told this station was one of the only remaining possible ports, now that all of your worlds are at war. How typical of humanity."

"Yeah, and now Loyan has this station too," said Pati. "The Loyans are everywhere. How the hell'd they come up with this many ships to send? They must have ten thousand ships at this point."

"Is that possible?" Qas asked. "I don't think Sovena has even a third that many."

"In the end days of the war over Earth, each of the dozens of sides had a hundred thousand ships," said Serlay tonelessly. "The *Call* was originally one of them. It was found, intact, by Avorna and Brasna, and we repurposed it. But it was only one of so, so many."

"All that from one planet?" said Pati, eyes wide. "Your people must have done nothing but make ships."

"This is true. But by the end, there was nothing left to make ships from, and no shipyards still standing. So we fought with guns, then with rocks and sticks. And then we fought with disease, starvation, and fire. And then everything came to an end, but still, we tried to kill one another." Serlay looked at each of them. "Only when nearly all of us had died, and our planet was poisoned beyond repair, did we bother to make peace. Your people are making the same mistakes. It will end badly."

There was silence for a moment.

"It won't ever go that far," said Qas dubiously.

"Won't it? Will you fight the Loyans with all your strength and all your hate?" Serlay asked them.

"They stole my home away from me," said Pati. "Killed my friends. I'll fight them."

"And what about Sovena?" Qas asked. "I can't allow them to take my homeworld."

Siphany felt like she should say something, but she had no idea how to say *I won't ever fight. I can't.*

Not this war.

Serlay shook her head, her eyes ancient and worn. "I've heard of your planet, Pelagar, which chose to die rather than submit to their enemies. You are fools, just as we were. The curse of our people."

"Shouldn't we be figuring out our next move?" Isan piped up from her end of the table, where up till now, it seemed she'd been trying to ignore everything happening around her.

Serlay nodded curtly. "Indeed. Since none of you have any ideas, I will proceed as I was going to before. The crew I put down on Haeld is now in a war zone. I am going to evacuate them, and we will attempt to continue our mission."

"What?" exclaimed Qas. "That place is the front lines, now. It'll be impossible to get in and out."

"Silence," said Serlay with enough force that Qas closed their mouth in shock. She eyed every one of them. "This is my ship. It goes where I want it to. There is no discussion. I am grateful for your help. But in the end, I am the captain."

Qas seethed. Pati actually seemed to relax a little; maybe some kind of clear command was good for her. Isan didn't move a muscle, distracted by something else.

Siphany felt nothing but relief. Let everything be someone else's responsibility for a while. This wasn't her ship; she was no longer a captain.

She *had* no ship. For the first time in her adult life, there was no place in the universe Siphany could call her own.

Pati and Qas started asking questions, trying to coax some details about what the *Call* could do and how they could possibly get into Haeld space without being utterly destroyed. Serlay effortlessly batted them away, revealing nothing. Eventually, the meeting was done, and Serlay left to set the *Call* on course for Haeld. The rest of them followed.

Siphany, alone in the conference room, stared out the window. She looked to where she thought her ship might have been, but there was no way for her to see it now. She put a hand on the window, pressing her head against it.

They came to a halt, and she felt rather than heard the shift engines powering up.

Right before they shifted, Siphany thought she saw the distant, undulating form of the Whale, swimming through the void.

Why, she thought as the stars blurred and her stomach flip-flopped. *Why did you save us?*

*

SIPHANY PACED THROUGH the rest of the ship as they traveled, marveling at the change in the mosaics now that they were brightly lit. Some of them had their own spotlights, highlighting and setting off specific complex pieces and patterns.

Somewhere above, Serlay and the others were guiding the ship back toward Haeld. Siphany couldn't be bothered with that, not right now. All she wanted was to walk, see the mosaics, and think.

Besides, there was so much more ship to explore. Lurbira talked to her, pointed out things she remembered, told her stories.

After a day or two, Siphany found she had developed the outlines of a routine. She fed Kit, walked the halls, slept, ate, and played the flute at vague approximations of set times.

It wasn't much, but for now, it would have to be enough.

*

SIPHANY WAS PLAYING her poor battered flute in a long, narrow room somewhere deep below decks when Pati found her.

"Hey," said Pati, and Siphany stopped playing. "You're really good on that thing. I used to listen to you play it back on your ship and think, 'Wow, she's pretty good.' Right?"

"Thanks," said Siphany.

"I thought you'd want dimmer lights than this." Pati sat next to her. She seemed like her old, fluid, energetic self again. "It's so bright in here."

Siphany remembered the terrifying darkness she'd been plunged into when the power went off and shuddered. "I'm okay with it being a little bit brighter, for now."

"How are you doing? I've been looking for you. Qas and I are worried."

"Not Isan?" Siphany said lightly.

"Isan's worried about Isan, as far as I can tell. And Serlay's too busy being captain and ordering the rest of us around."

"That sounds fun."

Pati grimaced. "Less fun than you'd think. But how *are* you doing?"

"Fine." Siphany couldn't really look at Pati, fixating instead on a swirl of paint someone had inelegantly slathered onto a nearby wall. The colors seemed all wrong. That blue and that orangish-brown shouldn't go together.

"You sure? You had a rough time of it back there."

"So did everyone else." Siphany tilted her head. The painting was oddly abstract, nothing but colors and whorls. There wasn't even really a pattern.

"Yeah, but we're talking about *you*," Pati put an arm around Siphany's shoulder. "Qas and I talked about that too. It sounds terrifying. You were in your EV suit, alone. In the dark. Lurbira was dead. For twenty-two *hours*."

Siphany examined the painting intently, ignoring Pati. In fact, what made it so notable was the absence of any kind of pattern. There was nothing else like it on board. Siphany stood, shrugging Pati's arm off. "Hang on. I need to look at this painting more closely."

"Sif—"

"Be right back." Siphany crossed the room to the painting, examining it closely. It was almost as if a child had done this. But there'd been no children aboard the *Call*. According to what Lurbira had told her, none of the people here had been able to have children. That was why they'd been selected for this mission. Everyone else was too concerned with keeping the human race going back on Earth.

"Lurbira," she said into the air. "Who made this? It's so different from anything else on board."

There was a pause. Then Lurbira said, "I don't know," through the room's speakers.

"You don't? You're sure?"

"Who the fuck cares," Lurbira said sullenly.

"Aha! You made this, didn't you? When you were young!"

"Maybe," grumbled Lurbira. "You gonna tell me how ugly it is? Don't bother. Viernan pretty much beat you to it. *I* wanted to paint over it, but Avorna insisted we keep it."

"Well, sure. You made it. Of course she'd want to keep it."

"I'm shit at painting. I can't do art or anything creative at all. I thought it was an Artificial thing, but nope, plenty of us can make beautiful stuff. I'm just programmed to suck at it. Thanks so much for bringing it up; I wanted to relive that."

"Sorry." Siphany traced the color whorls. "It's…jarring. But now that I know, it's also very you."

"Oh, please," said Lurbira. "It's just paint on a wall."

"It's bold and uncaring about what anyone thinks of it. You were using whatever colors you wanted to. I bet you really enjoyed making a mess out of the wall."

"Oh, I did," said Lurbira, and Siphany could imagine her grinning as she said it. Not that she could actually grin anymore. "I got to make a huge mess, and I had a blast. I thought it was pretty too. But everyone on this stupid ship was an art critic, it turned out. You've seen this place. It's crammed to the gills with mosaics, statues, paintings, whatever. It's like a floating museum."

"It must have been a strange place to grow up."

"If you can call what I did growing up, yeah."

Siphany touched the paint on the wall. Some of it was still kind of lumpy.

She glanced back to see what Pati thought, but she had gone. Good.

*

SERLAY CALL FOUND Siphany as she stared out a viewport.

"Lurbira said you were here," said the captain.

"And so I am," said Siphany, not interested in company. "How about that."

"She was just as sarcastic as you. I miss the old computer. It was much nicer and more obedient than Lurbira."

"You ever find those spare parts for her?" Siphany asked nonchalantly, already knowing the answer.

"No," she said frostily. "There are none. Avorna either took them with her or someone jettisoned them."

"You're thinking the latter. Was it Brasna? Viernan?"

"Viernan and Lurbira never got along. But I'm not here to talk about her."

"What, then?"

Serlay folded her arms over her slight chest and gave Siphany a severe look. "You're walking around this ship like a ghost. I know losing your own ship was hard. I very nearly lost this one; I know what that's like. But I need you to snap out of it at once. If we're going to retrieve our people from Haeld, I need everyone."

Siphany turned her attention back to the stars. "Why should I help you? I don't remember agreeing to that mission."

"You're a *guest*. Aboard my ship."

"True," said Siphany, sighing. Qas, Pati, and Isan had been guests aboard her ship, once, and what she'd said went. Serlay was captain here, not Siphany. "Without us, though, your ship would still be a drifting ruin back there."

"Don't overstate your importance. The Whale came to you. Why not to me as well? Everyone who steps aboard this ship is a member of a team of equals and nothing more."

"And you're in charge of the team," said Siphany dryly. "Got it."

"It's a system that works well. The others from your crew are adapting themselves to it."

"They're just glad to have something to do. You know what's happening out there. The whole galaxy's gone mad. There's nothing but war and death everywhere."

"Yes. I know." Serlay joined Siphany at the window. "You're caught up in forces you can't possibly control or even affect. You've lost your nation and your home. You feel like your whole world is coming to an end."

"Something like that."

"My world came to an end, once. But we discovered there's life after the end. There's always another step to take."

Siphany had no idea what to say to that. It sounded like nonsense people made up to make themselves feel less awful inside.

And yet…Serlay was right. There was life after the end. She was alive. She could still take steps instead of simply being carried along.

"But you're right," Serlay was saying. "I didn't ask. So now I will. I've asked the others, one by one, and you're the last. Will you help me save my people?"

"No." Siphany was possessed by a sudden, wild idea.

Serlay actually started in shock.

"Unless," said Siphany after a beat, "you help me rescue Lurbira's people too."

The speakers crackled to life. "The hell, Sif! What are you doing?" Lurbira demanded.

"There are seventy or so Artificials on Haeld," continued Siphany, ignoring her. "It's occupied by Loyan. Artificials will have no rights or freedoms under the Loyans. They could be brought back to Loyan and, I don't know, melted down. Imprisoned. Made to do whatever the Loyans want. They see the Artificials as tools, nothing more. So, *Captain*, you're going to take everyone away from there, out into the galaxy. Your ship has the power and the space to do that. You can easily take on the Artificials as well as your own people."

Serlay Call considered.

"One Artificial aboard was more than enough, thank you," she said, but Siphany saw her resolve weaken.

"They're among the last of their kind. They deserve saving," insisted Siphany. "Surely, you must know about that too."

Serlay nodded ever so slightly.

"Besides," Siphany said. "I won't help you if you don't."

"Your help isn't as vital as you think," said Serlay coldly.

"You asked," said Siphany as firmly as she dared. "That's my offer."

"Lurbira?" Serlay Call asked the air. "Should we help the other Artificials?"

Oh crap, thought Siphany. Of course, she'd ask the one person who hated the Artificials on Haeld.

"Well," Lurbira said slowly. "Half of them are smug, stuck-up assholes."

Siphany winced.

"But…Harban's nice," Lurbira continued. "I'd hate to see him get caught by Loyan, if he's not caught already. And…Siphany's right. There aren't many of my people left. So yeah. We should save them."

"Very well. We'll do it." Serlay fixed Siphany with a firm look. "I don't owe you anything. So don't start thinking it. I'm doing this because Lurbira said we should."

"Right," said Siphany, relieved.

"I need your help to run this ship and to plan. Be in the control room in an hour. Shower first." With that, Serlay turned and exited the room.

"Sif, why do you want to help the other Artificials?" Lurbira asked after she'd gone.

"Because they need help. They helped us, once, remember?"

"Sure, but—"

"And they can fix you," Siphany insisted. "Harban can fix you. I know he can."

"Maybe. I hope so. But that can't be all of it."

"I wanted to make her do something. And I did, didn't I?"

Lurbira laughed. "You did. Hey, you should go see Pati. She's been really worried about you."

Siphany groaned. "Can it wait?"

"No time like the present to go explain why you've been acting so shitty," said Lurbira. "Take it from me. You don't want to let that opportunity pass you by, not ever."

*

PATI WAS IN her spacious quarters, and she greeted Siphany at the door with something between a smile and a glare.

"You came, huh?" Pati said. "About time. Did Serlay talk to you? She said she was going to."

"She did. I'm helping. I'll be up in the control room in a little while. I wanted to come see you first."

"Was it your idea? Or hers?"

"Lurbira's, actually," said Siphany, abashed.

"Lurbira?" repeated Pati, surprised. "Oh. Wasn't expecting that. Come on in."

Pati stepped aside and let Siphany enter. The door slid shut behind her.

Pati's quarters were decorated in soothing violets and grays, with swirls of deep blue here and there. "Nice place," said Siphany.

"Apparently, it belonged to a guy named Brasna. Lurbira's been telling me stories about him. She's just a chatterbox lately. It's like she has to give everyone a guided tour."

"Maybe it gives her something else to think about." Siphany shifted her weight, uncomfortable. "Um. So. We're going after the other Artificials on Haeld as well as the crew of this ship."

"Really? We are? How'd you convince Serlay to do that?"

"I gave her an ultimatum." Siphany sat at a functional-looking table and crossed her legs. "And Lurbira helped a little."

"Ah," said Pati, sitting across from her.

Silence hung heavily between them.

"Hey," Siphany began and then stopped. She had no idea where to go from here. "Uh."

"Let me help you out. I tried reaching out to you, and you blew me off. You've been avoiding me ever since."

"Something like that," mumbled Siphany.

Pati waited.

"I'm sorry," Siphany amended. "I shouldn't have done that."

Pati visibly relaxed. "It's not like I don't understand. I did the same thing to you, remember?"

"You did." Siphany grinned at Pati. "I didn't even hit the booze."

"No, that's champ-level stuff," said Pati, grinning back. "Heh. This is going to be one weird relationship; we'll just spend days in our corners sulking."

"Yeah," Siphany said, heart fluttering. "Relationship?"

"Can't sneak anything past you." Pati moved her now-long hair out of her eyes.

"I like that," said Siphany shyly. "The hair."

"It doesn't bother you? It's bluenet."

Siphany shrugged. "It bothers me less than it used to."

"That's good. I mostly did it to annoy Qas. It worked too."

Siphany grinned.

"So. Ah…I really wish we'd had time for that dinner back on Derstan."

"Me too. If only the invasion had come a few hours later," said Siphany, feeling suddenly shy.

"Damn Loyans. Always fucking things up."

"Pati, I…"

"There's something here between us," said Pati, her bright eyes intense. "I've been too stuck up my own ass these past weeks to really think about it. But we've been friends a long time, at least in Hydras."

"I miss Hydras."

"So do I. I hope it'll come back someday. But…"

"I know," said Siphany softly.

"I want to see if there's more to us than just friends." Pati reached across the table and took Siphany's hand. She smiled that dazzling smile, and Siphany's heart beat faster. "I hope there is."

Siphany hesitated. She wanted this. She knew she did. But…

"What is it? Sif?" said Pati, frowning. "Is it Qas?"

"No, it's not Qas." Siphany tried to get some kind of handle on her emotions. It wasn't Qas, right? Damn. This wasn't going like she'd hoped at all. "I…shit. I'm sorry. I like you. I like you a *lot*. You're fun and attractive, and I…I think I want this. But I haven't had a relationship with anyone in a decade. I don't know what I'll be like. I'm not sure I'm ready. And right now…"

"Is a bad time," finished Pati, failing to hide her disappointment. "Right. I felt that way a couple of weeks ago. I also felt really hung over."

"Very hung over," confirmed Siphany.

"True. But I got past it—all of it. Maybe you will too."

"I think I will." Siphany gave Pati's hand a squeeze. "But I'm not quite there yet. Give me a little time."

"So why'd you come by, then?"

"Just to say sorry for blowing you off, before. I know you were trying to help, and…" Siphany shrugged. "That's it."

"Hey, could be worse," said Pati, grinning. "You could have barfed everywhere and woken up in a strange bed with a pounding headache."

"You're very hard to carry," Siphany said wryly.

"I know it. All my friends said so."

"It's been a bad couple of months, huh?" asked Siphany softly.

Pati's smile wilted a little. "Yeah."

Pati stared at the ground for a moment.

"Sif?" she asked at last. "You think we'll get Derstan back someday?"

"I don't know. I hope so."

Pati shook her head. "Nothing's ever going to be the same again, will it."

"No. It won't."

"But we won't always be at fate's mercy, either." Pati glanced at the signs, sigils, and wards posted all over the walls. Brasna, apparently, had been just as superstitious as the rest of them. "Fortune always comes around again. So Serlay says, anyway."

They sat together, Siphany unwilling to remove her hand from under Pati's, for a long while.

*

SIPHANY ENTERED THE control room, cleaned up, and forced herself to think positive thoughts. Captain Serlay Call merely grunted at her appearance.

"Siphany," she said. "Lurbira and Qas both say you're very good at plotting out smart shift points. I want you to get us to Haeld as quickly as possible."

"I can do that." Siphany sighed. "Or I would, if I could read your panels."

"We've made a few changes. Lurbira's translated for us. She's reconfigured your panel, at least. You should be able to do your job."

Siphany glanced at the navigation panel, and a lump formed in her throat. It looked just like the one on her old ship.

"Oh." She blinked her eyes to clear the tears and started running through the commands. "Oh, this is perfect. Thank you, Lurbira." Siphany looked back at where Lurbira's body sat, inert, connected to the ship's computer by dozens of wires and cables.

"No problem," said Lurbira through the intercom.

"Good," said Serlay sharply. "Get us to Haeld. At once."

"If you don't mind me asking." Siphany began plotting a course. "How do you plan to get this ship into the war zone and save your people?"

"We will simply ask," said Serlay matter-of-factly. "Our people have nothing to do with this war. The Artificials may present more of a problem, of course. But our people will be ready to go."

"The Loyans may try to shoot us on sight," Siphany protested.

"They would have shot *you* on sight," said Serlay smugly. "This ship is not a party to your senseless conflict. We are simply trying to evacuate refugees. It's logical that they would allow this." She frowned. "No planet wants refugees. Not even Haeld. Not now."

Siphany exchanged glances with Qas at the engineering station. They shrugged fatalistically.

"And that's your plan," said Siphany, dubious.

"It is the only plan that has a chance of success. Do you seriously expect me to go in with guns blazing? To kill and burn and destroy? Childish. That would lead to more war and death, and there is no guarantee we would win."

"And after that? Where are we going?"

"Out and away from the war zone. As far from here as we can. We'll continue our mission. There are other arms of the galaxy that humans colonized, after all."

True. There were supposed to be colonies everywhere. Ten thousand years of spreading humanity had left a mark on the galaxy, to be sure. Many of those other worlds were so distant that the worlds of the Mid-Perseus Arm rarely heard from them.

What else might be out there?

Siphany thought about leaving all of this behind. The future seemed to bloom before her eyes. She wasn't sure she liked it, but what difference did it make? The future always came.

"All right," she said firmly. She began to plot a course for Haeld. "Here's to the future."

"Indeed," Serlay said coldly.

Chapter Sixteen

THE *CALL* SHIFTED through space farther than Siphany's ship had ever been able to go, covering the distance with remarkable speed. The Earth-built shift engines, differently tuned than what Siphany was used to, meant some obstacles were less trouble for the *Call* than for local ships.

War news trickled in. The total blackout of the asynchronous net began to lift, and suddenly, there was information. It quickly became clear why the blackout had ended—Loyan had won.

The Loyan advance was relentless and awe-inspiring. They'd swiftly taken twelve Stationbund stations by surprise, constructing a network of satellite states all over the sector. Two other minor planets, Kalala and Ianas, had surrendered after offering only token resistance.

And then there was Sovena.

When Qas found out about the horrific slaughter that was the Battle of Sovena and the relentless bombing campaign the Loyans had then subjected the planet to, they burst into hopeless, enraged tears. The Sovene fleet had put up a brave defense, but in the end, what was left of them had to retreat and regroup at Saralar, their last remaining major ally.

Sovena itself had had no choice but to surrender. And so, the war was all but over.

Serlay Call was nonchalant. "Better submission than a prolonged conflict. Better to suffer occupation than more war."

"Easy for you to say!" Qas snapped, furiously wiping the tears from their eyes, and stormed from the room.

"I'd better follow them," said Siphany, excusing herself. Isan, looking stricken, trailed along after her.

"Siphany?" she asked as soon as they were out of the conference room.

"Not now, Isan."

"But…"

"I need to see Qas. I'll be back."

Isan nodded shakily. Siphany tamped down the sense that something was seriously wrong and sprinted after Qas.

*

SHE CAUGHT UP with Qas in a wide central corridor of the ship, staring at a mosaic of beautiful, blue-white Earth as it must have appeared before the catastrophe. Tears ran freely down their face.

"I'm so sorry, Qas." Siphany put a hand on their shoulder.

Qas turned, despair in their eyes. "We should have been there! You and I! We should be there now, with our people… But there's no way to get there. There's no way anyone's getting in or out. It's *gone*, Sif, it's gone."

"It's *not* gone," Siphany insisted, fighting her own rising anxiety. When Qas got like this, they took her along with them. "Stop talking like that. It's all still there. It's…just occupied by the Loyans."

"That's the same thing. How can Sovena be Sovena under the Loyans? There's no freedom under their rule." Qas banged a fist against the mosaic of Earth, striking it in the ocean somewhere.

There wasn't much for me under Sovene rule either. The only freedom Siphany had ever found was either aboard Derstan Station or on her own ship.

Which was also lost…but permanently.

"I'm sorry." She put her arms around Qas. "Believe me. I am."

"You don't give a shit about Sovena at all," they said, pulling away.

"I do. It was my home. And you care about it…so I do too." She tried to give them a reassuring smile and failed. "I don't know what else to tell you."

Qas turned and collapsed into Siphany's arms, sobbing. Startled, she almost pulled back, but she steadied herself and put her arms around them and held them while they cried out their grief and guilt.

*

IT TOOK ABOUT an hour for Qas to calm down enough for Siphany to even begin to think of leaving them alone. They babbled and talked of old times, of life on Sovena before everything had gone to hell. They talked about their father, their brother, their old school, the town they'd grown up in… They were trying to catch it all, to capture that Sovena before it receded into the past forever.

Siphany tried to remember her hometown, but there were only a few jumbled images of a place that was too bright, too loud. She mostly remembered her mother dragging her by the hand, lecturing or singing while Siphany cried and fought. Not a pleasant memory. So she listened to Qas instead.

They told her their familiar old stories, and slowly, hesitantly, Siphany joined in. The two of them fell back into their old way of being together. The things they'd said to each other a million times in the past, shared old memories of how Sovena was when they were kids, old songs and shows they'd seen…

In the end, they just sat with each other.

"I've missed this," Qas said at last.

"So have I," admitted Siphany. "But…"

"I know, I know. It wasn't always like this. But maybe it could have been…given time. Do you ever wonder…?"

"I used to. All the time. I had all these regrets about you. Now, I just worry about today."

"That's fair," Qas said. "What am I going to do, Sif? I don't have a world to go back to now. My whole life…I don't even know what it was for."

"Maybe it doesn't have to be for anything. Maybe it's okay just to be alive and doing the best you can."

Qas smiled. "You used to say that to me, back in the old days."

"I did?"

"You did. And you were right." Qas sighed a heavy sigh, shoulders sagging under its weight. "I…I'm sorry, Sif."

"What?" asked Siphany, shocked. "For what?"

"For everything," Qas said quietly. "For leaving. For being too young and stupid to know what I had. There's…there's been no one else. You moved on in ways I couldn't. You should be with Pati. She's wonderful. But all I have is Sovena. My family is…still my family. They're all so cold and distant. So, what, am I in love with an ideal I have of Sovena? With something that is getting bombed into the ground? With something that never really existed? I don't know. But you know me. I'm a stubborn ass."

Siphany had no idea what to say to that. But something ancient was stirring in her heart. Here was the brave and vulnerable person she'd fallen in love with back at the institution. She'd thought that person had been buried by arrogance and time, but no. Here they were.

"Qas," she said softly.

"I'm trying to let it all go," Qas said. "I'm trying to tell myself that it's okay to go on. But it's been so hard."

"We're going to Haeld. We're going to save the *Call*'s crew and the Artificials. We're going to help *somebody* in this awful war, even if it's not Sovena. Maybe that can be enough for now."

They nodded, wiping away a stray tear. "You're so much wiser than I am. When did that happen? Or was it always that way, and I didn't notice?"

Siphany checked the time. "Qas…back home, the sun's coming up over the institution."

"And?"

She stood and spread her arms, just as the Form demanded.

Qas's eyes widened. "Sif…"

"I used to do it every morning. I never really forgot how. It was good for me. Routine. But it was also part of who I am. I didn't want to tell you because…because I was busy being a stubborn ass too." She held her hand out to them. "Come on. We can be Sovena together."

They rose and joined her, and they greeted the Sovene morning together in the windowless hold of the *Call*.

*

WHEN AT LAST Siphany left Qas, she found Isan sitting outside Siphany's cabin, eyes closed. Siphany had never known her to sleep. What was she doing?

"Hey." Siphany prodded her with a toe. "Isan."

Isan opened her eyes. "Siphany. Finally. Where've you been?"

"Please tell me you didn't wait here for me all this time."

"I had nothing else to do." Isan clambered to her feet. "Are you done with Qas? Can I talk to you now?"

"Of course. Come on in. Can I get you something?"

"No, I'm fine," said Isan as Siphany let her into her quarters and turned up the lights, trying to make Isan more comfortable. "I just…I would usually talk to Qas. But they're not doing so well, I guess, and this might not make them any better. I'm kind of afraid of Pati, and I don't want to talk to Lurbira or the captain."

"Which leaves me," said Siphany, feeling rather like the last kid picked for a team. "Okay. What's happening?"

Isan's hands were actually shaking. "Siphany, am I really sei?"

"Yes?" said Siphany, confused. "I thought you said—"

Isan ran her hands over her face, stretching it back. "I'm…I don't know anymore. I can't stop feeling this." She looked up at Siphany, eyes full of tears. "I still love Mother Junk."

Siphany's heart cracked. Isan continued.

"I—I want her to love me back. I want to go and show her who I am now, what I've done, so she'll be proud of me. But—but she'll never love me back, will she?" Isan slapped a hand against her arm in frustration, then flinched at the pain. "Lurbira was right. She said I was just a loyalty algorithm. And that's all I am, isn't it? I'm just a program pretending to be self-aware. I'm a sham. I can't let go of Mother Junk even after everything."

"Oh, Isan," said Siphany gently. She took Isan's hand. "I… Look…that's not… Damn. I'm really bad at this. Okay, let me back up." She took a deep breath. "When I was a kid—no. When I was a little boy, I loved my mother so much. She was the light of my world. I followed her everywhere, I loved the sound of her voice, and she always made me happy just by being there. But…she didn't love me back either. She loved things like music and bright colors and loud laughter; she loved being in a crowd of people. Those things scared me. I was overwhelmed by them. Whenever she took me out, I would retreat into myself, or I'd scream and cry and cry. So she started getting impatient with me. The rest of my family wasn't like this, so she didn't understand."

Siphany sighed. It felt like picking the scab off a wound, even now. "She took me to psychiatrists to try to 'fix' me. Therapists, healers, priests…you name it. She tried it all. They all tried to get inside my head, to connect with the 'inner me,' and convince me to control myself. That's a thing Sovenes believe too. The inner self is a sort of bedrock, and…yeah, it's Sovene. They want to try to reach that and not do anything physical, like body mods or drugs. But nothing helped. I just got worse as I got older."

She wrapped one hand around her upper arm, holding herself against the memory. "And then, when I figured my gender out and told her, that was it. It wasn't long after that they sent me to the institution."

Siphany shook her head ruefully. "I still loved my mother though.

She would come every year to see me on my birthday. Or…near enough. I looked forward to it. She never stayed long, but I convinced myself it was enough. Then one year, she didn't come at all."

"Sif…" Isan squeezed her hand. "I'm so sorry."

"Yeah. Well, she sent a note. A few lines saying she was sorry. She didn't even give an excuse. That's when I realized she'd…stopped caring. And a few weeks later, I finally let Qas talk me into escaping. The rest you know about. So… Look, realizing all the assumptions we have when we're…when we're new is all a part of growing up. Mother Junk loved her granddaughter, I think. But you're not her. You're someone new."

"But…am I sei?"

"Does the answer matter to you?"

"Yes!" wailed Isan.

"Then, yeah, I'd think so. Right?" Siphany looked up at the ceiling. "Help me out, here, Lurbira."

Lurbira's staticky voice crackled through the speakers. "She's right, kid. You're not just an algorithm if you're pulling yourself apart because you feel two different ways. I was like that, too, when I was new. You feel loyalty, but you don't want to because Mother Junk doesn't deserve that loyalty. Good! It's fine to be conflicted. It's conflict that makes us self-aware, makes us who we are. Someone with zero conflict in their soul is only following a program. So yeah. You're sei." There was a long pause. "But you were sei a long time ago, I think."

"Thank you, Lurbira," said Siphany.

"Thank you," whispered Isan. She let herself be gathered into Siphany's arms. "I'm sorry. Is it okay to—"

"This time," said Siphany with a smile.

Isan gave her a long hug and then let go. She took a deep breath.

"I…I'm hooked in to messages from her. From Mother Junk. Everybody from the Junk is. We have receivers and homing beacons. Except Lurbira, I guess."

"You are? Why didn't you say anything?"

Isan shrugged, looking miserable. "It's part of my implant. And I didn't want to talk about it?"

Siphany blew her frustrations out. "Fine. What happened? Did something happen to the Junk?"

Isan sniffled. "Um. Mother Junk's message said that everyone was being evacuated. Her included."

"Evacuated? Why?"

Isan shrugged. She looked like she was trying really, really hard not to cry.

"Where did they go?" Siphany asked.

"Loyan."

The implications of that settled in. "Oh, Isan. They were made to go, weren't they?"

"It has to be! They swore they'd never do that. But they did."

Once the Junk's purpose was served, they just took it. The Loyans were showing the Junkers their true colors at last. Everything Mother Junk had fought and sacrificed for, all the deals and the humiliation, now undone.

Siphany almost felt sorry for her.

"I know you lost your ship, and you and Pati lost the station. And Qas's planet was conquered and bombed. So…I don't know. I feel like I have no reason to be sad." Isan blinked back tears. "It's not like they're dead. It's not that bad. But…"

"They took your home," said Siphany quietly. She thought of poor Derstan, now occupied, and her ship, broken and dead in space. "They stole your people away."

"I hate this war," cried Isan. "I want it all back the way it was!"

"So do I. I'm so sorry, Isan. I am."

Isan closed her eyes, and her face relaxed to something approaching normal. Siphany marveled at the Synthetic's iron control and wondered where it had come from. Everyone had hidden depths.

"It's all right to be upset," Siphany said. "Even angry. You can talk to us about these things."

"No. Qas was so upset. I didn't...I didn't want to make things worse."

Siphany hesitated, then gave her a hug. "You wouldn't have. I'm so sorry."

*

WHEN ISAN FINALLY left her cabin, Siphany flopped on her bed, exhausted. Kit jumped up and nestled into the crook of her arm, where he started kneading her side and purring. Siphany was so tired that she didn't even mind the gentle pricking of his claws.

"Hey, Siphany." Lurbira's voice came through the intercom. "I have a really complicated emotional problem I need you to solve for me!"

"Goddamn it, Lurbira," Siphany wheezed, laughing despite herself.

"You okay?"

"Yeah. Just...tired. Did I do okay?"

"How the hell would I know? I'm even worse at feelings than you are."

Siphany stroked Kit's fur. "This is why we're friends."

"You bet it is," Lurbira said. "Feelings are the worst."

"They really are," Siphany agreed.

*

THEY APPROACHED HAELD more quickly than Siphany dared think. They could shift farther, and the *Call*'s powerful engines covered the distance between shift points shockingly fast. After only two weeks, they were almost there.

Siphany and Pati danced around each other, and Qas wandered the ship, looking hollow but determined. Siphany tried to engage with both of them when she had the energy to spare. She and Qas would practice some of the rituals from the Form several times a day in a beautiful space three decks down from her cabin, while she and Pati would get together to laugh and play cards to pass the time every evening.

The weight of unspoken needs hung heavy around all of them.

Isan started randomly hanging out in and around Siphany's quarters, finding ways to cook bland meals that Siphany liked. She would chat about nothing, such as the workings of the engine and the interesting bits of the ship she'd discovered, and it was all immensely relaxing.

Siphany was surprisingly grateful to have her around. Of everyone on the ship, except for Kit, Isan was the least difficult to be with.

It struck Siphany that being on a ship with other people was starting to seem very normal to her. It was even starting to be nice, if sometimes draining. Lurbira seemed to vanish into the computer most days, popping up at random moments to talk with Siphany or report on what other members of the crew were doing.

War news, when it came, was nothing but grim. The bombardment the Loyans had subjected Sovena to before the planet surrendered had been brutal, with Sovene cities in ruins, millions displaced, and awful death tolls. Siphany looked for the name of her hometown and found it had been attacked. She had no idea what had happened to her family. They might be fine, still in the house, or they might be in some miserable refugee camp with a Loyan flag fluttering over it. Or…

There was no way to know.

Siphany stopped looking through the reports. There was nothing new, nothing she wanted to know.

Instead, she focused her thoughts on the Whale that had, for reasons she still couldn't fathom, saved them. *I am the sei of Earth.*

What did it mean? Was it the only sei that had come from Earth? That didn't seem quite right. The Whale seemed like…more, somehow. Was that why it had helped?

Serlay might know, but Siphany's anxiety shot through the roof when she thought about asking her. Serlay was still very obviously put out about her ultimatum, and the last thing Siphany wanted to do was make things worse.

And so they shifted on toward Haeld.

*

IN THE HEART of the control room, Siphany watched, hands resting nervously atop the navigation console, as Haeld grew large on their screens. "I'm amazed the Loyans haven't challenged us yet." They'd shifted into the system hours ago.

"All their energy is focused on Sovena and Saralar," said Pati. "Haeld is old news."

"Their ships aren't unlimited," Qas said thoughtfully.

If Loyan is that thinly stretched, thought Siphany, maybe they aren't completely unstoppable after all.

"We're finally receiving a transmission," said Lurbira through the intercom. "Stand by."

"*Attention incoming ship, this is the Greater Loyan Province of Haeld's civilian traffic control. Halt at once and state your business.*" The terse voice spoke with the accent expected from someone from Haeld. Local control. Interesting.

"This is Captain Serlay Call of the Earth exploratory and diplomatic ship *Call*," said Serlay crisply. "We are on a peaceful mission and come into your system under a banner of truce. We seek peaceful exchange and understanding." She cleared her throat. "We also have people on your world. We wish only to retrieve them and go on our way."

There was a pause, then: "*Earth ship Call, you are in our records. Stand by.*"

Serlay nodded. "Standing by. Thank you."

The connection was broken. Serlay shot Siphany a smug look. "You see? Diplomacy and talk is better than fighting."

The voice returned. "*We have records, given to the previous government, of a number of Earth people living on the island of Nuaree.*"

"So that's where they were," murmured Lurbira through Siphany's console so only Siphany could hear her. "That was only a thousand kilometers or so from where we were. So close."

"Excellent," said Serlay. "We would like to retrieve them, and thank you for protecting them."

"*I'll have to clear it with the Foreign Office,*" said the voice on the other end.

"Go ahead and do that. In the meantime, are we cleared to orbit the planet?"

"We'll make sure there's an escort for you waiting there."

"That's not necessary."

"In these troubled times, we insist," said the voice with what sounded like a practiced patter. *"No one is to leave or approach your ship until we give clearance. Is that understood?"*

"Perfectly," said Serlay dryly. "Thank you."

The connection cut out again.

Siphany whirled around, furious. "What about the Artificials? You promised me!"

"I'll keep my promise," said Serlay coldly. "Don't worry about that. Lurbira, are you in contact with them?"

"Wait a moment. Yes," said Lurbira. "Yes. I've made contact with Harban."

Another long moment passed.

"Good," Lurbira continued. "He'll have everyone ready. They're still in the caves. Of course they are. Morons."

"Fine," said Serlay. "Siphany—Lurbira and I have come up with a plan."

"Why didn't you tell me?" asked Siphany angrily. "You never said a word."

"Because I am captain here," said Serlay in icy tones. "And I don't require your input." She gave Siphany an intense glare. "I had hoped the Haeld government would be more receptive to our presence. They are not. If we asked about the Artificials, that would merely alert the government to their presence."

"Right. No kidding. Which is why we need to get them off there."

"We will." Serlay gestured at Siphany, Pati, and Qas. "Do the three of you think you can fly our shuttles?"

"I can fly anything," Pati boasted.

"I think so," Qas said.

"I'll do my best," said Siphany. "What's the plan?"

*

THE THREE SHUTTLES dropped out of the belly of the *Call*. Siphany flew one, Pati and Qas the other two.

The Earth-made shuttles were huge; each could fit up to fifty people. They'd clearly been built with moving large numbers of people in mind. Siphany thought they might have been troop transports.

Given the numbers, they were going to need every single inch of space.

They slipped by the ominous gray bulk of the single Loyan battleship that was "escorting" the *Call*. The sensors on Siphany's shuttle picked up traces of the weapons lock the Loyans were lazily training on them.

That was something they'd have to deal with later. Serlay had said she had a plan for the Loyans, too, but she hadn't elaborated. It made Siphany very jittery to leave details like that out, but in the end, she didn't have any choice.

Siphany nosed the shuttlecraft downward, following Pati's lead. She checked her sensors. Qas was right behind her.

The island of Nuaree was dead ahead.

Haeld's new government had approved the transfer of the refugees off their surface with a cautious enthusiasm, as Serlay had suspected. Once they were sure this had nothing to do with the war and would get unwanted people off the surface, they'd endorsed the idea—but under close supervision.

As for the Artificials, Lurbira had quickly found when she contacted Harban through a secure channel that the new government had issued strict orders to bring in any Artificials for transfer "back" to Loyan for reprogramming and reassignment. The thought of that made Siphany's skin crawl. No wonder Harban and the rest of them had remained in the caves.

"They should be ready, right?" Siphany said over the radio, keeping vague in case the Haeld air traffic controllers were listening in.

"*They're ready,*" came Pati's voice. "*Serlay says she was in contact with her people. They know what's up. Don't worry about it. We should be able to get this done quickly.*"

Siphany's nerves had her vibrating, though, as they approached the island. "*On approach,*" Pati said. Siphany could barely see her ship in front of her. "*Landing area sighted and verified. All clear. Repeat, all clear.*"

"*Understood, all clear on this end too,*" said Qas from the hindmost shuttle.

"Are they there?" Siphany asked.

"*Yes, they're gathered on the far end. I'm setting down now.*"

Instructions appeared on Siphany's screen from the local air traffic control. *Stay on your course. Do not deviate from the flight plan.*

It sounded like a threat. She swallowed hard.

Siphany deftly brought her shuttle down for a landing, wincing as it settled onto the tarmac more roughly than she'd prefer.

"*Nice soft landing there, Sif,*" said Pati, needling her. "*Think you scratched the paint.*"

"What can I say." Siphany relaxed a little tiny bit. At least Pati was still talking to her. "I'm the champ."

Pati laughed. "*You're the champ!*"

Qas's shuttle settled onto the landing pad. At the far end, streams of crew from the *Call* rushed forward. Siphany belatedly hit the hatch control, and the heat and humidity of the outside flooded in. People clambered aboard. Siphany stood, watching intently, as they jogged up the ramp. One somewhat plump middle-aged woman dashed forward.

"We're here and ready," she said. "We got the plan. We're all agreed, and we're glad to try to help Lurbira's people. Everyone understands."

"Thank you," said Siphany, grateful she'd muted the microphone. "I'm Leshandre Siphany."

"Hello! I'm Avorna Call," the woman said, introducing herself.

"Avorna!" Siphany broke into a surprised grin. The woman who had taken care of Lurbira when she was new. "Lurbira's told me all about you. I think she'll be happy to see you again."

"I still don't believe it," Avorna said. "Lurbira came *home.*"

"She's waiting for you on the *Call.*"

The woman smiled happily, eyes bright. "I can't wait to see her again."

"Soon. We're ready to go. Will you let everyone know?"

"Yes." Avorna nodded. "Of course."

"*I'm set.*" said Qas.

"*I am too. Sif?*" said Pati.

The last of the *Call* crew packed into her shuttle, and she closed the hatch. She unmuted the microphone and said, "Done! Let's go!"

Siphany fired up the engines and opened the intercom. "Strap in, everyone. It could get a little bumpy."

Siphany hit the thrusters, and the shuttle lurched off the pad. "Sorry!"

She nosed up, following Pati's lead, Qas right behind her. They all rose in a graceful arc back toward the *Call*. Everything normal. Everything completely normal. *Relax, relax.*

"*Coming up on 10,000 meters,*" said Pati's voice through the radio.

"Acknowledged," said Siphany. The break point was 10,221.

Her altimeter ticked off the numbers.

And…*now.*

"System failure!" Siphany called abruptly into the radio, making sure she was broadcasting wide. "I'm losing boost! One of my engines isn't responding!"

"*Status,*" Qas demanded. "*Can you make it to the Call?*"

"I can't stay with you!" The preprogrammed downward arc commenced. Siphany ignored the happy green readings from all the engines. "It's bad! I have to set down!"

"*We'll land with you and transfer your people to our shuttles,*" said Qas. "*Haeld Civilian Traffic Control, did you read that? One of our shuttles is having engine issues, and we are setting down. Repeat, we are setting down.*"

"*Acknowledged, Call shuttle 2. Return to Nuaree field,*" said the Haeld controller.

"Can't make it," Siphany cried. "Engine and helm are only barely functional. Looking for a place to land."

"*Call shuttle 2, you are descending into restricted airspace!*" the Haeld controller said, sounding increasingly agitated.

"Can't be avoided! Sorry! I've found a platform. Shuttles 1 and 3, stay with me!"

Siphany nosed the shuttle down, muted the microphone, and shouted, "Hang on back there! I'm going to open the hatch as soon as we hit the ground!"

*

THE SHUTTLES CAREENED out of the sky, braking thrusters firing on full, and landed on the broken and pitted stretch of tarmac outside Sunshine Valley with a sickening, bone-crunching jolt. Siphany thought her teeth might rattle right out of her head.

The hatch was already opening.

Outside, seventy or so Artificials broke out of the tall grass and sprinted onto the tarmac.

There was consternation at Haeld traffic control. It was becoming very clear what Siphany was doing, and they had only minutes, maybe less.

"Come on. Move," shouted Siphany. "Move!"

"*Incoming!*" Pati said over the radio. "*Sif, Qas, I've got incoming aircraft on sensors! Shit! Five of 'em! We have to go now!*"

"*Full! Taking off!*" Qas shouted. Their ship began to lift off the ground.

"All in," shouted an Artificial voice behind Siphany.

"Done. Going," she said. The hatch slammed closed as the shuttle leapt off the pad. Pati's followed an instant later.

"*Going to full boost,*" called Qas. Their shuttle rocketed ahead. The sonic boom below must have been window-shattering—if there were any windows below left to shatter.

Siphany, last to leave, did the same. This was their secret advantage—Earth-built shuttles that should be as fast as any fighter aircraft. The Haeld military wouldn't be expecting that.

She hoped.

Static burst over their radios, and then Serlay's voice came through, clear and calm.

"The Loyan escort has been neutralized. You're clear to land."

The *Call* crew broke into cheers. "Captain Serlay!" cried Avorna. "That's our captain!"

"Full power now," said Siphany, feeding as much power as she dared to the howling, whining engines, pressing everyone back in their seats as they blasted ahead.

"Still incoming!" Pati said. *"Qas, you're falling behind!"*

"Come on, Qas," Siphany said, gritting her teeth. "Come on!" Siphany could now clearly see the Haeld fighter aircraft approaching.

The fighters were faster than the shuttles, even at full boost. Damn it!

"Call shuttles, you have committed an illegal action!" barked a Loyan-accented voice. *"Land at once and surrender!"*

"No way in hell, you Loyan scum!" Qas cried. *"For Sovena! Sovena!"*

"Shut up, Qas," shouted Siphany. Panic began to set in. "Shut up!"

"Head straight up," ordered Pati.

"They're firing!" said Qas.

Siphany's shuttle shuddered as a missile exploded off the heavily shielded aft. Siphany heard herself shriek and tried to concentrate on flying. *C'mon, Siphany, keep it together!*

"Warning shots," said Pati. *"Next ones will be live and on target! Boost! Boost as fast as you can! Burn the engines out if you have to! Get close to the Call!"*

Siphany shakily fed as much power to the engines as she could. The ship strained and wailed as indicators flashed warnings everywhere.

There were more explosions, but behind her now.

"*Here they come!*" Qas cried. "*Oh sh—*"

There was a burst of static.

"Qas!" Siphany cried. "Qas!"

She checked all her panels. Two shuttles. Only two. No, no, no—

No.

Three.

The sky outside turned from blue to black. *Space.*

"Captain!" cried Siphany. "Help!"

"*Lurbira's already firing,*" said Serlay's calm, icy voice.

A dozen bright orange projectiles flashed past the shuttles. Below, the five Loyan craft crackled with electricity, then plummeted like stones back toward the surface, their systems fried. Siphany caught a glimpse of a pilot bailing out.

"*Got 'em,*" crowed Pati. "*Nice shooting, Lurbira.*"

"*Fucked 'em up,*" said Lurbira, sounding strangely weary. "*That's what I do.*"

"That's my girl!" Avorna cried.

"*Get aboard at once,*" said Serlay. She sounded furious. "*Loyan military ships are convening on our location.*"

"*Shuttle 3 is damaged,*" a voice Siphany didn't recognize said. "*But we can make it to you.*"

Siphany's heart leapt into her mouth. Qas. Where were they? Why weren't they talking?

She couldn't do anything for them now.

Siphany angled the shuttle into the hangar bay, following closely after

Pati. Qas's shuttle limped in a few heart-stopping beats behind.

The bay doors shut behind them, and Siphany felt the *Call* begin to move.

"We're here," she said to the disheveled and thoroughly jostled cargo of humans and Artificials. Her nerves felt like they'd been set on fire, and she was shaking. "Everybody out!"

*

SIPHANY SPRINTED TO where Qas's shuttle sat smoking and scarred in the bay. Its hatch opened slowly, and people and Artificials limped out. Siphany ran up the ramp and straight into the hulking figure of Harban.

He carried a limp, blood-covered body.

Qas.

"Oh, no," said Siphany. "Oh, please, please…"

"They're still alive," said Harban. "Medical!"

Chapter Seventeen

TWO HUMANS HAD died on Qas's shuttle, and dozens had burns and other wounds. There was a hastily arranged and agonizingly long memorial service that Siphany somehow managed to get through, surrounded by grieving members of the *Call*'s crew, before she dashed back to the strange, round medical lab where Qas was quickly, inexorably fading away.

They had been badly burned, their entire body lacerated by shrapnel. The *Call*'s doctor, newly restored to her post and equipment, had hooked Qas up to an elegant series of small machines.

They had grown gaunt and haggard. Their studied androgyny slipped away as they lay unconscious, and under the sheets, the outlines of their body became clearer.

Oh, Qas. How Sovene of you to live your life this way but not change your body to match. I know you wanted to. I remember.

Be yourself, but don't alter Nature. That was in the codex. That line, which had kept Siphany away from the medication she'd needed, had once made her furious. But now, looking at Qas, it just made her sad. She doubled the blankets and sheets up, hiding the traitorous tells, and smoothed down their hair. There. Qas looked like Qas again, just a little bit.

*

THEY'D BEEN LUCKY, far more so than Serlay Call would ever admit.

The *Call* had shifted out of the Haeld system just ahead of a pack of angry Loyan warships. Now, they dodged constant patrols in deep space, weaving a path out and away from the Haeld system.

Serlay and her senior officers had been consumed with getting everyone organized while they plotted a course away from the conflict.

Siphany found her presence was no longer needed. She went to the control room, but of course, there was a pilot already there. The old crew had taken their former stations as if nothing had happened, as if they'd always been there. The life of the ship resumed all around her as the crew and the Artificials sorted themselves out. As for Siphany, she felt like nothing so much as baggage.

Siphany told herself being useless like that suited her. She had other concerns, after all.

*

THE *CALL*'S DOCTOR, Goren, called her in the day after they'd escaped from Haeld. "Siphany, good. I'm glad you're here. Qas is awake, and I need to talk to them."

"They're awake! How are they?" Siphany asked, feeling a sudden burst of hope.

Dr. Goren shook her head. "Not good at all. The damage in some places is too severe for us to actually repair with the equipment we have. We had to leave a lot of it behind when we left Haeld."

Siphany swallowed hard. "What does that mean?"

Dr. Goren sighed. "Let's go talk to them."

Qas was still flat on their back, covered in medical equipment and scanners. They groaned weakly as Siphany leaned over the bed.

"Hey," she said.

"Sif," they croaked feebly.

The doctor stood over them. "Hello, Qas. I'm Goren Call. I'm the ship's doctor."

"Ah," they said.

The doctor glanced at Siphany. "I know you're a Sovene, so I haven't gone ahead without your permission. But some of the damage is very, very bad. I can't repair it with what I have here. Our medical technology is far behind yours, I'm afraid. I'm sorry. But I can repair at least some of it…if I use bluenet."

"Bluenet?" asked Siphany, shocked. But of course, it made sense. Bluenet had originally been developed as a medical tool to help reshape damaged organs and flesh. It couldn't perform miracles, and it couldn't revive what was dead, but it had saved countless lives. "You actually have bluenet?"

"Yes, we have several dozen capsules. A doctor back on the island gave me a small supply for emergencies. Marvelous stuff."

"No," whispered Qas. "I…we don't…"

"I'll be blunt," said Dr. Goren. "The only thing keeping you alive right now is my equipment, and your body is failing faster than I have a chance to repair it. If we don't use bluenet, you will almost certainly die."

Qas closed their eyes.

The doctor looked over at Siphany, an eyebrow cocked as if to say, *Well? Make them see reason.*

She thought about the nanites running around in her system that made it possible for her to understand the doctor at all. She thought about the time the web of bluenet lines had coalesced around her body, *shifting* her. She thought about body change horror and what it meant to be Sovene.

"We're losing time," said the doctor. "It may already be too late."

She took a deep breath. *Please let this be the right choice.*

"Qas," she said gently. "Do it. Please. It'll be all right. I did it, and I'm fine."

Qas groaned weakly again.

"And…I want to see you alive. I want you up and walking and being annoying. Please. *Please.* Sovena needs you alive."

Qas looked at her and then over at the doctor. Then they sighed and nodded ever so slightly. Siphany squeezed their hand and stepped back from the bed, not sure she wanted to see this next part.

Before she could leave the room, the doctor removed a tiny bluenet capsule from her bag and placed it on Qas's forehead. It powered up, and a web of blue lines flew out from it, blanketing their body. Qas seemed to moan, and they shimmered blue for a brief instant. The doctor entered several complex commands into her tablet.

Then, just like that, it was done.

"Oh no," said Qas, despondent. "What did I do? Siphany? Sif…"

And then they sank back into unconsciousness.

*

THE NEXT DAY was nothing but torment. Qas wouldn't see her that night, though the doctor said they were getting better. They'd be up and about soon.

Siphany worried. It had been hard enough for her when she'd gone through it. Qas was so much prouder, so much more Sovene than she ever was.

She could only hope they would come through it.

Lurbira assured her she'd done the right thing.

"It was their decision, in the end," she said through the intercom to Siphany, alone in her cabin. "Right? Nobody put a gun to their head."

"Yes, but…you know how Sovenes are about this stuff," Siphany said. "It almost broke me, and I was *desperate* for it."

"I know. You still did what you had to. Being alive is way better than being dead. Trust me. It'll take a while, but they'll get past it. Ow."

"What?"

"Oh, Avorna and Harban are poking me in the sensors. Trying to get me separated from the computer. Don't worry; they can't hear us."

"Thank you," said Siphany.

"For what?"

"I never have to try to explain things with you. You always get it."

"Isn't that what friends are for?" asked Lurbira. "Oh. Sorry. Gotta go offline for a bit, okay?"

"Sure."

Lurbira went silent, leaving Siphany with a new reason to dread the next few days.

Please let them both come through this. She didn't know what she'd do, now, without Lurbira or Qas in her life.

*

AVORNA CAME TO see her on the second day out. "I wanted to at least say hello again," she said.

"How is Lurbira?" Siphany asked, grateful for the distraction. She knew Harban and Avorna had put their heads together to see if they could do anything for her. So far, they'd separated most her functions from the rest of the computer, which Lurbira said was a tremendous relief, but they hadn't put her back into her body yet.

Avorna shook her head. "Very bad, but we're working on her. Her body is so old, and the damage was overwhelming. I'm amazed she survived it at all. I'll transfer her completely from the computer when I have a functional body to put her back into, of course." She smiled fondly. "She's very impatient. Same old Lurbira, always in a hurry. But…not even Harban can create one from nothing. So, we have to work with what we have, and what we have is not much."

"I'm sorry to hear that," said Siphany, spirits falling.

"We'll be able to repair her back to some kind of functional," Avorna reassured her. "But it will take time. A few days for a barely functional body. Then after that, many weeks of repairs. Some we can't do. We don't have the tools or the materials. Harban says some of the other Artificials are willing to donate parts they can spare."

"That's…that's so kind of them. Lurbira didn't get along well with the other Artificials, so…"

"That's her way. But they are a very nice bunch. I've been getting to know them. As for Lurbira, we'll see. I'm hoping for the best."

"Thank you. She appreciates it, even if she doesn't say so."

Avorna nodded and then gave Siphany a long look. "She tells me you're her friend."

"Yes. And she's mine."

"I'm so glad. She had so few friends here," Avorna said with a wistful sigh. "She was so different. So…difficult. I'm glad she's finally found someone. Thank you for being so good to her. I think it made an impact."

"I'm glad. How's she taking…all this?"

"She's been her usual self," said Avorna with a fond little smirk. "Complains nonstop. But she seems a little calmer now that we're working on her."

"Good," said Siphany. "Good."

"Here, I wanted to give you this." Avorna handed Siphany a little red paper ornament. It had writing Siphany couldn't read on it. "It's for good luck. We have them everywhere. You've probably seen. Superstition, maybe, but sometimes, they actually seem to help. There's no harm in them, and sometimes, it's good to have a little hope. This one's for you."

"Thank you," said Siphany, cradling the delicate paper gingerly. "I hope it works."

"Me, too."

The computer terminal in the room crackled to life. "They're crap," said Lurbira's voice. She'd clearly been listening in. "But you always hung them around for some reason. Who knows why? Derangement."

"Hush, child," said Avorna with a smile.

"Listen to your mother, Lurbira," said Siphany, and she and Avorna shared a grin while Lurbira cursed them out.

*

QAS FINALLY ALLOWED her in to see them. Siphany rushed to their side and found them sitting up in bed.

"How do you feel?" she asked, hands shaking with nervousness.

They shrugged. "Better. I…I actually do feel better. Sif…" Qas looked up at her, and she saw the unspoken question in their eyes.

"It takes time to adjust," she said. "I did it, and I wasn't even dying at the time. It's hard. You'll remember. But it doesn't make you less human or a worse person. Remember when you told me that?"

They nodded slightly. "I do. Sif…thank you. It was the right choice, I think. I can't do anything for Sovena if I'm…yeah. But…it's going to take me time."

"Take whatever time you need," Siphany said, almost giddy with relief. "I'll be right here."

*

SHE SPENT HER time after that at Qas's side, or sitting silently in her room after visiting hours, ignoring both Pati's and Isan's calls. At last, frustrated, Pati sent her a message:

Isan misses you. I'm worried about you. When you're ready to stop being the champ, I'll be here.

Siphany smiled in spite of herself. "I *am* the champ," she whispered.

*

AVORNA CAME TO find her a day later. "We're ready," she said.

Siphany followed her up to the control room. Harban waited next to

Lurbira's inert body.

"She won't be perfect," warned Harban. "There are many sectors in her brain that aren't usable and will be difficult to replace."

"I have some of her old code," said Avorna. "I made plenty of copies. But that was a long time ago…and to say that her brain is made of lines of code is like saying a human brain is made of tissue and chemicals. It's technically true, but it misses the larger picture. It will take a lot of time and effort for her to integrate what I have."

"But she'll be herself," added Harban. "And she'll be independent again."

"I just hope she's happy," said Siphany, kneeling next to Lurbira.

"So do I," Avorna sighed. "It's all I ever wanted." She placed a hand on Siphany's shoulder, squeezing gently. "Go ahead."

Harban pressed a switch, and Lurbira jerked awake.

Siphany smiled through a blur of tears as Lurbira reached her hands up. Avorna took one, Siphany the other.

"Oh, shit. Shit, I think it worked. Thank you," said Lurbira with her own voice at last.

Chapter Eighteen

ON THE THIRD day out from Haeld, though, Serlay paged Siphany over the intercom: Come to the conference room right away.

Curious, Siphany found her way there.

Serlay sat at the head of the table, flanked by Avorna and Viernan, the prickly engineer who hadn't liked Lurbira. She stood shorter than Serlay and seemed to have a permanent scowl on her face. A number of the *Call*'s senior officers, including Goren and tall Brasna, the navigator, were there.

Harban was also there, looking worried.

"Siphany. Good," said Serlay. "Let's begin. Viernan? You called the meeting."

Viernan cleared her throat. "Yes. We have a problem. The ship may not be as fixed as we assumed."

"Explain," said Serlay, leaning forward.

Viernan pursed her lips and brought up a complicated diagram of the engines. Siphany's eyes widened as the implications of the power flow schematic became clear.

"The power is starting to drain rapidly," said Viernan. "Whatever was done, whatever you or any of these foreigners claim happened, it's only temporary. The reactor had a kind of fuel, but it's not what we usually use. It's much more quickly spent. It sometimes seems to evaporate before use, which I cannot explain."

"So that means we have a much more limited range than we thought," said Brasna.

Avorna shook her head. "This is incredibly unlucky. How bad is it?"

"Very bad," said Viernan. "We will be entirely out of power in twelve days if we continue at this speed and power level. The additional people on board make things more difficult, of course, but in the end, the result would have been the same."

There was a shocked silence around the table. Twelve days! That was hardly any time at all.

"We can't go back to Haeld," said Viernan. "They'd attack at once. The only other world within our range is Sovena."

"We don't want to go there either," said Siphany, trying not to think of what an occupied Sovena would be like. "The Loyans have the whole place locked up."

"There may be no choice," said Avorna. "If the engines are failing, what can we do?"

Serlay's face was stone. She stood and began to pace back and forth.

"Options," she demanded.

"Leave the ship when we get near Sovena," said Brasna. "Get into the shuttles. Land. Let them deal with us after."

"They could just shoot us out of the sky!" said Viernan.

"We might have to surrender ourselves. It might be the only way to survive," said Avorna.

"Survival is always preferable," agreed Brasna. "Damn. We should have just stayed on Haeld."

Siphany looked around the room. She couldn't imagine the terrible blackness returning. Had the Whale's fix been so cruelly temporary? Had it wanted them to find a place to make repairs? Had there been some problem with firing the weapons?

"It was a noble try," said Harban. He sounded resigned. "We appreciate the effort."

"There must be another way," said Serlay. "I didn't get all of you and my ship back just to lose everything again."

A glum silence settled around the table.

It was happening all over again, thought Siphany, fighting down panic, the old anxious feelings returning. The ship was doomed, and so were they. They were out of options.

Everything seemed closed in. She'd been so sure they would be okay this time, that they'd gotten away, that her future wasn't some dank Loyan prison, or worse.

It had all gone so wrong, ever since she'd had the bad luck to run into the Junker ship. But…there wasn't much hope now. The Loyans had no reason to grant them mercy. After all, she and Qas were Sovene by birth, Pati was Derstan military, Lurbira had committed all kinds of crimes against them, and Isan had betrayed them.

Isan.

Siphany stood up, smacking her hand on the table in triumph.

Everyone turned to look at her, shocked. "I have a really bad idea," she said.

*

ISAN STARED AT Siphany and a still chairbound Lurbira. "You want to find the Junk? Why?"

"Because we're screwed," said Lurbira.

"Whatever the Whale did to us, it's only temporary," Siphany cut in. "We're losing power fast, and we have no other good options. You said you have a homing beacon. Can you find the Junk?"

Isan's eyes grew wide as she comprehended. "It's empty! Only Loyans aboard. Yes. Hang on. Okay…" She closed her eyes. "It's out near the Sovene border. If I can have access to the nav maps, I can pinpoint it."

"Amazing," Siphany breathed. "Thank you, Isan. Are you sure this is okay with you? We don't have to."

Isan shook her head. "The Loyans drove everyone out. They probably don't have more than a skeleton crew aboard. It might as well be useful—and once we take over and move it, nobody will be able to find us."

"Good. Let's go tell the captain."

"There's some more bluenet capsules there," said Isan thoughtfully as they walked. "Maybe I'll use one. Maybe…maybe I don't have to be afraid to be me. Maybe I can ditch the old Isan. I don't like a lot about this body. It isn't really mine. Plus, I don't really want a gender. Gender is stupid, right, Lurbira?"

"Damn right it is," Lurbira agreed cheerfully.

"Good," said Isan, nodding. "Good."

*

A FEW SHORT days later, they assembled in the control room when it was time for the final shift. Lurbira wobbled nearby. She looked dazed and small, and she wouldn't speak to anyone. At last, she sat back down in the hovering support chair they'd provided for her, grumpy but herself.

"Please," said Siphany to whoever and whatever might be listening. "Please let it be there."

She exchanged glances with a very nervous Isan.

All the Earth people were making mystic signs or chanting something in low tones. Siphany even lit a candle and blew it out, making a wish. Another old Earth custom, they told her. Guaranteed to work.

When Serlay felt everyone had generated as much good luck as possible, she gave the order.

The stars shifted…

And there, in front of them, was the Junk.

"Report!" ordered Serlay, leaning forward.

"There's only one ship here," said Brasna. A Loyan military scout ship was docked at the station. They were apparently using it as a stopover.

"I'm reading about two dozen life signs," said Avorna, manning the sensors.

"Transmit the following demand," said Serlay. "Tell them to surrender and evacuate the station, or we'll destroy their ship."

Everyone looked at her.

"I won't do it really. But if we can get them out of here…"

"Transmitting," said someone.

"The station does move, correct?" Serlay asked.

"Yes," said Siphany. "It did last time. And Isan says it can even without a helper ship to push it."

"Good," said Serlay. But she seemed nervous. Everyone seemed nervous. The stakes were impossibly high.

"We're ready to storm the station and take it by force," said Harban.

"Disable their long-range weapons from here, take out that ship, and we can go in and mop up," said Pati confidently. "No problem at all."

Serlay nodded almost imperceptibly. "Stand by."

The minutes ticked by. Then…

"Response, Captain!" said an elated Brasna. "They accept! They want a small delegation to go on board and seal the deal."

"It's a trap," said Pati at once. "Captain, don't do it. Or if you do, send a team that can take care of themselves."

"Agreed," said Serlay. "We have to take the chance. Volunteers?"

"I'll be delighted," said Pati, baring her teeth.

"I'm going," said Siphany at once. "No way I'm not."

Pati leaned over to Siphany. "You sure you want to come?"

"Yes. I…I want to see it through."

"I'll go as well," rumbled Harban. "Several of my people will join me. We can take care of ourselves."

"I…as well," said Lurbira.

"Lurbira, no," protested Siphany. "You can barely walk."

"Harban…carry me," said Lurbira. "I still have really great weapons."

Harban looked worried, but he nodded his agreement.

"I want to go," said Isan. "It's my home. I know it better than any-one."

"Good. Can we dock?" asked Serlay.

"They have a flexible dock," said Viernan. "I can alter our docking mechanism to fit it."

"Do it," said Serlay. "At once."

*

THE *CALL'S* AIRLOCK doors opened, and Siphany stepped back onto the Junk. *Welcome to Peace Station*, said a sign on the entryway. Their "delegation" was Pati, Avorna, Isan, and Siphany, plus seven Artificials, including Harban and Lurbira. Harban carried a limp, damaged looking Lurbira on his back. A single nervous-looking Loyan soldier greeted them.

"I'm to bring you to the commander," she said. "This way."

The station looked so different now, without the constant press of people. The lights were lower, the smells different. Siphany noticed a few familiar plasma scorch marks here and there. Lurbira's handiwork, from what felt like years ago.

She wondered if the Loyans here still ate croppygreens.

The soldier stopped and listened to something on her implant. She nodded and pointed to an anteroom. "Everyone can wait here. You." She pointed to Siphany, Isan, and then at Lurbira. "You three. Come with me."

"Us? What for?"

"The commander wants to see you."

"No," said Harban. "All together."

"It'll just be for a moment," said the solider. "We insist. It's quite safe."

Siphany felt butterflies in her stomach, but she set her jaw. It had to be a trap. "I'll be all right. You're just outside."

"Let me down," said Lurbira. "I want to go with her. I can walk a little. Please."

Harban let her down. She clung to Siphany's side. Isan stepped forward and helped to steady her. The Artificial and the Synthetic exchanged nods.

Siphany glared at the soldier. "Go ahead."

"In here." The soldier pointed to a door. Siphany and Lurbira walked through—

—and came face to face with Mother Junk.

*

"SO," SAID MOTHER Junk as the door closed with an ominous clang. There was a commotion outside, and someone banged on the door. "Leshandre Siphany. Lurbira Call. And Isan the traitor, wearing the body and face of my granddaughter. Disgusting. You're here with a strange ship and a pack of Artificials. How wonderful."

"You're still in charge here?" Siphany asked, glancing over at Isan. The girl's hands shook as she stared at Mother Junk. "How?"

"It's *my* station. Mine! They had no right to take it from me. I came here as soon as I could. But my people were already gone. My people, my poor people. Where did they take them?" Mother Junk scowled at Siphany. "You have no reason to gloat anymore though. Your precious Derstan and Sovena fell weeks ago. You've *lost* the war."

"It's not over yet," said Lurbira.

"It will be soon, you worthless scrap. Then my poor children can leave Loyan. They can live their lives in peace, maybe even make a new Junk. Lurbira, you look terrible. I hope it's the effect of the plasma bolts we shot you with. They were designed to disrupt your higher functions. A pity we didn't actually kill you."

Lurbira glared at her. Mother Junk gave her a triumphant little smile.

"You need to surrender," said Siphany, trying to sound threatening. "Now."

"Why should I? What possible reason would I have to do that? You're right where I want you."

"You don't understand your position," said Lurbira. Her gun ports opened with an ominous little *click*. "We can storm this station. There are a lot of us."

"How wonderful." Mother Junk gave them a hard, determined look. "Your ship is attached to my dock. As I said, you're right where I want you to be. I won't surrender. You've taken too much from me, Lurbira and Siphany. I won't let you take my father's station from me as well."

"Mother Junk," said Siphany, panic rising. She didn't like the wild, desperate look in Mother Junk's eyes. "It doesn't have to be like this. We need a place to exist. We don't want to hurt anyone. Our ship is in trouble. We—we can share the station. Us and your people."

"Sif!" Lurbira said, shocked.

"No, it's true. We have weapons power now, but we won't in a few days. We need—we need a home. We want to come here. Will you let us come on board? We were expecting a military presence. But maybe—"

"No," spat Mother Junk. "Never. I'll never share this station with you. My father built this station himself. I'll destroy it before I let you have it. And that's what I'll do."

"Please don't," said Siphany. "You can let the past go, Mother Junk. I know it won't ever be the same again. You picked up a snake and were bitten, and it serves you right. I'm just sorry your people had to suffer. But even though everything is different now, it's possible to change, and make peace with the past. Let us share your station. We'll go somewhere and hide in deep space. We can work *together*."

"It's possible to grow beyond your original programming," said Lurbira quietly. "I did. Siphany has. So has Isan—she's sei now. If we all can do it, so can you."

"Grandmother, please listen," Isan pleaded. "I know I'm not your old Isan, but these people have taught me so much. They're not as awful as you think. We can live in peace here. We can even see if we can get the others back someday."

Mother Junk gave her a hard look. "Pretty words for a corpse." She pushed a button. "But I don't have to listen to you. I don't have to surrender. I don't have to give in at all. In about thirty seconds, this station's reactor will go critical. When it goes, it takes you, me, and your entire ship with it."

"No!" Lurbira snapped up her arm, intending to shoot Mother Junk where she sat. But the hard look on her face wavered. "I…I won't let you."

"Lurbira," whispered Siphany, heart pounding.

"Go ahead," said Mother Junk, smirking. "I doubt you have the power."

"No," said Lurbira, trembling. "Siphany!"

Siphany took Lurbira's hand.

"I can't," said Lurbira. "I—I can't do this anymore. I'm sorry."

Siphany squeezed her hand, her heart full of pride for a brief moment.

Mother Junk pulled out a plasma pistol and aimed it at Siphany. "Come near, and I shoot her."

Lurbira's arm shook harder. "N-no…"

"Stop!" begged Isan. "Mother Junk, stand down, please!"

"Isan," Siphany said, seizing the moment. "Isan, help us. Open the door—she can't shoot us all."

"Stay where you are, Isan," said Mother Junk. "Help me avenge our people. That's an order."

The station began to shake ominously as power built up.

Isan stepped forward. Mother Junk's eyes widened as Isan advanced.

"I'm ordering you," Mother Junk snapped. "Obey. You're a loyalty algorithm. Just like Lurbira always said."

Isan shook her head. "I am sei," she said simply. "And my answer is *no*." She launched herself at Mother Junk, moving faster than Siphany had ever seen her go, fists flying.

Mother Junk swung the pistol around and fired, but she was too late. Isan slammed into her, knocking her to the floor, her arm and shoulder singed and smoking from the plasma fire. Siphany bolted forward.

"You!" spat Mother Junk, trying to bring the pistol to bear. But Siphany was faster. She grabbed the older woman's fragile, narrow wrist and squeezed, jamming her thumb into Mother Junk's flesh just below her palm. She cried out in pain, and her hand opened, dropping the pistol. Siphany grabbed it and rolled away, holding it out in front of her, aimed at Mother Junk.

"Lurbira, the reactor," Siphany shouted.

"I got it," Lurbira cried, wobbling her way to the console. She entered a simple sequence, and the station stopped shaking.

Lurbira tottered unsteadily next to the control console. "Only a few seconds to spare. Don't say I never did anything for you."

And then she collapsed into an exhausted heap.

Chapter Nineteen

THE STARS SHIFTED, and the Junk settled into a new sector of space, aided by the dying power of the *Call*. Almost everyone had been evacuated onto the Junk, and the corridors and bays were full again. The people from Earth were busy discovering the joys of croppygreens, and the Artificials were carving out niches for themselves everywhere.

Siphany sighed and settled back into her chair. She played a few more notes on her flute, then put it back in its case.

There was nothing for her to do except go see Lurbira. She stood and stretched, knocking a protesting Kit off her lap, trying not to let the tension show in her face. The station was full, so full of people! Plus, it was cold, too bright, and the floors didn't have carpets.

But it was what it was. She told herself she would have to adapt. This was her life now.

Siphany started to pace around the station.

*

ISAN SAT ON the floor overlooking the croppygreen bays, doodling in a notebook with a pencil. Dr. Goren had used bluenet to heal her arm and shoulder, which had been almost entirely melted away by the blast. And then, Isan had used bluenet to change herself once again.

She was a dazzling array of colors, her skin a beautiful deep brown nearly the same shade as Siphany's, her hair a wild mass of pink and blue and silver, her eyes a sparkling amethyst. It was a splendid effect.

Still, Isan looked moody.

"How are you feeling?" Siphany asked, sitting down with her.

"Better. Still processing. But better."

"Did I tell you how proud I am of you?"

Isan smiled. "Every single day since we got here."

"Good," Siphany said.

"What's going to happen to Mother Junk, do you think?"

Before shifting away, they'd stuffed her and all the other Loyans onto their scout ship, which had been stripped of weapons, and left them with just enough fuel to make it to Sovena. It was easier than keeping them all here.

"They'll find her. She'll probably have a lot of questions to answer," said Siphany. "And then, I expect she'll try to find us. Does she still have that beacon?"

"I turned it off. I'm sure that makes a lot of the old Junkers sad. They probably think the station was destroyed now. But…better than her finding us."

"Do you still care for her?"

Isan shook her head. "I do. But…less now." She gave Siphany a genuine smile. "I'll be all right. Thank you."

"Thank *you*," said Siphany. "I'll remind you again tomorrow of how proud I am of you."

*

PATI WAS WORKING on some random component of the station. "This tech is sort of like what we have on Derstan," she said after greeting Siphany with a quick kiss. They'd started doing that, almost spontaneously. Siphany found she liked it. "So, it should be easy to improve. Some of the parts on the *Call* are good for something after all."

"Glad to hear it. How are you doing?" Siphany asked.

It wasn't a casual question. Siphany had felt herself torn between Pati and Qas, so she'd proposed the only solution that made any sense.

"Qas and I talked it over," said Pati. "They're interested. And…I have to say, I'm not averse. They get on my nerves sometimes, but there's a lot to like too. We've been talking about things we have in common. Addiction, that sort of crap, you know? So, you're sure about this?"

"Very," said Siphany. Trios weren't so uncommon, not even on Sovena. "I think it's a good place to start."

"We're going to need a bigger bed," joked Pati.

"We'll get one," Siphany promised. "And you can be a boy, or whatever else you want, whenever you want. Not that you need my permission. I should never have been upset with you. I know it's part of who you are."

"Aw, it's nothing." Pati looked thoughtful. "I have some great ideas about what I want to be next. I love this sort of change. You sure you're okay with it?"

"Like I said, it's who you are," said Siphany, meaning it. She remembered the horror of bluenet but also the relief and freedom that came after. Someday, she'd promised herself, she'd tell Pati all about that. "And I like who you are. So, yes."

*

QAS WAS BUSY writing something when she found them.

"Another letter home?" Siphany asked.

"Someday, I'll get to send them." Qas still looked gaunt and sickly but far better than they had. Dr. Goren was sure Qas would be fine now.

"Did you mention…?"

They shook their head. "No. I don't want to think about that too much. It happened. But…maybe I can forget."

Siphany took their hand. She understood that. "So you and Pati talked."

"We did. I'm amazed, Sif. I didn't think you'd come up with this solution."

"Oh?" said Siphany, trying not to be peeved. "Why not?"

"Because it's so different for you. I thought you didn't like it when things changed so much."

She thought about being mad at them, but instead, she shrugged and took Qas for what they were—blunt, but honestly caring. "I couldn't keep the past forever. And everything's different now."

"It really is," Qas said wistfully.

"At least something good came out of it, right?"

Qas grinned. They were so beautiful.

*

SIPHANY DESPERATELY WANTED to see Lurbira, but she had one last person she needed to talk to first. She looked for Serlay where she always seemed to be, aboard the *Call*. This time, Siphany found her in the engine room with Viernan, trying to make sense of the power the Whale had given them and why it had faded away so fast. Siphany knew Serlay would never stop trying to find a way to get the *Call* back up and running again to continue their mission—no matter how doomed it might be.

"Any luck?" Siphany asked.

"Not yet," said Serlay. "But I have faith. And Viernan has some ideas. The *Call* will fly again."

"I hope so," said Siphany honestly. "Can I ask you a question?"

Serlay pursed her lips and nodded, setting her tools down. She and Siphany walked a little way away from the nearly dark engine core.

"What is it you want to know?" Serlay asked.

Siphany took a deep breath. She hadn't told this to anyone, not even Lurbira. She wasn't entirely sure she hadn't hallucinated it. But she had to know. "When I saw the Whale, when it breathed power into the ship, it said something to me. And I was hoping you might know what it meant."

"Go on," said Serlay.

"It said 'I am the sei of Earth.' Do you know what it means? Have you ever heard it before?"

"Humph," said Serlay, considering. "Lurbira has explained 'sei' to me. But the sei of Earth? No. I haven't heard that before."

Siphany waited. "Do you have any idea what it might mean?" she asked after a long silence.

"No," said Serlay Call, a curious and almost hopeful look in her eyes. "But…I will think on it. Thank you for telling me."

Siphany gave her a small smile, and to her shock, Serlay returned it.

*

SIPHANY SOUGHT OUT the lab where they were working on Lurbira. She hadn't seen her friend much during the several days Avorna and Harban had been working on her. Several of the Artificials had indeed donated parts they didn't need, which Siphany thought was incredibly touching and generous.

Harban had smiled when she said that to him. "She's one of us," he'd said. "What else can we do?"

Lurbira was sitting up, looking clean and polished, and moving an arm back and forth. "Hey, Sif."

"How are you?" Siphany asked. "Feeling better?"

"Much. Getting sick of this stupid room. Though the company's okay," she allowed.

Harban and Avorna Call both grinned. "We love you too," said Avorna.

"Can I take her for a walk?" Siphany asked. "It won't be long."

"That should be fine," said Harban. "Don't stress her too much. I need to work more on those joints, but a quick walk shouldn't damage anything."

"Great." Lurbira hopped down. She stumbled and caught herself. "Ouch. Maybe not that much better. Okay. Let's go."

*

THEY WALKED OUT to the observation deck, which had three windows looking out on a starfield. Siphany sat down in front of one, and Lurbira, joints whining, sat next to her.

"Pretty," said Lurbira. "I used to come here sometimes. Mostly because Mother Junk was making me clean it."

"I almost don't blame her, you know," said Siphany. "She lost everything."

"So did you. So did I too. Almost."

"Almost." Siphany took Lurbira's hand in hers and squeezed.

"I did a lot of thinking," said Lurbira. "You know…I really did die back there. On the *Call*, when the lights went out. There was nothing left of me. I thought a lot about what I'd become. When I saw Mother Junk, and I knew what she was going to do, I was so angry. But…"

"You couldn't kill her."

"I'm sorry. I couldn't do it before, in the bay when they surprised us. I…I had the shot. I knew they were there. I just…couldn't."

"Don't be sorry," said Siphany. "I think you did the right thing. We all have to live with the choices we make."

"Yeah. Poor Isan though."

"I know. But she's doing a lot better now. It was never her fault that any of this happened."

"True. People just get caught up in things."

"They do," said Siphany, thinking about the first time she'd been on this station. "It's what they do then that really matters."

They gazed out at the stars for a while. Siphany hummed a little song, something she'd played back on her ship many times. She'd have to find new places to play her flute.

"You seem awfully mellow," said Lurbira.

"Do I? I don't feel that way. I'm worried about what happens next. But maybe things are working out. I don't know."

"So. You and Pati *and* Qas?"

"Yes," said Siphany. "We decided to try being a trio for now. We'll see how it goes. It may be a total failure, but it may work out really well. I know you don't like Qas, but maybe they'll grow on you."

"Like rust, maybe."

Siphany laughed. She felt strangely free.

"Look at you," said Lurbira, beaming. "Taking risks and everything."

"What you said to Mother Junk about all of us growing beyond our original programming…I liked that. The institution, Sovena, my old ship…they're all still with me. But I don't have to let them control me."

"It's a good thing—to move on. Isn't it?"

"It is."

"So what happens now?"

"I wish I knew," said Siphany sadly.

"I doubt we'll be safe here for long. The *Call*'s pretty much dead. We won't be able to hide forever. And when the Loyans come back…" Lurbira trailed off, watching something out in the darkness.

"We'll deal with it when it comes."

"We will. And at least we have a place to live again."

"So here's to home," said Siphany with a rueful smile.

"Yeah. Home." Lurbira suddenly sat forward in her seat. "Oh. Oh, Sif…look."

Siphany caught her breath. Out there, far past the station, a massive, dark shape undulated through the void.

The two of them sat there for a long time as the Whale, whatever it was, whatever it intended for them, slid slowly through the starry darkness beyond the windows.

Siphany's heart filled with something dangerously close to hope.

About the Author

Susan Jane Bigelow is a librarian and writer from Connecticut. She loves reading, spending time with her spouse and their cats, and wandering the green hills and wide valleys of her home state.

Email

susanjbigelow@gmail.com

Facebook

www.facebook.com/whateversusan

X

@whateversusan

Website

www.Susanjanebigelow.com

Bluesky

@whateversusan.bsky.social

www.ninestarpress.com

www.facebook.com/ninestarpress

www.facebook.com/groups/NineStarNiche

www.twitter.com/ninestarpress

www.instagram.com/ninestarpress

bsky.app/profile/ninestarpress.bsky.social

www.threads.net/@ninestarpress

9 781648 907746